Choose your Lane to love!

Fish Out of Water

"*Fish Out of Water* delivers an intense plot as well as a sizzling relationship between Ellery and Jackson."

—Gay Book Reviews

Red Fish, Dead Fish

"Deliciously tense… a satisfying mix of sweet angst and steamy suspense."

—Karen Rose, *NYT* Bestselling Author

A Few Good Fish

"*A Few Good Fish* is a riveting page-turner with high-stakes action scenes, an intriguing plot and two compelling, incredibly likeable central characters."

—All About Romance

Hiding the Moon

"This whole series is amazing, and this book is the cherry on top!"
—Paranormal Romance Guild

Fish on a Bicycle

"The problem for me with an author like Amy Lane is that she continues to exceed my expectations… Thank you, Amy, you're the best."

—Rainbow Book Reviews

By Amy Lane

Published by DREAMSPINNER PRESS
www.dreamspinnerpress.com

By Amy Lane

FAMILIAR LOVE
Familiar Angel • Familiar Demon

FISH OUT OF WATER
Fish Out of Water
Red Fish, Dead Fish
A Few Good Fish
Hiding the Moon
Fish on a Bicycle • School of Fish

FLOPHOUSE
Shades of Henry

GRANBY KNITTING
The Winter Courtship Rituals of
Fur-Bearing Critters
How to Raise an Honest Rabbit
Knitter in His Natural Habitat
Blackbird Knitting in a Bunny's
Lair
The Granby Knitting Menagerie
Anthology

JOHNNIES
Chase in Shadow • Dex in Blue
Ethan in Gold • Black John
Bobby Green
Super Sock Man

KEEPING PROMISE ROCK
Keeping Promise Rock
Making Promises
Living Promises
Forever Promised

LONG CON
The Mastermind

TALKER
Talker • Talker's Redemption
Talker's Graduation
The Talker Collection Anthology

WINTER BALL
Winter Ball • Summer Lessons
Fall Through Spring

Published by Harmony Ink Press
BITTER MOON SAGA
Triane's Son Rising
Triane's Son Learning
Triane's Son Fighting
Triane's Son Reigning

Published by DREAMSPINNER PRESS
www.dreamspinnerpress.com

Amy Lane

SCHOOL OF FISH

Published by
DREAMSPINNER PRESS

5032 Capital Circle SW, Suite 2, PMB# 279, Tallahassee, FL 32305-7886 USA
www.dreamspinnerpress.com

School of Fish
© 2020 Amy Lane

Cover Art
© 2020 L.C. Chase
http://www.lcchase.com
Cover content is for illustrative purposes only and any person depicted on the cover is a model.

Trade Paperback ISBN: 978-1-64405-889-3
Digital ISBN: 978-1-64405-888-6
Library of Congress Control Number: 2020943466
Trade Paperback published December 2020
v. 1.0

Printed in the United States of America
∞
This paper meets the requirements of
ANSI/NISO Z39.48-1992 (Permanence of Paper).

To the people who got me through quarantine on audio—I feel blessed to know you all in person: Mary Calmes, Melinda Leigh, Karen Rose. Your words are magic, and they saved my life. Also Mate. Because we went a little nuts together.

Acknowledgments

ANNA J. Stewart and Kilby Blades—thanks for the writing sprints, without which this book would still be a flounder in a sea of flounder.

Author's Note

ALL. FICTION.

Prologue
Unexpected Cargo

At a gas station in Victoriana, California, which is literally the middle of the goddamned desert....

ACE ATCHISON watched the RV pull away from the gas station across the two-lane highway from his garage with flat eyes, Jai, his employee and giant ex-mob muscle at his side.

"D'ya see that?" Ace asked grimly.

"Da," Jai said, voice also grim.

They'd been taking a break when the RV had pulled into the gas station. The vehicle—old, decrepit, gasping like a fish swimming in smog—had probably left parts strewn across Highway 15 heading from LA to Las Vegas. The guy who'd gotten out of it was possibly in his thirties, but they were thirty the hard way, and he moved like... well, a killer.

Ace and Jai had experience with killers. They'd each crossed that line when the situation had been dire, but it wasn't a habit for either of them.

This guy moved like he'd shoot a baby because the stroller crossed his path. Ace and Jai had been leaning against the minivan they'd been working on. The family who owned it was across the street at the Subway, getting lunch while Ace and Jai tried not to let the thing die here where there wasn't even a fucking hotel. They saw the killer open the door, shout something harsh into the RV, get gas, and then go into the mini-mart/food court for a soda, probably because that thing didn't look like it had any AC.

And the guy had left people sweltering inside it.

As they watched, the tattered yellowing draperies that covered the back window rustled, and two faces pressed against the glass.

Young faces, dirty, and then those faces moved, and two more appeared. And then came two more. And two more.

While Ace and Jai watched, they must have seen twenty faces. Kids, maybe fifteen at the oldest, peaked, terrified, all of them looking out into the sunshine like it was going to be their last chance to see freedom and space.

"You know," Ace drawled, keeping his fury inside. "I don't think that man is actually related to any of those children."

"I would doubt that very much." Jai kept his voice neutral, but Ace knew Jai had essentially been given to Ace because while he was a very good man, he was not necessarily a good mobster. Jai was not a fan of people who abused the innocent any more than Ace was.

But God, Sonny had barely survived their last adventure. Not that *he'd* gotten hurt, but Ace had gotten captured, and Ace's boyfriend… well, Sonny didn't do well when Ace was in danger.

Because Sonny's childhood had been a nightmare, just like that of those kids in the RV.

And that decided him.

Ace swallowed. Most of the time, he kept any illegal activities limited to defending or sustaining his immediate family. But this was evil in a way that ate a hole in his stomach.

"Should we take the SHO?" he asked, talking about the souped-up racing machine he and Sonny had built from sweat and tears and the last of their savings from their time in the service, after they'd bought the garage.

"Nyet," Jai muttered. "He is a coyote, not the main mobster. We take a car we can make disappear."

They looked at each other. "Ernie's," Ace decided. Ernie didn't technically live with them anymore, but he was still part of the family. Burton, his boyfriend, still went on missions, and Ernie came and stayed in Burton's old safe room when he did, going home only to bake and to feed the cats. Burton was on an op now. Ernie was adamant he wouldn't be gone long, and Ernie was a witch and knew those sorts of things.

"Da," Jai said, and both of them pushed off the minivan.

"Sonny!" Ace called toward the small house that sat off to the side of the garage. "Sonny, Jai and me have to go handle something. You need to come out here and finish this damned minivan."

Sonny had gone inside to start dinner, because it was getting near closing time, but he popped out of the house like he'd been waiting for Ace's call.

"The hell?"

Sonny Daye was a small blond man, slender, muscular, mean as a rattail dog. Ace strode up to his lover and gave him a short hard kiss on the mouth, and he melted under Ace's touch.

"We're taking Ernie's car to go stop something bad. We may need Burton to bail us out. And that family needs their minivan 'cause they've got three kids and this is no place for them to be."

Sonny's face paled at his first words, and Ace kissed him again.

"No fretting. Jai and me, we're good at this, remember?"

"But Ace—"

"We've got to go," Ace said, feathering a sort of caress down Sonny's cheek with his thumb. They were not soft men. That touch was sufficient to silence Sonny and give him pause enough to back off and let Ace go.

"So I'm just fixing the minivan? Seriously?" he said, but he'd already taken that step back.

"You're what?" Ernie said, coming out of the cashier's cubicle where he worked for them sometimes.

"It was an RV full of kids," Ace said shortly as Jai brought Ernie's little Sentra around the far side of the house. "We need something that can catch up but that nobody will recognize."

Burton worked covert ops—and Ernie was supposed to be dead. Between them, Ace, Sonny, and Jai kept Ernie in a revolving train of piece-of-shit cars with sketchy VIN numbers. Ace could literally leave this car by the side of the road, and it would disappear, never to be seen or heard from again.

Ernie's eyes went wide, and then he opened his witchy mouth and said, "Get the children to safety—this blood's not yours," just as Jai got up and jogged around the side of the car.

Ace nodded shortly. "That's really all I needed to know. Keep Sonny calm, willya?"

He didn't wait for the answer as he slid behind the Sentra's wheel, grateful Jai hadn't pushed the seat all the way back. Jai was nearly six foot seven, and that would be damned uncomfortable for Ace.

"You see which way—" Jai began as Ace peeled out.

"East."

"What is your plan?"

"Hope he doesn't want to go through the window of that RV," Ace said shortly.

"Is a shitty plan."

Jai's honesty wasn't always Ace's favorite thing.

"The question," he muttered, "is what we're going to do with the kids once we have them."

"I'll ask Ernie for suggestions." Jai pulled out his phone and started texting.

"Think your nurse friend can help?"

Even with his eyes glued to the road, Ace got a feeling for the pained expression that crossed Jai's features.

"I dislike dragging him into this," he admitted.

"Well, I dislike leaving *my* boyfriend back at home scared to death, but everybody's got to make sacrifices, Jai. The only way our little operation works is if we keep it under the radar."

"Da," Jai said reluctantly. "Let us get rid of the rattlesnake behind the wheel and see if there's more bad guys. Then we can make plans."

The RV moved as slow as frozen shit through a pipe. They could see it waddling in the distance, and Ace looked in his rearview mirror and noted at least five miles of nobody behind him and another five miles of nobody in the front. He stood on the accelerator of the little car, and it buzzed its heart out for them, making him feel bad for planning to kill it when this was over.

"You are sure he will stop?" Jai asked, displaying only a mild curiosity.

"You got your seat belt on?" Ace asked. His was on, like it always was, because speed limits were more of a suggestion for the faint of heart than a rule.

"Da," Jai said.

"Then, sure. He'll stop."

And with that, Ace zoomed past the laboring RV, then up the road a quarter mile, where he jammed on the brakes, hit the emergency brake, and allowed the resulting skid to carry the car 180 degrees around in a circle and land on the dividing line between both lanes.

He and Jai had about three heartbeats to regard the oncoming vehicle before the guy at the wheel—eyes looming like boiled eggs, even from the closing distance—swerved off the road and halted, skidding to a stop in a cloud of dust on the side of the road to Ace's left.

"I'll talk to him," Ace said. "You reconnoiter."

"I don't even think you know what that word means," Jai said.

"It means you circle around and bash him on the head," Ace said.

"Apparently you do," Jai murmured and slammed the door shut so Ace could pull to the side of the road and out of traffic.

As he was getting out of the car, he noted the driver of the RV had recovered a rifle from somewhere in his nightmare-mobile and had it cocked and ready as Ace stepped out.

"The fuck you doing!" he demanded, his accent thicker than Jai's and sharper somehow. Provinces, Ace thought. Countries he wasn't versed in. He'd been enlisted in the military. Nobody'd paid him to learn languages, but he knew this guy and Jai were two entirely different creatures.

"You were dragging something," Ace said, hands up, keeping his spine loose. "In the back. Looked like your tailpipe was about to fall off. Just being friendly, right?"

The coyote was wearing jeans that had been ready for the hamper five-to-ten wears ago and a T-shirt that had lost its original color pulled tight enough to expose a potbelly. His hair hung in lank strands across a pink, balding head. Ace bet that if he got within five feet of the guy, the smell would knock him flat.

"I do not hear anything," he said, not moving his eyes from Ace. "Get your fucking car out of my way, or I shoot you here and leave you and your...." His piggy eyes narrowed. "There were two of you."

"There were not," he lied. Ace had a face that did that well—he was aware. He didn't lie to Sonny or Sonny wouldn't ever trust him again, but this guy got no fucking loyalty from him.

"I...." Pig-eyes probably hadn't slept in a very long time because he squinted and looked away as though trying to remember. "I do not care," he decided, and then he cocked the shotgun and fired.

Ace had dropped to the ground before the thing was done cocking. He gave a quick roll, putting him up against the Sentra, slightly angled away from the man with the gun, and pulled his own service pistol from the back of his pants. Squinting against the flurry of dust, he swore. Jai could be back there, just beyond this asshole, and if he missed the bad guy, he could kill his employee, who was also his friend. That was no damned good.

The guy cracked the shotgun to load it, and that gave Ace time to scuttle backward like a crab and duck behind the car. The coyote fired again, twice in quick succession, and the front window of Ernie's car disintegrated.

"Who the fuck are you?" demanded the driver.

"Like I'm gonna tell you now?" Ace snapped, checking under the car to see which way his feet were going.

"Who sent you? Are you trying to steal my product?"

"What product?" Ace screamed, still telling lies. "All I saw in the back there was a bunch of kids!"

"Who sent—" The man's scream—Ace could imagine spit flying from his lips as his voice broke—cut off abruptly with a thud and a sort of groan and a crunch.

"Ace?" Jai's voice said clearly. "You are not dead?"

"Nope," Ace said, climbing out of the dust and gravel that littered the roadside. His work overalls were covered in sand, and the palms of his hands were cut up some by the small rocks in the roadside gravel, but he was relatively unscathed. He dusted himself off and went to smooth his short black hair back from his brow when his fingers encountered small sharp pebbles.

"Ouch," he mumbled, drawing blood. "Is that glass?"

"Ernie's car." Jai sighed.

As Ace approached he could hear the gurgle of blood their friend with the shotgun was making through a nose that had been turned to powder.

Ace hunkered down by the feebly struggling meat sack, wondering what was broken in him that he didn't feel like this *person* was human enough to deserve pity.

"How you doin'?" he asked, not particularly caring one way or the other.

"Mng mnib mmm…."

Ace blinked and translated. He'd been in enough fights as a kid and had seen enough violence as an adult to figure it out. "Yeah, I know he hit you. You were shooting at me. You're lucky your brains aren't leaking on the sand."

The writhing figure on the ground suddenly ceased struggling, and Ace used the Beretta still in his hand to gesture, making his point.

"So, you see, we need to know where these kids were goin', so we know to give them a special delivery of their very own. Don't worry, kids'll be fine. I know that was a problem and all since you probably left them locked in there with no fuckin' water. This way, you won't have to worry none, and you can just slither off into the desert and find another way back home."

"I'll… mmm…."

Ace rolled his eyes. "He won't kill you if he can't find you. I'd just make sure he can't find you. Maybe change your name, wash your pits, change your clothes. I'm pretty sure they'll be looking for an entirely different person." Some of the whimsy went out of his tone. "One who wasn't trafficking kids for God knows what to God knows where. Which you will tell us right—"

The sound of chopper blades took him by surprise. He and Jai looked at each other and then up as the small black helicopter that had suddenly appeared above them began a slow circle and started to lower itself to the ground.

And the guy on the ground took advantage of their inattention and grabbed Ace's gun—and pulled the muzzle into his mouth while Ace gave a jerk with his hand to pull it out.

He'd had the safety on, but the man's scrabbling hands clicked it off, and as Ace jerked, the gun went off, and gore spattered up Ace's arm and onto his coveralls.

"What the—" He stared, appalled, as a loudspeaker from the chopper began to blare.

"Put down your weapons and stand, hands over your heads. Put down your weapons and stand slowly, hands over your heads."

As Ace stood, horrified, he and Jai met eyes.

"The actual fuck," Jai said.

"You are telling me."

This was it. He was going to be arrested for a murder he hadn't really committed and let off for one he had. He knew it. In his head, he was reciting Ellery Cramer's number, because Cramer was a lawyer and knew about the worst thing Ace had ever done.

The figure who leaped from the passenger's side of the helicopter and bent down to run toward them was not a policeman, however, and he wasn't holding a weapon aimed at them.

"Are you Burton's friend Ace?" he asked. He was a handsome man, in his midthirties, with tired brown eyes and curly brown hair that had gone two haircuts past the military requirement under his cap. He was dressed in fatigues, with a few shiny stars and bars on his shoulder that showed his pay grade was so far beyond Ace's that he could have eaten Ace for lunch. The patch over his pocket read "Constance."

"So," Colonel Constance said, "you're the one he keeps tabs on in the desert?"

"Yessir," Ace said.

"Ernie said you'd come to stop this man from trafficking minors?" Ace nodded to the RV. "In there, sir."

Constance's dark eyes took in the gore on Ace's arm and the very, very dead man missing the back of his head at their feet. "So, uhm, what in the actual fuck?"

"That would be our question too, sir," Ace told him, a tiny part of him relaxing. Maybe he wouldn't need Cramer's number after all. "He started firing on us. My friend here subdued him, and I was just asking him some questions when he grabbed my gun and gave it a blowjob."

Constance's eyes widened, but other than that his expression remained impassive. "Think that was the happy ending he had in mind?"

Ace thought about it seriously. "He was real fuckin' scared," he said at last. "Kept talking about how someone'll kill him if he doesn't get his 'product' to its delivery drop-off." Sweat trickled down between his shoulder blades and coated the top of his ass. "Speaking of which, sir, is there any way we can get those kids out of there and give 'em some water." He grimaced. "I should check the car and see if Ernie's got some bottles or something in—"

"He's got three cases in the trunk," Constance said, shifting as he stood. "Uh, he mentioned that when he called Burton and had Burton call me."

Ace met those tired brown eyes with his own and wondered if his expression was that same mix of uneasiness and acceptance that Ernie's gift seemed to fill Constance with.

"That was right fortunate," Ace said with a slow nod. "Can we…?"

Constance nodded. "But you might want to take off your coveralls and wash off your hand," he said, and Ace grimaced.

"Well, Ernie said the blood wouldn't be mine."

Constance got on the radio while Ace and Jai let the kids out of the RV. They were all young—between eleven and fourteen, maybe—and all terrified.

And only a few of them spoke more than a few words of English.

"Russian," Jai said shortly. "And Polish. Some Ukrainian. I speak."

Ace followed him dutifully, giving each kid a bottle of water and a wet wipe so they could wash their hands and faces and maybe cool off a little. He'd rummaged through the trunk of the Sentra and had also found several five-packs of kids' T-shirts, rainbow colors, and exactly fourteen pairs of shorts in various kids sizes.

There were fourteen kids.

By the time Jai had talked quietly to every kid who spoke one of the languages Jai could get by with, each kid had gotten a camp shower—or rather, a wet-wipe in all of their places—and a clean set of clothes.

The clothes that they left in a pile next to the RV after they changed reeked of several days' sweat and piss. Most of the kids had chafing marks on their thin arms and on their necks from where filth-stiffened cotton had rubbed them raw.

"They are hungry," Jai said softly.

Ace gave him a flat look and pulled out several boxes of saltines and three jars of peanut butter he'd found in the same Walmart bags with the clothes.

And the whole time, cars passed them on the interstate, looking curious but never stopping, and Jason Constance argued angrily on the phone.

Finally he shouted, "I'll take them, then, goddammit! Because I'm not turning them over to mobsters so you can track the fucking money trail. Fine, have my stars. Come down here to the fucking desert and track the psychopaths that you people made and then tell me what a goddamned imposition it is to do the right goddamned thing!"

He hung up then, stabbing angrily at his phone, and Ace was surprised the unit didn't get pitched across the desert. He left Jai talking to the children and walked over to see what was doing.

"They're out of Sacramento," Constance said, body still shaking with rage. "They were supposed to be turned over to a mobster in Vegas. *I* would like to return them to their homes, but…."

Ace plucked the phone out of his hand as he went to pitch it and substituted a rock instead.

Constance threw the rock out into the desert, where it probably continued in a short, shallow orbit around the earth until it reached Canada. Oregon at the very least.

"I have a suggestion," Ace said, thinking he liked this man that Burton looked to very much.

Constance just stared at him. "Yes, and…."

"You gotta make sure me and Jai don't get arrested or shit."

"I can't guarantee civilian safety."

"Killed's on us," Ace told him bluntly. "We get killed, we pretty much had it coming. But how about you let Jai and me deliver this RV to wherever it's going. You seem to know the address. We stop and fix it up at the garage, we can have it running well enough to get to Vegas sometime in the small hours of the morning. Don't worry. Me and Jai can do what needs doing."

Constance regarded him through narrow eyes. "What *exactly* do you think needs doing?"

Ace wondered if it was a trick question. "Well, we need to set some high-grade explosive in that bustedass vehicle and drive it into the mobster's house and detonate it. And then get the hell out of there before we're recognized."

"That's a terrible plan," Constance told him flatly. He paused. "But only because there might be more kids in the compound and because you and your friend can't be seen."

Logistics! Ace grunted. "We can find an alternative. We could just deliver the dead guy to the live guys and skitter away."

Constance grunted. "I'll have Burton meet you. And the dead guy…." Constance looked around at the vasty nothingness surrounding this spot on 15. "He doesn't need to spend the night in the RV."

"Understood," Ace said. "But what're you gonna do?"

Constance looked at his pilot, who was sitting in the plane, obviously waiting for orders. "I think I'm gonna have Huntington over there fly to our base of operations and return with another vehicle."

"Make sure it has AC, sir," Ace said, looking over his shoulders to see that Jai had organized the children in the shade of the RV, each sitting quietly on the ground, legs folded, with water and crackers and peanut butter.

"Way ahead of you, soldier." Constance looked unhappily at the RV and chewed his lower lip. "I shouldn't ask you to do this," he said, sounding helpless. "But they want me to have soldiers drive the kids to Vegas and put them in danger and…." His eyes creased at the corners, making him look much older.

"Then don't worry about it," Ace said, shrugging his shoulders. "Right thing ain't always the government thing. I got no illusions."

"I used to," Constance said, sighing.

"Well, give your orders and then c'mere and meet your cargo. Jai's got names and family members from most of them." Ace felt the same bleakness that was saturating Constance's expression. "Most of 'em have families, sir. These children may not speak English, but they're missed."

Burton's CO squeezed his eyes shut and then opened them, command falling like a mantle on his shoulders again. "Then we need to do right by them."

"Yessir." Ace turned to go talk to Jai about the children, expecting Constance to go do his ordering thing with the helicopter pilot, but Constance surprised him with a hand on his shoulder.

"Ace?" he said, the first time Ace had heard the man say his name. "Sir?"

"Burton's friends reflect well on him."

Ace laughed outright. "Burton's a better man than I'll ever be."

Constance shook his head. "No, sir. But I'll let you keep yourself a secret. You seem more comfortable that way."

Ace nodded his head. "Man, I just wish all the assholes in the world didn't have to use this fuckin' road."

Constance chuckled, and Ace had no idea why. He just turned back toward the kids and figured the sooner he and Jai could get into that RV and get it back to the garage, the sooner Sonny might be able to forgive him.

Reflect well on Burton—ha! Burton was off saving the world or some such shit. Ace really only had one goal in life, and it was to keep his skinny blond dirty bomb of a boyfriend from detonating and killing them all.

It's a good thing Sonny was his favorite thing in all the world; the rest of it wasn't a hardship.

"Jai," he said, striding up to the big man as he sat on his haunches. "How about you and me go to Vegas and kill some mobsters."

Jai brightened. "You," he said soberly, "are the best boss in the world."

"Tell me that after Sonny yells at us for an hour."

"Da."

Meanwhile, back in Sacramento....

"PLEASE?" JACKSON begged, not sure if Ellery really understood how important this was.

"No." Ellery Cramer, Jackson's boyfriend, could be an amazingly sexy man. He had deep brown eyes, a decisive nose, a square—if bony—jaw, a brilliant legal mind, and a sense of humor that was both sly and devastating.

He could also be an unbearably prissy stickler for the rules.

"But I've only got a week to go!" Jackson wailed and then hated himself for it.

Ellery sat on the edge of the bed, all decked out in his summer-weight olive work suit and tie, even though it was their own damned legal office and he didn't have to go to court. He could have been wearing basketball shorts and a tank top if he wanted, but of course he wouldn't. Jackson had tried—*tried*—to set his phone alarm to get up before Ellery so he'd be all dressed and ready when Ellery was, but Ellery had caught on to that the week before and had started disabling Jackson's phone in the middle of the night when he got up to pee.

Ellery Cramer only did things right, and infuriatingly enough, that included Jackson's return date from his recent heart surgery.

"They didn't even have to crack open my chest," Jackson told him. Needlessly, of course, because Ellery had been in the waiting room during the entire procedure. "I was out in two days. It was practically outpatient surgery."

Ellery regarded him flatly. Jackson had been out in two days because hospitals freaked him out so badly they couldn't be sure his heart rate would slow down enough to let him heal, and because he got no sleep.

"It's just," Jackson continued, soldiering on in spite of the hard brown-eyed glare, "I really *have* been obeying all of the rules, haven't I? And I wouldn't ask if I didn't feel up to it. I promised, right?" He smiled prettily. Once upon a time, he'd been mostly sure he could get away with anything from a lover on a wink and a prayer. It wasn't that he thought he was handsome, but people tended to respond to confidence, and he had a certain swagger.

Ellery was not that lover. Never had been. But then, Ellery hadn't let himself get brushed off and had stuck around long enough to see all the demons that swagger covered.

Ellery was made of tougher stuff than the parade of one-night wonders that had marched through Jackson's bed before they'd met. And he knew it too.

"You did," Ellery said. "You *did* promise."

Augh, guilt! This was not supposed to be a situation calling for guilt.

"So, since I've been a model recovering patient," Jackson said, pushing up so the covers fell away from his bare chest, "and I feel fine, and you've come running with me for the last week and taken my heart rate after swimming too, I thought that maybe—just maybe—I could, you know, get back into the game early."

"No," Ellery said.

"Please?" Jackson closed his eyes because he didn't want to see himself turn into a big needy whiny baby. "Please, please, please, please, *pleeeeeeeeeze*? Ellery, I'm *bored*!"

"Read a book," Ellery said, his voice clipped.

"I've read books." Mostly textbooks. Jackson had been taking online courses over the last eight weeks in order to keep his PI skills sharp so he could better help Ellery at the firm. Ellery claimed Jackson knew as much about criminal search and seizure laws as Ellery knew, but Jackson thought Ellery was probably blowing smoke, because Ellery was damned smart.

"God, read a novel. Think of ways to redecorate the house. Go to the shelter and adopt a cat."

Jackson stared at him. "Adopt a cat?"

And finally—*finally*—Ellery looked away. "Look, it's what my mother said when she was here in the spring."

"She said our cat was inappropriate," Jackson told him, feeling miffed.

"He licks his balls at every opportunity."

"That's unlikely since *somebody* got him fixed!"

Ellery's brown eyes snapped. "I got him fixed so he wouldn't run away and break your heart. And my mother also said that the cat was going to need some company when we both went back to work. And since you're returning next week, I...." His brows drew down and his mouth pursed, and the resulting expression was grumpy and uncomfortable and very, very dear. "I don't want him to be lonely."

Jackson turned to the cat, who was sitting on the other side of the bed with his one remaining back leg shot up in the air as he—yes— licked where his balls used to be.

"Did you hear that, Billy Bob? Ellery loves you."

The battered, mostly-Siamese cat looked up, his tongue halfway extended from his mouth, and blinked one-and-a-half crossed blue eyes at him. He had a snaggletooth, an ear that had healed ripped, and he'd lost his leg when Jackson's old duplex had been shot up. His neck was as big around as Jackson's wrist, and he tended to thug walk, even on three legs.

The fact that Ellery spoiled the cat rotten almost—*almost*—made up for the fact that he'd gotten Billy Bob fixed while Jackson had been in surgery for a gunshot wound.

"I do," Ellery said primly. "And I would feel better about both of you if Billy Bob had some company."

Jackson looked at him, hurt. "Don't you want to help me pick out his buddy?"

Ellery glanced away again. "Well, yes," he admitted. "I do, but...." He swallowed. "Dammit! I'm starting to feel bad. You really *are* working hard at recovery, and Henry's getting better, but he's getting on my last goddamned nerve." Ellery took a deep breath and pulled some of his composure back. "He was in the military for ten years, and he tends to rely on orders," he said after a minute. "It turns out I don't mind a little independence." He sent a conciliatory little smile Jackson's way.

Jackson sat up completely and held a hand to his chest, hoping his heart was doing a victory lap and not threatening to quit again. "That's it? You're caving?" Billy Bob leaped off the bed in a fit of pique, and Ellery stood and backed up like a hunted man.

"No, I am not caving. I am making a *concession* to the fact that I'm not caving."

"Oh no," Jackson said, hopping out of bed. "I'm not going to get that kitten without you, and if I'm not getting the kitten without you, you have to let me come back to work."

Ellery stared at him, mouth moving like he was trying to find holes in Jackson's legal theory, and there were probably a boatload, but Jackson didn't care.

"So you start the coffee, and I'll get—" Jackson wrinkled his nose. Ellery had bought him a truckload of new clothes while he'd been stuck at home in Ellery's amazingly spacious house, and Jackson had sort of promised to wear some of them. "—dressed. In the appropriate wear for my job," he added, all virtue. "I'll be showered and out the door and ready to go in—"

"Five days!" Ellery countered, with an admirable return of his earlier resolve. "So help me, Jackson."

"I'll jockey from the office," Jackson pleaded. "Henry can do all the footwork. I'll just help Jade."

"Jade will strangle you," Ellery said seriously. "If you're in that office and underfoot, she will kill you."

"Jade loves me like a brother," Jackson returned, indignation lighting him up inside. Jade Cameron and her twin brother, Kaden, and their late mother had taken Jackson in when his own mother had bailed on the job of family while they'd all been in middle school. Jackson and Jade had spent part of their lives as on-again/off-again lovers of convenience, but in truth, the dynamic that worked best for them was as brother and sister.

"Which is exactly why she'll kill you." Ellery scrubbed at his face with his hands. "Look, Jenny Probst at the public defender's office wants me to take a pro bono case. I need some vetting. She's pretty sure the kid is innocent, but he won't speak up in his own defense. She wants some help getting him off, if she can. She says he wasn't made for jail. If you want, I can let you vet the case, look into it, maybe even help me interview him, but *you can't leave the office*. Is that understood?"

"Not even for lunch?" Inwardly he winced. God, he just had to push it one more inch.

"If you're good," Ellery said sweetly, "we can have lunch together."

Jackson paused, thinking that even though they'd been shut in together for much of the past eight weeks while Ellery and Jackson's family monitored his recovery, this was still an attractive prospect.

"Fine," he said, thinking. "Define good."

"I've got a meeting. I've got to go. But I'll send Henry back for you. You may pick the files up from the PD's office. Come *directly to our office* with them. Do not pass go. Do not save children from the burning building—that's what the fire department is for—and do not rescue kittens from trees."

Jackson grinned at him, so happy he could practically dance. "But if I rescue the kitten from the tree, does that mean I can *keep the kitten*!"

Ellery's eyes narrowed to slits. "No."

"But you're still going to send Henry for me?" Jackson asked, following as Ellery turned to go.

"Maybe."

"But we still get to have lunch together, right?" he prodded, on Ellery's heels as he strode down the hallway, barely pausing to scratch Billy Bob on the stomach where he now sprawled on the kitchen table without shame.

Jackson followed Ellery's scratch, and the cat doubled up, kicking with his back leg and biting.

"You traitor!" Jackson gasped, scooping the snarling animal into his arms. "You're supposed to love me best."

"It's the stomach, Jackson," Ellery said. "He gets one scratch on his stomach per day."

"*You*," Jackson said in outrage, "bogarted my cat!"

Ellery turned to him, his expression severe but his eyes dancing. "You could always spend the day getting another one so we don't freak this one out with too much attention."

Billy Bob had calmed down and was now rubbing his nose and whiskers systematically on Jackson's shoulder to make up for the several scratches that graced his forearm.

"*I*," Jackson said with dignity, "will be having lunch with you." He sobered. "Besides, we have a Jackson cat. We need an Ellery cat."

Ellery's eyes darted sideways and his usually pale cheeks sported red crescents. "What kind of cat is an Ellery cat?" he asked.

"A dignified cat," Jackson said. "Gray, like a pinstriped suit. Or tiger-striped, but dignified. Ooh, or black, like a little panther. Sleek and elegant." He looked at Billy Bob, who had flopped into the crook of Jackson's arm and was drooling complacently. "Something sane."

Ellery still couldn't meet his eyes, that shyness that sometimes took Jackson by the throat very much apparent. "We can look this weekend," he said, biting his lip, and Jackson dumped his affronted cat on the ground to press Ellery back against the connecting door between the kitchen and the garage.

"Lotsa things we can do this weekend," he purred.

Ellery's eyes danced again. "We do that a lot." But it didn't sound like he minded.

"Not full up yet," Jackson told him, moving in slowly so he could smell Ellery's aftershave, his clean precision, his minty take-on-the-day scent before moving in for the kiss. He captured Ellery's mouth and tried to devour that smell, that excitement, whole.

Ellery responded, mouth open, cupping Jackson's face with his smooth, manicured hands. The kiss ended before it really began, and Ellery groaned and leaned his forehead against Jackson's.

"I might not ever be full up," he said wickedly. Then he sighed. "But I am late."

"Fine," Jackson said, but then he remembered he'd won. "Henry and I will be by the office before lunch."

"Good. I've got some stuff you can do from the office then." He gave Jackson another quick kiss and slid out the garage door, leaving Jackson to dress for the day.

JACKSON DECIDED on cargo shorts—but ones in decent condition, and a new T-shirt—one they'd gotten from the Monterey Bay Aquarium with a sea otter on the front. It wasn't snarky, but it wasn't a suit and tie, and it was cute as hell.

He figured adulthood didn't have to be all bad, right?

He'd just finished washing morning dishes when there was a knock on the door.

Henry Worrall had served in the military for nine years before he'd been forced out by an abusive boyfriend, and his posture and close-cropped blond hair remained to prove it. But when Jackson opened the door, his lips twisted into a smile, and his blue eyes lightened fractionally, proving that a new perspective is only as far away as you make it.

"So, you're done with this vacation bullshit?"

"Don't attack the cat on your way in," Jackson said, turning to lead him into the house. "He's already had his share of blood today."

Henry snorted. "That cat could eat out your throat and then take out the neighborhood." Henry and Billy Bob had a long history of enmity under their belts. "Are you ready to do, like, real work again?"

Jackson grunted his frustration. "Picking up files is as real as it gets," he said reluctantly. "After that, you drop me off at the office, and I sit still like a good boy and do my desk work."

"Oh my God, are you whipped." Henry smirked.

"You're looking good today," Jackson said dryly. "Wipe any runny noses? Diaper any rash?"

Circumstances had landed Henry a job working at Ellery's firm, with Ellery's first partner in law, Galen Henderson. They had *also* landed Henry a living situation in which he mentored a group of young men who were supposedly grown and on their own. And making their living in pornography. Living in the "flophouse" for a few months before moving out with his boyfriend, Lance, had been partially responsible for mellowing Henry out from his straightlaced, straight-passing life when he'd first gotten out of the military.

Working along with Jackson, Ellery, and Galen to help clear himself of a murder he hadn't committed had done the rest.

And the mentoring had never really gone away. In Henry's words, a lot of the guys living in the two-bedroom apartment while they tried to figure out their lives had "more balls than brains," and Henry and Lance did a lot of counseling in the guise of hanging out with the boys from the flophouse.

In response to Jackson's question, Henry gave a solid grunt. "Yes. Yes, I wiped noses this morning."

Jackson gave him a sympathetic look. "Cotton?" he posed delicately.

"He's...." Henry grimaced. His first language wasn't really English. It was more like Repressed Male, and he spoke it well. "Sometimes, some people, you just want someone to show up and say, 'You. You are my Cinderella. I shall take you to a castle and we shall talk and be equals, but I will always, always take care of you.'"

Jackson shuddered. "Gah!"

"Yeah, I know," Henry said with a sigh. "Not my thing either. But seriously, and I say this with all the love in the world for this kid, he can pay rent, and he can shop, and he's going to school for a degree in something that will never get him money, but inside"—Henry held his hands to his chest—"he is never going to be not broken."

Jackson blew out a breath. "There's a lot to be said for broken but functional," he said after a moment. "Sometimes it takes the right person to be the glue."

Henry rolled his eyes. "Well, I'm his glue for now, but that's not healthy." He blew out a breath. "I'm just as glad he's out of porn, though. It's like every guy who came on to him was 'the one,' and that's not a good place for someone who's getting paid to put out."

Jackson grimaced. "No. No it is not." He snagged his wallet and a small messenger bag, then shoved his house keys in his pocket. Billy Bob was up on the table again, eating his second breakfast, and Jackson scratched him at the base of the tail because fuck that guy if he wanted to go nuclear.

Billy Bob purred and continued to eat, and Jackson figured they were good.

"Speaking of broken," Henry continued as they ventured into the oppressive heat of mid-August, "how're you doing?"

Jackson paused to give him an unamused look. "Heart's fine, Henry. All checked out. Eating well, exercising well, being a good boy. Wanna see my blood pressure and my last X-rays?"

"Nope, because Lance talks to your doctor and then he talks to me, and I know all that shit," Henry said mildly, apparently HIPAA laws be damned. "That's not the broken I was talking about."

Oh dear lord. "Feelings?" Jackson asked, appalled. "You want me to talk about my feelings? Werewolf fucking Jesus, when did that happen?"

"Oh my God, you people gave me so much shit because I was repressed when I got here. *You* wrote the book on emotional repression. I'm just asking you if any of the shit you had to sort when we were running around trying to clear my name got sorted."

"Oh, who cares," Jackson snapped. God yes, he'd been talking to Ellery's rabbi, who had appointed himself Jackson's personal counselor for life, and yes, he felt a little better about things than he had before he'd driven himself to the damned almost-heart-attack. But part of the reason he wanted to get back to the office wasn't so much to *avoid* the personal tinkering he had to do in order to make his relationship—and, face it, himself—work *better*, it was to have a place where he *didn't* have to confront hard personal truths.

Activity and puzzle solving was oh-so-much easier, and sometimes he needed a break from his own head.

"I do," Henry said brightly. "Emotional enlightenment works great that way."

"I'm fine," Jackson told him. "I'm practically giddy."

Henry paused as they neared the cream-colored Lincoln that Galen Henderson, who technically employed Henry as *his* private investigator, lent out to Henry so Henry could drive him to and from work. Galen had been injured in a horrific motorcycle crash nearly five years ago and had battled addiction to painkillers afterward. He could walk now and drive a car, but not without pain. His boyfriend liked to spare him that, so they'd hired Henry to drive for Galen when Henry had first come to Sacramento.

Then there had been the inconvenient murder charge, and Henry had proved to have a knack for helping Jackson search out the truth, so Jackson had gained himself a protégé, and Henry had gained himself a calling.

"Still having nightmares?" Henry asked softly as Jackson reached to open his door.

Jackson grunted and was about to blow Henry off when his last discussion with the rabbi flashed through his mind. *Allow other people to worry about you. It's a kindness—it gives them something active to do while you go help people.*

"What was it you said?" He rubbed his chest. "Always broken? My nightmares and I go way back. It's going to take a lot more than a really decent relationship during a real bastard of a year to fix that."

"Wow," Henry said, sliding into the car.

"Wow what?" Jackson did the same and belted up too.

"That's about as healthy as you probably get." He hit the ignition switch and grinned. "Excellent. Let's go kick some ass."

Jackson laughed a little and let Henry speed out of Ellery's expensive American River Drive neighborhood.

It really did feel like being let out of school.

THE PUBLIC defender's office was located in a squat, ugly, square butt plug of a building on Seventh and H, which was sort of the center of the legal district in Sacramento. Given that the city was the state's capitol, with plenty of lobbyists and representatives and senators floating around, the district itself was a little bigger than most, but still, Ellery's law offices were probably within walking distance of this particular public eyesore.

They had to park three blocks away near the levee, because ugh, that was downtown, and by the time they'd walked back to mount the granite steps, Jackson could feel the sweat of a humid August day trickling down his armpits and his back.

Henry, dressed in pretty much the same non-uniform in cargo shorts and a T-shirt, was the first to remark on it.

"God, I'm so glad we don't wear suits."

"Oh my God, right? But you have to if you testify. You've got one, right?"

Henry's slow breath of disgust told him that was a go. "Galen took me shopping right before you and Ellery offered me the job with the firm. I had no idea why somebody would buy me suits when he didn't want up my ass, but now I know."

"Technically we're probably supposed to wear slacks and collared shirts," Jackson told him, belatedly remembering that that's what the other PIs in his and Ellery's old firm used to wear. Just not him.

Henry looked at him in horror. "Are we gonna?"

"Oh God no. That's the other guys."

"Thank you, Jesus."

The lobby was utilitarian and plain, and they passed the security guard and the metal detectors before they were directed up to the third floor, where their particular public defender worked.

As they got in the elevator, they heard a disturbance, a man arguing vehemently, his voice thick with a Slavic accent. But that didn't stop Jackson from hearing "Jenny Probst" in the mix of shouting and, just as the doors closed, gunshots.

He and Henry met startled glances.

"Shit, was that guy gunning for—"

"Our public defender," Jackson finished tersely as they both watched the lift light up for the third floor. "You go jam the door to the stairs shut. I'll warn everybody to get down."

"And hide her," Henry shouted as the doors opened.

"No kidding, Junior!" Jackson stepped out of the elevator and sighted down the hallway filled with doors. Jenny's was third door to the left, so he had to get cracking.

He stuck his head into the first office and spotted the security guard leaning up against the wall, eyes scanning the office cubicles beyond. He nodded the guy over and said quietly, "There may be an active shooter downstairs, heading up here. Get everybody under their desks and tell them to keep calm. Lock the door until you can get an all clear from your buddies downstairs."

The guy nodded tersely and got on the radio as Jackson ran to the next door.

The ones on the left were individual offices, and the first two were locked, thank God. He warned one more large public office before heading for Jenny Probst's small office, throwing the door open right as he heard a ruckus back in the direction of the elevators and the stairs.

Henry came trotting up next to him as he opened Jenny Probst's door.

"I propped the door closed with an axe," he said breathlessly. "Good news is, it's wedged there pretty tight. Bad news is—"

"If he gets past it, he's got the fire axe," Jackson muttered. He must have missed the sound of breaking glass in his rush to get down to Jenny's office. Her name was emblazoned on the window, and short of breaking it and giving away an advantage *and* their position, there was no way to keep her whereabouts a secret.

"Jenny Probst?" Jackson asked.

The woman behind the desk had pale yellow hair and soft pink features. In her midthirties, if she hadn't been wearing the power suit, he would have pegged her for a soccer mom, but one who forgot to dye her roots regularly.

"Hello?"

Jackson's eyes searched the room. "Hey, does that lead to the office next door? The empty one without your name?"

"It's the copy room," she said, appearing puzzled. "Why?"

Jackson and Henry looked at each other as the shouting at the other end of the hall got louder.

"Lady, we need to get you in the fucking closet."

Oops, Here I Go Again....

ELLERY LOOKED at the kid sitting on the other side of his desk and then at his tearful mother and wished his people skills were more on point.

"Look, Ty, I know this wasn't fair."

"Dammit, there were sixty other kids at that party with X on them!" Ty Townsend burst out, and Ellery resisted the temptation to rub at his temples.

"I know."

"And they were all white kids, and I was the only brown boy in the crowd!"

"I know, Ty."

"Then what in the hell am I doing here?" he shouted, and Ellery's temper broke.

"The fact that you are here is not my fault! The fact that you're not letting me defend you *is*!"

Ty sat down abruptly. "What am I supposed to do?" he asked, wounded and angry and thoroughly confused, and not for the first time in the last weeks, Ellery wished for Jackson.

Jackson had a way with people. He probably could have had Ty eating out of his hand and a way to get Ty out of the charge of possession with intent to sell before Ty had even had to pay for his first consult.

But Jackson wasn't here, and Ty's mother had put a lot of money into getting Ty a lawyer who would not plead her barely eighteen-year-old son right into prison, and Ellery needed to pony up.

"If I'm convicted, I can't go to school at the end of this week," Ty said. "I'll lose my scholarship. I'll lose everything!"

And part of Ellery wanted to say, "Well, you shouldn't have grabbed the damned drugs as a party favor, then."

But the other part of him recognized the absolute unfairness of Ty's arrest when he had not been the one who'd brought the X and he certainly hadn't been the one to sell it—or use it.

They'd get to that if and only if they could save this kid's future first.

"Look," Ellery said, making sure Ty's eyes were locked on his. "I can't make promises because some of this is out of my control. But I will tell you this. We will talk to the police involved, we will talk to the other kids at the party, and I've got some tricks up my sleeve. I can't guarantee that this will disappear, and I can't guarantee that you won't lose your scholarship, but I will do my damnedest to make sure you don't see jail time. But I need some things from you first."

Ty looked like he was going to get angry again, but his mother—a comfortable woman wearing what looked to be her Sunday-best dress in muted shades of gold and brown—put her hand on his arm and gave him a pleading glance.

"Tyson, please," she said softly. "I... I can't have you in jail."

Ty grimaced and nodded. "Okay, Mama."

A mama's boy. Ellery was one himself, and he approved of the breed in general.

"So," Ellery said with a deep breath, "I need to know who gave you the drugs."

Ty looked at his mother and then sighed. "Look, this could be really bad if it gets out who told you."

"Was it a secret?" Ellery asked. "Your statement here says all the students had them."

"They did! We walked into No Neck's house—"

"James Cosgrove?"

"No Neck," Ty confirmed, and then he frowned. "Man, something was going around text about him this morning. Nate was losing his mind, but I had my own shit to sort. Anyway, he shook everyone's hand and told us that Ziggy would hook us up."

"And Ziggy would be Sergio Ivanov," Ellery said, making the note there.

"Yeah. Ziggy's this little squirrely guy—eyeballs always vibrating. He's not in high school. He pretends he is, but I could swear he's a couple years older. Anyway, I went to the kitchen for—" He looked at his mother. "—water."

"You gathered around the keg with all the other high school students. Don't bullshit me, Tyson. I can't help you if *I* get busted in one of your lies."

Tyson's broad, football player's shoulders slumped, and he gave his mother that look that only teenagers could have. The one that said their world was over, and they would take it all back if they could.

"So, yeah. I gathered around the keg, and Ziggy came up. He was always getting super familiar with us when we weren't, you know, loving him. But he came up and gave me this handclasp bullshit, and when he pulled back I had a dime bag with three pills in it."

Ellery frowned and looked at his police report again. "Three pills?"

"Yeah. And I was like, 'No, man, I'm already training. I leave next week,' and he smiles this really slimy smile and goes, 'Just a little party favor, yeah?' And I don't want to piss him off or hurt his feelings or anything."

"Why not?" Ellery asked, curious.

Tyson shifted as he sat. "I… I just get this really bad vibe off Ziggy. Like, this one time last year, at a football game, one of the guys got this real bad break. It was sort of scary, right? And I look up into the stands to see if Jaden's mom is up there, and I see Ziggy, and he's got this look on his face. This really shitty look. Like it was worth the price of admission to watch Jaden's leg snap backward like that. So I don't like Ziggy, but I don't piss him off either."

Ellery nodded. "Fair enough," he said thoughtfully. "So he hands you a bag with three pills in it, and you…?"

"I put it in my pocket and tell him it's for later. And I'm planning to throw it away." Tyson had a man's body: broad shoulders, arms like cannons, and a notable absence of neck. He was one of the best offensive tackles in the state. But the look that crossed his face then was even younger than the teenaged one. This one was a child, full-on vulnerable, and it broke Ellery's heart.

"I swear, Mama," he said softly. "I was going to throw them away."

Ralene Townsend wiped her eyes with her palm. "I know, sweetheart. You're a good boy. I've never doubted it."

Tyson let out a shuddering breath. "So I put them in my pocket, and I swear to God, not ten minutes later, the door bursts open, and it's the cops."

"Now, you say you were the only 'brown face' there. Can I ask if your school is mostly white?"

Tyson tilted his head. "Uhm, no, actually. It's a pretty good mix."

"Did it bother you to be the only person of color at an all-white party?"

"No." He shrugged. "Sorry. Not the only time it's happened. Black people deal with it, you know?"

Ellery nodded. "I, well, I guess I can't really understand personally, but I understand that the world works that way sometimes. I was just wondering if this was a rare occurrence or a usual one." Because while Ellery hadn't had a chance to put Henry on the case, he *had* asked to see the files of the other kids arrested at that party and had been told that Tyson was the only one.

Tyson frowned. "You know, now that you mention it, most of the parties I've gone to as a football player are pretty, you know, rainbow. 'Cause the team is pretty rainbow, and the school is all the colors, so it's not so much me against the world."

"So, this was a situation that only happened at No Neck's house?"

Tyson nodded slowly, and Ellery could see the wheels turning. "His family is pretty white. His grandparents were Russian, I guess, but we don't really talk about it. Do you think I was set up?"

"I can't say for sure, but we have lots of inconsistencies to look at when our PI gets here." Jackson had texted when he and Henry had arrived at the PD's office building; they should get there any minute. Ellery looked at the police report again, and then at Tyson. "Tyson, there are some differences between your police report and your story. Now, I'm going to ask you about them, and I don't want you to get upset. I just want you to know this is me, looking for the truth. I'm not taking this document at face value, that's why I'm asking."

Tyson blinked slowly at him, and in spite of his size, Ellery could sense the intelligence that had made him an outstanding student athlete.

"Yessir," he said. "What's different?"

"Three pills. You said the little stapled baggie only had three pills in it."

Ty nodded. "Yeah. I remember showing it to Nate Klein, and he showed me his own. He's got his own scholarship and we were like, 'Yeah, right,' before we both shoved them in our pockets."

"Three," Ellery repeated grimly, circling the passage on the report that said *three dozen*. "What did they look like?"

"Pink, with a little butterfly on them. Same as Nate's," Tyson told him, looking confused. "What else?"

"Okay, you said the party was mostly white. Were these kids clean-cut white or grungy white?"

"Honors-student white." Ty grimaced. "I remember thinking I didn't know No Neck knew that many honors students." He gave an abashed look. "No Neck's not the smartest kid on the team, you know? Like, some of us got scholarships to out-of-state schools, but No Neck got a scholarship to the local junior college."

Ellery grunted. "Okay. So I'm going to go out on a limb here and say that when the police report says 'suspicious characters,' they want me to think—"

"There were a lot of Black people at the party?" Tyson said incredulously.

"Or just a lot of shady people in general," Ellery muttered. "That's their reason for knocking on the door. Now, were you in easy visual of the door?"

Tyson suddenly got where this was going. "No, sir. I was in the hall."

"Did they search anyone else?"

"No, sir, they came straight to me."

Ellery let out a sigh. "Did anyone remark on it?"

"Well, yeah. Nate was all up in their face until someone shoved him down and drew their weapon. He tried to tell them the drugs weren't mine, but they shouted, 'Whose were they?' and Nate looked around and…." Tyson bit his lip. "Ziggy was gone."

Ellery rubbed his temples and wished for Jackson. Jackson would have vetted this folder first, and then they could have discussed it, and then, oh God, he wouldn't be the only one thinking that this setup was bad. So very, very bad.

"Okay. Tyson, I need to talk to my associates. Don't worry. We're still taking your case. But—and I know you're not supposed to leave town—but do you and your mother have a place to stay? One that your friends at school might not have visited or know about?"

"His sister lives in Fair Oaks," Ralene said.

"That's exactly what I'm talking about," Ellery said, relief washing over him. "Do you have any pets or anything to care for?"

"My dog, Captain," Tyson said. "He's a pit bull/shepherd mix. A rescue." His square-jawed face went sloppy with adoration. "He's super cute and so sweet."

"Okay, then, I would like to talk to you both tomorrow."

"I don't have money for—"

"Don't worry about the hourly," Ellery said. "Show us last year's income tax, and I'll have Jade come up with a reasonable fee. I just want your family and your dog to be someplace else while this is going on."

"But we take public transportation!" Ralene said. "We can't take that dog on the train!"

Ellery pursed his lips. "Give me five minutes," he said politely. "I'll be right back."

He stood and left them in the office looking out the peaceful window, which featured a view of some of the spectacularly large leafy trees Sacramento was known for. The entire office, actually, from the windows looking out onto the trees in the yard next door to the wall with Ellery's degrees on it, which was painted the color of a stormy blue-green ocean, was designed to make people feel serene and invigorated.

They could come here and take charge of their lives, with Ellery's help.

But first Ellery had to take charge of his very late and very wayward boyfriend.

The nest of rooms in the refurbished Victorian house were part of a bigger office complex. As far as Ellery knew, they shared space with a headhunting firm next door and an adoption agency downstairs, which to his mind sort of added to the normalcy of a defense attorney. Everyday people could end up in extraordinary circumstances.

He and Jackson had decorated the suite with strong, happy colors—the teal gray in his office, the soothing browns and tans in the vacant office, and Galen had a strong combination of brown and burgundy.

And fortunately his door was open so Ellery didn't feel bad about bothering his new partner.

Galen Henderson had been a stunningly handsome man before his motorcycle accident. His narrow, appealing face with its patrician features and bold nose was probably the toast of Miami. He wore his hair longer now, and kept a neatly trimmed goatee to help hide the scar that marred his temple and his cheek, but his brown eyes and sharp, sardonic gaze were still incredibly magnetic.

His Southern roots and Ellery's no-bullshit Yankee pragmatism were probably the things that would get the firm—now officially Cramer

& Henderson, with Henry and Jackson listed as PIs in smaller script beneath their names—off the ground and through their first year.

Of course it helped that Henderson was so excited about practicing law again following his hiatus after his accident that he was willing to follow Ellery's lead. Ellery had the feeling this man didn't let much else guide him.

"What's up?" Galen asked as Ellery poked his head in the door.

"Have you heard from Henry?" Ellery chewed his lower lip.

"Uhm… no." Galen frowned. "Wasn't he supposed to pick Jackson up and visit the PD's?"

Ellery grimaced. "Yeah. They left over an hour ago."

Galen's very expressive eyebrows "expressed." "Oh dear."

"I told him to do one thing," Ellery said, fighting panic.

"It could just be traffic," Galen soothed. "Here, let me text Henry. He's—"

"Less likely to ignore your call," Ellery finished darkly.

Galen nodded, completely on board with that.

"I need to go grab AJ for an errand. Tell me what Henry says."

Without waiting for an answer, Ellery strode to the empty conference room. He'd had Jade decorate this place, making it professional and comfortable at once. The chairs were roomy and supportive—and pretty, with sturdy wooden frames and fabric cushions—and the massive oval-shaped table in the center was heavy oak. At one end, with his laptop plugged into an outlet, sat a young man with long and tiny spirals of sunset-colored hair, and a pale brown face with pinpoints of dark brown freckles. He had a delicate chin and soulful eyes, and so much eagerness to help, Ellery always felt bad for asking him for anything extra.

But that didn't mean he didn't.

"Hey, Mr. Cramer." He smiled excitedly, and Ellery wondered why Ellery was always "Mr. Cramer," but Jackson was either "Jackson" to his family or "Rivers" to the people who really wished he just fucking wouldn't do whatever it was he did to piss them off.

"Hey, AJ. Look, I've got a favor. Are you game?"

AJ closed his laptop screen and nodded. "Yeah, sure. What do you need?"

Ellery outlined AJ's job as chauffer and then winced. "Wait, what car are you driving? Because there is a dog invo—"

"A dog? What kind? I love dogs!"

"I'm just wondering if there's enough room in your car," he said, hiding a smile. AJ drove a battered "student-mobile" that had started out as a loaner Jackson bought for the kids coming out of jail who needed a fresh start. Jackson housed them in his half of the duplex he'd been living in when he and Ellery had first met, and Jade and her boyfriend helped Jackson keep an eye on them from the other half of the duplex. The idea was they got free rent as long as they could prove they were trying to get jobs or get into school or do something productive with their lives. The first group of young men had moved out in early June—AJ's boyfriend among them—and the next group were mechanically inclined. Jackson got them their own loaner-mobile, and told them it was theirs to use as long as they fixed it up.

AJ's car didn't have the benefit of someone who knew cars—although Mike tinkered with it once in a while—so it was a primer-spotted, shoestring, run-on-a-dime sort of vehicle, and Ellery wasn't sure how well it would reflect on the firm.

"Hold on a second," he said.

Then he took his courage in both hands and went to talk to Jade.

Jade Cameron stood maybe five feet, four inches in her stocking feet, and her curves would send a race car on a spin. An African American goddess with a gimlet glare and a penchant for magenta both in her clothes and hair, she was one of the few people who had been there to take care of Jackson when the rest of the world had bailed.

Ellery was Jackson's person now, but before that happened, he'd had to get Jade's seal of approval. He was pretty sure the only reason she'd turned over the reins was that Jade was quite simply exhausted by the job.

"Uhm, Jade…," he began as he approached her at the built-in secretary's counter that separated the waiting room from the offices.

"What do you need?" she asked, looking up from her computer with a frown line already between her eyes.

"The Townsends need a ride to their house and then across town."

Jade's eyes widened. "We're doing that now?"

"There is something *very* wrong with that police report," Ellery growled, looking out into the waiting room and relieved to find it empty. "I don't trust them to be safe in their house, especially not if Ty gives me the names of the other people at the party where he was busted. AJ can give them a ride, but...."

She was already digging through her purse for her keys. "Isn't Jackson supposed to be coming in? I thought we were all doing lunch."

"Yeah. I expected him and Henry back about fifteen minutes ago. Think there was traffic? Maybe they stopped for lunch. Or coffee. Or...." Ellery wasn't aware that he was rubbing his chest until Jade looked from his hand to his eyes and then back again.

"Yeah," she said unhappily. "Maybe we should—"

At that point Ellery's phone buzzed, and he pulled it out of his pocket.

And tried not to hyperventilate.

Don't look at the news—we're fine.

"What?" she asked, taking in his expression. "What's wrong?"

"Do you have a local news channel on your computer?" he asked, and his healthy breakfast made unhealthy noises as she pulled up a news site. They both read the scrolling banner across the top together.

Shots Fired at Public Defender's Headquarters. Police Have Suspect Barricaded in Stairwell.

"Oh shit," Ellery said, his heart pulsing in his throat.

"Are we fucking serious here?" Jade asked.

Which was exactly what Ellery texted Jackson.

Are we fucking serious here?

Jackson returned, *I told you not to look!*

Where are you?

Hiding with Jenny Probst behind the giant copier in the supply closet.

You do that a lot, Ellery texted, and he could almost hear Jackson's filthy laugh in return.

It's not as romantic as it sounds.

Is Henry with you? And Ellery wasn't sure whether to hope yes or hope no.

Yes. He's the guy who barricaded the door. Ellery, he was coming specifically for Jenny. Do you know why?

He thought about it. The Townsend case was hinky, but he already had that file because Jenny had dropped it off the day before. The guy currently barricaded on the stairwell wouldn't know that, necessarily, but then it could also be the case file Jackson was supposed to pick up.

Or it could be something completely unconnected.

I'd need to see the file she wanted you to get, but it could be something totally unrelated. You know that, right?

His response was an emoji face with rolling eyes.

It's possible, he maintained stubbornly, partly because Jackson on the phone arguing was *not* Jackson out in the thick of things taking unnecessary chances.

She's sort of hysterical right now. I may go get the case file just so I have something to do while I'm waiting.

"Werewolf fucking Jesus," Jade muttered, and Ellery stared at her. "The fuck is that?"

"I don't know. We saw a meme, we decided to make it a thing. But seriously, tell him no!"

Please don't, Ellery typed, aware that his fingers were shaking.

No response.

Ellery pulled up Henry's number and texted, *Tell him to stay put*!

You tell him!

Tell him I'll kill him myself!

Keep your shorts on. He's back.

Ellery stared at his phone, sweat trickling down his back, heart pounding like *he* was the one in lockdown, waiting for an active shooter to pound through his door.

When Jackson's name flashed across his screen, he swore softly, "Werewolf fucking Jesus."

And smiled.

I'm fine. Everything is fine. Got the file. I think cops took the shooter down with tasers. Give us an hour, we'll be there.

There was a pause while Ellery caught his breath, and the phone screen flashed again.

Want us to bring lunch?

Ellery started to laugh softly and a little hysterically.

Don't sweat it. Jade and I will walk down.

His phone erupted then into a lot of texts saying mostly it was hot outside and not to bother and it was no big deal, but Jade was already running down the hallway to give her keys to AJ, and Ellery was heading for Galen's office to brief him, and seriously.

Ellery had given him one lousy thing to do.

In Jackson's words, *fuck* that guy!

AJ DROPPED Ellery and Jade off about a block from the public defender's building before driving away with Ralene and Ty Townsend in the back of Jade's SUV, a little confused but very grateful.

Jade and Ellery joined the throng in front of the building, watching as two EMTs transported a guy handcuffed to his stretcher out of the building, two policemen on their heels.

Henry and Jackson followed—both of them looking casual and happy and 100 percent abso-fucking-lutely fine—escorted by a very familiar young detective. Sean Kryzynski had blond hair and blue eyes like Henry, but Sean's narrower face, his more expressive eyes, his smaller build, marked him as another kind of creature entirely.

When Ellery had first met Kryzynski, or K-Ski as Jackson and Jade had taken to calling him, he'd been super idealistic and super sure that Jackson had done something wrong in his past to deserve all of the bullshit the department threw at him. After a year of working together—sometimes willingly, sometimes not—Kryzynski had started to trust Jackson a little, and Jackson had stopped treating the guy like a raging yeast infection under his balls.

Kryzynski had lost a little of his new-detective polish, but he'd gained some wisdom—and some lines around the eyes—over the past year.

Ellery considered him a friend, and he was pretty sure Jackson did too.

"You have no idea who this guy is?" Kryzynski said, for what sounded like the umpteenth time.

"He was the guy who shouted Jenny's name and apparently fired his gun into the air. And I'm guessing he can run like the wind." Jackson's hand shifted as he walked with Kryzynski down the stairs, and Ellery was suddenly aware of the messenger bag at his hip.

Go, baby, go, he thought silently, because oh yeah, they really needed to read that file.

Kryzynski nodded. "You had to see the video replay. He seriously would have made it to her floor if you hadn't barricaded the door."

"All Henry's doing," Jackson said mildly.

"Jackson's idea," Henry said, sounding bored. "He was supposed to be taking it easy today."

Kryzynski gave a real smile, one that reached his tired cop eyes. "First day back?"

Jackson grimaced. "Wasn't supposed to be."

Henry and Kryzynski both chortled.

"Oh, it fucking figures," Kryzynski said. He glanced up and spotted Ellery and Jade on the sidewalk at the same time Jackson and Henry did. "And guess who's here to reinforce sick leave."

Ellery gave a sigh and met Jackson's apologetic gaze. "Wouldn't dream of it," he said. To his surprise, Jackson stepped forward and gave him a brief kiss on the temple before moving to his side.

"I swear to God, Ellery, it wasn't my—"

"Fault. Yeah, I get it." A reluctant smile pushed at the corners of Ellery's mouth. "I mean seriously, what are the odds?"

Kryzynski blew out a breath. "That this is related to something you two are doing? I'd take that bet. So what are you doing?"

At that point Henry's stomach made a loud, obnoxious, unmistakable sound.

Jackson chuckled and Ellery said, "I think we're going to lunch. You all want in?"

Henry nodded and then grimaced. "Is it okay if I go get Galen? If we're having a powwow, it feels rude to leave him alone at the office."

"Text him first and make sure he's not busy," Jackson said. "But yeah."

"Tell him to grab the Townsend file from the top of my desk," Ellery prompted. "I want Sean to see that one too."

"Uh-oh," Kryzynski said, eyes growing sober. "Am I going to like this?"

"I hope not," Ellery said briskly. "'Cause if you do, you're not the person I thought you were."

Kryzynski groaned and rubbed the back of his neck. "You guys. You guys are like the cherry on the shit sundae, you know that?"

"Bad day already, K-Ski?" Jackson asked sympathetically.

Kryzynski shook his head and glowered. "I don't want to talk about it. Love life's fine, thank you. Absolutely peachy."

Jackson and Ellery exchanged looks, but Jackson was the one who said it.

"How's the fireman?"

"Older than I am," Kryzynski said sourly. "And he won't let me forget it."

Someone called Kryzynski's name, and he nodded to another detective down by the curb. "Look, guys, give me a restaurant not too far away and I'll meet you there. Make it cheap and make it… franchisey, okay? If I have to eat kale today I might kill someone."

"Understood," Jackson said. "You go talk to whoever, we'll go pick up Galen, and we'll meet you at the Mongolian barbecue place a few blocks from here."

Kryzynski's eyes went to half-mast, and he damn near drooled. "That guy by the car is my partner—I may have to drop him off at Mercy San Juan so he can check in on our wild man in the stairwell."

"He get tasered pretty good?" Jackson asked, his eyes lighting up like this would not disappoint him at all.

"Twice," Kryzynski said with satisfaction. "I think he bit the tip of his tongue off and wet himself. Asshole. I feel no pity."

"Meet in an hour, then," Jackson told him, taking charge effortlessly like he did. He looked at Jade and Ellery. "Good news is, Henry brought Galen's car. It's got air-conditioning like a *boss*."

Ellery became aware of the sweat trickling down his back and the absolute airless thickness of the heat around them.

"I may forgive you yet."

Jackson grinned. "Like I said, it was not my fault."

They turned and started walking for the parking lot, and Ellery let his hand brush Jackson's as they went.

"*That*," he said grimly, "remains to be seen."

Fish in a School

GALEN ACTUALLY declined lunch, asking instead for Henry to bring him something when they were done. It was just as well—parking was fiercely competitive in front of Ellery's office. At this rate, Henry would be able to take Galen home before the most miserable part of the day, and Ellery didn't have to move his car so they could all go out, which meant nobody had to die when they all got back.

They hit the place right after the rush, so they didn't have to wait in line to pile their bowls with frozen slices of meat and raw vegetables. By the time Kryzynski got there, everybody was eating, and Henry and Jackson were giving the details about what had happened earlier in the day.

"This story again?" Kryzynski drawled as he slid into the booth next to Henry.

"This is only the first time they've heard it!" Henry defended before resuming the narrative. "So, Jenny Probst and I were hiding behind the copier, and Jackson's like, 'Hey, what's the name on that file anyway?' And Jenny sort of blanked out for a second before going, 'Uh, Dostoyevsky?' And Jackson says, 'Like the writer?' and Jenny goes, 'Uh….' And Jackson disappears."

"I did not disappear," Jackson told him, rolling his eyes. He gave Ellery a furtive glance. He seemed to be taking this whole thing in stride so far, but Ellery had seemed to be okay on other occasions regarding Jackson's safety when he really had been on the verge of losing his shit. "Look, remember that the bad guy—"

"We have no idea who he is," Kryzynski supplied. "We're trying to get his fingerprints because he doesn't have any ID on him, but so far no luck."

"And is Mr. No Luck still unconscious?" Jackson asked.

"Mr. No Luck whacked his head when he fell down the stairs," Kryzynski said with a grimace, "so yes. He might be unconscious for another two days. Christie—my partner, Andre Christie—stayed with him. He'll buzz me if he wakes up anytime today, and we'll have someone staying tonight."

"Okay, then," Jackson said, "more about Mr. No Luck anon—"

Henry snorted, holding his hand up in front of his mouth so he didn't spray noodles everywhere.

"Anon," Jackson repeated. "Look, you guys, I was stuck at home for eight weeks. I read a lot. Anyway, this story ends with me looking on her desk. It was *not* Dostoyevsky, which makes me glad the poor woman was staying in her office with a cop until her husband came to pick her up. It was Dobrevk, which was damned close. So I have the Dobrevk file right here, and Ellery has a file he thinks might be hinky too—"

"It's at the office," Ellery said. "Since we didn't pick up Galen, I didn't get it."

Jackson grimaced. "Well, we'll look at it later. You give us the gist now. I think it would be a good idea to show and tell so we can figure out why the unconscious guy was so damned excited to break into the lawyer's office. What do you think?"

Kryzynski was unwrapping a set of chopsticks before digging into his own bowl of meat, veggies, and noodles. "*That*," he said soberly, "is a fantastic idea."

Jackson opened his own file and nodded to Ellery. "Ellery goes first."

Ellery started to go over the Townsend file from memory, and Jackson took notes on the back of the Dobrevk file.

When Ellery was done, Kryzynski burst into a long, colorful bout of swearing.

"Goddammit," he muttered. "God*dammit*. What in the hell is that? Why would the police report say a pocketful of drugs and the kid maintain there were only three? Who would gain from such a stupid lie?"

"It would get a conviction," Ellery said, like explaining to a child.

"But why? Why pick on this one kid? What was so special about this one football player that these guys had to go after him?" Kryzynski rubbed a hand over his short blond hair, his hard blue eyes flashing. "It's so dumb. I thought.... I mean, after last year, you know?" He looked at Jackson pleadingly, and Jackson got it.

"You thought all the dirty cops were put away," Jackson said softly. Last year at this time, he and Ellery were working their first case together, trying to clear Jade's twin brother's name. Kryzynski had been skeptical, at first, that the authority he trusted so implicitly could be as corrupt as any criminal, but Ellery had believed in Jackson, and Jackson had believed in the truth.

"Yes!" Kryzynski snapped. "Yes! Is it so much to ask that everybody who works this job not be a scumbag?"

"You have no idea what happened here," Jackson said softly. "When we get back to look at the file, let's see which cops were on the scene. Let's see who signed off and searched the kid. Maybe a dirty cop, sure. But maybe someone was putting pressure on him elsewhere. This kid was singled out for a reason, one he might not even know. But if we can get hold of some of his friends, some of the people from that party, maybe we can figure out what happened."

Kryzynski nodded and shoved his bowl of noodles away. "Okay. Yeah. You're right. But this looks bad, Jackson. The one Black kid at a party singled out for a drug bust for drugs that really weren't his? Wait. What are you smiling about?"

Jackson hadn't realized he was until Kryzynski said something. "You… do you hear yourself? Who do you believe, Sean?"

Kryzynski blinked tired eyes. "Ellery. The kid, I guess. I mean, you guys don't sell bullshit. If Ellery's taking this case, the kid must be telling the truth."

"Damn." Jade blew out a low whistle.

"Right?" Jackson said, nodding at her.

"Wait. What's the big deal? And everybody finish your goddamned food. Kryzynski! Jackson! I'm talking to you."

They all looked at Henry, who glared back at them.

"What? I mentor a bunch of bulimic fucking porn stars. You guys eat your fucking food or I'm gonna lose my fuckin' mind. And somebody tell me what the big deal is!"

"I believed them," Kryzynski said after a moment. He pulled his bowl back and took a bite. "A year ago, I would have dismissed this kid's story. Stupid teenager. Not necessarily because he was of color, but because he wasn't a cop."

Henry's mouth parted, and he nodded slightly. "But now you can fix the problem because you're willing to see the problem."

"Yeah," Kryzynski said. He took another bite. "Jackson, finish your food, and then it's your turn."

Jackson rolled his eyes. "Ellery threw too much in the bowl. I'll finish what I finish. But about my file…."

He opened it up and grimaced. "Okay, first of all, it's a seventeen-year-old kid being tried as an adult."

Everybody winced. "For what?" Henry asked.

"Murder," Jackson said. "But it's so odd. The police report here… it looks on point, but we'll have to do some interviews again. Tage Dobrevk, young man from a good family, Russian…." He frowned. "Wait. I know this kid. That's weird."

Ellery looked at him. "You know this kid?"

"Yeah. That new crop of ex-cons at the duplex. One of them is his cousin. I met Tage two weeks ago when Sascha got out of jail. He was there with his parents and brother and sister, helping Sascha move in, talking about how Sascha had to work really hard to go straight. I *remember* this kid." He peered at the police report closer, thirsty for the details.

"Okay. This is… this is weird. They found Tage in an apartment laundry room, unconscious, with a dead guy next to him. They were both covered with the dead guy's blood. He'd been knifed pretty savagely and had bled out in minutes. Tage said he had no idea what this guy was doing in the room, and the police were inclined to believe him, but then…."

He kept reading, his stomach knotting up like crazy.

"But what?" Ellery asked, nudging him.

"But then his parents entered the room, and the cop says the kid looked at his father and started to cry, and then he wouldn't say anything else. Not in his own defense, not to explain, nothing. They put him in with—oh God. Ellery—he's in gen pop. We've got to get him out!"

Jackson stood up before he even knew he was going to and slid out of the booth. "This kid is in general population. Ellery. He's been there since last night. We've got to… you've got to rescue this kid. He's maybe five seven, one twenty sopping wet. This kid's gonna get hammered. Oh my God!"

"Jackson, sit," Ellery said, taking the file from him. "Sit. I can go to the jail and visit him after lunch. Nobody's going to let me in now, so just cool your jets."

Jackson's knees got a little wobbly as he sank into the booth, his chest filled with retroactive panic. That kid—that sweet kid who had played with his brother and sister, who had worked hard at boosting his cousin's spirits—*he* was in jail?

They had to fix it. They just had to.

"Okay," Ellery said, and he slid his hand, warm and firm, onto Jackson's thigh. "So more about the case. Who was the dead kid?"

Jackson took a breath. Yes, this was important, and as Ellery pointed out to him often enough, he was no good to anybody if he ran off half-cocked.

"Uhm, Cosgrove. James Cosgrove. Caucasian, just turned eighteen, goes by—"

"No Neck," Ellery said, staring at Jackson. "His name is No Neck. What school does Tage go to?"

"Capitol Valley," Jackson said, and Ellery nodded grimly. "Same school?"

"No Neck was the guy hosting the party Ty got busted at."

"Hunh," Jackson said, brain working overtime.

"What is that sound?" Henry asked. "I hate that sound!"

"You get used to it," Ellery told him blandly.

Jackson ignored them. He looked at Henry. "Junior, you and me got some explaining to do."

"I am with you, brother," Henry said. "Now eat your goddamned noodles, so we can go get that other file and K-Ski here can stop having a conniption. God, you guys—all about the fucking drama."

Jade took the last bite of her noodles and smiled. "Aren't they, though? Better than popcorn and a movie."

THEY HAD just finished lunch and pushed their chairs in, with a plan to go to the office so Ellery could make some calls and make an appointment to interview his new client, Tage Dobrevk, when Jackson, Henry, Jade, and Ellery all got a text from Galen at the same time.

Someone is attempting to break into our office. So far no luck, but hurry.

"K-Ski," Jackson said as they all bolted from the restaurant, "do you have a light and a siren in your unmarked?"

"Get in," Kryzynski told him as Henry ran to the Town Car, Jade and Ellery on his heels.

The unit—an unmarked black SUV—made good time weaving in and out of traffic, light flashing, and Jackson had Kryzynski kill the siren as he pulled up to the office complex and parked in a miracle space along the street. Jackson hopped out almost before the vehicle had stopped and went hauling through the breezeway, around the corner, and up the stairs.

Sure enough, a wiry blond man a little on the short side was rattling the doorknob and shaking it, swearing, a switchblade in his hand as he jiggered the lock.

He heard Jackson's footsteps on the stairs and read his intent in one quick heartbeat.

"Cop," he sneered, the faintest of accents clear in the vowel.

And with that, he took two bounding steps toward the stair railing and vaulted over, landing with a crouch and a tumble one story below.

"Kryzynski," Jackson called, "get him. He's got a knife!" He practically hung over the railing to see what happened next.

Kryzynski rounded the corner just at that moment and ran, full-tilt, into their suspect, who was fleeing the scene.

As Jackson hammered down the stairs, he saw the detective stagger back, hands out, as the kid took off, footsteps pounding the concrete of the breezeway before he disappeared around the corner. Jackson drew even as Kryzynski's knees buckled, and Jackson saw the welling of blood spilling over the white shirt beneath his suit coat.

Bright red blood, and K-Ski's face blanching shock white.

"Oh fuck," he muttered. He helped the officer down and hauled his new shirt off over his head, folding it quickly to apply pressure. "Radio, Sean. Where's your radio?"

"Belt," Kryzynski panted. "Left side."

Jackson grabbed it, remembering all of the protocol they'd drilled into him at the academy. He radioed in an "Officer down! Repeat, officer down!" with one hand while staunching the blood with the other, his own breath coming in quick little bursts. When prompted, he gave the address of the building and their location, then identified himself as a civilian giving first aid.

He set the radio down to use both hands and made eye contact with Kryzynski, trying to offer reassurance.

"How's the breathing there, buddy? You doing okay?"

Kryzynski nodded. "Maybe my lung. Chest hurts."

"Hope it's not your liver, 'cause that sucks large."

Kryzynski let out a short, breathy laugh. "You *would* know that."

"Yeah. I can give you the ins and outs of the hospital. It'll be great. I know the best nurses."

"Male or female?" He said it lightly, but his whole body was trembling, lines of pain making his young face old.

"Both," Jackson said. Then, "Hey, you want me to call someone?"

Kryzynski closed his eyes and nodded. "Yeah." A faint spittle of blood filmed his lips. "Yeah. Head of the Oh-Four. He won't hear this call in his—" He struggled for breath. "—area."

"I can do that," Jackson told him. He caught Kryzynski's hand. "You're going to be fine. I can hear the ambulance now. You got a pool at your place?"

He shook his head no, eyes still closed. "Shitty cop apartment."

"We'll hook you up. You can hang out, pet the cat, put your feet up. People will be jealous. Wonder why *they* didn't get stabbed after noodles. It'll be great."

Sean's lips curled up in a smile, and he let out another small laugh. One that sputtered more blood.

The EMTs clattered through the breezeway first, and Jackson squeezed Kryzynski's hand before he stood up. "Hang in there, Sean. I'll make that call. You've got people, okay?"

He backed away slowly, shaking, and watched as the two professionals—one of whom he knew well—began to call stats, checking Sean's vitals, calling the hospital and asking for blood and preparation.

The EMT he knew—a round, fortyish guy with thinning brown hair—looked up and caught Jackson's eyes. "Not you this time. That's a first."

Jackson couldn't even grimace. "Sucks to be on this end," he said numbly, and the guy nodded and then went back to his job just as Ellery came hauling ass through the breezeway, Jade on his heels.

"Jackson?" Ellery grabbed his arms and shook him. "Where are you hurt? Where are you bleeding? Why aren't they working on you?"

"It's Sean, dammit," Jackson snapped, and Ellery pulled away long enough to really take in the scene.

When he realized it was Kryzynski on the stretcher, he gave a definite wobble. Jackson caught him, a flood of emotions from relief to guilt to fear hitting him hard in the chest.

"I'm fine," he said, a little gentler. "But someone needs to check on Galen."

"On it," Jade said. "Did he get in?"

"No. Bad guy was still working on the lock." Jackson frowned. "See if you can get Galen to open the door from the inside. The guy didn't have gloves, and he was handling the doorknob. There should be prints."

Jade nodded and took off, and Jackson and Ellery were left watching the EMTs work. Where were the police? Normally when Jackson was working a case, Kryzynski was all over his ass. Where were the cops when it was one of their own?

"He...." Jackson frowned, trying to remember every detail. "He jumped the fucking railing, if you can believe that shit. Landed...." In his mind, he could see the tumble, the way the guy had rebounded, the way he'd still had his knife in his hand, turned out. "He's trained," he said. "He was young, really young. Looked like a high school student, but he held that knife like a pro. He was heading out the breezeway when Sean came running in after him, and they collided. I don't even know if the kid meant to stab him. They bounced off each other, Sean went down, and—"

"And you called for help," Ellery finished. "It's not your fault, Jackson."

Jackson shook himself. "I tried to warn him. We don't have a protocol," he said helplessly to Ellery. "Cops have a protocol: who goes in first, who comes next, how you approach a suspect. Me and Sean, we... we didn't have a protocol."

For the first time in the ten years since a sniper's bullet had ripped away his career, Jackson actually felt his time in the academy rattling through his bones without the contempt he'd carried for so long. Had he done it right? Sean had let him go first. Had he done it right? He'd called warning. He remembered that. Clearly. He'd warned him. God, *had he done it right*?

Jade came clattering down the stairs while Jackson watched the EMTs put a stabilized Kryzynski on a stretcher and ran him to the back of their unit, which was double-parked on the street.

"Galen's okay," Jade said, puffing a bit. "I told him about Kryzynski." She looked at him, her eyes sharp. "Are you okay? You don't look so good."

"I'm fine," he said, the words coming out a little harsher than he meant them. He shook himself and looked at her. "I'm sorry. I'm fine. I... the kid vaulted over the goddamned railing."

Jade let out a low whistle. "That's not your usual move," she said, and Jackson smiled a little. "Uh-oh, here comes the po-po. Looks like your day just came to a screeching halt."

Jackson nodded and remembered his promise. "Jade," he said, voice low, "Sean's boyfriend is apparently the captain at fire station oh-four. I have no idea if he's out or what the deal is, but could you find the guy and let him know? This is not their district. He won't hear about it, and I think Sean would like him there if he can be."

"I hear you," she said. She squeezed his arm. "He's going to be okay, baby. I've seen you look way worse and be back on our ass, giving us shit, the next day."

They all looked as Henry pulled up to the one spot in the miniscule parking lot by the stairs. It was just big enough for four cars, and today, Ellery's Lexus was one of them, and Galen's Town Car was the other.

"Go warn Henry to stay away," Jackson said as the responding officer approached him. "This is going to be ugly."

"On it," Jade said and disappeared.

On his other side, Ellery stayed right where he was. "I'm not going anywhere," he said firmly.

Jackson managed to give him a weak smile. "I'm glad," he said, voice soft. Then he took a deep breath and turned to face the music.

And God, he hated this tune.

Forty-five minutes later, they were still standing outside. They'd moved to the breezeway to be in the shade, but the two officers—a thin, blond woman in her forties and a huskier, bronze-skinned man about ten years younger—were both dogged and irritatingly dense. In the corner of his mind, Jackson wondered why there weren't detectives there, why this wasn't a bigger deal. There should have been press, bells, whistles, clown cars!

But no, he had these two yahoos, who were definitely not the city's finest.

"So you don't know who stabbed the officer?" the woman, Lindstrom, asked for the fifteenth time.

"If I did, I would have said so," Jackson retorted.

"You'd think so, right?" her partner, Craft, sniped. "But all I got from you is that the guy in the offices texted you that someone was breaking in."

Jackson and Ellery both held up their phones with the text on it.

"You could always go ask Mr. Henderson," Jackson said evenly.

"Why can't he come out here?" Lindstrom asked, her voice gaining a nasty edge.

"Two reasons," Jackson said, wishing for a weapon in a way he didn't think he was capable of. "The first being that you haven't asked him to come down. The second being that he has a disability, and it would really be more courteous for one of you to go up, you know, maybe check out the door? You haven't even checked for prints, and I know our paralegal had Mr. Henderson open the door for her so she didn't disturb any prints on the outside."

They ignored him.

"What, is forensics on strike?"

"An off-duty cop got stabbed by a housebreaker," Lindstrom said. "That's all we're seeing here."

"How would you know?" Jackson asked, irritated as fuck. "You're not *looking*. This cop solved a lot of cases in the last year. He just got his detective's shield before thirty, for sweet fuck's sake. Do you think he did that by taking the easy way out? The very least you could do is *print the fucking doorknob*!"

"You said the perp looked young," Craft badgered. "What makes you think he'd even be in the system?"

Jackson frowned. "The way that kid moved," he said after a moment. "He vaulted over the railing and onto the ground, but he was ready for the fall. He's practiced—tumbling, parkour, something. He kept his grip on the knife through the roll, and he had it out when he ran into Kryzynski. This was not a punk kid. He may not have known jack about breaking into an office, but he was *not* new to holding a weapon or running from the law."

Ellery studied him for a moment, and Jackson saw his eyes narrow. He'd thought of something, but he was not telling the police that. Ah, Jackson knew that feeling, but it hit him that Ellery had only learned of it this last year.

"Does this mean something to you, Mr. Cramer?" Lindstrom asked.

"No, ma'am," Ellery lied smoothly. "But what does mean something to me is that you haven't even called your forensics team when we've told you repeatedly there are fingerprints. This man *stabbed a detective.* Shouldn't we be talking to someone higher up on the food chain?"

They both glared at him sourly. "I'm not sure if you heard this, but there was an active shooter in the public defender's office this morning. Most of our forensics team is down there picking up shell casings and trying to figure out who the guy was. He didn't have ID, you know."

"I know," Jackson said. "Detective Kryzynski was the guy who took that guy down."

They both nodded, and Jackson heard the obvious, unasked question. Why weren't these guys asking why two defense attorneys would be hit in the same day?

His gaze flickered to Ellery, and Ellery clearly had the same thought. Ellery's eyebrow arched up incrementally, and Jackson realized that was two things Ellery knew that Jackson didn't.

That file, he thought. The one with the other kid's case; that was the thing Ellery knew and Jackson didn't.

They needed to see that file.

"Do you think this was revenge?" Lindstrom asked, sounding excited by the idea.

"How could that even be possible?" Jackson snarled. "This guy wasn't at the original scene. He didn't know me or Kryzynski. He had no idea the bunch of us would be eating lunch together when that text came through." Jackson glared at them and then looked at Ellery and nodded.

It was time to wrap this up.

"Is my client under arrest?" Ellery asked smoothly, and both the cops flinched.

"No."

"Then he's free to go," Ellery said. "You've kept him out here covered in blood with no shirt for nearly an hour. It's high time we leave."

"Where's he going?" Lindstrom asked.

"Our law office. Don't worry. We'll leave the doorknob unmolested until five o'clock this evening so you can get forensics down here."

"They should be here shortly," Craft told him, and Ellery gave them both a curt nod before pulling out his wallet and giving them a card. "Here's our information, although I know you have it down already. Please call us if you have any more questions."

"Hey, we didn't say you could leave."

Ellery gave them both a disdainful glance. "You have no reason to keep us here. And our friend is in the hospital. We would like for Mr. Rivers to go get cleaned up so we can visit. You may know the man—*he's a cop.*"

Jackson had texted Jade, and she held the door open for them as they approached. Jackson noticed that the doorknob had been dusted, and he looked at Henry.

"You got 'em?" he asked.

"Got 'em." Henry held up a perfect photograph of a neatly powdered black print on his hi-res camera phone. "Waiting for you to log in."

Jackson had learned how to lift a fingerprint in the academy. Although it was a task more often handled by the local forensics team, Jackson hadn't wanted to be left out. He'd taken classes in using the database that housed criminal fingerprints on file and had urged Ellery to buy the equipment capable of taking Henry's picture and converting it to a biometric scan. He'd passed the knowledge on to Henry, a lot of it by phone as he'd recovered and Henry had taken on some of the PI duties at the firm. He was anxious to get back into the seat and help again, but first he had to—ugh!—get all of Sean Kryzynski's blood off his body.

"Password is Billy Bob Wants His Balls Back. Capitalize every word and put exclamation points in between them, with a five at the end. Are there extra clothes still in the drawer?" he asked as Henry ran off to start the process.

Jackson started keeping an extra set handy in his early days, when he and Ellery had both worked at the area's biggest criminal-defense firm. Even though he hadn't been on the street in seven weeks, he was pretty sure he still had some old clothes in Jade's office.

"Ugh. Yes. I was going to make you take them home and replace them with something decent," she muttered.

Jackson took a deep breath and tried to remember his new-and-improved Jackson resolution, and part of that involved not wearing clothes rotting off his body out of sheer perversity.

"I wasn't supposed to be back," he told her, rummaging. He found them, folded neatly, behind six reams of copy paper and a case of pens. "I'll try to remember some of my newer stuff when I come back in tomorrow." He looked up and found everybody staring at him. "Yes," he snapped. "I'm coming in tomorrow. Kryzynski's in the hospital, and someone tried to break into our office, and we've got a seventeen-year-old kid in jail about to be tried as an adult and another kid whose life might be ruined because someone was trying really hard to make it so. This is no time for me to extend my vacation."

Ellery gave a reluctant nod. "Fair," he said. He grimaced. "I don't suppose we can ask you to be careful?"

Seven weeks of recovery, but Jackson hadn't been the only one recovering. Ellery had been pulling his tattered faith and hope for Jackson back around his own heart, trying to sustain himself for living with Jackson and all his copious damage.

"Of course you can," he said gently. "I'll have Henry with me. You heard him at lunch today. Man, that kid'll make sure I eat right, take my vitamins, don't walk into any gunfights. I promised you all." He looked at Jade and Henry and even Galen, who was leaning on the doorframe to his office, taking in the show. "Life just got good. Don't want to check out yet."

He remembered Kryzynski, squeezing his hand with a pain in his chest not unlike the thing that Jackson'd been recovering from for seven weeks. "But that doesn't mean we're getting any sleep until we know who did this to our friend."

"Truth, brother," Henry said gravely.

Jackson nodded and turned toward the bathroom. God, he needed a breath to himself.

And he needed to wash the goddamned blood off his hands.

Two Fish, One Pond

JADE HAD canceled everybody's afternoon appointments because she was a powerhouse of efficiency, and Ellery wouldn't have been able to afford her if she hadn't been devoted to Jackson.

When Jackson emerged from the bathroom ten minutes later, wearing a tattered black T-shirt that read My Way or My Way in bright pink letters, and a pair of jeans so transparent they were mostly indecent, everybody else had set up in the conference room, and Ellery was passing copies of the files and the police reports around the table.

"Jade has scanned copies of these and sent them to Crystal, and she's giving them to our old firm—"

"Feisty, Llama, Hamster and Clopper," Jackson inserted, and Ellery rolled his eyes for form. The actual name of the place was Pfeist, Langdon, Harrelson and Cooper, but since they'd fired Ellery for doing the right thing—and Jackson and Jade had quit in protest rather spectacularly—Jackson refused to use it. Ellery had understood the firm had made a business decision. A defense attorney with a well-developed moral compass was not going to make them as much money as one who would just plead people out whether they were guilty or not. Jackson and Jade held grudges.

"Yes," Ellery returned blandly. "Feisty, Llamas, Hamsters and Cloppers now hold our future in their hooves. Or paws. Or whatever. Anyway, I also sent copies to my mother."

Jackson looked panicked. "Did you instruct her *not* to come over?"

"She lives in Boston, Jackson. She's not just going to hop a flight over because I sent her an email."

Jackson shook his head. "She will too. She's been out *three times* in the last year. We can't get rid of her!"

"She was out to help take care of you," Ellery said patiently. "I had to go back to work, remember?"

Jackson shook his head. "Next time, *you* stay home and let Lucy Satan defend criminals. She's terrifying. She'll scare them straight."

Ellery gritted his teeth and refrained from telling Jackson that his mother's name was *Taylor*. It never worked. Jackson's uneasy relationship with Ellery's mother seemed to include both affection and exasperation, equally mixed, and Ellery wasn't going to solve it now.

"Well, she has her own firm," Ellery said, "and we've got a job to do."

Jackson sobered. "Got it. Okay, so we have five sets of eyes here and a lot of highlighters. Yellow highlighter for connections you see between the two cases and blue for inconsistencies. Everybody gives a twenty-minute review, and then we compare notes." He glanced at Ellery. "You good with this?"

Ellery gave a faint smile. God help him if he wasn't, since Jackson had just captained the meeting with ease. But it was a good plan.

"Ready if you are," he said, picking up his highlighter.

"Go," Jackson said, taking a set and a file from Jade.

Exactly two minutes of silence passed before Jackson said, "Motherfucker!" at the same time Ellery said, "Are we serious here?"

They locked eyes, and Ellery nodded. "You saw it?"

"Oh yeah."

"Anybody want to share with the class?" Galen asked, voice sandpaper dry.

"For the record," Jackson said, "the two incompetent and/or corrupt flatfoots on the Townsend case were the same potatoes who just tried to grill me downstairs."

"So which are they?" Henry asked. "Corrupt or incompetent?"

"I'm guessing a little of both," Jackson murmured thoughtfully.

"We *just* watched them botch evidence," Ellery said. "And that was for another cop. But they'd have no way of knowing they were helping someone they knew." He took a breath, his eyes going to the police report. "Unlike this, where it's so obviously a setup. I'm with Jackson here. Someone bought off a couple of low-level cops who weren't getting promoted anyway." He looked at Henry, who had been on Jackson's computer scanning the prints. "By the way, have we gotten any hits?"

"Still running," Henry said. "We don't have the giant server that they do at the FBI or the police office. It's gonna take a while."

"Gotcha," Ellery said. "I have no idea what you guys are doing. It's like with Crystal back at Fingerling, Hamster, et al." Everybody was so grim, he felt like he had to play that game too. Jackson gave him a wink to let him know he'd done okay. "Anyway, fingerprints could help, even if they won't be under chain of evidence."

"I can't believe they wouldn't even look for a guy running down the street with a bloody goddamned knife," Jackson muttered, then frowned again and uncapped his highlighter, hitting the page with unnecessary force.

The whole table stopped and stared.

"What?" he asked irritably.

"C'mon, Rivers, share with the class," Henry drawled, and Jackson blew out a breath.

"Let me ask Ellery something first," he said, and he bumped Ellery with his shoulder and pointed to Ellery's note. *Ziggy=Sergio Ivanov.*

Ellery looked at it and arched an eyebrow.

Next to Ellery's note, Jackson wrote, *Description?*

Ellery frowned. *Let me ask Ty.*

He pulled out his phone while everybody else read, and texted Ty Townsend, asked for a photo of Ziggy Ivanov, then put his phone away and resumed skimming the two files. After about ten minutes of silence, there was a general shift in the room, and Ellery looked up from his last page to see people making eye contact.

He grabbed a legal pad from the center of the table, and everyone else followed suit.

"Okay," he said. "Let's hear it. What do you have for me?"

"Henry first," Jackson prompted.

Henry nodded, making quick notes on his own legal pad.

"First thing, that Townsend kid was definitely a hit. There was nothing about that bust that was normal."

Ellery met people's eyes and got a general nod.

"I'd want to look into the drugs: Who was the distributor? Where did they come from? Who just shows up at a party with a backpack full of three-treat baggies and starts passing them out? Was this someone the whole school knew or just the guy who invited them?"

"No Neck, the dead guy," Jackson prompted, and Henry nodded again.

"So that's a place to start. No Neck's parents, No Neck's friends, the kid with the party favors—"

"Ziggy Ivanov," Ellery supplied, meeting Jackson's eyes. They were still waiting on Ty's return text.

"Yeah, those guys."

"But let's start with someone friendly," Jackson said. "Nate Klein. He's in the file as Ty's buddy who tried to tell the cops that everybody had a baggy and the bust was no fair. Nobody listened to him, and he's not mentioned in the police report, but Ellery mentioned him after the interview with the kid."

"Ooh," Henry said, making his lips do the pursing thing. "Good catch. Make him a priority?"

Jackson nodded, still studying the sheet in front of him. "Yeah."

"Solid."

"Okay, the cops," Jackson said. He grimaced and looked at one of the files in front of him. "*Not* the two cops on the Dobrevk case. The two cops on the Dobrevk case were not excited about arresting this kid—you can tell. And they called forensics in and are processing the entire scene in spite of the kid's apparent willingness to go down for the crime."

"So they know something's hinky?" Henry asked.

"They do," Jackson said, then grimaced. "And this is where we'd need a department contact to get hold of them for an interview." He looked up at Henry. "Nobody knows you yet. Maybe you should take that one, over the phone first. Ellery, do we have an interview with the Dobrevk kid lined up?"

"End of the day," Ellery said. "You owe Jade something really awesome, by the way."

Jackson gave his sister-of-the-heart a smile. "We might get a new kitten. Want to help us pick it out?"

Jade grimaced. "No. No. And no. And don't ask Mike to come with you either. You two go into a shelter and the shelter will walk out with you. You'll have cats, he'll have dogs, the world will be pandemonium."

Jackson gave her a fond smile. "Okay, well, I'll think of something. Thanks for getting that interview, sweetheart."

"He's a baby, and he's in jail," she said simply.

"Yeah, but you're still made of awesome."

She gave him a pert grin, and he winked at her.

"So," Ellery said, interrupting their byplay because that interview was looming near. "Jade, any impressions?"

"Mm, they singled Ty out because he was Black, but not because he was Black."

Ellery's brain popped. "Excuse me?"

"Okay, so, you invite a party full of white people and one Black person. Why?"

"I've got nothing," Jackson said. "Ellery? You talked to this kid."

"He said that usually the school was much more diverse than that party," Ellery said. "Why?"

"It's like they invited one Black kid so the police could arrest the one Black kid. It didn't matter *which* Black kid. They just wanted the cops there to take care of that."

Ellery tried to wrap his brain around the idea, and then Jackson put it into perspective.

"Like the whole setup was a diversion?" he asked, one eyebrow up.

"Yes!" Ellery said, finally seeing it. "Like... like they wanted those cops there, instead of where they would normally be."

Jackson nodded slowly. "That is a theory." He looked at Henry. "Okay, Henry, put that on your list of things when talking to the police. Where would those two officers normally have been? What duty did they get pulled off of to make that bust?"

"Okay." Henry chewed his lower lip. "How about you guys go to the jail and I'll make some phone calls. Then you and me go to the police department this evening."

"Was gonna go visit Kryzynski," Jackson said. "They took him to Med Center. I texted Dave and Alex to buzz me when they know anything."

"The morning, then," Henry said firmly. "Jackson, I don't know the department. I know they may hate your bisexual ass, but at least they know you. Some of them have got to have a soft spot for you there, you think?"

Jackson shrugged. "I don't know. They seemed pretty impressed with what we did on the Sampson case, but that may have been Jade's driving."

There was general laughter around the table, and Ellery took charge of the meeting again.

"So, Galen—wait! Hold on a minute."

Galen rolled his eyes but allowed Ellery to check his phone. Ellery looked at the picture of a kid. Well, mostly a kid. He could have been anywhere from fifteen to twenty-five. His size and the delicacy of his features said teenager, but his eyes, hard and narrow, said hard-boiled ex-con. He showed the picture to Jackson, and the effect was electric.

Jackson sucked in a breath, and his jaw clenched and eyes flashed. "Fuck. Me. New plan. Henry and I drive to the police station now, and we question every cop we can find who dealt with either case. Then we meet Ellery at the jail, and then we go see Kryzynski. We need to give the cops that kid's name, 'cause he's the one who stabbed our favorite detective and gave Ty Townsend party favors just to lure two incompetent flatfoots away from whatever they were supposed to be doing."

"Oh damn!" Jade said, and Ellery gaped.

"Do you think he was after the Townsend file?" Ellery asked, trying to make a picture.

"No," Galen said, and Ellery remembered he hadn't had a chance to contribute.

"What are you seeing?" he asked. Galen had a sharp mind. Although his focus was on corporate law, he tended to see larger patterns that might be helpful here.

"Remember, this kid was at the party of the kid killed in the other case. Lots of white kids at that party where Ty was arrested, and that's small potatoes next to cold-blooded murder. I'm betting this is all about the Dobrevk case. In fact, if you want to do your friend Tyson a favor, maybe keep him out of it. If they know we've tied him to the Dobrevk case, he just became a witness—"

"And he's in more danger than before," Ellery said, glad AJ had moved the kid across town.

"That's what I'm seeing," Galen said. He eyed Jackson and Henry. "So maybe don't mention Ty Townsend while you're talking to the police either. The Dobrevk cops seem to be straight shooters. We should maybe only talk to them about the Dobrevk case."

"What about getting Ty off?" Ellery asked. "Kid's future is at stake."

"Can you get him off just by being a stellar lawyer?" Jackson asked, batting his eyes.

"Can you maybe ask Nate Klein some questions that will help me?" Ellery retorted.

Jackson nodded. "We can do that. Nate goes on tomorrow's list, first thing. Henry and I have to leave about thirty seconds ago if we want to do our thing at the police station in time to meet you at the jail." He frowned. "Jade, darlin', we have to take you home tonight, don't we?"

"If AJ does not get his ass back with my SUV, then yes," she said. "Did Ty make it home?"

Ellery nodded because that had been in the text. "Yes. He said he, his mom, and his dog were settling in with his sister. They got there a few minutes ago. I guess traffic was sort of a nightmare."

Jade rolled her eyes. "Fine. Jackson, Henry, you two take the Town Car. We'll figure out vehicular bingo while you're gone."

Jackson grunted. "You know, maybe I could buy another car."

"No!" Jade and Ellery both shouted, and he grimaced. He actually *had* a car—a supersonically tricked-out SUV with bulletproof panels and a stripped-down interior that could bring urban assault to the finest war zones in the nation. It was not, however, fuel efficient, nor, being painted a bright pearlescent oyster color, was it inconspicuous. But Ellery couldn't help it. Jackson hadn't had a lot of luck with vehicles in the past year. The Tank, as they'd nicknamed it, was Ellery's last try at buying him an SUV that he couldn't destroy. It actually had *been* destroyed—and then rebuilt—and Jackson didn't get any more cars for a while.

Besides being an expensive hobby for Ellery, it was also hard on his heart.

"Or I could continue to bum rides from everybody else," Jackson said blandly.

Ellery regarded him with narrowed eyes. "That sounds like a fantastic idea. Doesn't that sound like a fantastic idea, Jade?"

"Yes, Ellery. That idea sounds like it could save the universe. Henry, do *you* mind giving Jackson rides around town?"

Henry hadn't been there when Jackson's old car had been shot up, or the replacement vehicle wrecked, or the second replacement *also* shot up, or the Tank's original version *blown* up. But apparently he still got the gist.

"Nope," he said, giving Jackson an evil grin. "Not even a little."

Jackson rolled his eyes. "You all suck," he said. "Just remember, not *one* of those cars was actually destroyed in a car *wreck* when I was driving."

"Yeah, baby," Jade told him. "That's the takeaway from all of that."

Jackson sobered and stood, taking the top sheet of his legal pad and a pen. "Okay. So this one's complicated, and there's a lot of angles. We may have to have one of these sit-downs tomorrow. Galen, I know you've got your own shit, but—"

"Your Detective Kryzynski is a friend," he said, nodding. "And we have young people in danger." He gave a thin smile. "Honestly, this is so much more exciting than corporate takeovers in Miami. I had no idea."

Jackson nodded, and before Ellery could give a more elaborate thank-you, he said, "'Preciate it," in that terse, hypermasculine way that seemed to mean more.

"Jackson, a moment, please?" Ellery said, standing. "Galen, Jade, I'll be right back."

Galen allowed one of those bland Southern smiles that told Ellery he was fooling nobody, but Ellery didn't have any other way to do this. He ushered Jackson down the hallway and into his office and closed the door behind him. He didn't even need to turn around before he felt Jackson's heat, pushing him into the door.

"I don't need to say it, do I?" Ellery asked, leaning into Jackson's body anyway. A little more substantial than he'd felt in June. He'd put on maybe fifteen pounds, maybe even a teeny bit of healthy fat. His color—lightly tanned face, slight pink to his cheeks—was good. But Ellery only had to close his eyes to see the bluish tinge to his lips from eight weeks ago. He only had to feel under Jackson's shirt to count his many, many scars.

"I like it when you do," Jackson said softly, kissing the corner of Ellery's mouth.

Ellery opened his eyes in surprise. "Really?" A year they'd been doing this. A year since Jackson had first hit on Ellery and had then retreated because Ellery wasn't a one-night stand. A year since Ellery had first held Jackson in bed as he'd screamed through the nightmares that would probably haunt him forever.

A year since Ellery had decided that, whether Jackson knew it or not, Ellery's job, the thing he'd *really* been born to do, was to take care of Jackson.

Ellery hadn't realized how desperate he'd been to know Jackson appreciated that until right now.

"Yeah, really," Jackson said, kissing the other corner of his mouth. He leaned close enough to whisper in Ellery's ear, and Ellery splayed his hands across the hard definition of his chest. "Every now and then, knowing you want me to be careful is what gets me home."

Ellery closed his eyes against the times it almost hadn't and for a moment opened his heart to the fact that Jackson was here, now, and he was willing to be careful, just for Ellery.

"I want you home tonight," Ellery said.

"Every night," Jackson promised. This time, he took Ellery's mouth for real, and Ellery allowed himself to be soothed, allowed Jackson to convince him that he was strong, that he was capable of making decisions in his own best interest and not kill himself being a hero.

He moaned a little, shaking, and when Jackson wrapped strong arms around his shoulders, they released the kiss, and he rested his head on Jackson's shoulder.

"Hey, Counselor," Jackson whispered. "What's wrong?"

"I saw the blood," Ellery said roughly, the memory surging of Jackson standing in the breezeway, staring at the EMTs with dazed eyes. "I saw the blood, and… I just…."

"Mm." Jackson squeezed him tighter, and although Ellery was not a small man, he felt cared for. "I know. I wish I could tell you I wouldn't trade places with him."

"Jackson!" Ellery pulled away, alarm in his eyes, but Jackson wouldn't back down.

"I don't want people hurt in my place," Jackson said, unyielding. "I keep playing it in my head. The kid vaulting the railing, me calling that he had a knife. Kryzynski's not stupid, but the kid had some momentum, and I couldn't stop him. I couldn't block him, I couldn't help Sean and… and I hated it. I hated the blood and the way he was afraid and there wasn't anything I could do."

He took a deep breath, and Ellery tried to still the hammering of his heart. He should have known. Ellery was afraid because it could have been Jackson. Jackson was shaking because he thought it *should* have been.

"There was nothing you could do," Ellery said. "Jackson, there was nothing you could *do*. I know you'd switch places. I *hate* it," he added passionately, "but that's the man I love. Please believe me—believe yourself—there's nothing you could do."

Jackson nodded, gave a hard shudder, and held Ellery tight again. "I'll meet you at the jail," he said, his voice under control again. "I'll text you as soon as Dave or Alex send me word."

Dave and Alex were his friends from UCD Med Center, and Ellery was grateful for them. Jackson would have worried himself sick if he hadn't had a way to know about Kryzynski.

"Play nice with the policemen," Ellery said, trying to smile.

Jackson leaned back and regarded him with sober green eyes. "I'll try not to worry you any more than I have to," he said, and then he kissed Ellery again, quick and hard, like he was trying to warm Ellery's soul.

Ellery let him, thinking of all the times he'd blown off the concern, tried to cajole Ellery out of the worry, pretended like he didn't court danger with every step.

The acknowledgment was new, and it was hopeful. That he knew Ellery worried, that he'd try not to worry him more, was considerate in ways Jackson had been learning to be throughout the last year.

He'd taken to the new wardrobe, he'd let the car thing slide, he'd been taking care of himself because he knew he was important.

If Ellery was honest, there had been times this last year when he'd thought he'd never see Jackson Rivers be this much of a grown-up, and he'd learned enough in that time to take the win.

"I only worry because I love you," he said, not sure if Jackson got that.

Jackson winked. "It's why I can deal," he said. His expression sobered, and he placed one last kiss on Ellery's forehead before moving himself toward the door and slipping out. "I'll text you when we're done," he said, and then he was gone.

Ellery permitted himself a lean back and the count of ten to pull himself back together before he walked down the hallway to finish talking with Galen and Jade.

GALEN WAS still studying the two files when Ellery reentered the conference room, but his smirk was unmistakable. "All those last-minute instructions delivered?" he asked, his eyebrows raised.

"Mostly to come home in one piece," Ellery replied, not sure if he had it in him to play coy.

To his surprise, Galen's smirk disappeared, and the look he returned was all compassion. "I understand he has a problem with that. Well, if it's reassuring at all, *my* boyfriend used to forget sunscreen fairly constantly, and he's practically self-combusting. I finally told him that I'd love him even if they had to cut off his nose from skin cancer, but he might feel a bit self-conscious."

Ellery couldn't help it; he covered his mouth to stop a snicker. He'd met Galen's boyfriend, a rather manic, skinny ginger porn-mogul who liked to film guys having sex, and also tried hard to make sure they were grown-ups when they *weren't* in the bedroom. Ellery came from a family strong in liberal politics but academic and professional. It hadn't been until Ellery had actually met John Carey that he'd realized that sex work didn't have to be sleazy, and that the more professional it was allowed to be, the more protected the workers. He'd met some of John Carey's employees. They were sweet young men, and John himself was exactly the kind of "idea guy" who would run off and cook his fragile freckled skin until it peeled off his face.

"Poor John," he said. "I bet he swims in zinc oxide all summer."

Galen huffed out a breath. "He has the most *obnoxious* hats."

Ellery couldn't help his smile. "The only way I could get Jackson to wear new clothes was if I made sure his new T-shirts were as obnoxious as the old ones."

Galen met his smile and nodded. "So, let me tell you what's bothering me about these two files," he said, his expression flattening out to his shrewd-lawyer look. "Ms. Cameron, if you move in a little closer, you can take down my notes, and we can all share the same brain."

Jade did so, and Ellery noted that her own smile gentled as she leaned in. Galen's bone-deep Southern courtesy had that effect on her.

"So," Galen said thoughtfully, "when a corporation is planning a takeover, a number of things have to be in place. One company's stock has to be cheap enough to buy, the other company has to have enough liquid cash to purchase it, and all the trustees on both boards have to be in a place where this looks like the smartest option. You both understand?"

Ellery met Jade's eyes, and they both nodded.

"Good. There's a lot of moving parts. But a lot of movies—many of them heist movies—have been made about tweaking each of those moving parts to make sure the outcome is orchestrated rather than random, right?"

"Right," Ellery said. "Distract the president of one company while the other company is buying stock. Cause a disaster in one company so the stock sales plummet. Trade information before it's due out to do the same thing. Acquisitions and mergers are pretty cutthroat, from what I understand."

Galen nodded. "Exactly. Now, I can't tell you what the corporations *are* here. Maybe drugs, but drugs are commonplace, and…." He grimaced as though looking for the right words.

"Most drug dealers aren't that smart," Ellery said, thinking about the ones they'd dealt with at the beginning of the summer. "And if they are that smart, they're trying to commit fewer crimes instead of more of them, to keep attention off their activities."

"*Exactly*," Galen agreed. "So I can't tell you who is taking over what. But think about this. This Ziggy Ivanov had to set up Mr. Townsend and get the attention of the world's dumbest policemen to come arrest him. There had to be a reason for that. What were they distracting the policemen *from*? Then the next night, they framed the Dobrevk kid for the murder of a witness to the original crime. Ziggy is the guy moving from crime scene to crime scene, but he's motivated by something. He doesn't strike me as a mastermind. The guy who went after the files in the public defender's office is probably higher up the food chain. He failed, so Ziggy is called in as a Hail Mary. Ziggy is a low-level corporate fixer, but one who wants to move up. That's why he's so very busy. He's ambitious. Is the guy who tried to get the file at the PD's office under guard?"

Ellery nodded. "Sean's partner is there—at a different hospital from Sean."

Galen nodded. "That is fortuitous," he said. "I wouldn't be surprised to find that more than one attempt is made on our coma patient's life."

Ellery nodded. "Loose ends. The Dobrevk file is about tying up loose ends."

"Exactly," Galen said. He gave a brief smile. "Corporations and criminals. People are forever surprised at how similar they can be."

"Not you, though," Ellery noted.

Galen's smile went feline. "Indeed."

"I'll go text Sean's partner, Christie," Ellery said. "I think Arizona and I need to have a conversation anyway."

"Your friend at the DA's office?"

God, the man was sharp. "Everyone's got one," Ellery said, and Galen's laughter warmed him as he turned to leave.

He paused at the doorway. "So I think if we take you to the jail, then Henry can—"

Galen waved a bored hand. "John's coming to pick me up in an hour." He smiled charmingly at Jade. "If you like, my dear, we can give you a ride too. It's not the kind of day one wants to be mucking about in traffic."

Jade looked at him with naked gratitude. "Ellery, can we keep him?"

Ellery laughed. Galen had shown up on his doorstep looking for some help for Henry, who was the brother of a friend. He'd taken one look at the office—which had still been under construction at the time—and decided he'd like to practice there.

"I can't imagine making him leave," Ellery said. "He's very useful."

Galen inclined his head modestly, and Ellery headed for his office. He'd thought he and Jackson were going to have a nice easy day today, but it seemed every time Jackson stepped onto the scene, the world had saved its hardest cases for him.

Big Fish, Little Fish

JACKSON WASN'T bad as a passenger. Fact was, Galen's Town Car was pretty luxe, and Jackson got to spend time staring out the window and churning the world over in his head.

For about fifteen seconds before Henry started talking.

"You know," he said conversationally, heading for Richards Boulevard, "seven weeks, and there was no drama—"

"You lie," Jackson said, rolling his eyes. "I seem to remember your boyfriend stuck in a closet while you took down an armed drug dealer."

"She was a middle-aged nurse in over her head. It was nothing."

"Yes, but I wasn't there. That was all you—you can't say there was no drama," he goaded.

"Man, all I'm saying is after you almost died, I was pretty much spending my days running license plates and juvie records and increasing my Google-Fu. Now we're heading for the police station when the one cop who doesn't seem to hate your guts is…." His teasing note dropped. "Well, he's not there to help us."

"Yeah," Jackson said, wishing Henry had left this alone for another hundred years. His pocket buzzed, and he pulled out his phone.

Your boy's going into surgery—give him an hour or two. No cops in the waiting room.

Jackson looked at "Nurse Dave's" text and swore softly.

"Well, he picked our side, so we're on his," he said and texted back. *We're trying to find who did it. We'll be there this evening. Tell him we're coming if he wakes up.*

Knew you wouldn't let him down, Dave texted back. *Alex would like to request chicken wings and pizza if you can grab some on your way.*

Jackson smiled, thinking fondly of the two nurses who had kept him sane when he'd been incarcerated, erm, stuck in the hospital ten years ago. *Depends on when Sean wakes up. But if we don't get them before, we'll get them after. Deal?*

You're a good man, Rivers. We'll take care of your boy.

Thanks. Tell him we're on it.

Jackson tucked his phone in his pocket again and pounded his head back against the headrest.

"He's okay?" Henry said with a worried frown.

"Yes, sorry. Didn't mean to panic you." Jackson had forgotten that Sean Kryzynski had been one of the first people besides Jackson and Ellery who Henry had met when they'd been defending *him* against a murder charge. Henry had been pretty new to town then, and he only had so many friends. He'd be as worried as Jackson. "He's going into surgery. They probably have to reinflate his lung at the least. He should be out and stable by the time we get there this evening."

He hoped so. He knew there were complications, chances for the body to give out. That knife could have nicked an artery, punctured an intestine, hit things in the body that no knife should be around. Just because the front of Jackson's body looked like a patchwork quilt didn't mean that Sean Kryzynski had the same sort of luck.

"You don't sound too sure," Henry said, and Jackson hated himself.

"I'm worried," he burst out. "Guy went down, held my hand, trusted me when I said I'd get in touch with his boyfriend. There aren't any cops there. *Why aren't there any cops there?* God, that pisses me off. I know his partner is doing guard duty, but this is… this is boys in blue. Someone should be relieving him so he can come have Kryzynski's back. Kryzynski's CO should be there, making sure he knows people care. Our office should have been swarming with cops. *Swarming.* It is driving me batshit, and that kid is all by himself in the hospital. It's not fair."

"No," Henry said softly. "It's not. But don't worry. I texted Lance while you were changing. You've got your guys, I've got mine. Kryzynski'll know we're worried about him, and he'll know we're on his case."

Jackson grunted. "I forget you have someone there too. Lance freaking out yet?" As Jackson remembered it, Henry's doctor boyfriend hadn't been too thrilled by Henry's new and dangerous vocation, and Jackson couldn't blame him. But Henry had been career military before he'd been forced out by a vindictive ex, and he didn't mind a little danger.

He was also bright, and interested in seeing the world in a different way than his father had seen it, and that kind of perspective was really useful when it came to dealing with law enforcement.

"Not on text," Henry confirmed. "He saves the real freak-out until I'm home."

Jackson spared a moment for envy. "That's only because he doesn't see you at work."

"Hey," Henry said grimly. "From what I can see, Ellery's nagging is the only reason you're still breathing, so don't knock it."

"Wasn't planning to," Jackson returned, voice mild. "Where are all the fucking cops, though? I mean, maybe the two yahoos were right. They could just be stretched thin. But maybe they didn't call in the right code either."

"Who are we looking for when we get to the station?" Henry asked, negotiating Richards Boulevard with ease. They both noticed the homeless encampments getting thicker as Henry approached the squat white building, and Jackson sighed. It was so hard to stay safe when you had no home and the local shelter that served meals was fairly close. Maybe being near to the police station helped them feel less vulnerable, but it didn't make the place any more approachable.

"Park around the back," Jackson told him. "And we're looking for Adele Fetzer and Jimmy Hardison. They're the officers on the Dobrevk case. Their paperwork was signed off by Lieutenant Christine Chambers, Homicide, so that's the second floor."

"When was the last time you were here?" Henry asked, finding a parking spot with surprising ease.

"Last year. I doubt they've forgiven us for that, either. Be prepared to take flack."

"Always."

Jackson grinned at him, pleased by Henry's general willingness to stir up some shit. Good quality in a partner, and he and Henry had worked pretty well together when they were clearing Henry's name.

His phone buzzed as he was getting out of the car.

"Ellery?" Henry asked as Jackson checked it. The heat hit him like a wave, and he actually had to catch his breath before he answered.

"Wants us to look for larger patterns." Jackson frowned. "I feel like I need a good run around the block to figure that one out."

"Yeah, that's above my pay grade," Henry muttered. "But sure. We'll look for larger patterns."

Together they ventured through the public entrance to a clean and relatively new and efficient lobby. The smell of too many sweaty people was still strong—there definitely weren't enough windows to go around—but body odor and burned coffee aside, Jackson felt himself respecting the purpose of the place.

Sure, he'd seen his share of corruption—and dammit, something was wrong here again, and why did he have to fix this shit?—but most of the employees were here because they believed they could do something useful, something important with their time. He'd read the Dobrevk file, seen indications that Fetzer and Hardison had been trying to keep Tage Dobrevk out of prison and that they doubted he'd been involved in the first place. If he could keep his attitude in check, maybe he could help that kid who'd already had a two-day pass to hell, and maybe he could get some people down to see Kryzynski, because it sure would be nice for him to know his department had his back.

"Can I help you?" the desk sergeant asked as they approached. Thirtyish, Latinx, very pretty—and very pregnant, Jackson noted with a smile.

"Please tell me they let you put your feet up behind that desk," Jackson said, sympathy in full force. That pregnant in August. There oughtta be a law.

Desk Sergeant C. Kensington allowed a dimple to pop on her pretty, round face. "Oh my God, that's why I took this job when it came up. I knew shit was going to get *real*!"

"Right? And better here than somewhere in the heat."

She nodded, her tight double french braid not even shifting by a shiny raven-wing hair. "Ugh. Once we hit May, I wasn't playing around. It was like an inferno!"

"Well, I'll tell you what," Jackson said. "How about my friend and I go get you some ice water? Crackers?"

She gave him a wide-set pair of soulful brown eyes. "Ice cream?" she begged pitifully. "I thought it was a thing you only saw in movies but... ice cream?"

"On it!" Henry said crisply. "Any flavor?"

"Yes," she said, nodding enthusiastically. "Any. Flavor."

Henry laughed gently. "I saw a minimart about a block away—is that the closest place?"

"Yeah." She sighed. "Never mind. By the time you got it back, it'll be melted." All vitality seeped out of her, and Jackson and Henry met eyes.

"You leave that to me," Henry said staunchly. "If you can help my friend there get in to see the people he needs to talk to, I will hook you right up."

Her lips parted ever so slightly, and her eyes grew terrifyingly bright. "Really?" she whispered, and Henry and Jackson nodded.

"I'll get you in to see God himself," she said, and her fervor was undeniable.

Jackson and Henry did a low five below the eye level of the Formica desk—but it wouldn't have mattered if she'd seen them.

Jackson was *in*.

Fortunately, so were Fetzer and Hardison, both of them sitting in the almost vacant briefing room, working on their tablets across the table from each other as they completed their paperwork for the day. The room itself was set up like a classroom, with tables lined up by columns, all of them facing the front podium where the chief briefed them every morning in preparation for their day.

Adele Fetzer, fiftyish, African American, with a smile of both cynicism and hope, noticed him first. She nodded to Jimmy, who was about the same age and had graying blond hair and a ruddy complexion. He looked up from his paperwork, and his eyes widened.

"Rivers?" he asked tentatively. "That's your name, right?"

"Yessir," Jackson said, and let some respect color his voice. He hadn't been tight with Fetzer or Hardison, but neither of them had given him reason to believe they were crooked, or even mean. They'd worked different shifts than he had, and as far as he knew, they held no grudges.

"What can we do for you, Mr. Rivers?" Adele asked, head tilted. "Who used to be a cop."

"I work for a defense attorney now," he said, snagging a plastic chair from another table and swinging it around so he could straddle it and prop his arms on the back. "Cramer and Henderson. Don't worry, you haven't heard of us. But you will."

"Dirty/pretty killer," Hardison said without missing a beat.

"And the Sampson drug ring," Fetzer added, both of them regarding him with no humor—but no enmity either. "You've been busy."

Jackson nodded. "It's been an eventful year," he said. "And we were at the public defender's office this morning"—he watched their eyes widen, so he knew he had them—"picking up a file for a young man named Tage Dobrevk."

Ooh, he'd hit a nerve. Both of them leaned in, glancing at each other furtively.

"Was that what the shooting was all about?" Fetzer asked, voice hushed. "Because nobody is telling us dick!"

"They don't know," Jackson said. "We were there to pick up the file when we heard the guy shout the name of the lawyer who had it. We got there in time to hide her in the copy room while my colleague barricaded the guy in the stairwell. They took him down with Tasers, but he's out cold. But they tried again. Did you guys hear about that?"

The confusion on their faces made his stomach hurt.

"Detective Kryzynski—you guys know him?"

Fetzer blinked. "Good guy," she said.

"In the hospital," Jackson told her brutally. "Because a kid with a switchblade was trying to break into our law office, and between him and the guy this morning, we figure...." He let them make eye contact, the way good partners did.

"They both wanted the same thing," Fetzer reasoned. Then she frowned. "Is Kryzynski doing okay? We have not heard about that!"

"He's actually by himself," Jackson said. "I told him we'd get the guy, but we're visiting later this evening. I...." He remembered waking up after two weeks in a medically induced coma to discover his hospital room had cards and stuffed animals from Jade and Kaden, but not a damned thing from his department because he'd been wearing a wire trying to bring down his corrupt partner. "I think it would mean something to him to know he had friends in the waiting room."

Fetzer nodded seriously. "Mercy San Juan?"

"Med Center," Jackson told her. "I can't believe you guys don't know." He grimaced, and let some of his anger slide down his spine. "To be honest, the two flatfoots at the scene were...." He pursed his lips, and tried to remember he was being a nice guy. "They weren't you guys," he said after a moment. "We couldn't get them to even call the forensics team, and we had prints on the doorknob."

"So they don't know who did it?" Hardison asked.

Jackson kept his expression neutral, but he arched one eyebrow.

Again, that partner eyeball communiqué. "You're a PI, right?" Hardison asked when it was over.

"I am."

"You're a pretty good one, right?"

Jackson gave a one-shoulder shrug. "I get by."

Fetzer snorted. "You're a hot dog—we can see it. Do *you* know who did it?"

Jackson gave them a cat and canary smile. "Wanna see a picture?"

Their eyes lit up. "Oh, do we," Fetzer said. "You're not going to give us crap about it?"

"I'm not trying to defend the kid who knifed my friend," Jackson told her, voice hard. "I'm trying to defend the kid who got charged for a murder I think this kid committed."

Fetzer swore softly. "You are just a bag full of grenades today, aren't you, sweetheart?"

Augh! He'd pushed too hard. He knew it. He took a deep breath. "We've seen some connections between this guy and some other people in the community. For example, your murder vic, No Neck—"

"James Cosgrove," Hardison said. "Aged eighteen. Not too bright, not too rich, big guy who liked to throw parties."

Jackson nodded. "That's the one. Did you know that the night before his death, he hosted a party where a kid got busted for drugs?"

They frowned. "It happens," Fetzer said.

"One kid. They walked into the house, looked for the one Black kid at the party, and searched him."

Fetzer got it first. "Was he the only kid with drugs?"

"No, he was not," Jackson told her.

"Where did they get the drugs?" Hardison asked curiously.

Jackson felt like he was back on an even keel again. "Would you like to see a picture?"

"How do we prove it?" Fetzer snapped. "All we know for certain is you've got a picture on your phone. Big deal. I've got hundreds."

Jackson nodded. "Me too. Mostly of my cat. But I've got a picture of something else. It won't hold up in court," he told them, "because we couldn't get forensics to come take the print, and it's in the sun and will probably be too degraded if they get to it tomorrow. But *we* took the print, and I have a scan of it, and we're running it right now. We got it off the doorknob—the doorknob our scumbag on my phone was holding while he was trying to break into our office before he—" Jackson had to take a breath for this. "—before he stabbed my friend," he finished. "Are we interested in this at all?"

"Very much so," Fetzer said. "And we'd like the names of the two officers on scene because they should have called for backup and forensics. It's not right," she said, looking at Hardison. "That boy's in the hospital and nobody's there."

Hardison nodded. "Nope. Someone'll be there." He pulled out his phone and started texting.

"I'll give you all of it," Jackson said, feeling easy in his stomach again. The world was not all evil. Not all of it.

"That's real generous," Fetzer sneered. "What do you want in return?"

"Tell me about the Dobrevk case," Jackson said, meeting her world-weary cop eyes with a hardness of his own. "I read that file twice, and I don't see how you guys came to the conclusion that he did it."

"We didn't," Hardison snapped. "That's no fucking fair. That kid was barely coherent. We got there and the EMTs were busy pronouncing the dead kid, and suddenly this kid sits up and starts babbling—"

"In Russian," Fetzer clarified. "He must have made some sort of sense, because his father burst in, and they, you know, had one of those conversations without words."

Jackson smiled faintly. "You guys have been eyeball talking since I walked in."

And that got him his first smile from Fetzer. "Is that so? What have we been saying?"

"You've been saying this case is driving you nuts, and you don't like the idea of that kid in gen pop any more than I do."

"He's in gen pop?" Fetzer asked, her voice pitching the same way Jackson's had when he'd heard.

"Hopefully not for long," Jackson said grimly. "We just got this file today. Mr. Cramer is headed to the jail as we speak, trying to get that kid tried as a kid and taken out of general population. We're doing our best, but we really need some more details."

"All right, then," Fetzer said, nodding grimly. "Here's the details. We get called to the scene, like I said. The EMTs are already there, and the dead kid is on the ground with his throat slit. Dobrevk is on the ground knocked out—he had a concussion or I didn't raise three boys. He's sitting up, babbling in Russian, and his father comes in and tells him *something*, and he goes limp. Still. I tried to talk to him, I had Jimmy here talk to him in case he didn't like the Black or the woman. He just shut the fuck down and cried."

"You don't think he did it," Jackson said.

"I know he didn't," Fetzer told him. "He couldn't even look at the body."

"But your lieutenant was on site?"

"Chambers. Got called because it *was* a murder, and because the kid who got killed was some sort of local football hero. Anyway, Chambers had us arrest him and then signed off on it. But Jimmy and me, we would have brought him in for questioning, maybe, turned him over to the detectives on site, but we didn't see that kid as the killer." She grimaced. "We've seen a few, you know?"

Jackson nodded. "You said his father was there. Were his mother and the other two kids?"

Fetzer's eyes went so wide, the whites showed all around the irises. "Two others?"

"Yeah. I know this kid. He has a brother and sister, look a lot like he does—sort of sandy hair, small pretty faces, big gray eyes. Girl dyed a pink stripe in her hair, but it might have washed out."

"But…. Jimmy, you remember, right?"

"Yeah," Hardison said. "His father—we went in to arrest the kid, and his father starts to wail, loud, in English. He's all, 'My son! My son! My only child, my son!'"

Jackson's breath stopped. "Oh, I think we have a motive," he said, not sure he even should have spoken.

"For killing the bigger kid?" Fetzer asked, horrified.

"No, for lying about it." He watched as they both met horrified gazes and saw the dawning comprehension steal across their faces.

"Someone's got his brother?" Hardison asked.

"And sister," Jackson added. "That's what his father was trying to tell him. Not to say anything."

"Because whoever killed the big guy with no neck…," Hardison began.

"Has the younger kids," Fetzer picked up. She frowned. "But who? And how do we even start?"

Jackson held up his phone. "Maybe give me your number first," he said, "and I'll send you this kid's picture and prints. His name is Sergio Ivanov, but people call him Ziggy, and you need to run his prints through *your* computer and tell your lieu that you have a lead on the guy who knifed a cop. One of you go do that *right now* while I pick the other guy's brains, because I've got a timetable and punching the time clock is not on the agenda. Let's talk."

Hardison rattled off his cell, and Jackson texted him the info before the big guy lumbered out of the room.

Fetzer broke out her notebook and her own phone, and they got down to business.

Twenty minutes later, Hardison walked back into the room, and Jackson's phone was absolutely bursting with addresses and contacts. He and Henry were going to be running their asses off tomorrow.

"Chambers briefed?" Jackson asked.

Hardison shook his head. "No. I mean, yes, I gave her the information and told her it came from a credible source, but… well, she's a transfer. She doesn't know you from fucking Bambi, and she said she'd take the info under advisement."

Jackson rolled his eyes. "Famous fucking last words," he muttered. "Well, when we're done here, I suggest you go back and tell her why she might want to listen." He turned back to Fetzer, wondering if he was going to have to tell these two well-meaning, reasonably intelligent police officers about Ty Townsend in order to secure their cooperation.

He hated the idea—he really did. Galen's advice was sound—and bringing Ty into it went against his first instincts. But God, there were too many balls in the air here for him to keep that one spinning when he might just maybe be able to trust someone else to handle it. If he could get these two cops to intervene, maybe they could get Lindstrom and Craft to drop the case.

"So about the Townsend kid," Jackson said delicately. "Do you guys really think he did it?" And now that Hardison was back in the room, he was treated to the vibrating eyeball schtick again. He gave a sigh and swung his leg back over the chair, standing up and stretching while he waited for an answer.

"You know who the arresting officers were," Fetzer said mildly.

Jackson nodded and moved his hands over his head, taking care to stretch out his chest and upper back. Physical therapy was important for heart patients too. "I do know," he said. "I was wondering if you had… opinions."

Hardison rolled his eyes, and then he and Fetzer shared one of those speaking glances again. "Of course we got fuckin' opinions," Hardison said finally. "But you don't speak ill of the department outside of the department."

Jackson thought about leaving it alone for a nanosecond, and then his hands found his hips and his mouth opened all by itself. "That was so much comfort when I was lying in my hospital bed for a year, and I had one fucking visitor from the department," he said and then wished for a ball gag, just to make things kinky *and* uncomfortable.

This time, they couldn't meet each other's eyes. Or Jackson's. "We'll make sure that doesn't happen to the Kryzynski kid," Hardison said gruffly. "We already promised."

"Good," Jackson said, straddling the chair again. "Because our firm is full up on PIs, and you people need him on your side."

Fetzer let a low, sweet laugh erupt. "You do not mind your words," she said after a moment.

"Well, there seem to be a lot of people who mind them for me," Jackson told her, feeling a sunny sort of benevolence again. "So about those two arresting officers—what do *you* think they were doing at that party?"

"They had a tip," Fetzer said grimly. "A CI they use." She swallowed like she tasted something bad. "I don't know why, but I do not like the sound of the guy's voice, even over the phone."

Jackson frowned. "You've met him?"

"No. But he's got a thick, gravelly voice. Not the voice of that kid you showed us. He just sounds smug. You can hear him through an earbud. Hell, Lindstrom was talking to him in the ladies one day, and I could hear him through the walls. I just...." She shuddered. "I know it's superstitious as hell, but I wouldn't trust that guy."

"Any sort of accent?" Jackson asked.

"German," Hardison said, surprising him.

"Not Russian?" Because that kid who'd knifed Sean had sounded Russian.

"Nyet," Hardison said and then laughed at his own joke. He sobered for a moment. "I took German in high school. It's less liquid, more phlegm."

Jackson rolled his eyes. "Gross. Moving on. Look, that bust, the Townsend bust, if I told you we think it was a distraction, could you tell me where you thought those guys were *supposed* to be that night?"

"Where was the bust made?" Fetzer asked, eyes narrowed shrewdly.

"I thought I'd told you," Jackson said. "Dead kid—No Neck Cosgrove's place."

The open mouths were not a good sign.

"How…?" Fetzer bent her head and rubbed the back of her neck. "Wouldn't Chambers have caught that?" she asked. "Shouldn't somebody have turned this over to a detective?"

Jackson shrugged. "I would think so. I don't know how it was missed."

"Augh!" Fetzer wore her hair in a tight graying braid, much like the desk sergeant's, and Jackson watched her wrestle with the urge to run her fingers through her hair. "This is no damned good at all!" she said finally, and Hardison shook his head.

"It's Chambers," he said after a moment. "She means well, but…." He shrugged. "Green. She legit could have missed that because she wasn't looking."

"I hope," Fetzer said sharply. "Because…. Because there are too damned many questions here. And I've got three years to go before my pension!"

"I've got two," Jimmy said dispiritedly, and at Fetzer's wounded sound, he gave her a tired grin. "I was going to hang in there for you. Don't go getting all girlie. My wife would never forgive me. She wants to start a Jimmy Hardison survivor's club."

Fetzer gave her partner a tired smile in return. "Good. I'll hold you to that." Then she looked at Jackson. "Look, we know who you are and what you did. And you probably expect the whole department's crawling with snakes. But there's crooked and there's green and there's lazy—and none of these things are the same. But you're right about one thing. This shit can't stand. These cases are linked, that Townsend kid should *never* have been busted, and whether he was part of this or not, James Cosgrove was barely eighteen and his parents are devastated. And the Dobrevk kid's a victim too. So you're right. We've got some shit to sort, and I'm grateful you brought it to our attention."

Jackson held up a hand. "Oh no. Stop right there. I'm not leaving this shit. We're getting the Dobrevk kid out of gen pop, and we need to get the Townsend kid off for reasons that have *nothing to do* with the rest of this shit, or he's a target. You see that, right? He becomes a material witness for this other shit, and his life is *over*. And that's if they don't shoot him dead."

Fetzer and Hardison stared at him, trying to digest. "Well, what, kid? You're going to save the world all on your own?" Hardison sneered.

"I've got help," Jackson told him, feeling grumpy. "And I wouldn't mind if you guys did your share. But you can't write us off because we're about to clean up your mess, and you'd better not get in our way."

The two seasoned officers stared at him. "You don't think much of yourself, do you?" Fetzer asked.

And Jackson hated to bring this up again, but he and Henry were keeping to a schedule here. "Dirty/pretty killer," he said, eyes narrowed. "Sampson drug ring. And there is some shit down south that you don't even want to know about. So don't fuck with me here. I gave you solid details on a 245 with a *cop*, and I'm going to get that kid out of gen pop if it kills me." He grimaced. "And it might. Believe me, my boyfriend is fucking tired of me ending up in the hospital here, so if we could avoid that last one, that would be great. So yeah. We're going to clean up a mess. It would be *fantastic* if we had some help from the good guys instead of having to worry about them fucking with us instead."

They went eyeball to eyeball again, and Jackson had had enough.

"Don't look at each other," he snapped. "Look at *me*! You guys can excuse anything you want to each other in the name of department solidarity, but I've seen past that curtain, and you know what's behind it? Blood and fucking despair. I'm the guy who didn't jump on the fucking bandwagon, and it almost backed over my head here. You got a guilty conscience, you own it up to *me*!"

"Oh my God," Hardison muttered, and *his* hair was short enough that he could run his fingers through it. "You are not going to let up, are you?"

"*My friend's in the hospital and there's a kid in jail!*" Jackson shouted, and both of them flinched.

Fetzer held her hands up. "Okay," she said after a moment. "You're right. You're totally right. Tell us what you need, and we'll see what we can do."

Jackson held up his hand and ticked the points off on his fingers. "Kryzynski needs people," he said. "I need to know what Lindstrom and

Craft were *supposed* to be doing when they were busting Ty Townsend. I need you guys to run Sergio Ivanov, and if your lieutenant isn't going to do anything about him, I need his fucking information because *I* will."

"We don't need a fucking vigilante!" Fetzer snapped, showing the spine he'd known she'd possessed when he'd walked in the room.

"Do you think he's working alone?" Jackson said, remembering Ellery's text as he'd entered the building. "Do you think these incidents are just isolated mayhem? There is something going on that we don't know about, and that kid is the key. If you're not going to investigate, *we* will."

"Sergio Ivanov," Hardison said quickly, "we're on it."

"And if you can get me the name of Lindstrom's CI, I need to hear it. Any info at all. Because they were manipulated away from something by this guy, and it would be helpful to know what."

He blew out a breath, and his phone started buzzing. He checked it and saw Henry with: *Where the fuck are you? She's going to ask me to be this baby's godfather and then deliver it on my feet if you don't get me out of here!*

"That's all I can think of for now," Jackson said, his mouth twisting up. Thank God for his punk-ass partner who was *not* going to let him take things too seriously. "Now we gotta go. Our next stop is the jail, and we can *not* let Tage Dobrevk down."

"Isn't Tage a Swedish name?" Fetzer asked.

Jackson blinked hard. "You know, that'll be the first thing I ask him," he said, shaking his head. "You've got my number. If you can get Chambers up to speed, do that. God, you guys—there's a line where incompetence gets criminal, and you all are riding it hard, aren't you?"

"Fuck you too," Fetzer muttered, but the words lacked heat, and he saluted her behind his back as he walked away.

HE FOUND Henry surrounded by cops, all of them looking hopefully at him for ice cream. Lucky for Henry, he'd bought a small ice chest and filled it with Popsicles, as well as the desk sergeant's cookies and cream.

Henry gave out the last of the free Popsicles, and the crowd thinned out, leaving an almost tearful Sergeant Kensington forever in their debt.

"Oh my God," she gushed to Henry. "You have no idea. That was the nicest thing anyone has done for me in… I absolutely can't remember. I can't even *tell* you how much I needed that."

Henry grinned at her and winked. "My sister was pregnant in August. I was told I was lucky I was deployed, because the family isn't sure how they survived."

Kensington laughed, but Jackson's heart gave a little ping. Henry's family had pretty much disowned him when he'd come out, and that was before they realized he'd been engaged in an abusive relationship with his sister's husband. Watching him put a little good ol' boy in his voice for this nice woman who'd done them a favor made Jackson a little proud of his baby PI. When they'd met, Henry wouldn't have been able to do that.

"Well, ice cream helps," Sergeant Kensington said. "Please let me know what I can do to return the favor."

Jackson thought about all those people excited about ice cream and how this woman should have been a little spoiled by her team long before two scruffy PIs came in looking for something. This place had a morale problem. Fetzer and Hardison were promising, but morale was raised by everybody.

"Are you in charge of sending flowers?" he asked abruptly. "Like if someone's sick or hurt or something?"

Kensington frowned. "I'm not sure if *anyone* is. The captain—"

"Captain Green?" That's who had been in charge the year before. He'd promised changes after Jackson and Ellery had busted a corrupt officer in his force, but Jackson had been skeptical.

"Captain Green's on medical leave," Kensington told them. "We've got an interim here, Captain Carlton."

Jackson shook his head. "Well, you've got a detective in the hospital. Do what you can to rally around him, okay?"

She looked shocked. "Oh my God. Who?"

And Jackson had to say it again before he and Henry left, practically at a run because they were getting close to being late.

"Augh!" Jackson muttered. "I don't know if they were crooked, but *God* their communication sucked ass!"

"Yeah," Henry said. "My unit in Iraq was a lot tighter than that."

"It's new people. New, shifting in, uncertain. It's… they need some fucking leadership there. It's making me crazy."

"You need to let it go," Henry said as they got to the car. "You absolutely can't solve everything in one day."

"Oughtta be a fucking law," Jackson grumbled. "God, it's like I took that time off and the department fell to shit without me, which is stupid because I've only been here a handful of times since last year!"

"Except that's any sort of system," Henry explained patiently. "There's always new people, there's always uncertainty, and there's always people who will make it in under the wire. Do you know why you know about this problem right now?"

Jackson slid into the vehicle and squinted at Henry in confusion. "Because we caught a case."

Henry nodded. "Because there are checks in the system. So don't get your panties in a knot. You can't fix everything."

Jackson rolled his eyes. "You are taking the fun out of my world," he groused. "Nobody at the fucking hospital!"

"And you *did* fix that," Henry told him. "God, were there not any kittens in trees for you to find?"

Jackson couldn't help a small smile, but he wasn't going to let Henry talk him out of his irritation. Fetzer and Hardison were both good cops, and they deserved better than Lindstrom and Craft.

But then, so did kids like Tage Dobrevk.

Jackson had Henry drop him off in front of the jail, telling him to go get their favorite nurses pizza and buffalo wings and check on Sean.

"You sure I can't see you interview the kid?" Henry asked, and Jackson pinched the bridge of his nose.

"I wouldn't mind you there," he said honestly, "but until I know Kryzynski's okay…."

Henry caught that and nodded. "Yeah. You're right. Buddy check. It's all good."

Jackson grimaced. "It's not like I do anything spectacular. I mean, there's secret arcane words and a few passes with a wand, but you can pick that up on YouTube."

"Ha-ha. Fine. Whatever."

"Besides," Jackson said reluctantly, "it's rough, seeing kids in jail."

Henry grunted. "Yeah, I get that."

Jackson shook his head. "No, man, it's really rough." He shuddered. "But it's worse seeing them dead, so I gotta get a move on."

He slid out of the car and into the lengthening shadows of late-afternoon August.

The jail facility in Sacramento was recently renovated and not nearly as squat as the PD's office. White granite, with some graceful curves to the architecture and a stretch of lawn out front, Jackson imagined it was probably a comfort to family members visiting that it didn't look like the dank cells of the Spanish Inquisition, but that didn't make it a picnic either.

After submitting to a wanding and a pat down at the entrance, Jackson showed his ID and gave his name to the admitting officer, who escorted him down the hall to the conference rooms. Ellery was already there with the ADA, the stunningly beautiful and knife-edged deadly Siren Herrera.

A guard stood in one corner of the room, arms crossed disapprovingly, and next to Ellery at the table was a barely grown teenager in an oversized orange jumpsuit, staring ahead with giant gray shell-shocked eyes. One side of his otherwise paste-white face was black and blue, and his eye on that side was brick red. He was shaking even as he sat.

"Mr. Rivers," Herrera said, nodding to Jackson.

Jackson nodded back and then pulled his chair on the other side of Tage. "Hey, kid," he said softly.

Tage actually looked at him, his eyes growing wider and shinier as he did. "Jackson?" he whispered.

"Yeah. How's Sascha?"

Tage's lower lip trembled, and he cast a watery look at Herrera. "I...."

"Ms. Herrera," Ellery said, his voice hard. "We need a few moments alone to confer with Mr. Dobrevk. You have my paperwork on not trying him as an adult, on setting bail, and on keeping him in the infirmary until he's transported immediately out of here."

Herrera nodded. "You do—"

"I've also given you a motion to dismiss because there was no evidence—none—that my client was even capable of the murder he's accused of."

"Lieutenant Chambers felt like there was enough evidence—"

"Lieutenant Chambers didn't know what she was looking at," Jackson interceded. "Her two beat cops were there, they briefed her on the scene, and she looked at Tage and said, 'He's here, he must have done it.' There is nothing to indicate this arrest can stand up in court, and if we put the first officers on the scene up on the stand, they'll tell a jury exactly that."

Herrera's eye twitched. "They were the first on scene?" she asked, her voice squeaking.

"Yes. Chambers was called in because of the severity of the crime."

Herrera closed her eyes. "I hate you guys," she muttered. "If this was in the PD's office, they would have pled this down by now!"

"Well, we got the same police report you got," Jackson said, crossing his arms in front of his chest. "What didn't you see?"

Herrera glared at him, and then glared at Ellery. "Where's the other guy? I liked him better."

Ellery raised his eyebrows. "The other guy is training. Wait until he gets his wheels off. He'll be just as obnoxious, trust me."

She snorted. "Look, we can't just let the kid out of jail after he's been charged."

Jackson stared at her. "Of course you can. That's why there's such a thing as dropping charges." He glanced at Ellery. "Look, we've got how much longer here?"

"Fifteen minutes," the guard said behind them.

"Could you go outside and argue with her?" Jackson begged. "Me and Tage will stay here and chat." He looked at Tage and nodded. "He knows I'm not his lawyer, and nothing we say here is confidential."

Tage blinked and shuddered. "I understand."

Herrera let out a long breath. "God. Nothing's easy with you two, is it?"

"I keep telling you," Ellery said mildly. "If Arizona kicks a case to you with our names on it, it's going to be a pain in the ass that she's tired of dealing with. Just kick the case downhill."

Herrera's eyes sharpened. "That's making an awfully big assumption about me," she said. "I care if I'm prosecuting a guilty person or not."

"Then stop complaining," Ellery said simply, and then he stood, gesturing toward the door. "And now, if we can give Jackson some time with the victim—"

"Accused," Herrera snapped.

"He had a concussion," Ellery told her. "Oh my God, Siren, you need to start reading the police reports with a better eye for detail."

"I really fucking do," she murmured as they left, and Jackson grinned. Well, even good students had to learn the same lesson once or twice. When the door shut behind them, Jackson turned toward Tage.

"How you holding up?" he asked quietly.

Tage's lower lip started the full-on wobble. "Sascha called his friends in prison, and word got here. They've been protecting me mostly, but...." He squeezed his eyes shut, and Jackson took in the damage to his face.

"Nobody's there twenty-four seven," he said softly.

Tage nodded, entire body shaking. "I don't know what to do," he breathed.

Jackson leaned his head closer to hear, and the guard behind him—a giant slab of beef with a ruddy face and thinning brown hair—said, "Sit back, please. We need to see space between you and the prisoner at all times."

Jackson nodded at the guard and pulled back. "Okay, buddy, I'm going to tell you what we think happened, and then you can blink twice if I'm right, how's that?"

Tage stared at him. "What you *think* happened? Isn't that why I'm here? Because the cops *think* they know what happened?"

"Yeah," Jackson said. "But they don't know what I know, so listen up."

"Yes," Tage said, voice limp and dead. "Go on."

"What I *think* happened is that No Neck and Ziggy were in your laundry room when some bad men came to your apartment building. You were actually doing laundry because you're a good kid, and the police report says there was a basket of laundry scattered on the floor and covered in No Neck's blood. So you get down there, see that Ziggy has actually taken a switchblade to No Neck's throat, and you stare at him, shocked. While you're staring, someone comes up behind you and knocks you on the head, hard. You go down, and you don't wake up until you're surrounded by cops and there's a dead body next to you. How am I doing so far?"

"I don't know this Ziggy," Tage said, his voice showing uncertainty—and maybe a little hope. "But otherwise, I'm very impressed."

"Good," Jackson said, nodding. He looked at the guard. "I'm reaching for my phone." The guard nodded and watched while Jackson pulled it out and summoned Ziggy's picture. He showed it to the guard and then showed it to Tage. "This is Ziggy."

It was like he got hit by lightning. Tage's face went from pasty to green, and he let out a little whimper.

"That," Jackson said, tucking his phone back in his pocket, "was Ziggy."

"I can't," Tage said, shuddering. "I can't tell—"

Jackson shook his head. "Not going to make you," he said. "Let me finish your story."

Tage nodded weakly.

Jackson continued. "So, you wake up, and you're horrified because that kid almost had his head cut off, and while you start babbling, which is perfectly understandable, your father comes down. And he looks at you, and you know something's wrong. And he starts to wail 'My son, my only son!' and you realize your brother and sister have been taken. Probably by Ziggy's pals, which you didn't know about because you were out cold. How you doing?"

Tage slow blinked. And then quick blinked. And then kept blinking until Jackson held up a hand. "I'm going to take that as yes."

Tage actually nodded his head.

"Now, do you know where your brother and sister are?"

Tage shook his head no.

"Do your parents?"

Tage lifted one shoulder, and Jackson got it.

"They might, but they're afraid, so they're not talking."

Tage nodded again.

"Okay. So, if we let you out of jail, will you and your family be safer or less safe than they are now?"

Tage's hands were cuffed to the table in front of him through a bolted-down bar, and at Jackson's words, he simply laid his head between his arms and cried.

Jackson looked at the guard, who shook his head no. No touching the prisoner. His body actually shook with the need to comfort.

"Please," he begged. "This kid—he doesn't belong here."

"None of them do," the guard said flatly.

Jackson tasted bile. He got it. He'd met some guys who would have used that gesture of comfort to disembowel Jackson and then rip their hands out of the handcuffs to get away. Jail, prison, these were ugly places where ugly things were done, and not everyone he and Ellery defended was innocent.

But this kid was.

"Kid," Jackson said, keeping his voice low. "We're going to do everything we can to get you out of here. We're going to do everything we can to keep your family safe. But I need to know something—anything—that will help us find your brother and sister, that will help back up your story. What was No Neck doing there? His house was at least a half mile away. Can you at least tell me that?"

Tage turned his head and blinked at him. "He has family in the apartment complex," he said gruffly. "His uncle's family." He shuddered, his chin crumpling. "It is not a good place, their apartment."

Jackson nodded. He got that. Some of the apartments in midtown were like that: solid, working-class families in one unit, gangsters-R-us in the next. A complex like Tage's—the kind with two-story clusters of apartments spaced closely around the apartment grounds, a pool in the middle, and laundry rooms in every cluster—wouldn't have security footage. The laundry room itself was a small white-tiled affair with six machines total and two chairs and a folding table as the barest amenities. According to the crime scene photos, Tage had been found in the center aisle, right next to No Neck, except Tage had been breathing.

"A name, Tage. Something to go on. The police have nothing but that the beat cops don't think you did it."

"Siderov," Tage whispered, so quietly Jackson could barely hear him. He glanced at the guard, who was listening intently, eyes narrowed.

"We're going to try to get you off," Jackson said, as though repeating Tage's word. "Are you sure you can't remember anything else?"

Tage shook his head, but in that same tone of voice he said one word, one that made Jackson's blood run cold.

Jackson breathed out carefully through his nose and without looking at the guard, said, "Don't worry, we won't bother your father. He's dealing with enough already."

Tage closed his eyes and let out a shaky breath. "Thank you," he said, this time loud enough to hear.

At that moment, Ellery and Siren Herrera walked back in. Herrera looked torn. The brown eyes that fell on Tage were not without sympathy. Ellery looked furious, a spot of color on each pale cheek.

Jackson gave him a bland smile and said, "Counselor, can I have your legal pad?"

Ellery frowned but handed the folio over without hesitation. "Wha—"

Jackson raised an eyebrow at him, which was all he needed. Then he wrote—left-handed, hand curved over his pen—two words. He handed the folio back to Ellery, who did a slow blink and then gestured to Herrera, and they left again.

"Tage," Jackson said. "This is important. If we get you someplace safe, whether it's in the jail or in protective custody, I need you to do me a huge favor."

Tage sat up a little and wiped his face on his shoulder. "What is it?"

"Don't talk to anybody. Not police, not friends, not even Sascha, although I think he wants only what's best for your family. Can you do that for me?"

Tage frowned. "But you just asked me—"

"I did. But Ellery and me, we're it. Someone walks up to you in the yard, in your cell, and says, 'How'd it go with the lawyers,' you tell them we're full of shit and you'll probably be in for life. It's not true!" he added hastily as Tage's face registered his horror. "But you have a face like an open book, kid. I need you to not let anybody read you who doesn't need to. Can you do that for me?" While he was speaking, Herrera and Ellery slid back into the room but remained quiet.

Tage didn't notice them. He swallowed, throat working. "We do not share our souls here," he said weakly.

"Good. You keep that up. No soul sharing." Jackson smiled at him kindly. "I'll tell your father you are okay."

Tage's lower lip wobbled, but he nodded.

"And you keep your eyes open, hear?"

Jackson glanced up at Herrera to make sure she wasn't going to give him crap.

"Infirmary tonight," Siren said. "Cramer, you can accompany him there and make sure the nurse on duty has him in the infirmary cell. I'll have a number for bail first thing tomorrow."

The naked hope on Tage's face hurt to see. Jackson pinned him with a no-bullshit gaze.

"We'll be here at eight with a suit," he said. "But in the meantime, I don't give a shit *who asks*—what's your answer?"

Tage's eyes stayed focused on Jackson's face, but they could both see the guard in his peripheral vision. "My lawyers are shitty. I'll be in jail for life."

Jackson let out a long breath. "Deal." He looked at Ellery and then leaned forward, just far enough to keep his voice low. "Don't eat anything tonight."

He pulled back, and Tage's eyes were enormous. "Da," he said numbly.

And then the guard said, "Time to go. Infirmary?" He looked at the ADA.

"Yes," she responded. "Please escort Mr. Cramer and the prisoner there, and then Mr. Cramer back."

"I'll—" Jackson began, but Herrera shook her head.

They both sat suspiciously as the guard unlocked Tage's manacles from the table and then escorted him, chains hobbling his thin ankles, out of the room, Ellery on his heels. Jackson watched them go helplessly and then sagged in his seat.

"God, that kid had better be alive in the morning."

Siren Herrera regarded him evenly from those sharp brown eyes of hers. "What makes you think he won't? And make it quick. I just pulled the infirmary card."

"Kid was terrified. Wouldn't say anything. I got two words from him, and when I got the first one, I looked up and the guard was practically in my pants. His cousin, Sascha, was on the inside for three years, stolen property. He had contacts who were supposed to keep Tage safe, so where did he get those bruises?"

Herrera blinked. "Okay, so we've got a terrified kid who may or may not have decapitated—"

"His brother and sister have been kidnapped and trafficked," Jackson said bluntly. Those were the words on the legal pad. *Kids sold.* "We've got a name—one I have to run—and contacts I need to talk to. We have a place to start, but none of it is any good if that kid doesn't make it through the night. And even if we get him off scot-free, the odds of him being safe until we get these people arrested and in prison are not great. But he'd rather be gunned down in the street than killed in his cell, Ms. Herrera. Trust me."

"Do you have a suspect for this killing at least?" Herrera asked. "I can't go to my boss with nothing."

Jackson pulled his phone. "This kid. Sergio Ivanov. Police just issued a BOLO for him in the matter of Sean Kryzynski, the police detective who was knifed outside our office after trying to steal *this exact* file," Jackson told her. "Did Ellery tell you that?"

Herrera shook her head. "No. Are you sure it's this one?"

"Well, someone stormed the damned public defender's office this morning, looking for a file that was going to us. We had a choice between two files, but the other one led to this one, so I'm pretty sure this one's it."

"What's the other one?"

Jackson shook his head. "Nope."

"Nope?" Herrera laughed, a little shocked. "You can't withhold evi—"

"This kid's a target, Siren, and he might not make it through the night. That other guy in the folder is not. And he won't be unless—"

"Unless someone hears his name," she muttered, proving she wasn't stupid.

"It's a matter of trust," Jackson said. His eyes darted outside, where Ellery and the guard had disappeared, Tage between them. "We trust that you're going to do your best to keep that kid alive. You need to trust us that we're not going to let a killer go free."

She squeezed her eyes shut. "He probably weighs 110 pounds," she muttered. "He... he doesn't belong here."

A tiny part of Jackson relaxed. "Then let's work to get him out."

She nodded. "Human trafficking. This is such bad news."

"You are telling me. God, how are we going to get those kids?"

She scowled at him. "Two kids? That's all you're worried about? Two kids?"

"No. I'm worried about all of them, dammit, but these two kids I know, and these two kids I can do something about. You tell me how I fix the whole damned world and I'll do it. But I can't. Two kids. What used to be a happy family." He breathed harshly against the tightness in his throat. "Sometimes that's where we have to start."

"Do we even know the names of these kids? There's nothing in the police report." Herrera closed her eyes wearily. Jackson knew Ellery's hours; he was pretty sure Herrera's were comparable. Ten-hour days and work on the weekends. Welcome to the glamorous life of the ADA.

"Sophie and Max," Jackson said, remembering the way Tage had played with them, teasing them, giving them things to do to make their cousin Sascha feel like moving into Jackson's old duplex was a cause for celebration. "Their family is pretty tight. Tage's not going to say a word until he knows they're safe."

Herrera nodded. "They lie to us, you know."

Jackson looked at her quizzically. "Who lies? About what?"

"We're told that the people who come through those doors into the jail usually have no family, are abusers, nobody will miss them. And some of them—" She shook her head and shuddered.

"Some of them really are monsters," Jackson agreed. He'd seen the psychopaths, the conscienceless, the abusers, the monsters. One or two of them had been cops, but by no means all of them.

"They are indeed," she murmured, and then, echoing his thought to the word. "But not all of them."

Jackson thought of that kid, his narrow shoulders, the fragile way he'd held his jaw. "No," he said gruffly. "That's why we're here."

She nodded and gave him a grim smile. "It's easy to forget that." They both saw Ellery through the wire-embedded glass, stopping to talk to the guard by his side, and Jackson stood and gave in to the urge to stretch and yawn.

"Long day?" she asked.

Jackson shrugged. "First day back."

"From vacation?"

Jackson blinked at her. Sometimes he had to remind himself that not everybody Ellery met was classified as a friend. Ellery wasn't great at small talk with colleagues.

"Medical leave," he said, waiting to see if she knew about him and Ellery or not.

"That's funny," she said, frowning. "Ellery said his partner had been out on medical lea… oh!"

She blinked at him, the expression dispelling some of the arctic coolness she projected by mere virtue of her cheekbones.

He batted his lashes prettily. "Not what you expected?"

She raked him up and down with her sharp black eyes. "Let's just say I'm personally disappointed."

It was Jackson's turn to blink. Wow, how had he missed the signs? "Well, that's flattering, and a year ago I might not have been such a disappointment."

Her full lips curved into a smile. "What happened a year ago?"

Jackson's eyes flickered to Ellery, the way the sharp brows snapped down in the middle because he was displeased, the strong, bony jaw, the lean mouth that could be mobile and full with kisses and humor.

"Oh," Herrera said again. "I guess there *is* someone for everyone."

Jackson ignored her, watching the guard's posture, his hands clenched at his sides, the ugly expression of distaste on his face.

"Excuse me," he murmured, stepping through the door and into the guard's personal space.

The guard's clumsy swipe at his head wasn't exactly a surprise. Jackson dodged back neatly and was dismayed when the guard's loose fist whooshed past Jackson and into Ellery's jaw.

Ellery wobbled on his feet, and Jackson caught the guard's hand as he yanked it back, and twisted the man's arm behind him, forcing him to lie facedown on the floor.

"Herrera!" he barked, relieved when he heard her coming from the conference room.

"I saw that," she said, lunging for the phone on the wall. "Herrera, Conference Room Two. We have an incident. Repeat, an incident. We need a supervisor here stat!"

Jackson was pressing most of his weight on his elbows into the guard's back as he struggled, but he managed to check Ellery out from his position on the floor.

"Counselor, how you doing?"

"Ou. Ch," Ellery managed, rubbing his jaw. "How do you do that for fun?"

Jackson let out a weak laugh. "Mostly I duck. Sorry about that. He wasn't really focused—I didn't expect it to get to you." Jackson put some more weight on the small of the guy's back. "Why did you do that?" he asked, right as a group of really angry men with guns, Tasers, and billy clubs came charging down the hallway.

Siren Herrera stood in front of them, hand out, in what was a balls-out act of bravery.

"Your man swung on a civilian," she said. "We can resolve this in-house, or we can press charges, but we're not doing a thing until you get him in hand so Mr. Rivers here can stop restraining him."

The group of five men slowed to a halt, and the leader eyeballed Jackson as he struggled to keep his perch on top of the much bigger guard.

"The actual fuck, Mayer!"

J. Mayer—or that's what it said on his nametag—turned his head and rested it on the floor. "He got in my space," he muttered.

"He was threatening Mr. Cramer," Jackson retorted. "His body language, his raised voice—I was trying to de-escalate the situation, and he swung."

"True story," Herrera said, backing him up. Jackson sent her a grateful look, and she gave him a hard nod. "We saw their argument from the conference room, but—" She turned to Ellery. "—I'm afraid we don't know what it was about."

Ellery was still rubbing his jaw, and Jackson saw a mild swelling already erupting.

"Could somebody get this asshole so I can get him some ice?" Jackson demanded, and immediately two of the other guards were at his side. Jackson slid off and waited for them to cuff Mayer before moving away completely.

"I'll go get an ice pack," said a younger guard, smaller, with dark hair, dark eyes, and skin of the palest clay color.

"Thanks," Jackson said, as M. Garcia took off for the infirmary.

"Great, now that *that's* taken care of," the lead guard said, "what exactly happened here?" He was an older man, retirement age, with thinning brown hair, a mustache, ruddy skin, and piercing blue eyes. His nametag proclaimed him to be J. Codromac, and he looked both Jackson *and* Mayer over with a canny gaze.

"Officer Mayer and I were talking about our client," Ellery said, wincing as he spoke. "Mr. Dobrevk was in Mayer's custody when he received a beating that bruised his face and ended up with Mr. Dobrevk having to spend the night in the infirmary. I wanted to know where those bruises came from, and Officer Mayer was more concerned about his sterling reputation than his prisoner's health and welfare."

"For the last time, I don't know what happened to that punk kid," Mayer burst out, still facedown on the ground. "This isn't a day care. People get hurt!"

"Seventeen-year-olds who weigh a hundred pounds apparently do," Jackson retorted. He looked at Ellery. "Is the boy okay?"

"The medic *was* very surprised he hadn't seen Tage yet," Ellery said, glaring at Mayer.

"Mr. Mayer assured us he'd been seen to," Herrera said, surprised.

"Kid was fine," Mayer snapped. "Was just a little bit of a roughing up."

Jackson's eyes narrowed in speculation. "Which he didn't get at the hands of the prisoners," he said, because Sascha's contacts had put a "no touch" order on Tage.

Codromac's eyes widened too. "Help him up," he said to the other guards, and Jackson scrambled out of the way as they hauled him up by the armpits. Once he was there, Codromac searched Mayer's face with those shrewd blue eyes while Mayer stared through his skull.

"Go home," he said. "Come in tomorrow. Let's hope that kid's okay."

"But—" Mayer began.

Codromac just shook his head. "Three weeks retraining, no prisoner contact. You're in the video room. Would you like to try for a suspension?"

Mayer growled, his face red with helplessness. "I can't," he said. "I just… I have to be here."

The words, the phrasing, the "have to." Jackson opened his mouth to ask "Why have to?" but Codromac beat him to it.

"You and me, we need to discuss that," he said quietly. "But right now, go change. No phone calls. Another word out of you and it turns into suspension without pay. You two, escort him to the locker rooms. Take his weapons."

Mayer looked like he was going to cry, but he nodded angrily, and the two guards at his side moved to do what was asked.

Jackson opened his mouth to protest, and Ellery and Siren did the same. Codromac held his hand up with the authority of someone who had been wrangling people at their worst through one political upswing after another.

"You three I will speak to outside," he said.

He escorted them through the confines of the entryway with the shaded trees in the front, taking a deep breath of the still-thick air of early evening. "You forget what free oxygen tastes like in there," he said, and they nodded. Something about the man instilled respect—even in Jackson, who had probably just risked his life by taking out a guy in uniform.

"So that guy's crooked," he said after a moment. "And I didn't know. But I don't think the union will do anything with him, not based on what we've got now. Suggestions?"

Jackson looked at Ellery, who nodded and picked up the ball.

"This case has a lot of Russian names in it," he said delicately. Nobody liked to say "Russian mob." Not in Sacramento, where the big players had been street gangs until the last ten years. But there was no denying the prevalence of Russian names here—or the tactics. Trafficking, police manipulation, the casual brutality against the young men, and the missing children. This wasn't an ordinary street gang. This was damned serious.

Codromac grunted. "I'm a stubborn bohunk, and I still know what that means," he muttered. "I'm not excited that one of my men is tied to this, but you think I should keep him away from the Russian guys?"

"Keep him away from the *vulnerable* guys," Ellery said. "I think if Mayer had help, there would've been a partner who would have alibied him. That wasn't the case here. Mayer may be dirty—and possibly being coerced—but he obviously doesn't expect anybody to have his back. If you can't get him out, just put him someplace he's got more accountability and less time alone with people who can't fight back."

Codromac nodded. "I will have a talk with our CDCR officer before I leave tonight." He blew out a breath. "Won't make me real popular, but I retire soon. Figure I got all the friends I need. You law people"—he made a dismissive gesture, throwing all three of them onto the same side and into the same pot—"do what you need to do. I'm just a dumb bohunk, like I said. I've got no use for lawyers." He paused and gave them all a hard glance. "Unless they're saving some poor kid's life who's got no more reason to be in prison than I've got in a fish bowl."

Jackson had to work not to smile. As easily as he'd taken out Mayer, he thought he could sort of like this guy.

"Watch out for him," Jackson said, feeling a slight surge of protectiveness. "All animals get mean when they're cornered."

"We'll keep Mayer out of gen pop until CDCR is done with him," Codromac agreed, and the lines at the corner of his mouth deepened. "That kid too." This time he pinned Herrera with an icy gaze that belied his assertion of being a "dumb bohunk" who knew nothing about the affairs of lawyers. "Don't know what your office was thinking. That there's a fucking travesty."

Herrera nodded. "Yessir. Well, mistakes were made."

Codromac snorted. "Your superiors were taking advantage of a rookie is more like it. Give 'em hell, girl. You all go fix the world. I'm going to go read one of the broken bits the riot act, and let's see if we can keep that kid alive."

And with that, the head officer at the county jail turned around and stumped away, average man, average height, a great deal more character than was first apparent riding his average shoulders.

"I like that guy," Jackson mused and then frowned at Ellery, who was holding the ice pack gingerly to his jaw. "Let's get to the car, Counselor—there's ibuprofen in the glove box."

Herrera frowned at them, the weariness Jackson had seen while they were waiting for Ellery's return weighing down heavier on her than ever.

"He didn't have us file an incident report," she said unhappily. "We should be up to our eyeballs in paperwork."

"A thing I plan to investigate tonight," Ellery told her, probing at his jaw. Jackson resisted the urge to knock his hand away. Not here. Not now. "But Jackson and I have a stop we should make." Ellery met his eyes. "Is he out of surgery yet?"

Jackson reached into his pocket and pulled out his phone. It had buzzed while he'd been talking to Tage, but the middle of the county jail wasn't where you lost concentration.

"Yeah," he said. "Henry says he just got out about ten minutes ago. They're waiting for him to come out of the anesthesia." Jackson smiled a little. "He says the waiting room is full, but that Dave and Alex appreciated the food."

Ellery raised an eyebrow and nodded. "Good."

As though remembering what had happened to Kryzynski, Herrera's features hardened into fury. "Oh for fuck's sake. We have *got* to get that kid out of jail."

"And his family into protective custody," Ellery agreed. "And hopefully Officer Codromac can keep him alive until that happens."

She shook her head. "God. Just... this situation isn't going to unfuck itself, but if we're the good guys, we need some help!"

"We're doing the best we can," Ellery said mildly, following that up with a wince.

"C'mon, Mad Max," Jackson said, tapping his elbow to get him to move. "Ibuprofen. Now."

"You're awfully bossy," Ellery muttered. "You need to teach me to hit back."

"First things first," Jackson said, jerking his chin toward the car, which he'd seen parked in a rare and precious spot along the curb. "I need to teach you to duck."

"I'll call you tonight, Ellery," Herrera called after them, and Jackson paused long enough to look back.

"Watch yourself," he said, swallowing. "This sitch—it's apparently open season on lawyers, and I don't think they care which side of the bar they're on."

Her eyebrows rose. "Thanks. We've got our own PIs. I'll tap someone when I get back to the office."

"Call them now," Jackson urged. "I'm not shitting around. Kryzynski got stabbed when we were coming back from lunch. This bullshit doesn't make a formal announcement."

She gave a hard nod and pulled out her phone. "I hear you," she said. "On it."

Still, Jackson kept an eye on her as he helped Ellery into Ellery's beloved silver Lexus and didn't draw a deep breath until she was in her own little red sport coupe and it was pulling away from the curb.

He'd started the air-conditioning in the meantime, and he reached into the space in the center console and pulled out the jumbo-sized bottle of ibuprofen and one of the waters they kept stashed there.

And a small packet of crackers that Ellery kept because he liked to think Jackson wouldn't remember to eat if he wasn't nannying Jackson within an inch of his life.

"Here you go, Counselor," Jackson soothed, handing over the stash. "You know the drill."

Ellery washed down the ibuprofen without comment and followed it up with a couple of crackers to help ward off the stomach burn. When he'd gotten that down, Jackson allowed his shoulders to relax and brought up tender fingers to probe Ellery's bruised jaw.

"Sorry," he muttered. "I shouldn't have—"

"What?" Ellery asked, his smile pulling up one side of his mouth because the other was swollen. "Not ducked? That's counterproductive." He grimaced. "It happened so quickly."

Jackson shook his head and cupped the side of Ellery's face that *wasn't* bruised. "It didn't," he said, lips twisting. "The guy was like a coiled spring, even when it was just me and Tage in the room together. You guys came back, and Herrera and I could see him cranking tighter and tighter. That's why I got so close. He was going to take you out. You gotta watch guys like that. If they think the uniform makes them better than the rest of us, they're not going to let anything stop them from cheap shots."

Ellery nodded, swallowing hard. "Good advice," he said, his voice wobbling a little. He leaned into Jackson's touch, and right then, in that moment, let his guard down.

Jackson rubbed under his cheekbone with his thumb. "Not used to the hitting, are we?" he murmured.

Ellery shook his head. "No."

"Good. Nobody beats on you. That's a rule."

He gave a tiny smile. "I like that rule," he admitted, nodding, and Jackson gave him a gentle kiss on the cheek.

"Me too. Now let's go before we start necking and the entire prison system takes us out on general principle."

Ellery rolled his eyes. "You exaggerate," he said, trying hard to keep his voice authoritative, and Jackson backed up and gave him his space.

"Says the man who just got clocked in the face for being right too much," Jackson countered, pulling the car out into traffic.

"That's not why I got clocked in the face," Ellery muttered. "I got clocked in the face because Mayer was an asshat who thought because he was seven feet tall he could beat up on us short people."

"You are six feet if you're an inch," Jackson scoffed.

"Five eleven," Ellery told him. "You're six one."

"That's not true." Jackson frowned. "We're the same height."

"We are not."

"I can't believe we're arguing over this," he muttered.

"I can't believe we've known each other for seven years and you don't know how tall I am."

"I can't believe we've been together for one year...." Jackson's voice trailed off, and he did the math. Mid-August. That's when he and Ellery had gotten together. A couple of furious days fighting the long-simmering attraction between them, then giving in to it.

Followed by three weeks in the hospital and Ellery moving Jackson into his life whether Jackson wanted to be there or not.

And now, Jackson couldn't even imagine his life without Ellery. His treacherous brain replayed Mayer's swing in slow motion, and then, because that wasn't nearly the worst thing that had happened to them, he saw Ellery standing in front of a dusty aluminum hangar in the desert, his body blowing back as he placed himself in danger because that sudden anger, that passion for the people wronged, had taken hold of him at the worst time.

"And what?" Ellery prompted, and Jackson tried to remember where he'd been going with that.

"And just that," Jackson said, swallowing hard. "I can't believe we've been together for a year."

"Are you freaking out?" Ellery asked suspiciously.

"No." Jackson breathed carefully, his throat unexpectedly tight. "No," he repeated, keeping his eyes stoically on the road. He hit a stoplight and flickered his gaze toward Ellery, who was leaning against the headrest in an unguarded pose because he trusted Jackson and Jackson needed to remember that. "Just no getting hurt, okay, Counselor?"

Ellery's warm brown eyes met his perceptively. "Same goes for you, Detective."

Jackson let out a harsh bark of a sound and switched his gaze in time to see the light turn green. "Doesn't seem to be my problem today." He scowled as he pressed the gas pedal. "And I'm saying, there oughtta be a fucking law. And somebody should text Lance and tell him to wrap Henry in a big quilt and then put him in a steel box and then wrap *that* in bubble wrap. I am *not* okay with the way this day has gone, do you hear me?"

"So noted," Ellery said dryly, and a silence threatened to steal over the car.

One Jackson felt compelled to break before he turned onto Alhambra. "Ellery?"

"Yeah?"

"We should do something. It's an anniversary. I know we took that trip when I was healing, but… you know. A nice dinner. Something. A year. It's a big deal for me." He let out a little laugh. "I mean, you know, for one thing, I never expected to live this long."

"It's a big deal for me too," Ellery said softly. "I never expected you to love me."

"That's just crazy talk right there," Jackson said, eyes fiercely on the road. "I'm not sure why that would even enter your mind."

"Gratitude," Ellery murmured. "Thanks for small miracles to the powers that be."

"I'm thankful for you too," Jackson said, and Ellery's hand on his knee grounded him, helped him navigate the tricky emotional waters they were both swimming. He took a deep breath and reminded himself that neither of them could fall apart now. He covered Ellery's hand briefly with his own. "I'd be even more grateful if you could, I don't know, maybe learn to frickin' *duck* the next time somebody swings at you? Please? For me? Since we're getting all sloppy about feelings right now?"

Ellery chuckled softly, and this time the silence, healing and thick with things they weren't willing to say right now, stole over the car.

A Familiar Pond

ELLERY COULD think better once the ibuprofen worked, and those blissfully quiet moments in the car helped him gather his composure around him like a shield.

Of course, Jackson's worry helped a little. Jackson hated people fussing over him because he was used to picking his own pieces up off the ground and sewing them together. He interpreted worry as criticism that he couldn't do the job right. Ellery had been raised by loving—if frighteningly competent—parents who had taught him, in careful steps, how to care for himself and how to reach out for help if he needed it. Worry was part of the process, one that Ellery had once been afraid Jackson wasn't capable of.

Turns out, Jackson could worry just fine if it was Ellery's health involved, but that was okay. Ellery didn't mind feeling cared for; that wasn't one of his demons.

Hating to leave that kid in custody… well, that *was*.

Ellery had figured it out as they'd been walking through the corridors toward the infirmary. They'd passed three other prisoners being escorted by their own guard, and Ellery had seen a glance pass from the leader, a giant of a man with a shaved head and a scar slashing down the side of his face, to Tage, and for a moment he'd been worried.

Then he'd seen the outrage on the man's face directed toward the guard at Ellery's side, and he'd put together a few things.

He'd grilled the onsite medic within an inch of his life as they'd set Tage up in a small open-grilled infirmary cell for an overnight stay. Mayer had stood impassively at the door, eyes focused on Tage with an unhealthy ferocity.

And Ellery had feared for the young man's life.

He'd gotten a promise from the medic—a burly man who had learned his trade in the military and who could probably take out an entire infantry unit and then doctor their wounds—and then allowed Mayer to escort him back.

But he hadn't been silent, and his pointed questions had elicited... well, an expected response. Ellery had expected the guard to get hostile. He'd been planning to report the incident to Mayer's superior as it was.

He hadn't expected the violence, but Jackson had. Jackson's instincts were a lot better for that sort of thing, and Ellery was grateful. Jackson got himself out of as many messes as he ended up *in*, and sometimes that was the only reason Ellery could let him, in good conscience, walk out the door.

"I liked that guard, though," Jackson said out of the blue as they neared the sprawl of the Med Center complex. Ellery startled out of his own thoughts to respond.

"Codromac?"

"Yeah. After the police station, I'm telling you, watching that old guy was sexy. It was like competence porn right there."

Ellery chuckled. "Glad to know that's your kink. Was the police station really that bad?"

Jackson's mouth thinned. "I... remember last year? We took out the bad guys and thought, 'Hey, they have a clean slate!'"

"I do," Ellery said, but his own mouth thinned. "They still treat you like crap."

Jackson nodded. "Some of them. But we were right about those two officers who had Tage's case. They were on top of it. They didn't think the kid did it, they wanted to treat him like a victim, not a suspect, but their lieutenant, green, trying to prove something, jumped in, and the DA's office went, 'Yes! Prosecute the young 'cause it makes us look strong!' And the one crooked prison guard was like, 'Okay, we gotta rough this kid up 'cause someone says so!' and...."

They both shuddered.

"One weak link, some miscommunication, and a public defender who didn't see the disconnect, and that kid could have been dead," Jackson finished. "I mean, on the one hand, I'm glad it's not corruption, but on the other, you've got guys like Sean, guys like Fetzer and Hardison, and they deserve better than an undertrained lieutenant and a DA out for numbers instead of real justice."

"I agree," Ellery said. "System's broken. Let's leave it all and go run a restaurant in Jalisco."

Jackson blinked. "Jalisco?"

"Supposed to be a wonderful place for American expatriates," Ellery said blithely. "Do you have your passport?"

Jackson slowed for the hospital on their left and prepared to turn. "You made me get one," he said, "when we went to visit your family over Thanksgiving. But I'm not saying we should chuck it all and run off into the wild."

"Then what are you saying?"

Jackson picked the parking structure and not the ER ground-floor parking. "I'm saying that the system is helping these guys. And I would wager, whoever Sergio Ivanov works for, whoever is trying to set Ty Townsend up and frame Tage Dobrevk, they're counting on the brokenness. That's why all the panic about Tage's file getting to the hands of someone like you and me." He frowned. "Which means...."

Ellery's jaw gave a throb, and he shut up and let Jackson think.

Jackson blinked. "Gah! I've never had a case with so many leads! But Henry and I *have* to interview the people in Jenny Probst's office. Somebody leaked where that file was going." He squeezed his eyes shut. "I'm going to have to spend all night making a to-do list for Henry and me."

"Why don't you split up?" Ellery asked. "I mean, twice the work, twice the people."

Jackson pulled the Lexus into a parking slot and stopped before glaring at him. "And leave Henry out there alone? Are you shitting me? After the way *this* day has gone? If that kid buys it, his boyfriend will *kill* me!"

Ellery chuckled as they both got out, and Jackson walked around the car to take the ice pack from him and check his jaw again.

"How bad does it look?" Ellery asked, fearing the answer.

"You're still dead sexy," Jackson said with a slight worried smile.

"I look like an extra from a horror movie, right?" He hated that his vanity was coming into play, but he prided himself on looking professional, and a swollen face did *not* keep up that image.

"You look like you got clocked in the jaw for a good cause," Jackson said, giving his cheekbone a brief caress. "But do me a favor, Counselor."

"Learn how to duck. We covered that." Ellery's heart picked up speed, just being near him. Weird how that happened but never, ever unwelcome.

Jackson shook his head. "Leave the pissing people off to me, okay? You're supposed to be the reasonable one. We need to keep it that way."

Ellery shrugged. "Well, given the way Herrera was looking at us, she seems to think we're both crazy."

"She's right. But we want to make your crazy secret, stealth crazy, like a secret weapon, okay?"

The criticism was leavened by Jackson's closeness and the concern in his eyes, and Ellery leaned into him, testing Jackson's usual public space.

Jackson rewarded him with strong arms around his shoulders, and Ellery took the comfort—real comfort—with the care Jackson intended.

"Gotcha," Ellery murmured against his shoulder. "Stealth crazy. I'll work on it."

Jackson stepped back and smiled faintly. "Only masters of crazy can implement that kind of thing, if the challenge makes it worth it."

Ellery chuckled briefly, and Jackson's hand went to his phone. He pulled it out as they started walking through the parking structure, and the tightness that had never left his eyes since he'd shown up at the jail relaxed slightly.

"He's awake," Jackson said, texting. "And he's asking for us."

"Well, that man's earned the right to ask for whatever he wants," Ellery told him primly.

Jackson's fierce grin was enough of an answer.

His bravado faded a little as they approached the hospital entrance. Ellery might have been the only one to notice it, although Jade might have. Jackson's steps never faltered, but his jaw was clenched tight enough to pop a vein in his forehead, and his face—tanned skin with a faint ruddiness from lots of time in the pool—blanched under the wheat color.

His bottle-green eyes were almost lost behind their squint, and every deliberate breath grated on Ellery's nerves.

Jackson had spent, by Ellery's count, nearly a year and a half of his life, at one time or another, under a hospital roof. By their last stay, together as it were, his hatred had morphed into a full-on phobia.

When Jackson had gone in for surgery, the doctors had released him early because it was either that or sedation. Just being at the hospital made his heart rate spike higher than was good for anybody, much less a patient recovering from heart surgery.

"You okay?" Ellery asked, keeping his voice extra casual.

"Peachy." Which was sort of Jackson code for "I'm losing my shit, thank you, but I'll be damned if I let anybody see."

"Of course," Ellery acknowledged. As they were walking, he got close enough to bump Jackson's shoulder and brush their fingers together. Jackson's pinky finger, cold and clammy, curled around his for a minute before they separated.

Ellery knew that if Jackson had his way, it was as much comfort as he'd ever be offered in the matter.

KRYZYNSKI'S CONDITION was listed as critical but stable, and they were told he had a night in the ICU before he would be released to standard care. The waiting room was down a stark white corridor, and it was clotted with cops. Henry stood in the hallway, talking to an intensely beautiful man with almond-shaped brown eyes, dark hair, and faintly dusky skin. Lance Luna, his doctor boyfriend, looked at Jackson and Ellery as they rounded the corner with a combination of irritation and gratitude.

"He kept saying you were on your way," he said as they approached.

"We apologize," Ellery said. "There was an incident at the jail, and we were held up."

Henry squinted at him. "Who hit you?"

"That's the incident," Jackson said grimly. "And one of the guards hit him."

"Hit *Ellery*?" Henry asked in surprise. "I would have thought it would've been you!"

"It was supposed to be me," Jackson retorted. "But I ducked and Ellery—"

"Didn't," Ellery said with a brief smile that still hurt. "It's not Jackson's fault I irritated the guard."

"And it's not Ellery's fault that he was taking payoffs to beat on a seventeen-year-old kid who had no business being there," Jackson rasped. "Junior," he said to Henry, "I hope you're ready to run your ass off tomorrow. We have got some *plans*."

Henry nodded, looking very sober. "But before that happens...."

"How is he?" Ellery asked. "You said he was asking for us?"

"He is," Lance told them. He looked at the watch on his wrist and made a frustrated sound. "I'm on my break. I can get you in, but not for long. I'm sort of working here."

"We appreciate your help," Jackson said. "Maybe Dave and Alex can take over?" Ellery looked at Henry and saw his grin.

"I am just crushing it with the catering today," Henry said. "Ice cream for the pregnant cop, pizza for the nurses. I should change my career."

"Did any of those people tip?" Jackson asked, at the same time Lance said, "I bet it would be safer!"

Henry smirked. "No, nobody tipped, and yes, yes it would be safer, but I would be both broke *and* bored, so I think Jackson's right and I should stay with my current job."

Lance rolled his eyes. "Of course Jackson's right," he muttered. "But if one of your nurse friends can come supervise, you can stay a little longer. C'mon."

He turned and beckoned to them to follow him across the corridor, but not before a harsh voice called out from the full waiting room.

"Rivers! What in the hell are you doing here?" An older officer, still in uniform, charged out of the room.

Jackson turned, his expression neutral. "Kryzynski asked for me."

"I'll just bet he did. Aren't you the one who got him stabbed in the first place?"

Ellery bet the other cop didn't see it, the tightening around Jackson's eyes, the slight softness to Jackson's lower lip. The shaft had hit home, but nobody was going to know Jackson Rivers was bleeding.

"Interesting that you're only wondering about that now," Henry said, moving up to Jackson's other side. "'Cause when we were at your precinct, not a soul had heard about it."

Jackson turned slowly to Henry with big eyes and a slightly parted mouth. "Henry," he said, voice toneless.

But Henry was unstoppable. "We couldn't even get your two flatfoots to call a detective and do forensics on a doorknob that had prints at the scene. But we show up because an injured detective wants to talk to us and suddenly you're interested? Damn, son—talk about a day late and a dollar short."

"Henry," Jackson rasped.

"You think you rate talking to a detective in the hospital, you little punk?" the officer snarled. "We did not know. That is not our fault!"

Jackson's head snapped around. "No, but it's somebody's. Communication in your department is for shit, Carruthers. I don't give a damn who's in charge, but if your patrol officers can't maintain protocol, what good are they?"

The officer, Carruthers, had tanned skin and what had probably been ginger hair, bleached thin and blond by too much time outside. He narrowed his eyes at Jackson, and Lance grabbed Jackson and Henry both by the shoulders and yanked them around, herding them toward the unit itself. When he got there, he waved his ID in front of a sensor, and the heavy barred doors swung open to let them all in, Ellery bringing up the rear.

"Henry," Jackson and Lance both growled at the same time.

"Don't let them talk to you like that," Henry muttered back to Jackson.

Jackson closed his eyes and squeezed the bridge of his nose even as he dodged a piece of medical equipment that Ellery couldn't name but after all of Jackson's time in the ICU looked unsurprisingly familiar.

"Henry, I told you to forge some relationships with the police department," Jackson said, voice despairing. "You can't do that when you take some old fart's head off for being an old fart!"

Ellery held back a laugh. Well, he did have a point.

"I *did* forge a relationship," Henry complained. "That desk sergeant wants to have *my* baby now, on top of the one she's about to push out."

Lance stopped them in front of a sliding glass door that led into an almost spacious cubicle. There were two stuffed chairs, an office chair, and a love seat in there, along with a small unit designed for visiting family to set their things on.

The office chair was occupied by a giant of a man, well over six feet tall, with iron gray hair and a weathered, fortyish face, who was leaning forward, hands dangling between his knees, really working a scowl of irritation.

As Lance let them into the room, the stranger stood and said, "Here's your new crew, Sean. I hope they treat you right."

"Jesse," Kryzynski murmured in a thin whisper. "Don't be mad."

The man, who was wearing a dark blue SFD T-shirt and what had to be big and tall jeans, shook his head. "I'm not mad," he said. "Just disappointed. I'll be by tomorrow."

He stalked out, glaring at Jackson on his way, and Ellery suppressed a wince. Well, one day back and Jackson had made more enemies than friends without even trying.

Of course he had.

"Ouch," Jackson said, taking the vacated office chair and moving it closer to Kryzynski's bed. He didn't sit down right away but instead engaged in one of those complicated masculine handshakes that Ellery had never gotten the hang of. Sean seemed to know how to do it, though, because he made languid hand motions as Jackson pulled in to an abbreviated mock chest bump, and he smiled when Jackson had finished.

Testosterone levels in room: restored.

Henry took one of the club chairs near the wall, and Ellery sank into the one nearest Jackson.

"How we doing?" Jackson asked, and then—because this was one of his strengths—he sat back and listened.

"Fabulous," Sean wheezed, still sedated, blue eyes sleepy. His blond hair, usually a thick shock of it, combed into submission, was plastered to his forehead, and his color was so pale he was almost gray against his sheets. "Was so jealous of Rivers getting that two-month vacation. Had to take one of my own."

"Two months for a punctured lung?" Jackson asked.

"And a hemothorax," Lance corrected. "They spent two hours draining the blood out of his pleural cavity and closing off bleeders before they could reinflate the lung. He's got four bright and shiny new pints of blood in his body. How's that feel, Mr. Kryzynski?"

"Like it needs more morphine," Sean said woozily.

"Pussy," Jackson murmured affectionately, and Sean managed a slight smile.

"Who hit me with the pigsticker?" he asked. "I owe him one."

"We'll be sure to pay up," Jackson said. "And you remember us talking about the kid who was at both crime scenes?"

Sean closed his eyes. "Ziggy," he said. "Great. I got knifed by some asshole named Ziggy." He took a few breaths that seemed to exhaust him. "My taste in criminals is almost as awesome as my taste in boyfriends."

"I cannot comment on that," Jackson said, and Ellery returned his speaking glance. Whatever had gone on between them, it had not looked like things were going well. Jackson turned back to Kryzynski, and Ellery noticed that the skin around Jackson's eyes was so tight, Ellery could see a vein throbbing in his forehead.

Great.

"I don't have the breath," Sean wheezed. "Rivers, not your fault. You warned—" He took another struggling breath. "—me."

"We dragged you into this bullshit," Jackson said grimly. "We'll do you right. You should see the waiting room. Wall to wall cops. They love you in there."

Kryzynski smiled faintly. "That's sweet. My partner has been yelling at me in text for two hours. Seems to think—" Long breath. "—I left him the boring stuff to do something… exciting."

"Little does he know of the enforced boredom of the next two months," Jackson told him grimly. Ellery tapped him on the knee, and Jackson nodded. "Look, Sean, we've got about a minute before Lance here drags us out by the ear."

Lance grimaced and nodded, but at that moment, he spotted someone beyond the door.

"You've got two now," he said, and Ellery watched as a tall, muscular man with pale brown skin and dark pinpoint freckles walked into the cubicle. Lance nodded at Henry, who waved him out and then took a moment to smile and wink at one of Jackson's favorite nurses.

"Dave," Jackson said. "How you doing?"

"Shocked," Dave said, holding an elegant hand to his heart for a moment before beginning his activities at Kryzynski's monitors. "I am stunned and shocked that it's not you lying here, baby. But not disappointed."

Kryzynski's mouth opened in what would normally have been a short bark of laughter. "He keeps hogging… all of the attention."

"He *does*," Dave told Sean. "Damned inconsiderate of him. But I'm betting you wish he'd found other ways to share."

Sean actually managed a full smile. "Damned… straight."

"We shared the case with you *before* you got shish kebabbed," Jackson told him. His voice was steady, chiding even, but Ellery could see how every heartbeat in this place was taking its toll. "Is there anything you can tell us about this guy before we go?"

"Good teeth," Kryzynski said. "Super straight. Smelled… like a businessman. And chalk."

"Wow," Jackson said, admiration tinging his voice. "You *are* a good detective."

"Don't… be an ass."

"No," Henry said from his place by the wall. "That's good info. Jackson and I can put together some things with that."

"Was there anything else?" Ellery urged.

Sean's eyes were at half-mast, and he was gazing at Ellery with dreamy focus.

"You're so pretty," he said.

Ellery gave Dave a pointed glance. "Did you up his morphine?"

Dave shrugged, unrepentant. "He was about fifteen minutes past due. We don't like post-op patients to hurt, right?"

"Not a problem," Jackson said, pulling in a shaky breath. "Another hit for my friend here." Jackson stood up, bent over, and squeezed Sean's hand gently. "We are friends, right?"

Sean gave one of those dreamy smiles. "I'm in the club. Did you hear that, Nurse Dave? I'm in the club!"

Dave gave him an isn't-he-precious look. "I know, sweetie. But I gotta tell you, the dues are a bitch."

"But I'm in the club." Sean's eyes were almost closed, and Jackson gave a "follow me" nod. They all paused outside the door, waiting for Dave to record his vitals and make sure he was sleeping comfortably before he came out too.

"He's going to be okay, right?" Jackson asked as Dave was sliding the door shut behind him.

"He should be," Dave murmured back. "You know how these things go, baby. Barring infection and embolism and all the other nasties that can attack post-op, he should be just fine."

Jackson swallowed and nodded. "Good. You know, he's—"

"In the club," Dave said softly. "I've met him at your house, Jackson. We'll do him right."

"Thanks, Dave." Jackson gave a weak smile. "I'll take any updates you or Alex can give me."

"Thanks for the food, sugar." Dave gave a wink, and Jackson shrugged.

"That was all Henry. He's like a mama bear, I swear. Feeding everybody. It's embarrassing."

Henry gave him a killing look, and Dave shooed them off. "Go. We'll tag you later."

Ellery turned to follow them, but Dave stopped him with a look. "Your boy okay?" he asked, eyes flicking to Jackson.

"Hospitals," Ellery said briefly. "But he had to come."

"Yeah. You know, you could have a shrink prescribe half a valium for him—" He broke off and rolled his eyes, as though he'd just heard what he'd said. "Or not," he muttered. "It is just as well that boy didn't end up here this go-round. I think he's done all the time he possibly can."

Ellery nodded. "Yeah, well, keeping him healthy is a full-time job."

"Good thing you're on it," Dave told him, winking.

"Thanks for keeping an eye out for Sean. It'll help Jackson sleep."

Dave grinned. "Just invite us to the next do. Practically made our year!"

"Ours too." Ellery gave a brief nod and strode through the ICU, catching up with Henry and Jackson at the corridor. What he was thinking was that he and Jackson should have another party, because the people in their lives seemed to enjoy them and because Jackson was always so bemused to find he had friends.

What he walked into was a strategy session.

"The jail to get Tage Dobrevk out," Henry said.

"Check."

"Jenny Probst's office to ask who knew about the file."

"Check."

"Ty Townsend's place to ask him who was at the party."

"Check."

"His best friend's place to get his story."

"Check."

"Tage's parents to figure out where his brother and sister went."

"Check."

"I thought you said they were Russian," Henry replied with a straight face.

Jackson's eyes widened. "I will beat you," he said, perfectly serious. "I will beat you and feed what's left of you to my cat."

"There won't *be* anything left of me after you drag me all these places. Dammit, Jackson, split the fucking *check* here!"

Jackson turned to Ellery. "Bad news, Ellery. I'm about to turn our junior PI into cat food."

Ellery tried to appear bored, but he really wanted to give Henry a raise. "Jackson and I will deal with Tage's family," he said before pointing at Henry. "You take Ty Townsend."

"What do you mean, *we*?" Jackson asked, startled.

"I need to be there when they release Tage, and you need to talk to his family. You can drop me off at the office after that, and you and Henry can compare notes."

"I don't like this plan," Jackson announced. "Henry—"

"Isn't stupid," Ellery said shortly. They strode past the corridor where the police were still congregating, waiting on news from Sean.

Jackson took a breath. "I'll be back."

Ellery made a sound of dissent, but Jackson was already on his way.

"Let him," Henry said softly. "He'll feel better. He's not okay with Kryzynski being here."

"So he lets those assholes beat on him and that makes it okay?" Ellery snarled.

"Yeah," Henry said with a shrug. "A little."

Ellery was afraid that if he rolled his eyes, one of them would pop out. "I am underwhelmed by that logic," he muttered, and at that moment, raised voices down the corridor stopped them both.

They heard the ruckus, and the clatter, and then Jackson came flying out the door, stopped by the wall on the other side of the corridor. He ran a hand over his mouth, and looked at the back of it, grimacing a little at what he saw. Then he glared back in through the open door and snarled.

"Somebody get that man some ice!"

And with that, he turned around and walked back to them, split lip bleeding, and a bruise by his eye growing puffy as they watched.

"We can go now," he said, not looking back. Henry and Ellery kept pace with him as they headed for the entrance.

"You had to," Ellery said, irritation dripping from his voice.

"Oh yeah."

"Couldn't *not* do that."

"Nope."

Ellery let out a long breath, and Henry said, "How bad *was* the other guy?"

"Heh heh heh heh heh…."

As they burst out of the front glass doors into the balmy night, the security guards at the entrance glaring at them suspiciously, Ellery noted that Jackson's pallor was much closer to normal, and the tightness around his eyes had eased.

Well, maybe some men needed valium, he guessed.

Some men did not.

"God!" Jackson burst out, running a hand through his hair. "Is it really this late?"

"After eight," Henry told him with a yawn. "It's been a bitch of a day."

Jackson eyed him with concern. "You're going home now, right?"

Henry lifted a shoulder. "Movie night with the flophouse guys. I'll probably crash on their couch until Lance gets home."

"Good," Jackson said. "Get some food, get some rest. Text me when you're on your way to Jenny Probst's. I want to know what you come up with."

"Deal. After you get Tage situated, we can meet at the office and go from there."

Jackson nodded and was going to head to the parking structure when it was obvious Henry was turning toward the lot. "Henry," he said before they split.

"Yeah?"

"Be safe."

Henry rolled his eyes. "Get some sleep, Rivers. Aren't you still on leave?"

And with that he moved off to his vehicle, leaving Jackson and Ellery to continue toward the parking structure.

"Just had to," Ellery said grimly into the silence.

"Shut up."

"Couldn't let me have the bruises, could you?"

"You got the bruises. There was enough to share."

Ellery snorted. "Thought it would make you look prettier, right?"

"I didn't do it for attention," Jackson muttered.

"Sure you didn't," Ellery goaded, liking him riled so much better than helpless and hurting.

"Counselor…," Jackson warned as they entered the close darkness of the structure.

"Jackson Rivers, action hero, can't stand to not have any—"

Jackson whirled, grabbed Ellery's hips, and pulled him close into Jackson's overheated chest, taking his mouth savagely. He thrust his tongue in without apology, swallowing Ellery's moan as Ellery melted into his arms.

"Any what?" Jackson taunted.

"Wha?" Ellery managed before Jackson kissed him again. Ellery could taste the faint tang of blood, but mostly Jackson, and they'd made love the night before, but that didn't mean that Ellery didn't want more of him, and more and more and more.

"You said I couldn't stand to not have any." Jackson grinned wickedly, his eyes sparkling in the darkness.

"Any action," Ellery said breathlessly. "Can't stand not to have any action."

Jackson chuckled. "I'll show you action, Counselor," he said, and then he kissed Ellery again. The kisses were wonderful, urgent, and God, Ellery never had a day when he didn't want Jackson Leroy Rivers.

But he could sense the underlying tension, the slight tremor in Jackson's hands, and when things might have gotten out of hand for two grown men in a parking garage, he pulled back, gentling Jackson, calming him down.

"Shh." He rested their foreheads together. "Home first. Dinner second. Stress relief third."

Jackson grunted. "Do you really think I'm only here for the stress relief?"

Ellery suppressed a shiver. "God, I really hope not," he confessed. "But, you know. Let's just get away from the hospital."

Jackson let out a breath. "Yeah," he said after a moment. He didn't move, though. "Thanks, Ellery."

Ellery straightened. "I have no idea what you're talking about."

Jackson turned and started walking to the car, his knowing chuckle echoing through the garage as he went.

Worms and Hooks

"JACKSON, EAT."

Jackson pushed the sautéed chicken and veggies around on his plate. "I'm not hungry," he muttered and then gave Ellery an apologetic glance. "I'm sorry," he said dutifully. "I'm not trying to be difficult."

Ellery let out a sigh and pulled his fingers through his wet hair. Both of them had gone for a swim after they'd gotten home. It was still thick and wet outside, so they'd come in to the air-conditioning for a late dinner.

It had been nearly ten o'clock when Ellery had shooed him into the shower while he cooked. Jackson was trying to be grateful, but....

"I know you're not," Ellery said on a sigh, closing his eyes. "I could go swim another twenty laps myself. God, this case!"

"Why do they have to be so young," Jackson wondered. It had been haunting him since he'd seen the two case files side by side. "Whatever is going on, *whoever* we're dealing with, they're smart, they're organized, and my God, they don't mind using children." He shuddered. "It was so much easier when the psychopaths were just... you know, psychopaths."

Ellery shook his head and, for one of the few times in Jackson's memory, looked bleak and at a loss.

"I.... You know, that's the one crime I could never defend. My mother told me it was a possibility someone would ask me to do it, and I just... couldn't."

"Hamster, Fingerling—"

"Pfeist, Langdon, Harrelson and Cooper knew when I signed on," Ellery said. He shrugged. "We all had a line. Some people wouldn't defend drug offenses, some wouldn't defend weapons offenses. I wouldn't defend crimes against children." He shuddered. "You have to see something defensible, I suppose, in order to do your job as a defense attorney. I couldn't. I just—"

"Couldn't," Jackson murmured, taking in Ellery in his "leisure" wear. Tonight it was a pair of linen pajama bottoms and a clean white

T-shirt. He'd probably take the bottoms off before coming to bed, but he was remarkably prim about things like clothes and when to wear them and what their function was.

Jackson was in one of the practically transparent pairs of basketball shorts that had survived the great clothing purge of Jackson's recovery time, and a black Fitz and the Tantrums T-shirt with more holes than lettering. He may have vowed to make an effort to dress better when he represented the firm—and Ellery—but even Ellery conceded that he could wear whatever he wanted when it was just the two of them alone in their home late at night.

But looking at Ellery working so desperately for order, trying to make the world a better place—one in which the bad were punished proportionately and the good were allowed to make their living—and seeing that he lived his life that way, gave Jackson faith.

"I couldn't see you defending anybody who would hurt a child," Jackson said honestly. "But even abuse and neglect—those are terrible, don't get me wrong. But sometimes they're crimes of desperation, of poverty. Latchkey children who are unsupervised because their parents are working to put food on the table and pay rent. The parent who's desperate over both those things and loses his or her temper. Those crimes can be... I don't know. They're awful and cyclical and all of those things, but they are at least functions of being human. Desperately flawed human beings, but *human* beings."

Ellery nodded meekly, and Jackson was struck by his vulnerability. It hit him—perhaps for the first time—that Ellery's insistence on order, on wearing the right clothes for the right function, on following sometimes inconvenient rules, was a defense against the fear of the things he couldn't control.

"These people," Ellery said softly. "Whoever would take Tage's brother and sister and traffic them, whoever would set him up, would try to steal Ty's future and slit James Cosgrove's throat...."

They both shuddered.

"Monstrous," Jackson said after a moment. "Tim Owens was monstrous, but I could see into his brain. I could see the human inside the monster." Tim Owens had been a serial killer who'd worked for the police force under an assumed identity for *years*. But Jackson could still remember following his twisted logic, his obsession with Jackson, with the "dirty/pretty" people just fallen into life on the streets. "Martin

Sampson's father—I got it. It was ugly, and it was awful, and it turned my stomach, but I got it." Sampson Senior had molested his son and then, when Martin refused to sell drugs or recruit his friends anymore, killed him. "But this? This is organized, and it's far-reaching. Tage Dobrevk was a kid in the wrong place at the wrong time, and I'm hoping he'll be alive when we get there in the morning to spring him. Ty Townsend was the same, but he was *engineered* to be in the wrong place at the wrong time. And don't get me started on Tage's siblings. And we only have one face to it, Ziggy Ivanov, and he feels like a front man. He's not small change, maybe—a mover and a shaker—but he's not a mastermind."

"What makes you say that?" Ellery asked, the directness of the question sharpening his features. Maybe he needed to make sense of it as much as Jackson did.

"Because a mastermind wouldn't have been breaking into our office," Jackson mused. "That's desperation. That's 'Oh shit! Our guy didn't get to the file at the PD's office. We need to get where it was going!' Stabbing Sean wasn't planned. He was literally on his way out the door. But…." Jackson bit his lip, remembering the two bodies colliding, Sean staggering back holding his hands over his stomach.

Ziggy's footsteps pounding down the pavement before Jackson had realized what that meant.

"He's no stranger to violence," Jackson said. "He probably killed James Cosgrove." He grimaced. "God, poor No Neck. It would be nice to know why."

"Loose end for setting Ty Townsend up," Ellery hazarded.

"Yeah." Jackson chewed his lower lip. "But maybe not. I mean, No Neck would have been an in. Whatever they were doing, Ziggy had the cop equivalent of a CI in a population he was interested in manipulating. Why kill him?"

"Good point," Ellery said. "But you know what we *really* need to know is—"

"What in the fuck are they doing!" Jackson burst out. "Drugs, human trafficking. Is it all of the above? Is it just a massive move on the streets to saturate a particular neighborhood with mob contacts…?"

He stopped and looked at Ellery in surprise.

"It's a massive move on the streets to set up the mob so deep they can't be unearthed," Ellery said, as stunned as Jackson to find he was right.

"There's an epicenter," Jackson said in wonder. "There's a.... We can't see it yet, but Ziggy, the poor bastard in the ER, Tage and his family—all of this is circling around something."

He scrubbed his face with his hands. "So. Many. Leads," he muttered after a few minutes. "God, we need to put this together soon. Tage and his family need protection."

"We need sleep," Ellery said decisively. "But first...." His lower lip wobbled. "Please, for me?"

Jackson looked at the plate of food in front of him and took a bite. It was good even cold. He took another bite and glanced at Ellery. "I'll finish it off on one condition," he said, hating how naked Ellery seemed without the protection of his sense of order, his sense of rightness.

Ellery arched a skeptical eyebrow. "Don't say it."

Jackson summoned up a wicked smile. "Heh heh heh heh." He took another deliberate bite, licking the fork.

Ellery's shoulders gave a little wiggle as his spine straightened, and his head assumed a haughty tilt. "Are you trying to seduce me over cold chicken and vegetables—" He paused, his eyes growing limpid again, before he added the endearment. "—Detective?"

"I'm trying to seduce you," Jackson said unrepentantly before taking another bite.

"Why would you want to do that?" And he'd meant it to be arch—Jackson could tell—but it sounded lost.

Jackson shoveled in his last bite, chewed deliberately, and swallowed before wiping his mouth. "Because we've both had a rough day, and we need to remember what's good."

Ellery's smile was particularly luminous. "*You're* good," he said softly, with that faith that used to terrify Jackson.

Jackson swallowed again, took a last sip of water, and stood. "Only with you," he said, extending his hand. Ellery took it and for once left the dishes on the table, letting Jackson pull him up into what Jackson had planned to be a mauling kiss.

It turned into a hug. Jackson nuzzled his neck for a moment, knowing he'd smell like soap and clean man and a little like Ellery himself. It was a surprisingly exotic smell, spicy and rich, because Ellery wasn't an average man.

And tonight he needed comforting.

He sighed in Jackson's arms, melting, and Jackson kept up the nuzzle, then ran his nose along the shell of Ellery's ear, turning it into a caress. Ellery slid his arms around Jackson's waist, and Jackson trailed his lips down the side of Ellery's neck, using his tongue and tasting a little, trying to pull that exotic, wonderful scent into his soul.

Ellery tilted his head, giving Jackson access, accepting comfort in a way that told Jackson he needed it desperately. Poor Ellery. Worried about Jackson all the time, worried about his business, worried about his clients. Jackson had started their relationship assuming that *he'd* be the one to take care of things, only to find his life neatly managed, his body and soul neatly cared for, by the man in his arms. But Ellery wasn't a god; sometimes he really needed someone to take care of *him*.

Ellery gave a little gasp, and Jackson trailed kisses along his jawline, being very, very careful of the swelling where the guard's punch had landed. "Tell me if it hurts," he murmured.

"No," Ellery said, tilting his head back and giving Jackson access to his throat.

"No, it doesn't hurt, or no, you won't tell me?" Jackson teased between kisses, between nibbles. The T-shirt Ellery was wearing, a silky, pricey affair, gaped to expose Ellery's collar bones, and Jackson trailed more kisses down the line.

"Nothing hurts," Ellery assured him. "Not when you're doing—" Jackson nipped lightly at his neck. "—ah… that."

"Heh heh heh." Jackson captured Ellery's earlobe and sucked, adding a little nip to it, delighted when Ellery shuddered in his arms, leaning against Jackson for support.

"Jackson?" Ellery begged.

"Bed?" Because Jackson would undress him here, strip his clothes off and make love to him standing in front of their dinner plates and the dining room table, but that's not what he wanted.

"Bed," Ellery breathed.

"Good."

Jackson turned and offered his hand, leading the way into the darkened bedroom. He paused for a moment to shoo the cat off the bed and pull back the covers, but he didn't turn on the light. Tonight's mood demanded the intimacy of the dark.

Once Billy Bob had stalked off in offended dignity, Jackson turned toward Ellery to find him still dressed and realized his Counselor needed more from him tonight than he'd allowed Jackson to give him in a long time.

"C'mere," he ordered, and Ellery approached obediently, allowing Jackson to shuck off his shirt and run his palms down Ellery's rib cage, the leanness of his stomach, before pushing at the soft pajama pants. Jackson sat on the bed and kissed Ellery's sternum, the soft skin of his stomach, using his tongue to tease along the line of his boxer briefs.

Ellery moaned slightly, and Jackson ran his hands along the backs of his thighs, teasing the inside of the boxer briefs with his thumbs. Ellery's back rippled, and he thrust his hips forward, and ah! There he was, full and erect, pressing against Jackson's chest.

Jackson could have teased him some more, but Ellery needed tonight. Jackson removed his boxer briefs instead, pleased when Ellery's sizable erection flopped forward, right at mouth level.

A sign if Jackson had ever seen one. He opened, took Ellery in without preamble, and Ellery moaned again, a little louder this time. So many other lovers, but Jackson could never remember their taste. Ellery's taste was the thing he craved—every morning, every evening— because it fed his soul.

Down to the back of his throat. Jackson was good at this, opening up, pushing forward until his lips met Ellery's pubic hair, his skin. He swallowed, milking the cockhead, then pulled back, allowing it to get passionate, sloppy. Welcoming the sting along his scalp as Ellery tugged at his hair.

"Oh… oh God, Jackson."

Jackson did it again, again, sliding his hands along Ellery's backside while he deep-throated, parting Ellery's cheeks with his thumbs.

"Ohhhh…."

Jackson would have smiled, but that would have meant letting Ellery's cock out of his mouth, and now he was the one who needed, needed it to fill him, needed more of Ellery's taste inside. He let some spit dribble onto his fingers and parted Ellery again, this time timing his breach of Ellery's entrance with the thrust forward along his cock.

"Ah!" Ellery spurted a little, precome filling Jackson's mouth, and Jackson swallowed again, savoring the taste. He thrust a little farther inside, and Ellery broke. "Now," he begged. "Please. God, baby, I need you."

One more time along his cockhead, and then just when Ellery whimpered and threatened to come, he pulled back. "On the bed, Counselor. Be sure you can see me when I fuck you."

Ellery nodded meekly and then, to Jackson's surprise, thrust his hands inside the neck of Jackson's awful old shirt and yanked, ripping it off his body.

Jackson laughed and stood, taking Ellery's mouth in a mauling kiss that left him pliable and breathless. "Told you," he said, ducking his head to pull a nipple in his mouth.

"Told me what?" Ellery demanded, holding Jackson's head in place, begging for more.

Jackson pulled off the nipple with a pop. "Told you old clothes have their uses. Now lay down and spread 'em."

Ellery did, some of the sadness gone from his movements, the moment lightened by his playfulness. Jackson loved him like this—loved him all the ways, in fact. Bossy and irritated, pliant and needy, and now excited and sensual, luxuriating in the touch of someone he loved.

Jackson grabbed the lube from the bed stand, pausing just a moment to grease his cock, enjoying the feel of the slick as he rubbed.

He added a little more to his fingers and knelt at the foot of the bed, teasing Ellery's entrance as he lay splayed out for Jackson's pleasure, just like he'd commanded.

Power like that could go to a guy's head. Both of them.

"You done—ah!—teasing me yet?" Ellery rasped as Jackson thrust one finger in and circled.

"Nope."

Ellery took hold of his cock and squeezed, his entire body trembling.

"I'm gonna come without you," he taunted, and Jackson shoved both lubed fingers in to the knuckle, enjoying Ellery's shudder, his cry into the dark, the way the vulnerability had fled, leaving him powerful and pleasured and happy.

"The hell you will," he said, spreading his fingers. "You'll lay there and take it."

"You're not... oh... oh God! Jackson!"

Jackson pulled his fingers out, not wanting to push too far. Some nights, when he knew Ellery needed it, he could be rough, could just thrust in with a little lube and know Ellery would be with him, greedy for the manhandling, for the bite of pain. Some nights he could tease until his lover was begging.

But not tonight, when Ellery needed the reassurance of Jackson inside of him as much as Jackson needed to know Ellery was whole in heart as well as body, needed to know nothing was going to hurt him as long as Jackson was there.

Jackson moved up until they were chest to chest, and his own dripping cock was poised at Ellery's entrance.

"You ready for this?" he breathed, pushing enough to tease.

"Yes," Ellery begged. "Please."

Jackson thrust in slowly until his head popped through, and Ellery *hmm*ed in his throat in welcome. "Good?" Jackson asked.

"More."

"Excellent."

Jackson snapped his hips forward, burying himself to the hilt, luxuriating in Ellery's full-throated cry of welcome.

He'd planned to go slow, to take Ellery apart inch by inch, to put his lover first in every moment, but Ellery dug his nails into Jackson's biceps and begged.

"God, Jackson, fuck me hard. I need...."

And so did Jackson. He needed it hard, needed it fast, needed it *now*. He lunged, hips pumping, chest heaving, suddenly needing Ellery's sex more than he needed to breathe. He pounded hard, relentlessly, chasing his own orgasm in the haven of Ellery's body, drunk on Ellery's cries of want, of pleasure, of joy.

"Oh God, Jackson. Right there—yes! Please. Oh God. So close!"

Jackson sat back and threw Ellery's knees over his shoulders, giving Ellery room to grab his own cock as Jackson thrust. He did, beautiful, abandoned, eyes squeezed shut as his body clenched around Jackson. All at once Ellery gave a cry, and his ass squeezed so tight around Jackson's cock that Jackson couldn't move.

That and the sight of come shooting across Ellery's pale abdomen, his chest, was all Jackson needed to send him over.

"Jackson!" Ellery cried and Jackson pumped come into his body, spending everything, heart and soul, as his vision washed black and then white and his molecules came undone.

Ellery spread his legs and allowed Jackson to fall forward, sliding out of his body in a gush of spend. Jackson paused and licked up Ellery's stomach, tasting Ellery's own spend, pausing at his nipples to suck, making his way along the tender line of his throat.

Their kiss was warmth and comfort and the intoxication of knowing they were both replete.

Ellery gave a satisfied sigh, and Jackson rolled to the side a little, kissing Ellery's shoulder.

"You good?" he asked, needing more than the sigh tonight.

"Much better," Ellery said, meeting his eyes in the scant light. They'd left the bedroom door open, and the light from the dining room spilled in. "You?"

Jackson kissed his shoulder again. "As long as you are," he said. That moment when he'd ducked and Ellery had taken the blow replayed itself behind his eyes. "Next time I won't duck."

"No," Ellery corrected. "You go ahead and duck. But next time I will too."

Jackson regarded him affectionately. "You, Counselor, take every blow on the chin. You are constitutionally incapable of ducking. I just need to factor that in."

Ellery chuckled, and the air around them lightened, dispelled by the lovemaking, by their playfulness, by their joy at being together. "I can too duck," he said. "I just need to duck *faster.*"

Jackson chuckled too and then kissed him again. "Stay here," he murmured. "I'll be back." He rolled out of bed and slid his basketball shorts on commando.

"Where are you going?" Ellery asked, rolling to his side.

"I'm gonna do the dishes and bring you ice cream in bed," Jackson told him, flashing a smile over his shoulder. "Do you mind?"

Ellery's lips parted softly, reminding Jackson of how often *Ellery* was the one doing the considerate-lover things.

"No," he said, smiling a little. "Not at all."

Jackson made short work of their dinner dishes and then grabbed a carton of rocky road ice cream, along with two spoons and a towel to hold it with. He made his way back to the bedroom, pausing to make sure all the doors were locked and the alarm was set and scooping Billy Bob up in his free hand before hitting the light with his shoulder and returning to the bedroom.

Ellery had turned the lamp on by the time he returned and was sitting up in bed, bare-chested, reading his phone.

"Anything interesting?" Jackson asked.

"Yes. I texted Jennifer Probst earlier, while you were in the shower."

"About the leak?" Clever Ellery—that had been on Jackson's to-do list the next morning.

"Yes. She gave us some names of people who would have known she was turning the file over to us."

"Ooh, more people to call. I like it."

Ellery glanced up from the phone and laughed. "No bowls?" he asked, setting down the phone.

"I set the dishwasher," Jackson protested. "And who eats our ice cream besides us?"

"Jade, Mike, Henry…." Ellery ticked the names off on his fingers and Jackson realized he was right.

"Come to think of it, Jade used to steal my coffee and ice cream when I lived alone too. And Mike always made himself sandwiches."

"Henry is new," Ellery said, reaching out for the carton.

"Well, yes. But he's damned competent."

"This surprises you?"

Jackson thought about it. "No. We knew he would be when we worked his own case in June. And you've been dealing with him for the last two months. If he'd really pissed you off, you would have said something."

Ellery took a bite and laughed. "This is true. And Henry's good. He'll do anything you ask him."

Jackson frowned. He heard the "but" in there. "And…."

"No, he's just not you. You have a way of reading my mind, that's all."

Jackson couldn't help it. He preened. "That's because you're mine," he said, puffing his chest out a little. "That's not Henry's fault. If he could read your mind like I do, I'd have to kill him."

Ellery rolled his eyes. "You would not."

"No, no. I definitely would kill him." Jackson nodded. "I work for the best criminal defense attorney in the world. He'd totally get me off."

Ellery laughed at his foolishness and retorted, "I think he just did!"

Jackson slid into bed next to him, only a little surprised to find Ellery had put his boxer briefs back on while Jackson had been doing dishes.

"I texted you the list of people," Ellery said, taking a bite of ice cream. "You might be surprised at two of the names."

Jackson looked at his phone and frowned. "Siren Herrera. Well, that makes sense."

"Yes," Ellery confirmed. "She's the ADA. She'd need to know she was working with me."

"So I need to find out who she told, who her paralegal is, who kicked the case up in the evaluations department. Yeah, we need to know who knew."

"Yes, and do you see that other name?"

Jackson scanned his phone and raised his eyebrows. "S. Mayer, Bailiff."

"Yup," Ellery said. "Think that's any relation?"

"Only one way to find out," Jackson murmured. Ellery offered him a bite of ice cream, which he took absently, eyes widening in surprise as the whole cold mass made its way down his throat. "That is a very coincidental name right there."

"Your nipples just got hard," Ellery said clinically.

Jackson looked up from his phone. "What? Augh!" Ellery used the spoon to put a tiny dollop of cold ice cream on one of his exposed nipples. "What are you doing?"

Ellery bent his head to Jackson's chest and looked at him wickedly. "Eating ice cream," he said before sucking the ice cream off.

"Nungh—"

Thirty minutes earlier, Jackson would have said he was all sexed out and guessed that he and Ellery would have done a little case work and then turned off the light, spooned a little, and gone to sleep.

Fifteen minutes later, Ellery slid out of bed to put the ice cream back in the freezer—a little depleted and a little meltier—and Jackson was a sloppy, gooey puddle on the sheets, with a pleasantly sore backside and the happy realization that he was never so glad to be wrong.

IT WOULD have been great if the good sex meant he slept until morning, but even after a doubleheader and a long day, Jackson's nightmares were still bound to come.

This one started as a memory of that afternoon. Of Ellery recoiling from the sloppy blow to the chin, but also of the blows not stopping. Jackson stood, paralyzed in the way of dreams, helpless as that monster of a man sat on Ellery's chest and beat him and beat him and beat him;

not like a movie beating, but a real beating, with blood pooling from the skin and the sound of crushing bone as his nose gave and—

"Jackson!" Ellery snapped, his voice irritated, calling to him in a way that nothing else could have, penetrating through layers of the dream until Jackson was abruptly lucid.

"Sorry," he mumbled, rolling over and engulfing Ellery in his arms, pulling him tight while he shivered, keeping Ellery safe and himself warm with Ellery's whole, healthy body in the night.

"Bad one?" Ellery murmured.

"Paralyzed by love," Jackson said, shaking, burying his face in Ellery's neck. "Terrifying."

"Shh… it's okay, baby. You can move. I'm okay. Everyone's okay."

Jackson nodded, allowing himself to be comforted, but as he closed his eyes, sliding back under, he wasn't thinking about Ellery or any of the people who made up his family.

He was thinking about Tage Dobrevk, in jail because he couldn't speak for himself for fear of harm befalling his brother and sister.

Paralyzed by love. A nightmare of the first order.

They had to find a way to fix it.

THE NEXT morning Jackson and Henry met up at the office at 8:00 a.m. and went over their list again. Helped by the info the PD had sent the night before, they refined their goals.

"Okay, new plan," Jackson said. "I take the DA, and you take the public defender's office. And this time forge some relationships and try not to piss anybody off."

"You're the one who got into the fight yesterday," Henry said mildly.

"Well, that was old business," Jackson said, trying for dignity and achieving only satisfaction. "Some fuckers want to hold on to the past even though it was crooked. You're the future. Keep it straight and narrow, Junior, that's all I ask."

"I am *maybe* four years younger than you. And that doesn't even count your emotional constipation."

Jackson was privy to a *lot* of Henry's past, and he knew all the signs of a fellow sufferer straining to outrun his demons. He arched a single eyebrow at Henry, who turned a healthy shade of pink.

"I'm still doing better than you," he mumbled.

Jackson cocked his head, staring at Henry in scientific fascination, like a new bug.

"Shut up! Fine. I'll hit the PD's office, you hit the DA's, we'll meet back here in the middle and go interview the parents. Are we good? Are you going to let me out of your sight? Do I need to take a weapon, Dad?"

"Shut up," Jackson muttered. "And be careful, dammit."

Henry rolled his eyes. "Oh my God. Listen to yourself. Try not to get shot, asshole." And with that, Henry stalked out of the conference room, flipping a salute behind his back and leaving Galen, Ellery, and Jade looking at Jackson in amusement.

"What?" Jackson glared at all of them, crossing his arms.

"Nothing," Jade said, her full mouth quirking. "Nothing at all. Not a damned thing. De nada. Zilch. Zero."

Jackson rolled his eyes. "Ellery, can we go now?"

"No," Ellery said. "I want Galen to repeat that thing he said yesterday about the larger pattern. It was important."

Galen smiled thinly. "I do believe I'm being patronized," he said, and it was Ellery's turn to roll his eyes.

"No, it was important." Ellery paused and gave Jackson a bored look. "And it will give Henry a chance to clear out of the parking lot so he doesn't run Jackson over with the car."

Galen's laughter—dry as lint—scuffed through the room. "That's the honesty I treasure. I told him to look out for patterns. There is something here we're not seeing. This is like a pattern of sabotage, a random trail of things that go wrong that shouldn't. Be on the lookout for things that don't fit, stuff that doesn't jibe with what you know. A guy in a nice suit with crappy shoes, a small-time thug with too much cash—"

"A guy who looks like a high school student who smells like a grown businessman and can vault over a fence and down a story while holding a knife?" Jackson said, eyes flicking to Ellery.

Ellery sat up a little straighter. "Yes. Sean did say he smelled like aftershave and mint. A businessman, like you said. The street hood and the high school student—those are disguises."

"Yeah," Jackson murmured. "And we've got a guard who's either taking payoffs or being coerced into beating down poor Tage. So a prison guard who's assaulting prisoners, a kid who didn't do it letting himself be arrested instead of fingering the grown man dressed as a kid who did. A house party that was probably held to get Ty out of commission and ruin his whole future."

"Where was that kid going to college?" Galen asked suddenly.

"USC," Ellery said, with that prompt recall of details that Jackson so admired.

"Hm...." Galen fingered his goatee.

"What?" Jade asked. "What is that sound?"

Galen cocked his head. "What do you mean?"

"That sound. That just wasn't right, was it, Jackson?"

"No," Jackson agreed. "But he's from Georgia. It's not his fault."

Galen shot Ellery a puzzled look. "What are they talking about?"

"You'll hear it eventually," Ellery reassured him. "Why does it matter where Ty plans to go to school?"

"We're talking big business here. The working theory was that they wanted to get the cops away from what they were really doing, but it was so elaborate. It's another thing that made me think corporate sabotage. So many moving pieces. Let me check with some sources. I have a theory."

Still pondering, Galen used the chair back to shove himself up to his feet, and without his cane, he walked steadily out the door and across the way to his office. Jackson knew he worked really hard to go without support as much as he could, and he admired a man who could stretch his limits, who could try to overcome his flaws.

Story of Jackson's goddamned life.

"Okay," Ellery said, looking at the clock on the wall. "While he does that, let's see if we can get Tage out of jail, talk to the DA's office, and maybe question Tage's parents while we're at it. Are you ready, Detective?"

"Always for you, Counselor," Jackson returned smartly. But on the way out the door, he paused. "Jade?"

"Yes?"

"I need you to do a couple of things for me. You got time?"

"Never. What do you need anyway?"

"I need you to have AJ run financials—a deep dive, Crystal has been showing him how—on a guard at the jail named J. Mayer. I'm sorry, I don't know his first name, but I'd check John or James or something common. He's crooked, and guys like that usually have something in their closets. A soft spot for someone to lean on."

"I can do that," Jade said, writing it down on a legal pad. "Or have AJ do it. What's the other thing?"

"When Galen gets out of his office, tell him that the crappy cops have a CI with a heavy German accent. Whatever angle he's looking up, that might figure, and right now, that piece doesn't fit anywhere else."

"German," she muttered as she wrote it down. "That's... well, interesting."

"Right? Apparently he sounds like a real bastard, gave the two *decent* flatfoots the fucking willies. I'm gonna take their word for it that we should look down that rabbit hole."

Jade gave a short laugh and wrote it down. "I'll tell him," she said, underlining it. Then she looked up at Jackson. "Baby?"

"Yes, ma'am?"

"Be careful."

"I've done my time in the hospital. Don't want to go back," Jackson reassured her.

"Thank God." Jade made a little shooing motion. "Now go. We've got shit to do."

"Yes, ma'am."

SIREN, GOOD to her word, had gotten her boss's signature to drop the charges. She called Ellery on the way to the jail, and Ellery called the Dobrevk family, so they were waiting as Ellery and Siren Herrera escorted Tage out of the jail.

They'd brought fresh clothes because the ones he'd been arrested in were still in evidence, and nobody wanted to wander around in a onesie.

Mr. and Mrs. Dobrevk were both small. Boris stood around five foot six, and his wife, Olga, was maybe two inches shorter. They dressed plainly, Mr. Dobrevk in corduroy pants and a button-down shirt, Mrs. Dobrevk in a serviceable skirt with tights and a blouse; traditional clothes from a country they both remembered.

The expressions on their faces when their son emerged were both agonized and relieved.

"You're okay?" Olga said, touching Tage's face lightly with her fingertips.

"Yeah, Mom," Tage said, capturing her hand. "It's fine." He smiled gamely at his father, who looked like the kind of man who was uncomfortable with emotion.

"That is good," Boris said, swallowing hard. He sent Ellery a surreptitious look. "You told them nothing?"

Tage looked at Jackson, and a grim smile lit his eyes as he said, "My lawyers were shitty and I'm going to be in jail forever."

Jackson nodded. "Good boy." He looked around them and said, "So, we need you to meet us at our office. Tage, you're going to want to shower, probably, get some food, reassure your folks, but we need to talk. Two hours enough time?"

He was thinking that if Henry was there to hear their story, the two of them could go question Ty and his friends with a little more knowledge under their belt.

Tage nodded but glanced at his father, who grimaced.

"Going back to our building with you," Boris said apologetically. "It is not safe. If they know you are out, not just your brother and sister, but your mother and I—none of us are safe."

Jackson's heart hurt at the crushed expression on Tage Dobrevk's face.

He and Ellery exchanged looks, but fortunately Jackson had a contingency plan.

"Okay then, we're going to try to get Tage into protective custody. Would you like to come with—"

"Nyet." Boris put his arm around Olga's waist. "No. No, this is our community. If we can't be part of our community, we have no lives. Tage, come with us. No one will see you. You can stay in the apartment."

"But what about Sophie?" Tage cried. "Maxim? Dad, they're going to—"

Boris's face was screwed up tight. "I have one son," he rasped. "One child. I cannot think otherwise."

"But no!" Tage turned to Jackson and Ellery. "If I go with you, if I tell people what I know, can they help my brother and sister?"

"Tage…," Olga whispered.

"We can't promise anything," Ellery said quietly. "We can't. But we can try. Jackson and I would take you to the DA's office and try to find someone who would listen."

Tage looked at his parents and swallowed, and Jackson would always think that in spite of everything that had gone on before, this was the moment the young man grew up.

"You two go home and be safe," he said, and the lack of irony was admirable. "I'll go and try to help Sophie and Maxim."

"Tage," Jackson murmured, just so he knew. "If you come with us to be put in protective custody, you might not see your parents for a long time, even if we recover your brother and sister."

Tage's jaw tightened. "Then Dad can say he has no children. It's fine."

Boris recoiled, and Olga cried quietly in his arms. "These are our people," he whispered.

"And I was your son," Tage told him, wiping his face on his clean shirt. He turned to Jackson. "Can we go?"

Jackson looked at Tage's parents, trying not to be angry. He didn't understand. They were abandoning their son, as far as he could see, abandoning their children so they could live with the comfort of their old life. But he hadn't walked a mile in their shoes. He hadn't left behind the familiar for the strange, only to find that the same people were in charge. "We'll keep him safe," he said, hoping he was being honest.

"Thank you," Boris said, looking wretched. Jackson felt a wave of what could only be described as relief wash off the boy. "We… we would like to know how they are, if you find out."

"Sure," Jackson said. He sighed. "Maybe. Are you sure? Are you sure you don't want to come with us?"

"We have other family," Boris whispered. "Not here, but in Carmichael, Citrus Heights. I'm the head of the house. If I betray…."

Got it. If the children left the family, the family couldn't be held responsible, but if the father followed the children, *everybody* was at risk.

"Great," Jackson muttered. He and Ellery looked at each other grimly.

"Then we'll go," Ellery said, his voice icy because he *obviously* didn't understand. "Please let us know if you change your mind."

They nodded miserably, and Mrs. Dobrevk darted out to kiss Tage on the cheek. "You're a good boy," she told him, voice breaking, before her husband pulled her way.

They escorted Tage to the car in tense silence, Tage's thin, battered face taut, his expression brittle.

"You hungry?" Jackson asked after a few moments. Ellery started the car to begin the short drive to the DA's office. Normally, they would have walked—it was barely half a mile—but something about having Tage exposed like that didn't sit well with either of them.

"Yes," Tage said promptly. "Like you said, I didn't eat in there. I couldn't sleep."

Jackson had figured this might be the case. He reached into the console and pulled out a breakfast burrito from one of his favorite places; he'd had Ellery get it on the way to pick Tage up. He'd thought he and Ellery would have more time to question Officer Codromac about Mayer, but Codromac had been unavailable, they'd been told. Apparently he was locked in a room with Mayer, watching training videos and reading him the riot act, so Jackson had left his business card and promised to come back later. Disappointing, but the burrito was still warm, and Tage took it eagerly.

Jackson handed him back some napkins and a soda, which the boy put in the holder by the armrest, and let him eat as Ellery pulled into another miracle parking space in front of the office.

"This whole area looks like it was built with those big Duplo blocks little kids play with," Jackson said musingly. None of the buildings were that tall, all of them were square, and most of them looked like you could stack them, one on top of the other, and build something taller but no more interesting.

"The seventies," Ellery said with a shrug.

"Hunh." Jackson turned around and saw Tage was still eating. "Ellery, you go on ahead. I'm going to wait until the kid's finished, okay?" He paused. "I'm going to take a detour to Sodhi and Pasternak's office."

Eleanor Sodhi and Ethan Pasternak were in charge of prosecuting human trafficking cases, and Ellery's eyebrows lifted.

"Just like that?" he asked. "Without me?"

Jackson shrugged. "I'll ask questions, that's all. You need to meet with Herrera. You can tell her what I'm doing. I just...." He knew that human trafficking got a decent budget; they might have the resources to protect Tage. "Call it a hunch, maybe, that we can get someone to take care of him there."

Ellery nodded and gave him a brief smile. "Your instincts are pretty good," he said, taking a deep breath of the morning air. "Don't stay too long in the car." The day promised to be hot, but the late-summer morning was surprisingly mild. Jackson figured they had about ten minutes before the car became a convection oven.

"Deal." Jackson watched him walk away and then waited until the kid took a breath while devouring the breakfast burrito.

"Tage, I'm going to ask you some questions. There's no one here to listen, and nobody has to know where I got the information, but we need something to go on here before I walk into that building and start looking for our bad guy information highway. Can you help me here?"

Tage nodded. "The boy who was killed—No Neck?"

"James Cosgrove?"

"Yes, that is his name. He has cousins who live in my building. There was another boy there. He… he hangs out with the high school students, but he is not one of us." Tage grimaced and took another bite, chewed and swallowed it quickly. "He is Russian, though. He visits the cousins in the building all the time."

"Cosgrove isn't a Russian name," Jackson remarked, but Tage shrugged.

"People emigrate, they change names, they get married. My name is Norwegian because my mother saw a movie. I don't know what to tell you."

Jackson grinned. "Hunh. That's good to know. Someone was asking me about that. So No Neck has cousins who live in the building. Does Ziggy know them?"

Tage looked uncomfortable. "Yeah—No Neck didn't particularly like Ziggy, but I got the feeling his cousins did. How'd you guess?"

Jackson shrugged. "We try not to be super shitty lawyers," he said. "So Ziggy used No Neck as an in?"

"I guess so," Tage said, chewing thoughtfully. "Just before school let out, everyone was getting all excited about graduation, about summer, and suddenly Ziggy is everywhere, asking people to parties, gossiping about who was hooking up with who. But always after school. I watched once as one of the teachers actually threw him off campus after school. I think the teacher told all the security guards to look out for him, because he started hanging out by the little store on the corner by the school. He'd catch up with people there."

"But you saw him in and out of your building?"

Tage nodded and, finally slowing down, took another reluctant bite. "No Neck's cousins aren't good people. Americans make a lot of movies about the Russian mob, but they never get how *everywhere* a thing can be when it's in your community—even in little bits. You drive down certain streets in our neighborhood and there are Russian and Ukrainian businesses everywhere. Maybe only one is mob, but if your parents use any of those businesses, go to those churches, they know the mobsters. They may be afraid of them, they may tell you to stay away from them, but they never defy them. It's too ingrained. It's like…." He chewed more thoughtfully. "Like one of my friends at school is Black, and he's so used to racist shit happening that sometimes *I'm* the one who's shocked, you know? Like certain teachers who say 'those kids,' and they don't mean *me*, they mean my friend, even though we get the same crappy grades and spend the same amount of time playing video games, you know?"

Jackson nodded. He'd grown up thinking of Jade and Kaden as his family, and the same thing still happened to him. He could never understand why people would be afraid of Kaden, the gentlest man he'd ever known, or would underestimate Jade's wicked intelligence because they were African American. And every time it happened, it left a wound in all of them—the kind of wound that made Jackson and Jade more determined to work for justice in the legal system. The kind of wound that had sent Kaden out of the big city. The injustice was still there where he and his family lived now, but it wasn't systemic. Ugly, but not built into the legal system and, as Tage had noticed, the education system too.

"So you're saying it's systemic. Everybody expects it to be there because it always has been."

Tage nodded. "So when my parents realize my brother and sister have been taken, and they're threatened with their safety, they wouldn't think of going to the police. For one thing, these men would kill them." He swallowed. "Sophie in particular—she's disposable to them. And Max could be sold, or he could be turned into a mobster. We just don't know. But—" He grimaced and took another bite. "—I don't think my parents are going to get them back, whether I go to jail or not."

"Why not?" Jackson asked, horrified.

"Because…." Tage's voice broke. "Things the guard said to me, about making it easier on my parents and letting the jail take me. He was telling me to let myself get killed. But he didn't… use them as a threat. He used them as an example."

Jackson took a deep breath and realized he had to work hard to keep his cold hands from shaking. "Do you think they're already dead?"

Tage breathed shakily and put the last bite of his burrito down. "No," he said gruffly. "I think—what were his words?—'You can be on the road to becoming pretty meat, just like them.'" He looked at Jackson bleakly. "They have been taken somewhere not here," he said, his eyes red. "I… I don't know how to find them."

Jackson nodded and gave Tage a look he hoped inspired confidence. "Well, lucky you, while I really *would* make a shitty lawyer, I'm not a half-bad investigator. I've got some ideas. But first, I need a name. It can be an obvious name or a whispered name. The name of a person or the name of a group. You gave me Siderov, but I don't know who that is."

Tage nodded his head and leaned back against the seat rest, closing his eyes briefly. "Dima Siderov. He runs—or owns or whatever—the apartment in my parents' building. You can't go there, though." He sat up. "He'll know. They'll all know, and they'll kill my folks."

Jackson nodded. "The name is the thing, kid."

Tage yawned, and Jackson almost took pity on him, but the idea of the kid asleep in the car, defenseless and vulnerable, did not sit well either.

He almost wished he'd driven the Tank.

"You ready? The sooner we move, the sooner we can get you someplace you can get some sleep."

Tage nodded and shook himself, and then grabbed the soda and took a hit, saluting with it before he dragged it with him out of the car. "Away we go," he said gamely.

"Good kid."

Jackson pulled out his phone and texted Ellery as they walked into the building. *Talk to Herrera about the leak—Tage and I are going to the HT department.*

A few years ago, before he'd hooked up with Ellery, Jackson had worked a case for their old firm in which someone who'd flown from Mexico to the United States on a work visa was then imprisoned and made to work in a factory with no pay and no option to leave. He'd killed his supervisor in an attempt to get away.

Pfeist, Langdon, Harrelson and Cooper hadn't been *all* bad. Lyle Langdon, Jackson's immediate supervisor at the time, had taken the case pro bono, and Jackson had gotten a chance to meet Eleanor Sodhi and Ethan Pasternak, the two DAs in charge of human trafficking offenses.

Eleanor was thin as a whisper, her long black hair elegantly coifed, only a few grays to indicate she had grandchildren. Certainly her snapping black eyes didn't give her away. Ethan was a stout, fortyish family man with the kind of fair skin that got ruddy if he so much as thought of a pretty day, and hair that was both blond and thinning.

Together, they looked at some of the worst evil the pits of hell could spit out and tried hard to set the world to rights again. Jackson figured they were aware that they couldn't do it by themselves, but the fact that they kept trying garnered his everlasting respect.

With Tage at his heels, Jackson made his way through the twists and turns of the DA's office, finding their underfunded, overwhelmed corner of the building from memory. He stepped up to the receptionist's desk and gave a game smile.

"Hey, I was hoping I could—"

"Jackson?"

Jackson stared at the tiny woman with the short-cropped black hair and the many freckles across her upturned nose. "Mira? Oh my God, is that you?"

Jackson stepped around the desk to give Mira Charleston a tight hug. She squealed and kissed his cheek. "Oh my God! How you doing? I haven't seen you in a dog's age. You still banging everything that moves?"

Jackson cast a half-guilty smirk at Tage, who smirked back.

"Uhm, no," he said, feeling his face burn. "Actually living with someone for a year now. He sort of won't let me leave."

Mira cackled. "Well, that was never our problem. I always had one foot out the door, and so did you. But God, it's good to see you." She held up her hand, and he saw a rock almost as big as her ring finger and an intricate wedding set.

"You too. And it looks like you're doing okay too. Congratulations!"

She beamed. "We have *kids*, if you can believe that shit. My cooter made two other complete human beings. I am *boggled*!" She held up a picture from her desk where two elfin children, maybe two and four, frolicked naked in a wading pool while a thin man wearing swim trunks, a beard, and a besotted smile sprayed them lightly with a hose.

Jackson had to laugh; happy families were a good thing. "Well, I am boggled too. I'd heard lady parts could do that, but you know, my brother's kids are like my only example."

"Oh, honey, you're born to be a dad. You and Mr. Right will figure it out." She batted her eyes at him. "So what favor do you need, and which kid am I going to have to sell to get it for you."

Jackson opened his mouth in true shock. "*Mira!*"

She blew out a breath and rolled her eyes. "Honey, we see shit so awful here that if we don't fucking laugh at it, it'll make us batshit insane. Besides, my kid daughter, the four-year-old, can take apart the toaster, the blender, and her bicycle if we so much as sleep in on a Saturday. Nobody's going to buy her. She's trouble."

Jackson nodded, understanding. Sometimes dark humor was the only kind life gave you.

"Well, I was hoping to talk to Eleanor or Ethan, but maybe you can help me. I've got a name of someone who is probably in the biz. He seems to have snatched our client's brother and sister. They're twelve and fourteen—" He looked over his shoulder. "—right, Tage?"

"Maxim turns fifteen next week," he said, his eyes going big and liquid.

"So yeah, they're a good age for…." He swallowed, not able to say it with Tage right there.

"Sex work," Mira said, dropping her voice. "I hear you. Were they snatched as part of a net? Were they just close? What happened?"

"Well, the same group of people who tried to frame Tage here for murder kidnapped the kids as insurance that Tage wouldn't talk. And then they tried to kill him in prison, and the assumption is they've been shipped off regardless of whether he talks or not. We're pretty sure they're counting on him to be dead."

Mira pursed her lips. "Oh, Jackson. That's some bad news right there. I mean, we've got a couple of bloodless gangs out there, but that sounds like one of our trifecta of scumbags. We've got MSTK, some outfit that seems to be run by American businessmen that we want really fuckin' bad, and a group from Russia that's kicking our ass. What's your name?"

Jackson looked at Tage who squared his shoulders resolutely and nodded. "Dima Siderov."

Mira's eyes got huge, her lips parted, and she actually gasped as though she'd been hit. "Oh Jesus. We have our scumbag. That's a case for Eleanor. This guy is her meat, and we want to make sure he's tender and sweet before we go after him."

Aha! A name—and a plan. "I'll be honest, honey, we don't even need to take the scumbag down. If we could recover the kids and get all the kids the fuck out of Dodge, I will take that as a win."

She made a face. The kind that Jade used when she was trying to say, "That's a beautiful dream, sweetheart, but it is just not going to happen."

Jackson girded himself for some bad news and some red tape and a need for an alternate plan. He'd meant what he told Siren Herrera. He could deal with the fact that chaos went on and on and on and he and Ellery could only do so much about it. But the people they could save he was by God going to save, because that's the only way he could sleep at night knowing the chaos was working overtime to grind people's lives into dust.

"Honey, I… with the way these guys function, the odds of them still being in Sacramento isn't great."

Tage gasped, and Jackson chewed his lower lip. "Where do they usually do business?" he asked.

"Well, Dima's a branch manager. There's human trafficking everywhere, and we've got all the vices here in Sacramento, right? Casinos, wineries, drugs? But LA and Vegas are bigger, and it's easier to lose the victims in the crowd. As best as we can figure, Dima's a lieutenant. He supplies the buyers down in Sin City and LA. In fact…." She frowned.

"What?" Jackson asked.

"I heard about something…." She let out an exasperated sigh. "Look, we work with a federal task force. You name the alphabet and someone's got a hand in it. It seems like I just heard some of the guys gossiping about something weird going down between LA and Vegas. There was a shipment that was intercepted or a rogue special ops something or other. God. I was listening as hard as I could too."

Jackson grinned. "Yeah, Mira, that's completely legit."

She wrinkled her nose impishly. "Hey, when these heroes with all the Kevlar think of you as just the secretary, you gotta have your parabolic mic on at all times."

"That's my girl," he said with admiration. "So if you hear something or remember something—man, it sure would be great to know if this group of kids has something to do with my boy here."

Tage was staring at her hungrily, like she'd somehow produced hope from a magic bottle.

"You think so? You think you know where they are?"

Jackson was going to caution him not to get too excited, but Mira beat him to it. Her life when the two of them had hooked up hadn't been easy. She'd been getting out of an abusive relationship that had dogged her since high school and had despaired of ever getting through college to be a paralegal. She knew about hoping for the best and having the hope just smacked the fuck out of you. He needn't have worried.

"Honey, I can't promise anything. It would be wonderful if we managed to get a hit on where they might be, but it's only nine thirty in the morning. I'm betting Jackson here has six zillion different stops before he's done today. Let's hope we have something a little more concrete before you get your hopes up, okay?"

Tage nodded, looking so dispirited that Jackson shoulder bumped him. "It's a good lead, though," he said softly and then looked back at Mira. "Look—I was going to talk to Eleanor and Ethan, if they have time."

She shook her head. "Eleanor's in court all day, and Ethan's taking depositions. I might get a chance to talk to them at lunch, but it's going to be a drive-by conversation. Tell me—as specifically as possible—what you need."

Jackson grimaced. "Okay. Dima Siderov lives in Tage's building—"

She blinked at him. "You lie."

"No, but let me finish. We think his boy set Tage up for the murder of one James 'No Neck' Cosgrove and then snatched Tage's brother and sister for insurance that Tage wouldn't talk until they could off him."

Mira stared at Tage. "And you're standing here breathing free air? Boy, you have a guardian angel, and you'd better give thanks to her every night."

Tage regarded her through sober gray eyes. "I would rather she look after my brother and sister," he said, sincerity in every syllable. "They are…." He swallowed. "Young. Sophie looks older, but she's only twelve. Max *is* older, but he's so gentle. I…." His voice trembled, and Mira nodded.

"Okay, baby. I hear you. So, Dima's on the move, and you would like any help we can give you." She chewed her lip. "Do you know *why* he ordered the hit on this No Neck person? I remember reading about the murder, but there was no motive, not even when—" She held her hand to her mouth. "You're the 'juvenile in for questioning.' Baby, you're not even eighteen?"

"No, ma'am."

"Jackson! Why was he in jail? Look at him! What did they do to him?"

"The guard beat me," Tage said simply. "But Jackson and Ellery turned him in to his superior. They are trying to find out who paid him."

Jackson gave the boy a faint smile. "You've been paying attention."

"Knowledge can keep you alive," Tage said with no irony and no play in his voice whatsoever.

"True that." Jackson looked at Mira. "Someone wanted him not to tell us what happened, and someone is paying people to keep track of his file. Did you hear about the gunman at the public defender's office?"

"That was *this*?"

He nodded. "And so was the cop who got stabbed. Dima's boy—Sergio Ivanov—was breaking into our office yesterday. Whatever it is they think he's seen or wanted him to keep quiet about, it's a big deal. We will take any information, Mira. His parents refuse to talk to the police, and he was unconscious for most of whatever happened. Herrera can't give him protective custody, and he's worried sick about his brother and sister."

Mira nodded. "Okay, this is pretty urgent. When did you know about trafficking?"

"For sure? This morning. Last night we couldn't talk to Tage without the guard who'd been beating him to a pulp. Herrera got him released this morning, and now here we are."

Mira nodded. "Good. Good boy. See, Jackson? Authority helps, right?"

Jackson rolled his eyes. "Sometimes. Right now we want to keep Tage safe, and we want to find the kids, but we've got Dima Siderov's location in return."

"But do you have Sergio Ivanov's?" she asked. "Because Sergio—he's a new player in all of this. I'm talking since Christmas, maybe."

"January?" Jackson asked, because God, that date wouldn't leave him and Ellery alone.

She shrugged. "But he's small potatoes. He was sponsored in from some guy who's not Russian. We don't even have a name for him. Just a big scary guy with a thick European accent."

"German?" Jackson asked, remembering his conversation with the two officers the day before.

She slow blinked at him. "Yes. Why?"

Jackson looked at Tage, how vulnerable he was, and thought about leaving him on his cousin's couch and hoping for the best. "I can tell you," he said, "if it will get our boy here two federal marshals with several layers of Kevlar between him and a stiff breeze."

She scrubbed at her short, spiky hair. "Gah! Jackson—I'm a *paralegal*—I do not have that kind of power." She grimaced. "You're just going to have to trust me on this one. You give me the name and the possible contact, and I will grab Eleanor by the hair if I have to and make her listen. They've got some law-student interns; maybe Ethan can throw one of those guys into the deposition or something. But I can't." She grimaced. "You're looking pretty fit these days. Think you can keep him safe?"

Jackson refrained from telling her that he was looking fit because he'd just gotten released from medical leave. "Guess I'll have to. And I don't have a name, but two cops in the first district have a CI with a thick German accent and an attachment to Tage's case that is"—he grimaced—"highly convoluted and really suspect. I can give you the cops' names. Maybe you can speak to Lieutenant Chambers and get an interview with them. Lindstrom. Officer Lindstrom in the first district. She's partnered with an asshole named Craft, and I don't think they're dirty but I do think they're being manipulated. I've—"

His pocket buzzed, and he checked it.

Herrera found the leak, and I need you here.

Jackson grimaced. "Did you get all those names?" he asked sweetly. "Because Ellery found the leak and—" He looked at Tage. "Hey, could I leave him here with you? If you've got a lunchroom or something, this kid could use a nap like nobody's business."

Tage picked that moment to let an enormous, soul-splitting yawn through, and Mira's bright brown eyes went limpid and Bambi on him. "Oh, baby, did you really just come from jail?"

Tage nodded and yawned again.

"No sleep at all, right?"

"No, ma'am," he said.

"We can do that," she told him. "I'll take you back in a minute."

"Let me give you cash for the vending machines," he said to Tage. "You're still growing."

Tage smiled tiredly, and Jackson knew there weren't enough candy bars in the world to cover his anxiety right now.

He turned to Mira to finish their business. "Look, here's my card with my cell. I'll be up to collect Tage in less than an hour, but if either one of your bosses wanders in before I get back, don't text me, *call me*. This is important, Mira. We need these people locked up and Tage's family safe." And then he remembered protocol. "And you may have to work with Siren Herrera on this one. Since Tage was her case, she's got some rights to—"

"Who?" Mira asked, and Jackson sighed.

"She's been in the DA's office for about four months. They have a habit of giving her Ellery's cases because she's new and they're tired of him kicking the crap out of them."

"Wait a second," she said, looking at the neatly lettered card. "You're not working for Pfeist, Langdon, Harrelson and Cooper anymore?"

Jackson shook his head. "No, Ellery formed his own firm. It's Cramer and Henderson now."

"Ellery Cramer? Didn't you and he help catch Tim Owens back in November? I seem to remember that being a big deal. How'd he get you to leave Pfeist?"

Jackson smiled at her and waggled his eyebrows.

It took her a minute. "Uh… oh. *Ooh!*" She nodded, as though impressed. "So he's your Happy Ever After," she said. "I was wondering who it would take to get you. Well chosen, sir. Ellery Cramer's a good guy."

"The best," Jackson said, loving to hear Ellery spoken about in the best of terms. He looked at Tage and smiled. "So you go with Mira here. Sleep on the couch in the lunch lounge. I'll be back. Can you handle that?"

"The bathroom is attached to the lounge," she said. "You should be safe and secret."

Tage yawned again, and Mira took his arm. "Come along, baby. Let's get you to bed."

"Motherhood suits you," Jackson told her as she walked away.

"I'll call you if anything happens," she told him over her shoulder. "Now go!"

Big Fish Walking

THE BAILIFF looked more like a thug than her husband did.

Stout, with square shoulders and a double blond braid wrapped around her head, "S. Mayer" was Suzanne Mayer. They'd lucked out when Ellery had asked about her—she was normally located in the courthouse, but the judge she worked for hadn't been hearing cases that day, and as a Sacramento County Sheriff, she'd taken an extra shift as an officer on duty for security. It had taken Arizona Brooks two calls to realize the woman was one floor down. When Siren and Arizona called her in, she'd sat, arms folded, her ruddy face as flushed as her husband's had been the day before.

"So," Arizona said, her tone that "we're just friends here" pitch she used to lure people on the stand into saying something incriminating. "You're not in trouble, Suzanne—"

"Sure," Suzanne grunted. "I believe that." She looked from Ellery to Siren to Arizona, one corner of her mouth lifting in a sneer.

"Do you have a problem with us?" Arizona asked, her own hands staying neatly folded in her lap. Arizona was a slim, fiftyish woman with Scandinavian cheekbones, cropped gray hair, and merciless gray eyes. She and Ellery had butted heads on more than one occasion in the courtroom, and neither one of them walked away unscathed. But she respected Ellery for wanting justice, and he respected her for respecting the law—as often as they'd butted heads, they'd also worked for fair and equitable plea bargains, and she'd helped him and Jackson more than once when she thought her office was serving politics more than it was serving people.

"I got a problem with two queers and a—"

"You can stop right there," Arizona snapped, and Ellery recoiled from Suzanne Mayer's obvious gloat. It didn't matter whether she'd gotten the word out or not, the racial epithet hung in the room as clearly as if it had been uttered.

"I think," Ellery said carefully, "that we're going to need a detective in here. Those weren't the words of an innocent woman. Arizona, can you get her boss in here and snag the nearest cop?"

"Lieutenant Chambers out of the first is in-house giving testimony in another case," Arizona said thoughtfully, and Ellery made what he hoped was meaningful eye contact.

"How about Andre Christie. He was pulling hospital duty yesterday. I bet we could have him here in ten minutes."

Arizona lifted her eyebrows. "If you think he'd want the case, call him," she said.

Ellery nodded, pretty sure he had the contact number Sean had given them the day before. "If you'll excuse me, I'll step out and do that," he said smoothly. He looked at Suzanne Mayer with a smug expression he cultivated for people he would never defend in court. "You know, I'm one of the best defense attorneys in the city," he said. "Too bad you just pissed me off."

And then he walked away. His old firm—the one that he had treated very professionally when they'd let him go because he and Jackson kept doing things above and beyond their pay grade—was still very friendly with him. He happened to know that Pfeist, one of the founding partners, had a brother whose firm handled most law enforcement defense cases in the city.

A gay brother.

And while lawyers were told to defend their clients without passion or prejudice, they were also allowed to hand cases over if they felt as though they couldn't defend their client objectively. And he'd met Ambrose Pfeist, who was a petty, irritating man with a swaggering god complex. One word from Ellery and Suzanne Mayer might have to pay out of her pocket to get representation that wouldn't plead her into a woman's correctional facility general population.

Ellery liked that idea very much.

He texted Jackson while his phone was ringing, and Andre Christie picked up while he was waiting for an answer.

"Christie."

"Detective Christie, this is Ellery Cramer, defense attorney. I'm a friend of Sean Kryzynski."

"I know who you are."

Christie's voice was neutral, and Ellery took that as a good sign.

"Are you familiar with the case that got Sean stabbed?"

"No, dammit," Christie muttered. "Oh my God, Sean is doped to the gills, and the idiots who worked the scene yesterday—"

"Couldn't fix a monkey with a banana," Ellery said dryly. "Yes, we've met. And it wasn't fair, but Jackson Rivers and I aren't letting it go. The people who stabbed Kryzynski were looking for a particular file. They wanted it lost in the system so they'd have time to kill the innocent kid who'd been booked for murder. We've tracked the leak who tipped his assailant off to where the case file would be to a bailiff here at the DA's office. Arizona Brooks wanted to call Lieutenant Chambers from the first district, but—"

"Not her," Christie bit out. "Please, for the love of God, not her."

"You want in on this?"

"You're at the DA's offices?"

"Arizona Brooks's office. How soon can you make it?"

"I'm at my desk. Give me ten minutes. Sean deserves better than what he's gotten."

"See you in ten," Ellery said. As he hung up and pocketed his phone, Jackson rounded the corner, his own phone to his ear.

"Who?" Ellery mouthed as Jackson drew near.

"Codromac—returning my call." Jackson slouched against the wall, making brief yesses and nos into the phone after that. Then, "We've got his wife at the courthouse, sir." He looked at Ellery. "Guilty?" he mouthed.

Ellery nodded vigorously. "And mean as a snake," he murmured.

Jackson grimaced. "She's apparently guilty as fuck. And not particularly nice about it." He paused. "Lawyered up, you say?"

Ellery extended his hand. "Officer Codromac?" he said into the phone. "This is Ellery Cramer. We met yesterday."

"I remember" came the mild voice. "You got your bell rung pretty nicely. How you feeling, son?"

Ellery tried not to cross his eyes. Such a nice grandfatherly man. "Like I'll be eating soup and pasta for a couple more days," he said truthfully, because all the ice and ibuprofen in the world wasn't making his jaw any less stiff. "Thank you, sir, for asking. You say Jarvis Mayer has lawyered up?"

"Yes, son, came in with his union representative this morning, looking smug as hell. They legally don't have to say a thing until they're assigned a lawyer. Wanted to kick him in the balls too, because sure as shit he's dirty."

Ellery felt his lips curl up like Snidely Whiplash or a cartoon cat. "You know, there's lawyers and there's lawyers, sir. I happen to know the firm that represents the law enforcement branch. Which kind of lawyer do you think would best suit Jarvis Mayer's particular needs?"

J. Codromac's laugh was low and dirty; not sexual, but it had a lot of living in it. "You do know how to talk sweet, Mr. Defense Attorney. I'd say Mayer needs a lazy lawyer. Do they make that kind?"

"Let me find out," Ellery said. "And I'll be sure to let you know who he ends up with."

"Thank you, son. You do wheel and deal better than you duck."

"Thank you, sir. Have a good day and thank you for all you do." Ellery hung up and gave Jackson a "here goes" look.

"Are you trying to deal under the table, Counselor?" Jackson asked mildly.

"That woman in there is not a nice person," Ellery replied. "And the first thing she did when confronted with the three of us was go for our most exposed, most painful nerve, which tells me she's caught dead to rights and she's going to try to catch us doing something emotional or something wrong. She's going to lawyer up, of that I have no doubt. But I don't want it to be easy for her." He pulled up Ambrose Pfeist's number and gave Jackson another grim look, relaxing only infinitesimally when Ambrose answered.

"Ellery! So glad to hear from you. I was so disappointed when you left my brother's firm and we didn't even get an application."

Ellery rolled his eyes. As. If. "Decided to start my own firm," he said. "I like the risk."

"Not a good quality in an attorney," Ambrose murmured. "Still— what can I do for you?"

Carefully, being as coy as possible, Ellery explained the situation.

"Oh dear," Ambrose murmured. "Are you asking me to sabotage their cases, Ellery? That's beneath you."

"No, sir," Ellery said. "I just need leverage, even if it's a delay or a bluff. We are working to get this boy's brother and sister away from the mob, sir, and these two witnesses are key. They are particularly vulnerable if they are convicted. The tiniest bit of fear could be a very good thing."

"Indeed," Ambrose said, and Ellery could hear the wheels turning and even smell a little bit of burning rubber over the phone. "I'll talk to Mr. Mayer's attorney and make sure I pick Mrs. Mayer's representation myself. Is the DA's office ready to deal?"

"I'll ask, sir. It's Arizona Brooks."

"Pfaugh!" Ambrose burst out. "If you can get the teeniest concession from that woman, my clients might not end up on death row. You do what you can on your end, I'll do what I can here." He paused. "I can see why you might not have worked out at my brother's firm, Mr. Cramer, but I do think I'm going to enjoy working with you from here on out." He paused. "You wouldn't happen to be available for drinks, would you?"

Ellery actually felt all his circuits blow at the same time.

"Mr. Cramer?" Ambrose's voice had the urgent tone of someone who had called his name repeatedly. "Are you quite okay?"

"I'm fine, Mr. Pfeist," Ellery said. "I'm, uhm, in a relationship. I'm not sure drinks would be appropriate."

"Oh, that's a shame." To his surprise Pfeist sounded genuinely sad about that, although in all their interactions, Ellery would never have guessed the man had been interested. "My brother says you had a thing for that detective—Rivers, was that his name? This can't be the same man. That man was… not worthy of your talents, Mr. Cramer."

Ellery dug his knuckle into his forehead to try to loosen the tension headache forming right there. "I'm afraid it is, and he's quite worthy, sir. You just have to know how to look."

"Well, you let me know if you're free. I would enjoy… drinks."

"Yessir. I'll do that. I'll talk to Arizona about making a deal. Let's see what I can do to put the fear of the California penal system into our leaky bailiff."

"You do that, sir. I'll enjoy hearing the results."

Ellery hit End Call and held a hand up to the back of his neck, not even wanting to look at Jackson.

When he did, he wanted to smack the smirk off of Jackson's face.

"Was that nice man hitting on you?" Jackson asked. "You can tell me. I can take it. Do I have competition?"

"Shut up," Ellery muttered.

"Hunh." Oh! And there was the sound Ellery and Jade had missed when Galen had said something sane.

"What? You know how I feel about that sound." As in, he was apparently starting to secretly love it.

"I was just wondering—do I need flowers? Chocolates? Should I bulk up? What's the other guy look like?"

"He's got warts and halitosis and diaphoresis," Ellery said, which was all, unfortunately, true. But not the main reason Ellery hadn't thought about dating him even when he'd been single. "He's also incredibly boring. I once watched his date fall asleep into his drink at a fundraiser, and Ambrose didn't even pause for breath."

Jackson all but puffed out his chest. "At least I'm not boring," he said smugly.

"No, you are not. But you have to blend into the woodwork when we go in here. Kryzynski's partner is on his way over to make this official, and Mayer *is* law enforcement, so it *does need* to be official."

"I'll keep my highly interesting, troublemaking mouth completely shut," Jackson said dutifully.

"No, you won't." Ellery sighed. "But if you could wait for Christie to get here, it might not bite us in the ass at the end."

"Heh heh heh...."

"What?"

"Isn't that redundant? If you're getting bitten in the ass, isn't it always in the end?"

"I could call him back and have drinks after all," Ellery told him, eyes narrowed.

Jackson blew out a breath. "Whoooooooo. See? Minty fresh."

"Stop it."

Then he flapped his arms.

"I will beat you," Ellery snapped.

"Really? But I have information on our mob-boss scumbag. Don't you maybe want to seduce it out of me first?"

"I'm trying to work here!" Ellery complained, and unexpectedly, Jackson sobered.

"It's bad, Ellery," he said softly. "Take the laughs where we can get them. This one might break our hearts."

Oh. "Let's work to make that not happen," Ellery said.

"Way ahead of you."

CHRISTIE ARRIVED a few minutes later, and Ellery could see how Christie and Kryzynski could probably be the shining stars of the department. Tall, slender, elegant, and perfectly coifed, Christie was a Latin counterpart to Kryzynski's fair-haired Polish ancestry. They both liked the nice suits, the perfect hair, and the consummate professionalism of the job. Only the bags under Christie's eyes betrayed a rough couple of days.

Poor Kryzynski. His being a part of Jackson's world must be driving his partner nuts.

They all shook hands, and then Ellery asked the obvious question.

"How's Sean doing? We visited yesterday but haven't checked in yet today."

"He's pretty doped up still," Christie said. He nodded at Jackson. "Your friends, the nurses? They're awesome. Keep him doped up at every opportunity. One of them put a picture of Justin Trudeau on his wall this morning and called it competence porn to keep his spirits up." Christie swallowed. "My wife's baking them muffins this afternoon. The boy got stabbed and dumped on the same day. Anything to make him smile."

Jackson chuckled. "Competence porn—that's good. I got Brad Pitt and Angelina Jolie ten years ago. Told me I could take my pick."

Christie gave a faint smile. "Good folks." He looked over Ellery's shoulder. "What should I expect in there?"

"She's hostile, bigoted, racist, and expecting us to go at her both barrels. However you approach her, you should know that I've talked with the man who will be providing her and her husband with attorneys, and he's very amenable to… slowing things down a little, to give us some leverage."

Christie nodded. "What about her husband? How does he fit into this?"

Ellery explained the situation quickly, including their end goal.

"We need to get a line on where the kids are headed," Christie assessed. "Which means we need to get some info on Dima Siderov and that little fuckhead who knifed Sean in the gut."

"Sergio Ivanov, aka Ziggy," Ellery confirmed. "Exactly. She's going to try to bait you. I think her game is to try to make us do something that she can have her lawyer use against us. It's her only hope. We have to be on our best behavior. She knows the ins and outs here, so all our best protocol."

Christie nodded and then gave Jackson an apologetic glance. "I am not casting judgments here, Rivers, because you have been a stand-up friend to my partner, but you are not exactly known for doing things by the book." He gave a little gesture with his hand by his own cheek to indicate Jackson's bruise from his dustup the night before.

Jackson gave a satisfied smile. "Good times," he said, voice dripping with nostalgia, and then he sobered. "I'm very aware that Ellery is the mouth of our operation, because he's got the brains to go with it. I know when it's time to stand back and be muscle and a pretty face."

Christie nodded. "Fair enough. Let's go have us a little conversation!"

The hostility in the room when they reentered was thick enough to cut with an axe. A knife wouldn't have made much of a dent.

"Sorry to be so long," Ellery said, bringing on his most congenial voice. "Was just having a little chat with Ambrose Pfeist." Arizona's eyebrows went up, and Siren looked from Ellery to Arizona as though trying to fathom what was happening.

Suzanne Mayer jerked as though she'd had an electric cattle prod shoved up her ass.

"You did?" Arizona said, her eyes widening as she improbably played the ingénue. "What did he have to say?"

"Not much." Ellery shrugged. "Just that they're having a hell of a time getting early court dates. People could end up in county jail for a while before arraignment. General population even. It's shameful."

"General population can be really dangerous," Christie agreed, taking up the thread. "Particularly if, say, you or your husband were in law enforcement before you were arrested."

Christie finished this with a direct look into Suzanne Mayer's eyes.

She glared angrily. "Who the fuck are you?"

"This is Detective Andre Christie," Ellery said smoothly and then decided on a slight exaggeration. "He's just coming from the hospital. His partner was injured yesterday when someone tried to steal a case file from my office. You might recognize the name of the file—Tage Dobrevk. Does that ring a bell?"

Mayer's ruddy complexion paled to paste. "I had nothing to do with a cop getting stabbed," she said.

"Except you did," Christie told her, his voice pitching, showing his anger. "Do you know what else I did yesterday? Besides wait for word on whether my partner was going to live or die?"

"I got no idea," Mayer said, but she was watching Christie carefully, like a snake might watch a mongoose.

"I sat by the bed of the guy who tried to shoot up the PD's office yesterday morning. He had a concussion and had been tased within an inch of his life, but you know what? That didn't stop him from talking in his sleep."

Ellery could actually hear her swallow, but he kept his face straight and expressionless because it was a masterful lie on Christie's part. Jackson had checked that morning as Ellery had driven them to the jail. That prisoner was still in a coma, eyes rolled back in his head, unconscious.

"Do you want to know what he said?" Christie went on, keeping his voice satin with an edge of broken glass. "Because I gotta tell you, it sure would make an interesting court transcript."

"Fiction, I'm sure," Mayer said, voice flat.

"Perhaps." Christie inclined his head. "Perhaps not."

Mayer took a deep, fortifying breath. "I need my lawyer now," she said.

"Sure," Arizona told her, pulling out her phone. "Ellery, did you want to call Ambrose, or should I? When did you say he could get an arraignment? Next week? The week after?"

"Wait!" Mayer said, a hint of desperation in her voice. "You can't put me in gen pop. They'll kill me and Jarvis if you don't get us in isolation." And finally, a hint of humanity. "Our kids are so vulnerable. We need to be able to move them out of school."

Ellery narrowed his eyes, and at the same moment, Jackson said, "Wait a minute. Which school do they go to?"

And the light bulb went on.

"Capitol Valley High," Mayer said. "The guy who asked for the info, he's one of the assistant coaches on my son's football team. It's the reason we gave it to him." Her eyes cut left. "One of them. Our kid's only a freshman but he's got so much promise, and the guy threatened to cut him from the team." She squeezed her eyes shut. "He loves it so much. It's the only reason he stays in school."

To Ellery, it felt like all of the oxygen had been sucked out of the room, and the room itself had been put on one of those horrible spinning carnival rides.

Tage Dobrevk, James Cosgrove, Ty Townsend, hell, even Ziggy Ivanov. The one thing—the *one thing*—they all had in common was the high school, and it was such an ordinary, everyday part of their lives that Ellery hadn't even seen the connection.

"What's the assistant coach's name?" Ellery said, giving Jackson a small nod. Jackson started to edge his way to the door.

"Schroeder," she said. "Baldwin Schroeder."

Jackson blinked. "Baldwin?" he mouthed.

Ellery's lips twitched. Well, it wasn't the kindest thing anybody had ever done to a baby, but it certainly didn't justify manipulating high school kids. Or trying to get them killed.

"What exactly did Mr. Schroeder ask you to do?" Ellery said, his voice losing some of its edge.

"He just wanted to know what would happen to the case file at first. Said he knew the kid. I have access to the lists of which PD gets which case, so it wasn't that hard. But then it got shifted to your office—" She nodded at Ellery. "—and things started to go to shit."

"What about your husband?" Ellery asked. "How did he get sucked into this?"

She swallowed, her eyes cutting left again. "That's when Schroeder started to get nasty," she said. "Told Jarvis that if something unfortunate didn't happen to Tage, something unfortunate *would* happen to Carlton."

Ellery could see Jackson's expression, and he was right on board. Carlton was almost as cruel a thing to do to a baby as Baldwin.

"That's not the only reason, is it?" Jackson asked cannily.

She took a steadying breath, as if to still her outrage. "No."

They all stared at her, and Jackson glared at Christie as if to say, "Do something!"

Christie cleared his throat meaningfully, and Mayer blanched.

"Our kid got busted with drugs," she rasped, eyes growing bright. "He swears he didn't know where the damned pink pills came from, but the SRO officer had him dead to rights, and Schroeder said he could make it go away."

He watched as Jackson's eyes grew huge—and knew his own were probably just as big.

Pink pills again. God*dammit.*

Jackson took a deep breath, and nodded, as though knocking the information into its rightful place. "So, this Schroeder," Jackson asked finally, nodding at Christie to tell him this was important. "Does he have a thick accent?"

"No," Mayer said, frowning. "A slight one, but not thick. What in the hell does that have to do with anything?"

"A lead," Jackson said mildly. "If you'll excuse me...."

He ducked out of the room, leaving Ellery there for the rest of the questioning.

In the end, Arizona allowed Mayer to call her union, and Ellery called Ambrose Pfeist and told him that Mayer had been cooperative. Christie read Mayer her rights and led her out of the office to central booking at District One.

Ellery watched them go and then looked at Arizona and Siren, shaking his head. "I am actually really glad that the rest of that mess is in your hands," he said.

"She'll lose her job at the very least," Arizona told him. "Her husband too. He might even see jail time, since his offense was violent."

Ellery scrubbed at his face with his hands. "So was all that enough to get Tage Dobrevk and his family protective custody?"

Arizona's eyes went wide. "Holy crap yes!"

"Oh my God," Siren chimed in. "Where did you stash that poor kid?"

Ellery tried to contain his smile. Jackson had filled him in while they'd waited for Christie. It only figured that an old lover had been the paralegal when Jackson had gone to the human trafficking division; he really had slept with half the state before Ellery had come along.

"Nearby," he said, keeping his voice mild. "You get the order to the judge, and we'll have him in your office in the next ten minutes." He remembered what Jackson had said about napping in the break room. "You, uh, may want to let him sleep on your couch."

Siren nodded, and Ellery actually saw the youth in her eyes, in her voice, which she was always so careful to hide with her ruthless professionalism. "Oh yeah, if any kid needs a safe place to sleep, it's that one."

"Alrighty, then." Arizona let out a breath. "Siren, I'm going to run that request to a judge personally. Could you, perhaps—"

"Do paperwork next to a sleeping teenager?" She sounded almost eager. "Because if you were the world's best boss, that's what you'd be asking me, right?"

Arizona chuckled. "And I *am* the world's best boss," she said.

Watching Siren Herrera do a playful fist-pump was one of the most delightful things Ellery had ever seen.

HALF AN hour later, Ellery and Jackson were on their way to the office after leaving Tage asleep on yet another couch, Siren working diligently on her laptop at his feet. They'd exacted a promise from Siren and Arizona not to leave the boy alone for so much as a second until the marshals got there.

"We hear you, Ellery," Arizona said. "We're taking this seriously."

"This kid has been through a lot," Ellery said. "And you need to listen to him. His parents are going to be hard to convince. You understand that, right?"

"We understand. But this is a matter for the DA now."

"The kid has rights."

Arizona crossed her arms and gave him one of those stares that he could have sworn she'd learned from his mother. "Ellery, I will not question your client nor put anything on the record without you in the room. That is a promise. He's a witness for my house now, and we're going to keep him safe."

Ellery took a deep breath. "Okay. Good. I... you saw his face."

She nodded soberly. "Yes. The system has let him down, and you and Rivers jumped in and took care of him. Now trust us a little, okay? I swear, I'm not the bad guy."

Ellery gave her a sardonic look. "Not this time."

She laughed shortly. "You know, you and Rivers do a lot of good, keeping us in check. Just remember that nobody signs up for the DA's office going 'Oh boy, I want to put innocent teenagers in prison so they can get beaten to death!' okay?"

Ellery snorted. "I'll try to keep that in mind."

"Then we're going to do fine. I'll call you as soon as he's in custody."

"Thank you."

And that was about all he could do. Arizona was right. Tage was her boy now, and Ellery and Jackson had to let go.

He was mulling all of this over, the silence in the car thoughtful, when suddenly Jackson said, "I can't believe it didn't hit us about the high school."

"Yeah. Not the same guy as the scary CI, though."

"No, but German. I'm afraid I don't know my Russian mob/German criminal past well enough."

Ellery thought about the first place Suzanne Mayer had gone to piss them all off and about Ty as a distraction. That thinking—that tribalism—didn't just extend to prejudice. Sometimes it extended to community too.

"Maybe it's enough that they're all pale people who don't kiss the wrong pale people."

Jackson snorted. "Pale people?"

"You know what I mean," Ellery said. "They're white. They think that's a link."

Jackson frowned. "You know, I had an exchange teacher once from a Slavic country. She walked into our classroom on the first day of school, and her eyes got really big and she ran out. She'd apparently never seen real people of color before. She was terrified."

Ellery made a choked noise. "Did you all educate her?" he asked, horrified.

"We ate her alive," Jackson confirmed. "And the white kids were the worst at it. Jade and Kaden kept their heads down. They knew the white kids could do it and not get in trouble. But they'd get taken apart because the system was inclined to believe the teacher, and she was already...." He trailed off thoughtfully.

"Biased?" Ellery supplied, trying to help.

"No. I mean, yes. But that kind of blank ignorance is... dangerous. Because if someone doesn't educate you the right way, it becomes a way to make people who don't look like you less than human. So if we're working with a group of mobsters who are already dehumanizing POC, that could explain what they did to Ty, using him as a distraction. His future didn't matter, and it was obvious. 'Go to party. Find the Black kid.' It's first-grade-level prejudice because they don't know enough about the people they're screwing over—or screwing with—to do anything more sophisticated."

"And if you're already dehumanizing people," Ellery said, following his line of reasoning, "it becomes easy to regard them as a product, like cattle. So shipping them off to Vegas or LA to work as underaged sex workers wouldn't be much of a stretch."

"Children aren't much use to them, especially the girls," Jackson agreed. "So assets but not...." His voice choked a little. "Not children." He shuddered hard. "Okay. I need a toilet brush for my brain now."

Ellery's stomach churned. "Make that two, thank you."

"But you were right. Pale people. But one of them is placed close to the source of studen—" Jackson stopped abruptly, and Ellery followed his line of thought and felt cold sweat prickle the back of his neck.

"Oh God," Ellery said, horrified. "We need to check the middle school and high school. How many kids have they had go missing lately?"

"Except it's August," Jackson said, also in horror. "How many people around this high school have gone missing since *June*?"

"Oh dear God." Ellery held on to his breakfast, but it was a near thing.

"Don't you hurl on me," Jackson snapped. "Come on, Ellery. We need you at full force today. You need to get Ty Townsend off that fucking charge without bringing any of this shit into it, or he and his mother are going to be on the chopping block next. They'll have to move out of state and change their names if this becomes a mob thing. You know that, right?"

Ellery nodded. "I need you to talk to Ty's best friend," he said. "I know you've got other things to do."

"That's where Henry and I are going next," Jackson told him. "And then we're planning to hit Lindstrom and Craft again to ask them about Ty's case. And then…." His voice dropped and grew grim.

"Coaches and principals, oh my?" Ellery supplied.

"Yeah." Jackson closed his eyes and smacked his head back against the headrest. "I hate the thought that there's someone attached to the school doing this. I know *some* pedophiles work as coaches, but Kaden's a coach too, and I know a lot of coaches who have given up nights and weekends just because they want to see kids do well. It's such a shitty thing to do, abuse that sort of trust."

Ellery grunted. "Like, say, your partner and academy sponsor trying to get you to be a dirty cop?"

Jackson sat up straight, his eyes practically popping out of his head. "I wasn't a child," he almost snarled.

Ellery didn't flinch. "You were still a victim," he said. "And it colored the way you thought of authority for the last ten years."

Jackson shook his head. "This wasn't even the same," he said. "I had power then, the power to say no. The power to walk away. These kids don't have that."

Ellery didn't state the obvious: the people Jackson had run to for safety had abused his trust, making him wear a wire for months and then using the information he'd gleaned to set up their own criminal enterprise. Jackson had been used too. Jackson had been victimized too. Jackson's humanity had been voided and sold to the highest bidder.

"No," Ellery said, because he was right that the children they were trying to find had even fewer choices—and fewer chances—than Jackson did. "Which is why we're going to track this thing down to the end. Don't hit the nice football coach, Jackson. We need to be able to arrest him first."

Jackson grunted. "Prison has a special place in hell for those people. You know that, right?"

"Hell has a special place in hell for them," Ellery agreed.

Jackson frowned. "You can't fool me, Counselor. I've been talking to your rabbi, you know. He told me some Jews don't believe in hell."

Ellery thought about the young people being betrayed by an authority figure, being shipped off to a strange city to be sold for sex before they even knew what it was themselves.

"I'm starting to change my mind about that," he said mildly.

"Don't," Jackson said, surprising him. Jackson's hand on his knee surprised him even more. "No cynicism. Not from you."

Ellery smiled tiredly. "You help me keep the faith, you know that, right?" He used Jackson's phrasing on purpose. "Do you think we should have Rabbi Watson over for dinner next week?"

Jackson grunted. "Make it two weeks from now. He shaved his beard, you know."

Ellery's eyes widened. "I had no idea. You didn't mention this to me."

"I was trying to purge it from my brain," Jackson protested. "I thought he *had* to have a beard. All the rabbis on TV do! But apparently they don't. He said he wore the beard to make him look older, but you know why I think he really grew it?"

"I have no idea," Ellery said, completely distracted—and happy for the distraction, at least for the moment. "Enlighten me."

"Because the man has a cleft chin! Like, a divot so deep it's probably hard to shave. Underneath that beard he looks like a movie star with a baby-butt chin! He grew the beard because he thought it would make him look older, and he's right. He shaved it and looked about twelve." Jackson harrumphed. "You would know that if you went to temple. I mean *I* don't go to temple because, hello, not Jewish, but I thought *you* had a pact with God or something."

Ellery made a pained sound. "Yes. I did. But then Rabbi Watson rather gently reminded me that *trying to bribe* God was—and these are his words, mind you—'A very non-Jewish way of looking at your relationship with the Almighty.'"

Jackson blinked. "Because it's like buying God's favor?"

"Yup." Ellery had been embarrassed to realize the rabbi was right. God, his bar mitzvah had been a long time ago. "I'll keep going once in a while—just so I don't forget stuff like that!"

"Well, I still think having him to dinner would make him happy," Jackson said. "That's a very *mitzvah* thing to do. You're a mensch."

"Oh dear Lord," Ellery muttered. "*Mitzvah* thing to do indeed! Are you sure you don't want an actual shrink to talk to?"

"An actual shrink wouldn't be nearly as entertaining as a guy who disguises his fountain of eternal youth with that amazing beard," Jackson told him. Then, a little more seriously, "Watson is human. He doesn't have to be a counselor because he's a rabbi. If he wanted to be, he could be a religious professor kind of rabbi. He took on the role of counselor because people trust someone whose whole study is about God. He feels like that's his mission to the world. So yeah, I trust the guy. I hope that's okay."

"We could practically make *you* a bar mitzvah," Ellery grumbled, turning off the motor. "You sure do seem to have learned a lot."

Jackson shrugged. "I was on medical leave for eight weeks, Ellery. I was bored shitless, and that guy was on my approved list of people you'd let me talk to. Of course I picked his brains. Smart guy. Very sweet. Let's have him and his wife to dinner. You already know how to cook kosher."

More like order it out, but Ellery half laughed and they both slid into the sunshine. "Sure. But, you know…."

And distraction time was over. "We've got work to do," Jackson said soberly. "Let's go catch some bad guys."

Extra Credit

"HAVE YOU eaten?" Henry asked as he got behind the wheel. "It's one o'clock. I'm starved. Let's stop some place—my treat."

"I'm fine," Jackson said, because truthfully, eating anything after that conversation with Ellery about human traffickers and the kind of mentality it took to strip a person of their humanity and make them cattle had seriously done a number on his stomach. By the time Jackson and Ellery had gotten to the office and had their meeting with Henry, lunchtime had come and gone. Ellery had asked Jade to call out for sandwiches, but Jackson had been just as happy to miss that action.

"Jackson."

Jackson ignored the warning in his voice and kept talking.

"So, did you ask Jenny to call Arizona and tell her what she knows about Suzanne Mayer?" Henry's morning had been pretty productive as well. It turned out that Jenny Probst had identified the picture of Ziggy Ivanov from Henry's phone after she'd told Henry that she'd caught one of the bailiffs who worked the courtroom she was often assigned to looking through her briefcase when Jenny had left it with a friend to use the ladies room. Jenny had snatched it back, and later that day she'd seen the bailiff with "a blond high-school-looking kid with serial-killer eyes."

And she'd ID'd the bailiff as Mayer, and Arizona had a solid case and more leverage, and that was always helpful.

It also helped to know that the leak didn't go beyond the Mayers and that the link was damned clear. Jackson had enough leads in this case already.

"Yes, I did," Henry said in exasperation. "You were getting phone numbers and addresses, and I was talking to Arizona Brooks, who, I have to admit, makes Herrera look like a kitten."

Jackson snorted. "Give Herrera some seasoning. She'll be a tiger soon enough."

"You sound like that's a good thing," Henry said.

"Well, not everyone who shows up in court deserves an Ellery Cramer defense," Jackson admitted. "For example, these assholes at the high school."

"I can't believe they're out there playing football," Henry muttered. "From one to three?"

"Yes, but that's because they've been there since nine already," Jackson responded. "God, this heat. It's barbaric."

Henry gave a mean chuckle. "You forget I spent eight years going on and off deployment to the Iraqi desert. This is bad—I mean, I know it's bad—but twenty miles, full kit, in 120-degree weather...."

"Yeah, yeah, you're tougher than me," Jackson admitted freely. "Well done, Junior. You go to the corner store and talk to Nate Klein." Ty Townsend's bestie just happened to be working today. "I'll talk to the asswipe football coach."

Henry grunted.

"You disagree?"

"Mm... well, for one thing, Rivers, and forgive me for saying this, but your poker face sucks, and you're an asshole to the people you don't like."

"No, I wouldn't find that offensive at all. Why would you think that?"

"Ouch," Henry said, voice arid. "I think your sarcasm slapped me in the kisser. And for another, you get kids. They trust you. I don't know, you have that look or something. Whatever. The kid you should talk to. I look like an Aryan asshole who might sympathize with another Aryan asshole."

"I look like an Aryan asshole," Jackson said, offended for Henry.

"Rivers, take it from someone whose father was a *real* Aryan asshole. You smell like a bleeding-heart liberal. I don't."

"So you put on your monster odorant, and you think you're ready to roll?" Jackson asked, stung.

Henry narrowed his eyes, and his lips moved. "Monster odorant...." The snort of laughter he made was so sharp, Jackson honestly worried about whether or not he could drive. "Oh my God. To make me smell like a monster!" Henry hooted. "Good one."

His grin then was so sunshiny bright that some of Jackson's sour mood evaporated. Henry had been a stereotypical redneck when Galen had dragged him into Ellery's office a couple of months back. Or he'd worked hard to appear that way. The truth was, he'd been lost, having just cut himself off from every toxic life pattern that had tried hard to shape him.

The person he'd shaped for himself was, in fact, kind and funny, if a little bit grumpy and bluntly spoken at awkward times. Making him laugh like that—at the person he'd worked so hard to be—was something of a victory.

That sort of thing gave Jackson hope. People could change. What he and Ellery did wasn't in vain. Working to help people, to make the world a better place, to make sure the system didn't eat the innocent or even the not-so-innocent whole, was important.

Tage Dobrevk was only seventeen years old. Ty Townsend had his entire shining future ahead of him. There might be dragons in the world, but that was why there were people who would slay the dragons too.

Jackson smiled a little, chuckled along with Henry, and let some of his funk fade away. "So okay, you go speak redneck to this guy. Nate Klein's in the little shop around the corner. He's got a scholarship to Sac State, so he's got to stay local, but he's apparently a nice kid. Drop me off at the mom-and-pop, and you go do your thing."

Henry grinned. "I'll make sure I smell like monster when I do."

Kensington's Groceries was one of those rare, true small grocery stores that big cities sometimes held on to. In a corner of the first floor of a much larger building, it had a produce aisle and a milk aisle, and while it did have a case for beer and some alcohol, that was only about 10 percent of its overall stock.

The kid wearing the traditional grocer's apron was busy with the rest of the stock, taking cans of beans from a handheld basket and stacking them neatly on a shelf that had been apparently stripped bare.

He was a good-looking kid—tall, more bulked up than most kids his age, but he had that ranginess in his shoulders and the thinness in the neck that said he was still growing. Dark hair, dark eyes, and Jackson bet he had his pick of cheerleaders if that was his thing.

"Nate Klein?" Jackson asked, putting his hands in his pockets and slouching a little to look as nonthreatening as possible.

It must have worked—or the kid must have had a good life—because he smiled earnestly and nodded. "Yessir, can I help you with something?"

Jackson noticed the small deli counter and thought of Henry's claim that he was starving.

"Yeah, can I get two sandwiches on sourdough and some conversation?"

Nate brightened, and he finished clearing out his basket. "Yessir. Here, let me go wash my hands. The sink's in the back."

He returned in two minutes, drying his hands on a paper towel. Jackson watched as the kid crumpled the towel and pitched it into a trash can, raising his hands by his head and mouthing, "For three! The crowd goes wild!" before pretending to run down "the court" and behind the deli counter.

Jackson had to laugh. "Bored much, kid?"

Nate grinned, his apple cheeks coming up to obscure his vision. "Well, it gets sleepy here after lunch. But you should see the place around eleven thirty. Line around the block. Mr. Kensington and I are usually working the deli nonstop for about two hours." He waved to the rest of the store. "It takes me a good half hour to get the place to look like it wasn't scavenged by locusts, you know? I don't mind a lull in the operation."

Jackson nodded. "I hear you. I'm glad I didn't catch you when it was busy. I sort of need to talk to you about something."

"So you said. Sourdough? We use the good stuff."

"Yessir," Jackson said, liking this kid very much. "I'll take one hot pastrami with pickles, and one chicken pesto with lettuce and tomato, no mayo."

"Good choices both." Nate got busy. "So, how do you know who I am, and what are we talking about?"

"Well, I got your name from Ty Townsend, and we're talking about how bullshit the charges against him are."

Nate paused for a second to look Jackson in the eyes. "So you're his lawyer? I told him to go find a good one because it was really bullshit. It was a total setup. I went home and told my parents, and after they chewed me out for even staying there when someone gave out party favors like that, they told me to make sure Ty got a good lawyer. They love him, you know. We've been buddies since we were in pre-K, and they were so proud of both of us when we graduated. Anyway, I'm glad you're here. What do you want to know?"

Jackson had to take a breath, his belief in humanity suddenly reaffirmed. "Okay, so we know it was bullshit. I want to know a couple of things. For starters, the kid who gave you the pills—Ziggy—what do you know about him?"

Nate gnawed his lip thoughtfully. "He's not really a high school student," he said bluntly after a moment. His hands paused mid bread slice. "Coach Schroeder is the only teacher who seems to know who he is. Calls him Ivanov, like he's a football player or a kid, but he's not in any of our classes. Ty and I…." Nate frowned. "We don't trust him. He was always trying to get us to go to parties and stuff, and, I mean, we were studying for our AP exams and our SATs and stuff. We didn't have time for that shit. I mean, Ty and me, we're not even in the same league as players, but we were both pretty good students, and, I mean, my folks would *kill* me, right?"

Jackson nodded. "No, that's what Ty told us. That you guys shoved the drugs in your pockets so you could throw them away later. But that you didn't want to piss Ziggy off."

Nate shifted from foot to foot. "I… I saw Ziggy one day, walking by the store. He had his arm around this girl. She looked like his sister, and she was crying. She was young—like maybe fourteen—and they were talking in what sounded like Russian. And at first I thought, 'Hey, maybe he's not as creepy as I thought.' He seemed to be comforting her, you know? And then, as they were disappearing around the corner, I saw his arm tighten, like, you know what muscles look like, when they're all taut? And it wasn't until I was walking home that I thought, 'Wait— was he *restraining* her?' And I started watching the news and stuff for amber alerts, but I didn't see one, and thought maybe I was imagining it. But… but I just keep thinking about that. And it hasn't left me. I've never trusted him, and I didn't want to, I don't know…. Call down the heat of God on him because of a muscle spasm. But…." Nate shuddered. "I just can't get it out of my head."

Jackson nodded and felt bad because he was going to color this kid's world a little darker. "Your instincts were right on, kid. You see Ziggy around—especially with any kids—and you need to call me." Jackson gave Nate his card and then wrote the department's general phone number along with Fetzer's and Hardison's names on the back. "If you can't get hold of me, get hold of these two cops and tell them what it's about. Ziggy, he's bad news. And those two cops aren't the same as the two who busted that party. Can you tell me about those guys?"

Nate resumed his sandwich making, obviously trying to gather his words, and Jackson gave him his space. For one thing, he was actually getting hungry, and for another, if he didn't feed Henry, Henry's newfound sense of humor might go up in hunger fumes.

For another, this kid had a sharp mind, and he might be able to give Jackson something important.

"Ty and I were toward the back. To be honest, I was heading for the bathroom so we could ditch the stupid butterfly drugs. God, making X look like candy? It's fucking creepy, you know? I've got a little sister. Someone could tell her that's a fucking vitamin, right?"

Nate's swear words got a little more pronounced as he got upset, and Jackson approved. But then something Nate said pinged something he'd seen in Ellery's notes on the police report.

"Ty said something about that too—little pink pills with butterflies on them. Have you seen those around?"

"Ziggy passes them around a lot." Nate shuddered. "God, I just keep thinking I should have beaten him up on general principle, but my folks didn't raise me that way."

Jackson's breath quickened, remembering that knife. "He's really fucking dangerous, Nate. Don't... the next time you see him, you call the cops or you call me, do you understand?"

Nate nodded. "Yeah. Yeah, I get it. What's he done?"

And Jackson sobered. "You heard about No Neck and Tage Dobrevk?"

Nate's eyes widened. "Tage couldn't have done that. Are you representing him too?"

"Yeah. And guess who was there before Tage got knocked unconscious at the scene?"

Nate shuddered. "Oh God!"

"So take this seriously, and don't let on to Ziggy you know he's dangerous. If he asks you to do anything, just tell him you can't. And then call me!"

"Okay. I hear you. Do... do we know why No Neck was killed?" Nate's voice trembled. "He wasn't a bad guy, you know? A little dumb and, God, insensitive as hell, but he was learning. Most of the time he was always smiling, always glad to see his team. We weren't tight, like me and Ty, but we were friends. Tage too. It just seemed so unreal! That two people I knew would... would be dead, or have done something that awful." Nate clenched his jaw and shook his head. "But Ziggy? Ziggy I could believe."

"Trust your instincts, kid. They're right on. And be careful around him. Don't let him know you know he's a bad guy."

Nate rolled his eyes. "Have you even *seen* me, mister? I can't hide *shit* with this baby face!"

And go self-awareness! "Well, do your best. Ziggy's pretty hot right now. Odds are good he's not going to be lingering around the high school set. Keep an eye out. And tell me more about this party."

"So Ty and I were back by the bathroom, getting ready to flush those creepy pink pills, and there's a knock at the door. Ziggy opens it and invites the two officers in."

Jackson frowned. "Did they identify themselves when they knocked? Say they were Sac PD or anything like that?"

"No, sir," Nate told him, looking puzzled. "But as soon as they stepped in, they told everybody to freeze."

"So of course everybody started streaming out the back door."

"Well, they would have, but the cops had their guns out already."

"Wait what?" Jackson blinked. "No. No no no no. You don't take your piece out if nobody's resisted. You don't take it out if it's a bunch of kids standing around a keg!"

"I *know*!" Nate said. "I almost wet my fucking pants. Anyway, Ty and I, we're good kids, right? So we just stand there like morons with our hands up, thinking if we do what we're supposed to, they go away. But they didn't. They walked straight to Ty and searched his pockets, and they found the little packet with three pills and arrested him and walked out."

The packet with three pink butterfly pills was starting to stick in Jackson's craw. "What happened to the party after he left?" Jackson said curiously.

"Well, for starters, everybody said it was bullshit," Nate said. He paused. "And then No Neck looked at Ziggy and…." He swallowed. "He had this hurt look on his face. He said, 'But Ty's my friend.'"

"What did Ziggy say?" Jackson asked, stirred with reluctant sympathy for the departed No Neck.

"He said, 'Yes, but not your family. You need to remember who your family is.'"

Jackson closed his eyes, hating where this was probably leading. "Did No Neck say anything afterward?"

"I cornered him in the kitchen," Nate said. "I was pissed. Told him I'd go to the cops myself. He said not to, said he'd do it." Nate's shoulders slumped. "And the next night, he was dead."

Jackson took in a sharp breath. "Okay. Okay, then. So you know Ziggy's dangerous, and there are a few things I need to find out. You got my card, kid?"

Nate nodded to where it sat as he finished wrapping the two sandwiches.

"After I pay for those, I'm going to watch you put that into your phone. Then I'm going to walk to the school where some guy named Baldwin is going to be lying to my buddy about why he let this Ziggy asshole around high school students."

"Baldwin?" Nate said, wiping down his work space before taking off his gloves. "You mean Coach Schroeder?" One full lip curled up in disgust. "Coach asshole?"

"Asshole? Why?"

Nate moved behind the register and threw his gloves away underneath the counter. "That'll be $15.98. But since you're helping Ty out, I can throw in some chips and two sodas for free."

Jackson grinned at him. "I'm down for that," he said. "Can I grab them on the way out?"

"Sure."

Jackson paid him and then threw a fiver in the tip cup, because the kid had been competent as hell. "So, why's the assistant coach an asshole?"

"Well, for one thing, he's not really a teacher. Coach Foster and Assistant Coach Herredia both get stipends for doing football, but they also teach in the school. Schroeder got the job part-time as... I don't know. Some sort of glorified water boy. But he's not a teacher, and he's always trying to 'get in with the kids.' It's creepy. He's been working with the varsity kids for the last two years but usually only the bench. I guess Foster and Herredia thought he could do less damage that way."

Jackson frowned. "What are his qualifications?"

Nate stared at him blankly. "Do I *look* like the principal or superintendent? I start *college* next week, remember? The only reason I'm here now is because we get the stadium to practice, when it's not two zillion degrees outside!"

"Well, you know, kid, you've been a fountain of information until now. I was sort of hoping it could continue."

"I dunno, mister. Come back when I'm all grown up or something." The kid rolled his eyes, and Jackson let out a snort.

"My ass. You're pretty grown up now. College is window dressing."

He got a grin in return, and then Nate Klein grew sober. "You're gonna get Ty off, right? I…." His voice stuttered. "He's worked so hard. I mean, you look at No Neck, and I guess there's worse things than not going to college but, you know. All that work." A flutter of a smile then, like a scared moth. "He was supposed to go to a big school and be a football hero and come back and brag to me. We had a deal, you know?"

Jackson nodded. "I hear you. We'll do our best."

He got an earnest nod in response. "That's all you can do, you know."

Augh! This kid's sweetness was killing him slowly. Nate Klein, Tage Dobrevk—even Ty Townsend, although Jackson hadn't even met the kid yet—they had no place in the same area populated by the Ziggy Ivanovs or the Baldwin Schroeders of this world.

"We'll try to make it count," Jackson told him. He took a step toward the door, plastic bag hanging from his hand, and then turned back. "So you may not know why Ziggy doesn't belong, but I understand that the teachers hated him. Can you give the name of a teacher you saw who wanted him gone?"

"Mrs. Eccleston," Nate said promptly. "I had her for American Government and Econ. Her classroom is right by the gate, so when Ziggy was just outside the gate, talking people up and shit, she could see him from her desk. Boy, did that woman kick up a fuss."

"Hardass?" Jackson asked approvingly.

"Marshmallow," Nate countered. "But she took care of us. And she thought Ziggy was dangerous."

"Interesting." Jackson pondered, thinking about the date. "Are the teachers there now, you think?"

"Oh yeah. School starts on Thursday of this week, if you can believe that shit!"

Jackson grimaced. "Yeah, no. My summer was a complete loss— I'm not even kidding. So if it starts Thursday, they should be back fixing up their rooms and stuff, right?"

"I hope so." Nate grinned, and then it died. "I was going to go with Ty on Wednesday. We made a plan the night of the party, you know? To go say hi to our old teachers."

It wasn't the worst thing that could happen, but it was a sharp reminder that somebody was trying hard to dick with Ellery's client. "Well, Ty needs to stay away until we get Ziggy into custody. Maybe give him a call and have him give you messages to take."

"Yeah. God. Okay. This sucks. We were going to do a sleepover before he left for school. I just…." He flailed a little.

"Miss your friend."

"Yeah."

"Well, we'll see what we can do," Jackson reassured him. "I'd like to wrap this up in time to call his school and tell them all charges have been dropped, but there's what I want to do and what I can prove." He took another step toward the door. "And to that end…."

"Yeah. Bye, Mr. Rivers."

"Bye, Nate. Don't forget to call me if you need anything or remember anything. Any help to fix this, okay?"

"Will do. Thanks!"

And with that, Jackson sauntered into the heat of the day, grateful for the sodas and the sandwiches as he took off for the school.

JACKSON HAD to pass the football practice field as he made his way to the administration building, and he looked across the grass to see Henry showing something on his phone to a stocky man in his late twenties, brown-haired, blue eyed, and as pretty as a field of daisies.

Henry's eyes flickered to Jackson as he sauntered by, giving him a brief nod but keeping his concentration on the man Jackson assumed was Baldwin Schroeder. Something about the way Henry carried himself— the stiffness of his posture, the way he crossed his arms, the neutrality of his expression—told Jackson that he was trying hard to hide his dislike of the person he was talking to.

Ah. That was what they called in the business a clue.

Jackson kept going, walking wide around the fence to head for the admin building, hoping he could check in as a visitor.

By the time he got there, he was drenched in sweat and so grateful for the air-conditioning he almost collapsed. There was something about the sun on the football field—probably the humidity—that made the heat so intense and so close it seemed to stop his breath.

He tried not to sweat all over the Formica counter and smiled at the grim-faced secretary behind the desk. "Hi, I'd like to talk to Mrs. Eccleston?"

"Sign in, please," the woman said sourly. The nameplate on her desk read Shirley Anderson, and Jackson wondered if she saved any of that disdain for her students or if she spent it all on him.

Jackson signed the register, and Ms. Anderson plopped a school map and a visitor's badge in front of him. "Put your name there and follow the map to here." She circled a destination. "It's in the K block, the portable on the end by the gate."

The gate actually backed up against the parking lot behind the football practice field—which had been open, dammit. He was heading, in fact, back to where Henry was, and given that the campus had a tendency to sprawl in the middle of the city, he wanted to whimper. Okay, okay, fine. Maybe he wasn't 100 percent yet, because the heat and the humidity really *were* sapping his will to live, but he was damned if he admitted that to *anybody*.

"Are there any water fountains on the—"

"You'll see them on the sides of these two buildings," she interrupted in a bored tone.

"Any vending machines with cold water?" he asked, and he had to admit, he was sort of pushing her buttons now because she was being a pill. He didn't usually get this response from people. He tried a pretty smile. "I've got sodas in here for my buddy, but I gotta admit, some clear water would be—"

"At the end of the building," she said, no smile in her icy gray eyes at all. "You'll see it. You should leave now before she goes for the day. They really weren't required to come back after lunch, but most of the teachers stayed to fix up their rooms."

"Gotcha," he said, still smiling.

Her hair was iron gray, and she compressed her lips so tight, they almost matched. "You can find it," she said heavily, and he turned to go.

"Hey," he said as his hand hit the release bar across the glass door. "You stay happy. You're the heart of the school, you know that?" And then he left before she could respond. Yeesh!

She was right about the vending machines, though, and he felt a lot better after finishing off an icy cold water in one gulp. He bought another one for Henry, because the sodas were nice, but seriously, nothing beat water, and then bought another one for Mrs. Eccleston on a hunch. Poor woman, having to work with *that* dragon? Jackson felt like the water was the least he could do.

His steps echoed on the cheap wooden ramp up to the portable classroom, and he had to admit, the sound had a familiar ring to it. There was something universal about cheap prefab buildings and schools bursting at the seams.

He opened the door partway and stuck his head inside, liking the bright posters on the walls that he got with that first glance. "Mrs. Eccleston?"

"Yeah? Can I help you?"

Given Nate Klein's glowing report, Jackson half expected the American Government teacher to be one of those sweet young things whom schoolboys fantasized about—and in that way, Mrs. Eccleston was a surprise.

Squat, fiftyish, with a good inch of gray between her dyed black hair and her part, the woman sitting at the desk was wearing loose shorts and an oversized gray T-shirt, neither of which was flattering on her. She wasn't attractive, not even in that lean, superfit way that a lot of women had when they hit this age. She was squishy and tired, and she'd obviously forgotten her coif and her public face when she'd come in to finish decorating her room. There was a step stool in the corner of the room and a series of posters and tacks, obviously waiting to fill up the last empty space.

"Hi," he said, coming in. "I'm sorry to bother you. I'm Jackson Rivers. I'm working for Ty Townsend's attorney, and I was hoping you could answer some—"

"Oh my God," she said, her eyes practically rolling back in her head. "Is that *food*?"

Jackson grinned. "Uhm, sure. How about… here." He pulled out the chicken pesto he'd meant for himself and the chips and soda, setting them up on her desk with plenty of napkins. "You sit down and eat, and I'll pin up the rest of these posters, and you can answer my questions. How's that sound for a bargain?"

Her eyes, which had sort of been lost in the folds of her eyelids, grew wide and limpid. They were a sweet brown. "That sounds like you, sir, are an angel from heaven. I forgot to eat and I didn't remember until *right now*."

He figured. And after that morning, facing the realities of getting Tage's family back, he was still a little queasy. The heat didn't help.

She sat down and dug into the windfall, and Jackson got started pushing pins. After a few minutes during which Mrs. Eccleston ate like she'd forgotten what food even was, she finally wiped her mouth, took a drink of soda, and sat back.

"I'm sorry," she murmured. "I just jumped a stranger for food. That's so embarrassing."

Jackson laughed and squared up another poster, this one featuring the title The Cost of War, with a list of everything from economic impact to the cost of the truth to social impact.

"No worries. I'm here to do two things. One of them is nice—Nate Klein says hello, and I imagine Ty Townsend would too, but I haven't talked to him yet."

"Oh, that's wonder—" Jackson heard the exact moment what he was really saying seeped in. "—ful," she finished weakly. "So, are you Ty's lawyer? I heard it through the grapevine that he was getting a good one."

"I'm the PI who works for the good lawyer," Jackson clarified, making sure the top of the poster was straight before sliding his hands down the front and pinning it from the bottom. "And we think Ty got a raw deal. In fact," he said, pinning first one tack and then the other, "we think he got set up."

"Oh thank God." He straightened to find Mrs. Eccleston taking a heavy swig from his root beer. "That kid has so much promise. I couldn't believe that he'd do something stupid—like getting caught with drugs—right before he was about to leave for school. His dad died when he was practically a baby, you know. His mom is just the nicest person. She started volunteering when his sister was going here. I...." She took another chug of the soda, then paused ruminatively. "You just worry about kids sometimes. But that kid I never worried about." She grimaced. "I worried about No Neck—I mean James—though."

He watched as she deflated where she sat, and his heart gave a little wrench. Ty Townsend and Tage Dobrevk were getting all the attention now because there was still time to save them. But James Cosgrove had been a victim too, and he seemed to have been forgotten.

"Why would you worry about James?" he asked. "He was going to college as well, right?"

She grimaced. "Yeah, but his heart wasn't in it. I don't know his family situation, but I know his original name wasn't Cosgrove."

Jackson frowned. "What was it?"

She frowned. "Something long and Slavic. I'm sorry. I'm pretty good at pronouncing names when I see them, but once they're out of sight? Not so much. But this school is about fifteen percent second-generation Russian immigrants and about thirty percent third- and fourth-generation Mexican immigrants."

"African American?"

"Around twenty percent. There's this terrible, terrible tension between the kids of color and the Russian immigrants. All sorts of hidden resentments. On both sides."

"I bet the Russian kids don't get told to go home, do they?" Jackson said grimly.

"No, they do not." Poor Mrs. Eccleston—she looked so defeated. "And when we can teach one of those kids to really open up? To love all his classmates, all his teammates, the same? That's a big deal."

"Was James like that?" Nate had said something like this, that he wasn't always the most sensitive of guys, but he'd tried hard to fix that and to do the right thing.

"He was." Mrs. Eccleston's voice grew thick. "It's so unfair. James started out sort of this big bruiser who had no plans to go to college. He told me when he was a freshman that his family didn't see any need for it. His oldest sister was already going, and he just didn't have the brains. Me, his math teacher, his history teacher—we kept urging him to try. We were like, 'Hey, you have to pass your classes to play football anyway, so why not just a little more?' And a little more, and a little more. And suddenly, he was taking his SATs and not doing half bad, and he applied to Sac State, and he was admitted. No big scholarship—he was a good football player, but not great—but he was a college student. We were really proud of him. I mean, kids like Ty? He was so bright, we had to wear shades the minute he walked in. But kids like James? He had to work so hard to get something like that. You're proud of them both, but with James, we really earned our stripes, you know?"

"It's hard when you lose someone like that," Jackson said softly.

She nodded and unashamedly wiped under her eyes with a clean napkin. He noticed that she had a stockpile of Kleenex under one of her shelves, and he ran her a box before she had to do that again.

"Thank you," she said. "I'm sorry. I just... I had all those kids. James, Ty... Tage, and I don't think he did it by the way. To have all those things happen so quickly—it's hard. We lost a carload of kids in a crash about ten years ago, and this feels the same. It's like every day I'm mourning all my hope."

"Well, at least Tage's been released," Jackson told her, pretty sure she wouldn't have heard this yet. "All charges dropped."

"Oh thank God!" She grabbed a couple of the aloe Kleenex. "Who are you, the happiness fairy?"

He gave her a lopsided smile. His phone buzzed in his pocket, and he pulled it out to check. When he saw Henry's text—a series of question marks—he responded with the room number and quick directions from where Henry was out in the field.

"Just doin' my job, ma'am," he said when he was done, tipping an imaginary hat.

"Except what *is* your job?" she asked, and he turned back to the posters.

"You mean besides helping nice folks such as yourself?" He kept the accent to let her laugh.

"Well, you said you were saying hi from Nate and Ty. What was the other thing?"

He hated to even bring it up, so he made sure he'd set the next poster up to tack before he began.

"There's two things," he said. "First of all, the party favors getting passed around when Ty got busted were little pink pills with butterflies on them. Is that something you've been told to look out for?"

She thought about it. "No, but—" She wrinkled her nose. "—I am not a big fan of our Student Resource guy anyway." She snorted softly, and Jackson wondered where this woman had been hiding when *he'd* been in high school. Well, this was the good school district. She'd probably been thanking her lucky stars she'd gotten hired here instead of where he, Jade, and Kaden had gone to school.

"What's he like?" Jackson asked, pulling his attention back to the job at hand.

"Young," she said dispiritedly. "And unlike most of the other SROs we've had, he got his job because he was connected and it was easy. The last guy was great—we had seminars at the teacher in-services, we'd get newsletters telling us the latest shit to watch out for. This guy just hangs out after school and talks to the kids and says he's patrolling—he doesn't even keep out the guys who don't belong here!"

"Like Ziggy Ivanov?" Jackson said, nose twitching.

"Who even *is* that kid?" she snapped, and he had to laugh, because she suddenly sounded no older than her own students.

"A pain in your ass?" he prompted, checking the number of pins he had in his hand.

"He does *not* belong here, and he's always leering at the freshman girls. It's *gross.*"

Jackson hoped she never learned how truly, truly gross it was. "Have you seen that kid lately?" he asked.

"No." He saw when the question hit her. "Why? Does he have something to do with what happened with Ty and Tage Dobrevk?"

"What if I told you he was at both crime scenes?" he said.

Her frown deepened. "But he and James were cousins. At least that's what James always said when I told him Ziggy wasn't a good influence."

Jackson remembered what Nate had told him. "Did he say they were cousins? Or did he say they were *family*?" he asked sharply.

And she knew what that meant. "Oh," she muttered. "Shit. He said family. Oh dear God—do I need to watch out for that kid?"

Jackson pushed the final pin in and stood back to admire his work proudly. "Don't confront him," Jackson said after a moment. "Don't say, 'I know what you did.' Don't ask him about it. Be normal. Tell him to get off school property or whatever, but then get out of his face and call me." He pulled out his card and then wrote Sac PD's number on the back, as well as Fetzer's and Hardison's extensions, which he knew by heart now. "Or call them. The point is—"

"Oh my God, you're slow." Jackson looked up as Henry burst in, and rolled his eyes.

"Hi, Henry. This is Mrs. Eccleston. She's given me a gold mine of information. Are you done flirting with the football coach yet?"

Henry made a gagging motion with his finger and open mouth. "Gross. It would be like flirting with a slime mold. Ugh. Poor kids. I'd rather sleep with an octopus. At least they're sensitive and have morals."

Jackson closed his eyes and then opened them again. "Did I mention Mrs. Eccleston the history teacher who is *in the room*?"

Henry rolled his eyes. "Please. She's not going to melt if I talk. Besides, the smell of food is making me faint. I can't be held accountable. Ma'am, if I may ask, where did you get that—"

Jackson held out his bag of food, complete with soda.

"—sandwich?" Henry finished. He threw himself into one of the desks with so much force Jackson watched the cheap metal legs bow. "Gimme."

Jackson set it down in front of him. "You're welcome. So did you get any info—"

"He's dirty," Henry said through a mouthful of pastrami on sourdough. "But not in the way we thought." He swallowed. "You are the best work partner ever. If I wasn't in love with someone else, I'd marry you."

"Be sure to tell your someone else that so your someone else doesn't shiv me if you get hurt," Jackson muttered. "How's he dirty?"

"How's who dirty?" Mrs. Eccleston asked curiously. "Did you want my chips?"

"No thanks, ma'am," Jackson told her. "Too hot to eat."

"And your assistant coach," Henry said, after swallowing.

"Sal?" she asked, looking legitimately surprised. "Herredia? He's an angel!"

Henry took another bite and nodded, chewing thoughtfully. They waited for him to swallow before he said, "He seemed totally nice and totally legit. It's the other guy. The guy who works the bench. Schroeder."

Her face closed down. "Yeah. He's related to our SRO. That guy's name is Schroeder too. They're both…." She grimaced. "You can hear it in people's voices. When they talk to a group of kids. There's the tentative people who don't know what they're doing and the confident people who do and the people who assume the kids are stupid and inferior, and they *think* they know what they're doing and they really don't."

"They throw their power around because they don't have the kids' respect," Jackson said, getting it.

"Yeah. Both the Schroeders. They bark out orders, and they don't get that the kids are doing what they say out of fear. Not out of respect."

Jackson and Henry met eyes. "I know the type," Jackson said mildly. "Henry, how did you know he's dirty?"

Henry chewed thoughtfully. "Besides being an asshole to the kids, he kept talking about sports statistics. On kids. You know who I know who used to recite statistics like that? At the drop of a hat?"

Jackson's heartbeat picked up in the good way that was the thrill of adrenaline when you found something you weren't expecting to find. "Bookies?"

Henry nodded decisively. "Man, we got really fucking—uh, fricking—bored in the desert. Someone was always betting on something. I learned everything I ever need to know about gambling watching my ex burn through both our paychecks on a Sweet Sixteen pick one year. God, he was an asshole. I hope it was worth it."

"Your ex, no," Jackson muttered. "And hey, way to spill your personal life in front of the nice lady who didn't ask to share lunch with you."

Henry stopped for a moment and looked horrified. "But you—"

"Didn't use pronouns. But that's fine. I'm glad you're all evolved and swearing in front of your history teacher now. Tell me more about the bad guy, Henry! That's why I sent you out there."

Henry took another bite of sandwich and slowed down enough to think, thank God. "He was looking at the kids like statistics," he said slowly. "And when I mentioned Ty Townsend, he got this... this smirk on his face. He said, 'That's a shame. USC will need to find another player. Maybe this one without his numbers.'"

Jackson rubbed his temple. "Wait a minute."

"What?"

Oh, the puzzle pieces were about to click. "Wait a minute."

"Waiting, dammit!"

"Wait—no—*fuck*!"

They heard the report of the gun just as the glass next to Jackson shattered.

"Get down," Jackson yelled to Henry and Mrs. Eccleston. "Ma'am, under your desk. Henry, you okay?"

"I'm under my desk," he called back. "Me and my delicious sandwich. We're chilling."

There were another couple of shots and more shattered glass as Jackson crawled past the window to take shelter back behind the desk with Mrs. Eccleston.

"Ma'am, you okay?" he asked.

She nodded, her squishy body tucked neatly in the recess under the desk. He noted that the desk was in a corner with two filing cabinets and a closet, providing her with cover on all three sides. Henry, on the other hand, was nearly naked.

Jackson handed her his cell phone, unlocked. "Call 911," he told her. "Tell them who you are and where you are and repeat the words 'active shooter' until someone says them back at you."

He left the phone with her and stayed low, snake crawling back behind a table that sat in front of the white board. There were boxes of books and art supplies under the table—unless someone was shooting through the wall to his left, he was pretty safe. Books were damned dense, and so were reams of copy paper.

"Henry, tip those desks over and surround yourself. You need better cover!"

"Where are you going?" Henry asked, doing what Jackson told him to.

"Heading for the door."

At that moment, a flurry of shots came at the door, but they didn't penetrate.

"What in the hell…?"

"Steel reinforced," Mrs. Eccleston said, her voice thready and bright with fear. "They wanted to put in a skylight. I asked for a better door."

"Henry, stay surrounded by the desks. I'm going to do a thing."

"Oh God," Henry muttered.

"Keep talking. Say something stupid."

Jackson turned and started to belly crawl toward one of the two shot-out windows, double-checking to make sure it wasn't the kind with the embedded wire inside. In the breathless silence, he could hear Mrs. Eccleston's shaky voice as she engaged the 911 officer, and Henry said, loudly and without context, "Don't worry, Jackson. I'm only bleeding a little."

"You'd better not be bleeding at all, asshole," Jackson muttered. He grabbed a box of Kleenex and held it above his head, waving it as if to get someone's attention.

"You told me to say something stupid!" Henry retorted, and Jackson couldn't be sure whether to smack him or kiss him.

"Mission accomplished." The Kleenex box remained un-shot-at, so he pitched it through the window and waited a heartbeat.

The response was more shots at the door, which told him everything he needed to know about how smart the shooter was. With a deep breath and a prayer, he vaulted over the bookshelf and through the shattered window, feeling some of the glass shred through his new cargo shorts and catch some skin.

Wasn't fatal, but God, Ellery was going to be *pissed*. He landed neatly in the gravel strip that separated the portable buildings from the fence that encircled the school and started running for the opening by the gate as soon as his feet touched the ground. The cuts on his thigh burned, and the blood sliding down his leg into his tennis shoe wasn't comfortable either, but he wasn't going to let that stop him. If the guy shooting from the other side of the portable building figured out he was there and caught him in this tiny crawl space, he'd be a big fat walking target and probably a dead man. He needed free air for any sort of self-defense.

He got to the corner of the building and peered around just in time to see cleated tennis shoes disappear behind a large, permanent structure about thirty yards away, the clopping sound of the cleats absurdly loud in the silence after the shooting. He called out, "Henry, collect the shells!" before taking off after those disappearing footfalls.

He turned left between two buildings and kept running until the space opened up to a quad area in the center of the school. The quad itself was empty except for a couple of teachers wandering around looking at each other uneasily.

"Hey!" one of them called out. "Did you hear shots?"

"Cops are on the way," he replied. "Did you see someone running by?"

"Heard someone—breathing hard. But didn't see them. Who are you?"

"Visitor. I'm signed in. Get back in your rooms and get down!"

The two men—both dressed like him in cargo shorts and T-shirts—managed to look alarmed. One of them followed the other back to what Jackson presumed was the closest room, and he was left alone in the quad, breathing hard, realizing that whoever it was, he'd lost him.

Fuck.

Irritated, he turned back toward the line of portables, tracking in the distance a line of cruisers, lights blazing, as they turned the corner around the football field and headed toward the back parking lot.

Goddammit, there went the rest of their day. It wasn't until he neared the portable building that he saw the damage to Galen's car.

A Little Chum

ELLERY HAD ten other cases on his desk besides the Dobrevk and Townsend cases, and he was working on those as Jackson and Henry went out and did their boots-on-the-ground thing.

But that didn't stop him from pondering the two cases in the quiet points. He was looking at his notes for a defense against a drug charge for a single mother—who, he was pretty sure had been asked to mule for her shitty boyfriend—and muttering to himself when he heard a knock on the door.

He looked up, saw Galen leaning casually against the doorframe, and gave a distracted smile. "I have the most comfortable office chairs on the planet. Come sit."

"I don't know," Galen said, moving in anyway. "The way you're talking to yourself, my life might be in danger."

Ellery smiled. Galen had pretty much pried his way into the firm after he and Henry had come knocking on the door, asking for help. He'd been new in town, and he'd needed to pass the bar in California in order to practice law, and Ellery had the feeling that in spite of being very much in love with his porn-mogul boyfriend, he'd been a little lonely.

Well, most of Ellery's friends now were people he'd gained from knowing Jackson, so Ellery could relate. It was nice to have a peer to talk to, someone who thought like you did without apology and who got the ins and outs of the job.

"You're safe," he said. "But this woman's boyfriend, on the other hand...."

"Deserves dire things?" Galen inquired delicately.

"Oh my God, yes. I can get her off the charges pretty easily, I think, but I want to put a stipulation that I'll only do it if she gets a restraining order and moves back in with her parents. This asshole is bad news."

"Mm." Galen nodded. "You can't fix their lives."

"If they would listen to my advice, maybe I could," Ellery grumbled, and Galen's wicked laughter was a panacea to his wounds.

"Well, yes, but then we're not so awesome at fixing our own lives, so why would they be?"

Ellery was about ready to retort "Speak for yourself!" but then he remembered Galen *was* speaking for himself. He'd made his share of mistakes—and owned up to them.

"It would just be so much easier," Ellery said instead, "if we could fix some of the things that were really broken."

"Like what?" Galen had tilted his head to indicate he was listening. Really listening.

"Like this assumption that women and minorities are disposable," Ellery ruminated, thinking about Ty Townsend and the woman in the case on his desk.

"If you're thinking about Ty Townsend, that's been bothering me too."

Ellery looked at him sharply. "What do you mean?"

"Well, you and Jackson have been running on the theory that Ty was targeted because of his race, but I've been thinking about what Jade said, and she was right."

Ellery's eyes widened. "She usually is," he said. "Explain."

"Well, yes, the setup was obvious. Someone aimed those two cops at Ty and said 'Get the Black guy!' And that is institutionalized racism, and it's deplorable. But the person who aimed the cops—Ziggy, and oh my God, why that name?—what was the motive again?"

"We think he was using Ty as a distraction," Ellery said, rubbing his chin with one finger. "That if the cops were at that party, they wouldn't be anywhere else?"

"Now that could be very true, but why *this* kid. Because Ty Townsend has prospects. Ty Townsend is *not* a disposable kid, is he?"

Ellery frowned. "They wanted Ty out of the picture for another reason?"

"Yes. And I'm not saying the distraction thing isn't a factor too. Has Jackson figured out where they should have been yet?"

"No," Ellery said. "I think it's on his list."

"Well, I've had AJ print out the entire roster of police calls for that night, and besides a dog barking and some asshole setting off what people think are explosives in his garage on the far side of town, there is nothing in the entire city that caught people's attention besides that party."

"So whatever it was, it must have flown under the radar pretty far," Ellery said. "And if it was that far under the radar, why—"

"Why call attention to it with the distraction. Yes." Galen nodded. "So you may have to revise the theory for that one. And there's one more thing."

Ellery nodded, thoroughly intrigued. "Go on."

"When AJ was looking for police calls, he started with the live feed from just this moment."

Ellery's eyes widened. "And…?"

"And weren't our boys supposed to visit Capitol Valley High today?"

"Oh no."

"Oh yes. There were shots fired about ten minutes ago."

Ellery was already on his feet when his phone practically tried to buzz across the table. He scooped it up off the desk, his heart dropping out of his chest in relief when he saw who was calling.

"Goddammit, Jackson!"

"I'm fine. Keep your socks on." Jackson sounded a little out of breath but, as he said, fine.

"I'm on my way," Ellery said into the phone, and then he glared at Galen. "You and me," he said succinctly, "are going to have to have a little talk about burying the motherfucking lede."

"There were no casualties at the scene," Galen replied mildly.

"That doesn't mean there's not blood on the ground!" Ellery took off through the door. "Jackson, stay put—"

"As it turns out, we sort of have to," Jackson said, just as Galen pulled his phone out of his pocket.

"Goddammit," he muttered, his voice sharp enough to actually slow Ellery down.

"What?" he demanded, pretty much from both of them.

And as Jackson's voice registered on the phone, Galen held up a picture that had obviously been texted to him by Henry.

"Somebody shot up John's goddamned car."

Ellery scrubbed at his face with his hand. "Oh my God."

"I swear to God," Jackson said earnestly, "neither of us was in it at the time."

Ellery's heart was thundering in his ears. "You're going to give *me* a heart attack," he said, totally and completely serious.

"Well, if you could hold off until you pick us up?" Jackson said, voice conciliatory. "Henry would take it as a personal favor."

Ellery ran his hand through his hair, breaking the gel that held it back and not caring.

"Ten minutes," he said, thinking about traffic. "I'll be there in ten minutes."

"Thanks, Ellery," Jackson replied with uncharacteristic humility. "We appreciate it."

Ellery's eyes narrowed. "Jackson, is there anything else I should kn—"

"The paramedics should be done stitching up my ass by the time you get here."

And that's when Ellery hung up on him.

"Jade," he said, his voice high and tight with tension. "Jade, did you drive today?"

"Yes...?" She obviously knew something was up.

"Could you, perchance, give Galen a ride home if we're not back by six?"

"Sure." Jade took a breath. "He's all right?"

And Ellery had to mirror her, or he was going to explode. "He said he's getting stitches from the EMTs on scene."

"Of course he is." She nodded. "It's been nice, these last months, not having to worry. Guess that can't last forever."

Her look of sincere sympathy actually helped him pull himself together.

"Hey," he said. "This time he told me before I had to see the bandages. That's progress."

And her surprised smile did the rest. "Damn, it's practically a whole new Jackson! But he's still bleeding a little, which I guess is okay, because we loved the old one too."

And Ellery laughed, the band around his chest loosening enough for him to hear the exact echo of words he'd said to Jackson not more than two weeks earlier.

"Yes, we did. Both of them. I'm going to go pick them up and see where we go from here." He paused and then turned back into his office. "And I'm going to take a minute to get my briefcase, just in case it's home."

Well, it was three in the afternoon. By the time they were done with the police, who knew?

THE EMERGENCY vehicles were still there in force. As well as, Ellery was happy to see, a forensics team.

Jackson was leaning over the back of the ambulance, posterior out, as an EMT—this one a dark-haired, thirtyish woman of Asian descent—finished taping a bandage to the outside of his upper thigh, with a little bit of tape on the buttcheek. He was still wearing what was left of a brand-new pair of cargo shorts. The back of them were shredded and covered with blood, as was the lower part of Jackson's leg and his tennis shoe.

They had, indeed, been stitching up his ass.

Two uniformed officers were talking to him while the EMT worked, both in their late fifties, an African American woman with some iron in her hair and a *lot* in her spine, and a paunchy white man with hair the color of rusty ginger.

"So all you have on this guy is he was wearing cleats?" the woman—her nametag said Fetzer—was saying.

"With mud on them, like he'd just come from the football field," Jackson said patiently, as though he was repeating himself. "We've gone over this."

"We've gone over this with your agenda, young man, but we don't know anything for sure."

Jackson grimaced. "Okay, so that's fair. My partner was just interviewing Baldwin Schroeder, one of the assistant coaches of the football team, for the same investigation we talked about yesterday. I was talking to Mrs. Eccleston, the social studies teacher. Henry came into the room, we bitched at each other like we do, and then there were bullets coming through the windows."

"And you decided to jump out the window unarmed and confront the guy or girl shooting," said the man, Hardison, sounding doubtful.

"Whoever was shooting wasn't that bright," Jackson retorted.

"And how do you know that?"

"Well, for one thing, they were shooting from the ground level. The portable is elevated about three feet. It's why you need a ramp up to the door. That's a lousy shot. The angle is what saved our lives. For another, after we dropped to the floor, they started shooting through the door. Now, on the one hand, that *might* get the teacher in the corner, but she's got this five-hundred-pound metal Army surplus desk, boxes of books and copy paper, and file cabinets surrounding her, so that's a hard shot to make when you're *not* firing blind. And this bozo fires into the door. Well, the teacher's a smart cookie. They offered to put Jesus lights in her ceiling—"

"What?" Fetzer said, almost like she was compelled.

"Skylights. It's like shining the light of God down on whatever student sits under the light. So, you know, Jesus lights. Anyway, she asked for a steel-reinforced door instead, because she's had kids try to take her room apart and thought it would be more practical."

"Than a skylight in Sacramento in August?" Fetzer said, eyes wide. "Yeah, I can see that. Poor kids getting cooked like bugs. Anyway, so there's a steel-reinforced door...."

"And the asshole keeps shooting into it. I waited until he emptied his clip, waved something in front of the window to make sure he didn't have a buddy on the other side of the portable, and hopped out the window."

The EMT at his side spoke up. "Hopped is an overstatement. You apparently sliced yourself out the window. But you're good to go now, sir. You begged not to go to the hospital. I pulled up your chart like you asked and saw the order, so my partner called in some antibiotics and some painkillers." She handed him a small slip of paper. "Get this filled from the pharmacy of your choice, and be sure to see a doctor if the pain persists or you pop your stitches." Her voice went dry. "It's that second one you probably have to worry about."

Jackson grimaced and straightened. "Thank you. I'm obliged."

She returned his medical card and shook her head. "You know, that thing looks really worn. Maybe you should try to minimize your risk or something. That's a pretty high price to pay to spot a cleat with some mud on it."

It was painful watching him try not to roll his eyes. "I'll take that under advisement," he said dryly and then turned to the two police officers. "So you see what I mean? Whoever shooting wasn't that bright, and they didn't have a clear objective other than to stop what was going on in that classroom. And I'm telling you, other than my partner eating lunch, it wasn't that exciting."

"What made that exciting?" asked Fetzer.

"He'd been whining about lunch on the way over. This way I knew he'd stop whining. That excites me."

Hardison let out a snort, and Fetzer looked around, her eyes falling on Ellery. Ellery took the cue and moved closer. He didn't reach out and touch Jackson, as much as he wanted to, and Jackson's gentle tap on his arm was more than he could have asked for.

"Fine, Counselor," he said softly. He looked over his shoulder where Henry and a short, round, middle-aged woman with a bad dye job were talking to another pair of officers. "So's Henry, and so's Mrs. Eccleston." Jackson grimaced. "But I think maybe you and me should spend part of tomorrow helping that poor woman move to another room. She's got kids coming in on Thursday, and a lot of her posters got shot to shit." He paused and then looked at the cops. "That's another thing. It was a handgun—Berretta, Walther PK—something small. Not an AK or anything meant to spray bullets. This was a one-shot-at-a-time gun, which means it takes some skill, and this shooter didn't have any."

"Lucky for you," Fetzer said. "I take it this is the lawyer you work for?"

"Ellery Cramer." Ellery held out cards to both officers, who each took one. "And I take it you've spoken with Jackson about this matter before?"

"We actually looked up the beat of the two people you asked about," Fetzer said softly, giving Ellery a sideways look. "There weren't any obvious calls that night, but…." She gave a gentle snort. "There's a couple of empty buildings—a big-bulk hardware store and a grocery store—on a big lot. It's on the same patrol area as your party. It hit me kind of funny. When that was our beat, we checked that place six times a night because there was almost always something hinky going on there. But going back over the logs, with the party bust and the paperwork, there was almost a two-hour gap patrolling that area—and Lindstrom and Craft only hit the place every other shift. I think maybe we should check that out."

Ellery nodded. "We think that besides being a distraction, there might have been something about Ty specifically that made our scumbags want to get him out of the way."

"Gambling," Jackson said, surprising him. Jackson nodded to Henry. "Henry was interviewing a coach—"

"Baldwin Schroeder," Fetzer said. "You gave us that name when we got here. He was out on the practice field when the shots were fired. We have him on film." She sniffed. "The person we have on film firing badly into that portable building was wearing baggy sweats and a hoodie over the face. And cleats, like you said. We followed the dirt off the cleats into the quad, but—"

"It had all been stomped off by then," Jackson said glumly. "Yeah. I saw."

"We know you saw," Fetzer said. She gave Jackson a pointed look. "That's when your damned blood trail stopped."

"Well, did you see where hoodie guy went?" Jackson asked, clearly uncomfortable with the mention.

She shook her head. "You saw that overhang over the lunch area? The cameras don't get the wall back there. It's a blind spot. The shooter ran in that direction and disappeared. We've got people looking at camera footage, but they've got two or three student functions going on there—swim team, cheerleading, student government. Kids were running around all over the back of that building. All the shooter had to do was ditch the hoodie. Are you sure you don't remember anything else?"

Jackson closed his eyes and thought carefully. "They'll ditch the cleats too," he said. "I don't think they fit."

Fetzer and Hardison were both standing, heads tilted.

"What makes you say that?" Hardison asked.

"They were too loud, like they were clopping because they were too big," he answered. "I had to hop out the window and run down the length of the portable. Someone younger, and not injured, would have been long gone. I shouldn't have even spotted a cleat going around that corner. But I did, and mud usually takes a lot of working to get knocked off like that. I really think he was wearing someone else's cleats. Maybe ask the football players if their shoes disappeared during break or something."

"Were they even football cleats?" Fetzer asked. "There was a rec-league soccer team using the upper field for practice too."

Jackson grimaced. "Well," he said, "you guys have more suspects to interview!" He swallowed then, rapidly, and Ellery noticed that he was awfully pale and had grown paler as they stood. "I'd show them pictures of Ziggy Ivanov if I were you, but it probably wasn't him."

"What are you going to be doing?" Fetzer asked.

"We should get you home," Ellery said, and Jackson shook his head.

"No, we need to talk to Ty Townsend about a few things. Like I said, I think we know why he was targeted for that drug bust. We also need to talk to a vice detective. Those pills with the little butterflies on them—"

Fetzer and Hardison both groaned. "We didn't get to that," Fetzer apologized.

"We're sorry," Hardison echoed. "We got busy with running the police activity on Lindstrom and Craft's beat."

"And it's not like you don't have your own beat to patrol," Jackson said, with what Ellery thought was a lot of grace for his usual style. "But I need some answers. Those pills sound very specifically branded, and if someone knows where they're coming from, besides Dima Siderov—"

Fetzer and Hardison both straightened like they'd been pinched. "Where did you hear that name?" they asked, almost in tandem.

Jackson flickered a glance at Ellery. Ellery stepped in, not liking Jackson's color at all but recognizing that they needed to have this conversation first.

"That's immaterial," Ellery said. "But we've heard it. And the drugs involved in the Townsend bust sound specifically branded, like Jackson said. If we knew which outfit they were coming from, we would have one more bit of evidence with which to get Townsend off, without involving Dobrevk in his defense."

"Is that kid safe?" Fetzer asked. "We heard he was in protective custody and the charges had been dropped, and that sounds good, but you never know for sure."

Jackson nodded. "He's safe," he said briefly, telling Ellery that even if Jackson was cooperating, he wasn't all bubbling with trust just yet. "But those pills could be important. So are Townsend's stats in Vegas."

Hardison was the one who made the connection. "Oh Jesus. People bet on college athletes all the time. If Townsend gets pulled before he even starts, they can advance someone else and make money."

"That's what we were thinking," Henry said, coming up behind him.

"How's our school teacher?" Jackson asked quietly—but then, his whole body was going quiet.

"In need of her husband and a lot of wine," Henry said. "And the principal, that guy over there?" He nodded at an extraordinarily tall, fortyish gentleman in a pair of khakis and a polo shirt.

"I see him," Jackson replied.

"Well, he told her that she had a month off with pay in her contract to deal with any repercussions from school violence. I told her to go for it," Henry said, and Ellery and Jackson both looked to where the woman stood, shaking, with a friend's arm around her shoulders.

"Why the foil blanket?" Jackson mused. "I'm so damned hot!"

"Not everyone's Superman like you are," Henry snipped back, and then he stopped and took a good look at Jackson.

"He's not looking like Superman," Ellery said quietly. "Jackson, how are you feeling?"

"I'm fi—" Jackson literally stopped himself in the middle of the word, closed his eyes, and rubbed the bridge of his nose. "I'm a little woozy," he admitted, wobbling on his feet. "Did I mention it was really fucking hot?"

"It is," Ellery said. "Henry's going to take you to my car and start the engine." Ellery pressed his keys into Henry's hand. "I'll finish here."

"I really am fine," Jackson said, nodding like he could make it so.

"You've been back for two days," Ellery told him, trying not to snap. Damn the man—two days! "Did you even eat lunch?"

"Yes," Jackson said.

"No," Henry said at the same time. "Bought *me* lunch, but I suspect he gave his to the nice teacher lady who's about to get a month vacation."

"That might never be enough," Jackson said soberly.

Henry nodded. "Well, no. It really might not ever be enough. But that's not our fault. I was eating lunch, and you were hanging up her posters, and if you hadn't made sure both of us were safe, someone might have shot until they hit something. Good call on having me stack the desks by the way. One of the shots went wide and came through the actual wall instead of getting stopped by the door. It glanced off that slick Formica and got lodged in one of those boxes of paper. Saved my life."

"We used to have lock-down drills," Jackson mumbled as Henry kept steering him toward the car. "The things you learn growing up in a war zone."

"You know where the water is!" Ellery called, and he saw Henry nod and Jackson drifting a little on his feet.

"Not such an action hero after all, is he?" Fetzer said on half a laugh.

Ellery gave her a look that should have dropped the air temperature from "incendiary" to "tolerable." "He had heart surgery eight weeks ago. We've been keeping him out of the heat until he got the green light to come back. He came back early because he thought these kids were important. Is there anything else you can tell us?"

Fetzer and Hardison both looked a little embarrassed.

"Well, now that you made us feel bad about that," Fetzer muttered, "no. But the guy who didn't cut up his ass collected shells for us using a piece of paper and an unsharpened pencil. We can get those to forensics and see if they can run the prints."

"Good," Ellery said, rubbing the back of his neck. "We can look up Ty's standing among the bookmakers, and see if anybody bet either against him or *for* anybody else who was up-and-coming. I'm pretty sure Jackson knows people."

"I can check with my sources too," Hardison said frankly. "Me and Adele's husband place a bet every now and then. We give our runner free pizza when we win."

Fetzer rolled her eyes. "If you only gave him food when you won, that kid would starve. But yeah, you check your sources, we'll check ours. And we'll let you know what our canvass of the kids coming out of activities tells us."

"And who got their shoes stolen," Hardison chimed in.

"If you could phone myself or Mr. Rivers with that information, I would be *very* grateful," Ellery told them. "Right now I need to make a phone call and authorize a police escort for Mrs. Eccleston, and I need to…."

He looked toward the car and saw Jackson, head between his knees, losing what looked to be mostly stomach acid on the pavement.

"Get your guy out of the sun," Fetzer told him. "I hear you."

Ellery turned toward the car without another word, texting Arizona as he went.

JACKSON WAS in the front seat, leaning against the headrest, door closed, air-conditioning on full blast as Henry ran the engine. Ellery knocked on Henry's door, and Henry slid out, heading for the back seat, but not before he had his own say.

"He bought two sandwiches," he muttered. "Gave one to the teacher, gave one to me. Wasn't particularly hungry all day."

Ellery thought about their morning and about the acid rumbling in his stomach and sighed. "Well, neither was I. I'm sure if he hadn't needed stitches in his ass—"

Henry tried bravely to contain a snicker, and Ellery let a smirk creep out.

"It's not funny," Henry said, obviously trying to be a better man.

"Only because it's Jackson," Ellery told him, losing against the smirk before clubbing it back into submission again.

"Okay, yeah," Henry agreed, letting a giggle escape.

They both sobered at the same time.

"Yes," Ellery conceded. "If Jackson hadn't been injured, he probably could have eaten something now and been fine. But there's a ticking clock here, and he's trying to race it. And I don't think he's going to be taking good care of himself until those kids are safe."

Henry rubbed the back of his head. "Well, Ziggy Ivanov's a problem," he admitted.

"And so's Dima Siderov. An even bigger problem."

Henry nodded. "Yeah. So everything we're doing is to what? What's our endgame here?"

Ellery had to stop and think about that one. Originally it had been to get Ty and Tage cleared of all charges. Tage had been cleared, but they were still trying to get Ty off. But the case had grown since then too.

"I need to think about that," he said, voice low. "Let's get Jackson some water, some food, his meds, and maybe get him home and let him rest."

"Good luck with that," Henry muttered.

"Well, food first." Ellery's stomach made an unmistakable—and unmistakably embarrassing—sound. He'd ignored the sandwiches Jade had brought in for the same reason Jackson had ignored his. "Would probably be a good idea for the both of us," he said. "And then we can come up with a plan."

THE CAR was quiet as Ellery found a chain sandwich place to park in front of. Henry offered to go inside, and Ellery let the car idle, checking Jackson every so often to make sure he was okay. His color was improving, and his breathing getting better too. After about five minutes, he sat up a little more and grimaced.

"My. Ass," he muttered. "Fucking why?"

Ellery let out a strained chuckle. "I have no idea. Why'd you skip lunch?"

Jackson had been wearing a faint smile, and it faded now. "Because I.... God. After this morning, could you eat?"

"No," Ellery said softly. "No. Tage's brother and sister are trapped in hell, and we are—"

"Helpless," Jackson muttered. "Except I keep thinking that if we have enough evidence, enough information, we can do something about it. We can get Ty off, we can find out where those kids are being taken. We just need the right amount of pressure to apply to Dima Siderov, and we can get it done."

Ellery looked at him with troubled eyes. "Dima Siderov is a pretty big fish," he said softly. "And he's surrounded by his own personal army of sharks. I'm not saying I'm not willing to go down fighting with you, but I was kind of hoping for a couple of years together before our bodies hit the floor."

Jackson winced. "Yeah. Me too." He let his tired eyes meet Ellery's, and Ellery saw an amazing thing.

Hope.

"Maybe we don't take down Dima Siderov all in one bite," he said softly. "Maybe we stick with Ziggy Ivanov and see if we can get him. Ziggy's a captain. He wants to go higher in the organization. If we can... I don't know. Not so much get him to turn on Siderov, because that's not going to happen."

"Why not?" Ellery asked curiously.

"Family. James Cosgrove wasn't thrilled with what happened to Ty Townsend. I think that's why he was killed. He said something to Ziggy about it the night Ty got arrested." Jackson sighed. "It was so sad. According to Nate Klein, James said, 'But Ty was my friend,' and Ziggy said, 'But he's not family.'"

"Mob family," Ellery murmured.

"Yeah, and Mrs. Eccleston backed it up. Cosgrove wasn't his original name. His family changed it. So his family is in with the *family*, and he asks somebody to back off Ty, and Ziggy executes a kill order, framing Tage and taking his brother and sister since he won't be there to stand up to them, since his parents won't or can't. So Ziggy killed Cosgrove, and he might know where the kids are. If we can get him to tell us where the kids are, we can save Dima Siderov for another day."

"So that's our solution," Ellery said. "Henry asked me what our endgame is. For right now, our endgame is Ziggy Ivanov and getting Tage's siblings back." He took a deep breath. "And we use Ziggy to help the DA build a case against Dima."

"And invest in Kevlar underwear," Jackson said grimly. "Because if Dima finds out about us…."

Ellery took a deep breath. "Maybe you should call your lawyer friend back this afternoon, after I take you home."

"Take me what?" Jackson sat all the way up and then collapsed back against the headrest again. "My head hurts," he said, his voice humble. "Why does my head hurt? My *ass* is what should be hurting."

"Dehydration," Ellery said. "Your body is not quite recovered, and you didn't eat. C'mon, Jackson, I know you're not dumb."

"Gah!" Jackson took a deep breath. "Some food, some water, and then we need to visit Ty so I can talk to him, okay? And we need to warn him and his family too. And Tage's parents. They might talk to us when they won't talk to the police." He leaned forward gingerly and fumbled for the glove compartment where Ellery had started to keep the ibuprofen after he and Jackson had become a thing.

Ellery watched him for a moment, trying to decide if he was angry or not. Jackson *had* made promises about taking care of himself, about being truthful regarding his health, and about balancing his own welfare and Ellery's peace of mind against his impulse to go out and do his job.

Watching as the man he loved fumbled for painkillers and then wash them back with a swig of water actually stilled the thundering in Ellery's own chest.

"Jackson, on a scale of one to ten, how do you feel?"

"Ellery—"

"Please. Humor me."

"A four, with room for improvement," Jackson said, closing his eyes against the sunlight.

"Given that Henry, Galen, and I still need to file an insurance claim before this investigation can move forward, how urgent is it that you come back with us after you go home and change?"

Jackson took another deep breath. "A five," he said reluctantly. "I can do some of the interviews on the phone."

Ellery swallowed and nodded. "You know, I shouldn't have hung up on you when you told me you were getting your ass stitched up."

Jackson let a pale smile slip through. "You were pissed. It's my second day out. What *should* you have done?"

"I should have made sure you were okay," Ellery said soberly.

Some of the tension eased from Jackson's smile. "If I was telling you I needed stitches, I was definitely okay."

Ellery snorted, some of his own tension fading. "You couldn't have thrown down a shirt or something? God, Jackson, it's like Sean ended up in the hospital and you were trying to keep up!"

"Oh hell no! I need to call K-Ski and then talk to his partner." Jackson let out a sigh. "By the way, poor Sean. I knew that conversation with the fireman didn't look good, but getting dumped on your ass in the hospital? That's not friendly."

"Yeah, you so expected me to do that the first time you ended up there," Ellery recalled fondly, remembering Jackson coming out of the anesthesia, wondering what Ellery was doing there and why he hadn't left yet. The panic, the worry; that had been new, but still, Ellery had known he couldn't desert Jackson then.

He'd never been able to leave. Not where Jackson was concerned.

"I'm glad you didn't," Jackson murmured. "I... I'm not sure if I tell you that enough. You had every reason to walk away back then, and only a few more reasons to stay now, honestly."

Ellery let out a short bark of laughter and reached over the center console to capture Jackson's hand. Just as their fingers brushed, Henry opened the back door in a huff, letting the soggy scorching air of August into the car.

"God, that took forever," Henry muttered. "I can't even believe how hard it was to order three simple sandwiches." He rooted through the bag and handed Jackson a paper-wrapped packet. "Here. Eat now. Your complexion is making me itchy."

Jackson took the sandwich from between the seats and did a double take. "Wait. Three sandwiches? Didn't I *just feed you*?"

Henry shrugged. "Yes. It was great. I think you should do it again. Sorry, Ellery, no change. Can I eat back here?"

"No!" Ellery said at the same time Jackson said, "Sure, knock yourself out, but be prepared to detail the car on the company dime if you spill."

Ellery backed out of the parking lot, huffing out in exasperation. "Jackson, it's not even your car!"

"And why is that?" Jackson asked bitterly. "You have bought me my last three SUVs. I *have money*. Maybe, before we go get a kitten together, we should get a *car*, don't you think?"

"No," Ellery and Henry said at the same time. Ellery let out a disgruntled breath and realized Henry was an ally. "Henry, you may eat back there, but please clean up any spills."

"Will do, chief. I've got a bottle of magic stuff back at John and…." He deflated a little. "Goddammit. I'm pissed. Shooting up John and Galen's car. There was no need for that!"

"I don't think it was on purpose," Jackson mused, nibbling on his sandwich in an experimental way, like a rabbit with a new strain of lettuce. "I think those were the shots that went through the entire room. There were only a couple. Unfortunately one of them went into the radiator and another went through the windshield."

"Well, I'm glad they didn't go into the kids on the practice field," Henry muttered. "But other than that, it still pisses me off. John and Galen didn't deserve this."

"Neither did poor Mrs. Eccleston," Jackson said glumly. "I swear, that woman was so happy to have someone bring her lunch, it made me want to start a movement or something."

"We'll check on her when the case is over," Henry told him, sounding bored. But Ellery recognized the words for what they really were, an unconscious way to soothe Jackson and keep him from fretting over how frightened the poor woman must be after the shooting, to keep him from feeling like he'd brought too much trouble to her door.

"Why *did* someone shoot at us while we were there?" Jackson asked. "That there is the big question. I mean, we assume it's to stop you and me, but why when we were in there with a civilian? What were they trying to stop us from learning?"

"Well, Sparky," Henry snarked, "that's what we're going to have to discuss. *After* you eat." He paused. "You made sure she was being watched over, right? In case whoever it was tries again?"

"Yes," Ellery interjected before Jackson could say anything. "I texted the DA, and she made sure there was a police presence at Mrs. Eccleston's home and an escort to work until the shooter is apprehended."

"Good," Jackson and Henry said at the same time.

"You know," Henry said into the silence afterward, "I was in the middle of a war, and I get why Kevlar was needed. Doing what Jackson and I do, I can see why I might need to get fitted for a lightweight tactical vest, just on, you know, the off chance someone's going to shoot at us.

But she's a *teacher*. She shouldn't have to worry about wearing a full metal jacket, you know?"

Jackson grunted in agreement, chewing—thank God—an actual bite of sandwich. "The idea that people expect that to be a job requirement is unreal," he said after he'd swallowed. "But in this case, I think it was very specific to the mob ties between Ziggy and Dima. You know, she told me that James Cosgrove wasn't his original name. I wonder if we could look up and see what his original name *was* and why someone would want to cover that up."

"And we never did get around to asking her about Ziggy," Henry said glumly.

"No," Jackson agreed, "but as Ellery just reminded me, I can do some damage on the phone this afternoon while you guys go out and get a rental for Galen and John."

Henry grunted. "So you're going back to the air-conditioning to rest? And we don't have to fight you or put you in an armlock or anything? Seriously?"

"Well, Ellery may want to hide the keys to the Tank, but if he does that, I've got no choice but to stay home and be a good boy," Jackson admitted.

On the one hand, Ellery's chest buzzed with the knowledge that Jackson's promises were being kept to the spirit as well as the letter.

On the other hand, he seriously considered taking the keys to the Tank.

Ducks, Row, Truck

JACKSON *WAS* a good boy when he got back to the house. He changed, finished his sandwich at the table, and then, ass hurting, brain jumpy and incoherent from exhaustion, he sat on the couch with the cat on his lap and let Ellery and Henry leave without fussing at them.

He actually napped for about fifteen minutes, but when he came to, his head was clearer, and he found himself sitting in the quiet with his eyes closed and Billy Bob purring in his lap.

His brain—usually busy and restless—went still, and he found the people and the events of the case appearing, in order, while he played with the pieces and tried to make them fit. He didn't get frustrated when they didn't fit immediately. He just went to the next piece and turned that around a little, and then the next.

No urgency. His body was spent. He'd promised Ellery he would take care of this body because it was the only one Ellery got, and Ellery was fond of it for whatever reason. For once, he couldn't urge himself toward healing or push his brain any further than it had already been. He had himself, the quiet, and the materials at hand.

After about half an hour, he sat up. Billy Bob—who had been drooling complacently on his clean T-shirt—extended his claws and let him know delicately that the cat preferred Jackson where he was. Jackson smiled slightly, snagged his phone from the end table where Ellery had left it charging, and opened his notes.

Family—James Cosgrove part of the Siderov
Family. Is ZIGGY part of the family? Did "family" shoot
at us because we were asking Schroeder questions? Is
SCHROEDER family?

*—Need: hard search on Siderov's family
members—see if AJ turns anything up on Ziggy or "the
German"
—Action: Text Mira and ask her too*

He looked at the note in surprise because it really seemed to help him think. Go figure. He almost died and came back with a more effective way to use his brain. He knew there had to be a benny, right?

But that wasn't the only thing that occurred to him. He kept typing.

*Ty Townsend—student athlete. Who would want
him out of commission?
—Need: info on who's making book on Ty and who
would benefit most if he loses his full ride and student
athlete status
—Action: Hardison says he can get it. Text
Hardison near end of shift to remind him.*

Okay, that was good too. He'd managed to make some contacts in the police force besides Kryzynski. Which reminded him….

*Kryzynski—his stabbing makes Ziggy pretty hot on
the street. Too hot for the "family" to handle?
Need: buzz on the street*

He tapped his finger on his lips for a moment because "buzz on the street" wasn't easy to get, particularly when you were laid up.

*Action: Call Kryzynski just because it's the nice
thing to do*

And that made him sit up as he remembered that Sean *wasn't* the only person in the hospital at the moment. In fact, he *had a contact* who could get him info on the guy who tried to shoot up the public defender's office the morning before.

But first, call Kryzynski.

"Hello, Officer Rivers," Dave said when Jackson was put in touch with Kryzynski's room number. "Are you behaving today?"

Jackson had to laugh. Dave and Alex may have been the best nurses at Med Center, but they had almost written him off when his heart had threatened to fail in June. They both agreed that they had seen far too much of him in the past ten years and they would rather he invite them to pizza, thank you.

"I am resting after lots of water and a good meal and a day of moderate activity," Jackson lied amiably, but Dave interrupted him before he could go any further.

"Deb Choi is a friend of mine, you big fibber. We just shared a soda on the back dock, and she told me about a PI who had to get his ass stitched up and then refused to come in for treatment. Don't try to pull the wool over my eyes, pretty boy. I can see right through you."

Jackson groaned. "Okay, well, the resting and hydrating and the good meal are the truth," he said. "But, you know, glass on the ass—not dignified."

Dave snorted. "I'm supposed to accept that? She said you looked like shit, by the way."

"Did you notice the hot?" Jackson complained, hating that he *was* complaining. "I didn't use to notice the hot, but I sure as hell am noticing it *now*."

Dave laughed ruefully. "Yeah, one of those things that doesn't always end up in the instruction books for recovering cardiac care. Okay. I guess you get a pass, seeing as you're all hydrated and fed and shit. Fine. I'll let you talk to my patient. *He* knows how to behave."

"I'm sure he's very docile," Jackson muttered, and Dave gave a bark of laughter as he handed over the phone. "Sean?"

"I preferred K-Ski," Kryzynski said. "When you call me by my first name, I think I'm dying."

Jackson snorted. "You're like a cockroach. Ain't gonna happen."

"Pot. Kettle."

And some of that rare peace stole over him. "Yeah, maybe," he admitted. "How you doing?"

"In. Pain."

"Sorry about that, big guy. I was hoping you were stoned to the gills. Don't be embarrassed. It's how I spent most of *my* time in the hospital."

"I can see why," Kryzynski said. "How are *you* doing?"

Jackson thought for a moment about lying completely, but he decided against it. The story might make K-Ski smile. He gave an abbreviated version of the case so far, from getting Tage into custody to the mob being involved in human trafficking, to how he and Henry had been taking a lunch break with a sweet middle-aged teacher when someone wearing outsized cleats had tried to shoot at them through a steel door, and finishing with having to bend over the ambulance bay, ass out, while he gave his statement. By the time he was done, Kryzynski was chuckling rustily into the phone.

"God. Only you."

"Very possibly. Anyway, I'm going to hit Christie and Mira up and do some cop work from my lacerated ass. I just wanted to make sure you're okay."

"That's nice. So the guy who got me—he's a mob soldier?"

"Yeah, we put that together this morning when we got the kid protective custody from the human trafficking division. We flashed his picture around a *lot* by the way."

"Rivers," Kryzynski gasped, interrupting with sudden urgency. "Why you? Why would they target you like that?"

Jackson frowned because this had bothered him and Henry too. "We're not sure. We've been poking a lot of hornets' nests."

"But did you poke them all with that picture?"

And Jackson had to think, and think clearly. He was suddenly very, very grateful for the past hour of rest. "Showed the DA's office, showed the cops, showed your partner. I mean, we were trying to get the guy who shanked you. We tried to make Ziggy *very* popular."

"'Preciate it," Kryzynski wheezed. "Did Henry show him to the guy at the high school?"

"I'm pretty sure, but I know I didn't have time to show the teacher lady. We were still talking to her. Does it matter?"

"Maybe, maybe not." Kryzynski took a deep breath. "Maybe I'm being para—" He breathed out. "—noid. But you saw the guy who got me. You can be a witness."

Jackson stopped talking for a minute. "But I'm not the only one who saw him. *You* saw—oh for fuck's sake! Put Dave back on the phone."

Dave spoke next. "What in the hell did you just say? He is looking *very* worried."

"Look, I'm going to call in some reinforcements, but I need you and Alex to do me a favor."

"What's—"

"Don't leave that room," Jackson said. "One of you needs to be in there at all times. Have your supervisor call me if you need to, but I need a police presence in that room. Turns out Officer Wheezy there is a *witness* to mob activity. Goddammit, it didn't even occur to me!"

"Well, it did *now*," Dave soothed. "And to be honest, there's been cops in and out of here all day. It's a pretty safe place to be."

Jackson thought about where he'd been showing the picture. "Unless some of them are dirty," he said. "Shit. Put Wheezy back on."

"I'm going to tell him that you called him that."

"Heh heh heh heh heh heh…."

"You are a bad, bad man," Dave praised. "Here's Wheezy."

"Dammit," Kryzynski wheezed. "Why?"

"Because I can," Jackson told him. "Now, I need you to think about this carefully—like your life depends on it. Andre Christie?"

"Rock. Solid."

"Okay. I'm calling him and having him arrange protection for you. Unless it's someone you know and trust, they can't stay. You understand?"

"What about you?" Sean asked.

"I was opportunity. Henry wanders up to someone involved and flashes Ziggy's picture. Think about it. Schroeder pulls out his phone as soon as Henry's gone, texts a buddy—"

"Why… shoes?" Kryzynski wheezed.

"I've got a theory about that too," Jackson reassured him. It had hit him while he'd been…. Dammit. He refused to call it meditating. God no. Absolutely not. He'd been napping, and that was his story, and he was sticking to it. "But let me call Christie first and get that ball moving. I don't want you there unprotected." He'd seen bad things happen when a criminal thought their loose end was unsupervised and vulnerable. One of them had almost happened to Ellery.

"Thanks, Rivers."

"Well, you know. You're growing on me. I'd hate to see shit happen to you, right?"

"You're embarrassing me."

"Good. Christie should be calling in a minute."

Jackson hung up and—after earning a baleful look from Billy Bob, who apparently thought all humans should become his couch—stood up and paced restlessly, his body accepting the food and rest and moving into recovery. After a couple of barefoot strides toward the kitchen for some water, he hit Christie's number.

"Oh my God, are we engaged?"

Jackson grinned as he started rummaging through the refrigerator. Maybe not water. Maybe soda. God. Sugar. Wonderful stuff. "Look, someone fired on Henry and me at Capitol Valley High today. And a totally innocent social studies teacher who is going to be in counseling for the rest of her life, but at least she's alive. I was just talking to your partner, and he reminded me that we'd been flashing Ziggy's picture around for two days, and—as we just discovered this morning—Ziggy has mob ties. Guess who likes to take out witnesses to crimes?"

"Oh my God!" Christie's horror sounded pretty damned genuine, so Jackson was going to take it on faith.

"So you can get him some protection outside his door?" Jackson asked. "And make sure it's not fucking Lindstrom and fucking Craft, by the way, because either they're dirty or they're dumb, and either way—"

"Not a good idea," Christie said smartly. "Okay, good. Who's with him now?"

"A nurse friend of mine who has promised that either he or his boyfriend are going to be there until your guys get there and talk to their supervisor about who is and who is not allowed into the room."

"Only cops that we okay," Christie said, his voice grim. "Only hospital staff on the prescribed list. I hear you. They may have to move him to a secure room. I'll let you know."

"Well, if they do, make sure Dave and Alex are part of his support team. They don't let people die on their watch. It's bad for their sex lives, so don't do it."

Christie let out a short bark of laughter. "Understood. I'm on that ten minutes ago."

"Good—I got calls to make, so late—"

"Rivers?"

"Yeah?"

"Thanks for having his back. Man, we watched him get pulled deeper and deeper with you and Cramer, and we were so worried about him. It's good to see you don't want him dead."

"Not even a little. Take care of him. He might be the only person in your department who doesn't hate us."

"Well, not the only one," Christie admitted. "Look, I'm going to get Sean secured. You need to call your girl at the DA's office. I think she's got news."

"Really?" Oh wow. Jackson really *could* accomplish a lot without running around getting his ass sliced. He snagged his soda from the fridge and decided to make an event out of it by getting one of those nice glasses Ellery kept in the freezer, along with some ice. Ooh. This could be like dessert.

"Yeah. I can't go into it now, but call her."

"Will do. Update me when you have K-Ski secured."

"Deal."

"Oh!" And let's hear it for clarity. "The guy in the coma…?"

"Still in the coma," Christie muttered.

"Has he been identified? And is he still under protection?"

"Yes and yes." Christie blew out a breath. "And I'm sorry for not telling you earlier. Avi Kovacs—brother to Alexei Kovacs."

Jackson frowned. "Should I know that name?"

"Only if you work organized crime in Vegas," Christie muttered. "That's the thing. Avi's third cousin or whatever to one of the biggest mob bosses in Sin City, but we have no idea what he's doing here."

All the air went out of the room, and Jackson remembered what Galen had said about a bigger picture. "Besides being involved in some sort of power transfer or takeover or whatever between Vegas and here?"

"Oh dear God." Christie sounded shocked. "You're right. Fuck me. Fuck this shit. We are in Mobland now. *Goddammit*, I did not want to be in Mobland with Sean in the hospital. Fuck me. I've got to go to our lieu and tell him all the fucking things."

"I'm… sorry?" Jackson wasn't sure how to feel about that. On the one hand, Christie was right; Mobland was not the place *anybody* wanted to be. On the other hand….

"Don't be sorry," Christie said tersely. "You probably saved Sean's life. Fucking Mobland. I'll scramble the troops, hit up the organized crime division, and ask about your trafficking case. If the DA's office *doesn't* have answers for you, maybe my guys do."

"Affirmative, and thank you."

"Try not to get shot again."

"That too. Later."

"Later."

Jackson hit End Call before adding ice to the frozen glass and then poured the cola. The charge of sugar on his tongue was sort of amazing. Just like the commercials promised, right? He took his little glass of heaven to the table and sat gingerly, pulling up the DA's office, human trafficking division, next.

Mira answered.

"Jackson? How you doing, sweetheart? Word on the street is you almost got your ass shot off!"

"More like fileted," Jackson admitted. "But it's mostly still there. How about you?"

"Well, you sure have been keeping us busy," she admitted. "We've got Tage in protective custody, but we tried again with his parents, and they still refuse it. I think they're trying to keep their extended family safe, but honey, I don't see good things happening there. If they won't cooperate, we can't even ask for guard duty."

"Do we have a lead on where Siderov is? Or Ziggy?"

"Well, Ziggy is pretty hot, but we've had a couple of sightings of him around town. Although not, oddly enough, at the high school."

"Do Ziggy or Baldwin Schroeder have a younger brother or sister?" Jackson asked. "Or maybe the SRO at the school, also named Schroeder? I need someone with a contact to, say, someone on the cheerleading squad or the swim team?"

"Let me check on that," Mira muttered, obviously working on her computer. "Why?"

"Because Henry flashed Ziggy's picture to a coach we think is implicated right before someone took a shot at us. I'm thinking—"

"He texted this person and they got hold of a gun?"

"Probably from the person who activated him—or even his or her own locker. Cleats too. Whoever shot at us had oversized cleats on—not their own shoes—and then disappeared into a group of kids who were just getting done with activities. And whoever it was, they weren't that smart or that good. The shots were off, the execution was bad. The only thing they did well was ditch the gun and blend into the crowd of kids. So I'm thinking Baldwin Schroeder, the coach, has a younger sibling, or his cousin the SRO whose first name I don't know does. Or it's Ziggy

Ivanov. Someone who could respond to that text immediately but….." He paused for a drink of soda. Bliss!

"Not expertly," Mira said. "I get it." He heard her tapping for a moment. "Okay, now I've got some news for you, but it's weird news."

"Is there any other kind?" Jackson asked, but only half facetiously.

"Not this weird. So we have gotten two calls today from the US military down in So-Cal, if you can believe that."

Jackson almost spit out his soda. Oh yeah, he and Ellery knew So-Cal. In particular, they knew tiny little pockets of the desert that held secrets and more secrets, and yes, some of them were military secrets.

"Stunning," he said, his voice robotic in his own ears. "Go on."

She obviously detected something odd about his tone because she continued, but slowly, as though afraid of what he was going to say or do. "So," she said, "one of these calls is from a Colonel Jason Constance, and he says a civilian has intercepted a shipment of young immigrants who are just about sex-trafficking age for the underaged set. Someone has interviewed these kids. They are all from the Sacramento area, and he wants to know if he can return them to us, if we can find their families and place them."

Jackson's heart was pounding arrhythmically in his chest, and he wasn't sure it had anything to do with the stress-induced heart murmur that had recently been repaired.

"Can you?" he asked, voice squeaking.

"We can!" she said. "We have an FBI interdistrict task force at our disposal for just such an eventuality," she told him. "But that's not the weird part. Do you want to hear the weird part?"

"Oh my God, I really do."

"Okay, first of all, this guy is calling from what sounds like a school bus from hell. I ask him when he took charge of the children, and he says two days ago, in the afternoon. He says he took the kids to a medical professional to get them checked out, and then he's had to change vehicles a couple of times because he was being tracked. I asked by who, and he said 'The mob? The military? Take your pick. I'm trying to stay one step ahead.'"

"Jason Constance?" Jackson asked, because the name was familiar. He'd never met the man personally, but one of those little pockets in the desert housed a couple of friends, and he was pretty sure Constance was the CO to one of those people he regarded as a friend. In fact, earlier on in the year, Constance and Lee Burton—the friend—had been watching over Jackson and Ellery and Ellery's mother in order to keep Ellery's mother safe from a hit man. Jackson hadn't seen them at the time—although he'd caught a glimpse of a thirtyish man with dark hair and big, sad brown eyes. They hadn't spoken personally, but he and Ellery had known they were there.

"Colonel Jason Constance," Mira corrected.

"Of course. Okay, that's weird. When did he say he'd be here?"

"Tomorrow morning. He was going to find another vehicle and travel by night. I told him to head for the courthouse. He seemed to be afraid someone would take the kids away from him, and like I said, it sounded like he was driving the school bus from hell. Anyway, so we get that phone call, and then we get a call from Constance's *direct superior*, who says that if we're contacted by a Colonel Jason Constance, he's acting without authorization of the US military and that he's armed and dangerous, and we should not accept any shipments from him, no matter what kind of shipment he brought."

Jackson went to take another sip of his soda and realized his hand was shaking. Oh God. Oh God, oh God, oh God. The last time he and Ellery had tangled with the military, they had almost died. *Ellery* had almost died. Jackson's heart was going triple time, and he wondered if he should take some of the nitro left over from before his surgery, or if he was just having a full-blown panic attack.

But these were *kids*.

And that steadied him. He knew who he was. He knew who Ellery was. Neither of them were the kind of people to turn their backs on children.

"So someone intercepts these kids, and Constance wants to return them home, and whoever was up in the food chain wanted to do something else with them," Jackson said. One of the things he *did* know about Constance was that he was in charge of a very secret, very important op. A rogue military leader had trained up a bunch of serial-killing psychopaths, one of whom had infiltrated Sac PD the year before. Constance's job was to track them down and take them out—or imprison them—but mostly not have them out in the world, wreaking havoc on the general population.

They couldn't lose Constance. Like Jackson and Ellery, he had a goddamned job to do.

"That's what it sounds like," Mira said. "And the thing that made me think of your case is that Constance said most of the kids were from the Russian and Ukrainian communities. There were a couple who spoke fluent English, and he was using those kids to keep the other kids calm. That sounds like—"

"Max and Sophie!" Oh holy hell. This was it. The miracle Tage Dobrevk and his family needed.

"Yes, it does," she said. "But first he's got to get here, and then he's got to get here before the other guy, Brigadier General Barney Talbot, intercepts him and takes the kids to do whatever he had planned."

Oh wow. "Constance is evading two bad guys," Jackson murmured. And one of them was his own commander, fuck all the fucking things.

"That's what we think," Mira confirmed.

"What do Sodhi and Pasternak plan to do?"

Mira's voice dropped. "Here's the thing: I actually talked to Constance, but Talbot? He went to voicemail while we were in a conference. I played the voicemail for them, and Pasternak—you know how he's so fair skinned?"

"Yeah?"

"His *scalp* turned purple. Like a beet. Like that's where the expression came from!"

Jackson imagined Mira's little upturned nose wrinkling in surprise, and he managed a smile. "That's amazing," he said.

"I *know*! Anyway, he looked me and Eleanor in the eye and said, 'It's a shame we never got this message, isn't it, El?' And Sodhi looks at me and says, 'Our machine eats them sometimes, right?' And I erased it while they were watching and said, 'What message? I'll have the FBI at the courthouse to greet Constance in the morning.'"

Jackson spit soda out all over his hand. "That's... that's... oh my God. Mira! That's... you could all get fired!"

"Constance wanted to get the kids to their homes. This other guy wanted to stop them. I swear to hell, Jackson, we see garbage humans get away with garbage human *excrement* every day, and here was a chance to have kids reunited with their parents and someone was trying to get in this guy's way? So yeah. But if you and Ellery wanted to be in front of the courthouse tomorrow around, I don't know, 6:00 a.m. or so, maybe bring some coffee. I think that guy is going to need some, right?"

Jackson swallowed. What Jason Constance should have was a hero's parade. Coffee was the least they could do.

"And a safe place to sleep and someone who's got his back," Jackson said soberly. "Ellery and I have that covered."

"That's good," she said on an exhaled breath. "I'm... I'm glad. To be honest, my hands haven't stopped shaking since I erased that message. Ethan and El are looking gray at the gills. It's good to know that someone—*someone*—knows what's going on."

"Even better," Jackson said softly, "I think I can talk to someone who might know more of the whole story."

"Oooh." Mira's voice dropped. "Look, even if you can't make it official? I'd *love* to hear the whole story. Seriously, Jackson, you dropped a monster on our lap, and then a leviathan jumped out of the toilet and ate it."

Jackson chuckled a little at the image. "Well, it was a monster, Mira. Let's hope the leviathan wins. I'll call you if anything changes."

"Deal."

He hung up and finished his soda, then rinsed out the glass. After which he went to the bathroom and washed his hands and took three deep breaths. Every time he called this number—every goddamned time—weird shit happened.

But Tage's little brother and sister might be on their way home, and Jackson needed to help.

He didn't keep the number in his cell. He kept it in his head and dialed from memory.

Ring. Ring. Ring. Oh hell. Burton was probably in the middle of an op. *Ring. Ring.* Jesus, this guy might be killing a terrorist or a psycho killer or something. *Ring. Ring. Ri—*

"Sorta in the middle of something right now," Lee Burton said tensely. "Make it quick and good."

Jackson barely bit back the retort of "Said your boyfriend!" because now was not the time—although it was a near thing.

"Why is your boss on his way to Sacramento with half the military on his ass and a school bus full of kids?"

Burton grunted. "Hold on a sec. Dammit, Ace! Not now," he cried. "Wait. What is Jai...? Oh Jesus fucking—"

The sound of the explosion was so loud it came across as silence over the phone, and Jackson stared at the device in his hand as though it would suddenly turn into a television monitor and *show* him all the things he was obviously missing.

He looked at the microwave clock, watched as a minute clicked off, and was about to hang up when Burton's voice came over the phone again.

"I'll kill him," he said, growling. "I'll kill them both. They have both obviously survived, but that wasn't cool. If I have to watch that asshole almost die again, I'm going to come unglued. Mother. Fucker."

Jackson heard the long, shaky sound of a cleansing breath and realized he was sweating in sympathy.

"So," he said, his own voice not too steady. "Everybody's okay?"

"Well, that mobster's not," Burton said. "But he was a scumbag anyway."

Oh Jesus. "Was that mobster's name Dima Siderov?" Jackson asked, because that would be too convenient.

"No," Burton said, dashing his hopes. "It was Alexei Kovacs. But Siderov reports to him, so, uhm, consider your hornets' nest officially kicked. Now, what about Constance?"

"He apparently has a brigadier general trying to stop him from delivering a bunch of kids he intercepted on a trafficking route—"

"Ace intercepted," Burton said succinctly. "And Jai." He pitched his voice to a furious whisper, obviously talking to two people who were nearing his location. "Yes, I'm talking about you two assholes! Which part of drive up and wait until I have a clear shot did you not understand?"

Jackson could hear Ace Atchison's voice clear as a bell through Burton's phone. "The part where there were no kids in that house and a room full of drugs and bad guys with guns."

"And C-4," Jai said. "Don't forget the C-4. That part is very important."

"Yes," Ace confirmed. "Jai saw the C-4 and thought that maybe one guy with a sniper rifle was not what the situation called for."

"So you two idiots thought blowing up half a city block was what the situation called for?" Burton demanded, obviously still seething.

"But Lee," Ace protested. "There's no city anywhere. We're out in the middle of the fucking desert!"

Burton took another one of those cleansing breaths. "Rivers, if I tell you I can get these two bozos to Sacramento by—when do you need them?"

"Tomorrow, in front of the courthouse, 6:00 a.m.?"

"Okay, yeah. I can do that. If I can do that, can I hang up and yell?"

"Knock yourself out," Jackson said. "He's your CO. You know what's best."

"Sure. Fine. See you then."

Burton obviously hit End Call, and Jackson was left alone in the kitchen as darkness washed over the room.

God, it was almost eight o'clock. He'd been on the phone for what felt like hours upon hours. Restlessly he went and put the thing in the charger and set about making dinner. Nothing fancy—broiled pork chops and rice—but it was done when Ellery walked through the door.

"Hey," he said, so happy to see his Counselor that his entire body almost melted with relief. "Does Galen have a car now?"

"Yes," Ellery said, covering a yawn. "And so do you. It should be delivered in a couple of days." Jackson washed his hands and moved to take Ellery's briefcase and set it under the working end of the kitchen table before moving back into his space.

He smelled like heat and a little like sweat and a little like his deodorant, which really wasn't bad stuff.

It all added up to Ellery Cramer, and after the intensity of rearranging the world by phone call, Jackson inhaled the basic smells of sweat and man with gratitude.

"You didn't have to get me a car," he murmured, nuzzling Ellery's neck.

Ellery's shoulders and body sagged a little, and Jackson thought fondly that Ellery went through most of his life with his spine straight and his armor in place, but in Jackson's arms, all of that melted away. His Counselor was soft and very, very improper when Jackson kissed his neck and nibbled his ear.

"Sorta did," Ellery mumbled. "I was being stubborn."

Jackson chuckled, moving to his other ear, sucking on the lobe a little and enjoying the salt. "You? Stubborn? No…."

"No, no." Ellery pulled away with obvious reluctance. "I have to say this or I'm just going to turn into a puddle and blow you."

Oh, and wasn't *that* an appealing image. "Heh heh heh heh heh heh…."

"Seriously, Jackson. Let me say this. And then we can…." His mouth, which had flattened into a grim line, went slack and lopsided. "Uhm, do that other thing."

Jackson grinned, and then, in a moment of delight, turned the tables on him.

"How about food. Have you eaten? You look like you need protein. Sit down. Rest, Ellery. Let me feed you. You should have food before you pass out. You can't neglect your health, you know."

Ellery's chuckle was both tired and a little hysterical. "Oh my God, you're being an asshole."

"I'm the asshole who cooked something that wasn't mac and cheese, so be nice and sit down." Jackson moved to the stove and started plating up their dinner, making sure to give Ellery a generous portion of steamed veggies 'cause they were good for you!

He set down the plate and some cutlery and then set his own place before moving back to the fridge and pulling out a chilled chardonnay.

Jackson had soda that filled him with deep delight—but Ellery really loved one, maybe two, glasses of wine.

He poured Ellery's wine and then a half glass for himself, and sat down to his pork chops, risotto, and salad. He'd taken over some of the cooking while he'd been on sick leave—mostly from sheer boredom— and he was rather proud of how much he'd learned.

Ellery was chewing on a bite of pork chop, eyes closed in appreciation. "Mm… this is good. Did you make the marinade?"

"Store bought, like the risotto in a box," Jackson confessed. "But that sweet-and-sour stuff? That was my idea."

Ellery tasted it. "Hey, that's great! What is that?"

"Balsamic vinegar and strawberry jam," Jackson told him, grinning. "You like?"

Ellery was regarding him in shock. "Balsamic… and…. What in the hell?"

"Sweet and sour." Jackson shrugged and took his own bite, smiling with a certain amount of self-satisfaction. "It totally works."

"Oh my God, it does." Ellery took another bite and washed it down with a sip of wine, and some of the exhaustion that had colored his movements as he'd come in washed away. "And you didn't give me a chance to explain about the car."

Jackson shifted uncomfortably and then winced. Gah! Stitches. On. His. Ass. The fuck! "You don't need—"

"I need to trust you," Ellery blurted.

Jackson looked at him in surprise. "Ellery, I'm not ever playing around on you. You know that!"

Ellery grimaced and nodded. "The fact that you think that's what I meant means I teased you about that way too often, and I'm sorry."

Jackson shrugged and took his own sip of wine. "I have a history," he said.

"And I'm so impressed with you," Ellery replied simply. "In just... all the ways. I look at you, and I think, 'No wonder he's slept with half of Sacramento. Everybody wants him. I don't blame them. He's amazing.'"

Oh my God. Jackson's face was on fire, and he couldn't even look across the table. "I'm a hot mess," he admitted. Ellery knew this. Jackson had taken all those people to his bed to keep the nightmares at bay, because a body in there with him usually meant he could at least wake up before he sat up screaming.

"And it was self-protection," Ellery said softly. "I know this. But that's not why those people came to your bed. They came because you made them feel good. And you still do—just not with sex. And that's amazing. But you have never even given me a doubt that way. In the last year, from the moment we first became a *we*, I knew I was important to you. You weren't going to play around because you and I were serious. I've never doubted—*never* doubted—that you would be faithful, because that's how your heart is made, Jackson Rivers. That's not the kind of trust I was talking about."

Jackson could hardly look at him. His brown eyes were so tired, but he was so earnest. It was one of the qualities Jackson had loved about him from the first. Ellery Cramer did and said exactly what he meant.

"I, uhm, I've scared you a lot," he said, knowing what this was about now.

"You think?" Ellery retorted, but he didn't follow it up with a snort of humor, or even with a sip of wine. "I know you don't think much of yourself, but *I* knew what I had from the very beginning. You are such a good man. And you cared for me, and I was—*am*—so afraid that you'll just throw that away because you don't understand how important you are to me. To your family. But look at this." He gestured to the dinner. "Look at *you*."

Jackson's face had still not gotten any cooler. "I have stitches in my ass," he pointed out, in case Ellery had confused him with someone else.

"Because you were protecting a terrified teacher, and your friend," Ellery said softly. "And not because you were trying to throw yourself away."

"I… I have a lot to live for," Jackson said simply. But it needed to be said. It hadn't always been that way, not even after Ellery. There had been a time—the longest, darkest night in November and its terrible aftermath—during which Jackson had looked at himself and seen who he'd been: the disposable boy, the junkie's drop piece, the department snitch, and meat on the OR table. He hadn't seen who he'd *become*, which was, he suspected, what Ellery was talking about now.

"Tell me," Ellery begged. "I just bought you your fourth car in a year. If you gave birth, we'd be handing our firstborn over to my mother's insurance broker. Tell me what you have to live for."

Jackson had felt less naked when he'd been leaning over the ambulance, ass out, getting stitches put in his backside. But Ellery was here, telling Jackson he had faith that Jackson wasn't going anywhere, and this? This emotional honesty? This was the price you paid for having a good person, a person you loved and desired, walk through the door and look at you the way Ellery looked at Jackson.

"You," he said softly. "Us. Our friends. Our family. Our jobs. A chance to do good in the world. A chance to chase some of the monsters away. My cat. A new kitten. Calling your mother Lucy Satan. Watching my brother's kids grow up. Working with my sister and putting her through law school."

Ellery's eyebrows arched. "I didn't know she wanted to go."

"I think she'd kick ass," Jackson said softly. "Don't you?"

Ellery nodded. "She'd definitely kick ass. But think of how much power she has now."

Jackson laughed and nodded, loving how much Ellery knew his family. How much he cared. "I'll ask her."

"But those are very good things," Ellery said. He gave a crooked smile. "And I appreciate—you have no idea how much I appreciate—being on top of that list. But the two of us, we did a lot of hard growing in this past year. And I don't think you're the same guy who would park your car in front of a drunk driver so he'd hit you and you could have your friend arrest him."

Jackson blinked and then remembered the incident. "Heh heh heh heh…." And then thought of three other courses of action that *wouldn't* involve wrecking his car or hurting his body. "Oh my God," he said, surprised. "You're… you're right."

"I am." Ellery's eyes sparkled.

"You're often right," Jackson said, his heart suddenly swelling. He knew it wasn't a heart attack because the feeling filled him with warmth of hope and not the chill of saying goodbye. And the breathlessness? That was all love.

"I am about this," Ellery said. "I have never worried about you taking care of my heart, Jackson. But I have worried about you taking care of yourself. And I'll always worry because you're not the kind of person to just sit and do nothing when someone is in need. I wouldn't love you like I do if you were. But now I know that if it's at all possible, if there's anything you can do to make it happen, you'll...." His voice grew thick. Choked with a year of worrying, Jackson knew now. Choked with a year of hoping Jackson could learn this simple lesson.

"I'll come home to you," Jackson finished for him.

Ellery nodded and used his napkin to wipe discreetly at his eyes. "So I bought you another fucking CR-V, because this one, I suspect, might make it longer than a month or two."

Jackson stared at his hands for a minute. "Ellery?" he said, feeling pathetic.

"Yeah?"

"You done with your food yet?"

"It'll keep," Ellery said with dignity.

Which was good, because Jackson needed to hold him badly. He moved without thinking to the other side of the table and sank to his knees, wincing as he strained his stitches. Well, fuck, so much for caring for himself. But it had to be done on his knees. He was so humble before this man. He buried his face in Ellery's middle and wrapped his arms around his waist and held him, just held him, while Ellery stroked his hair. The touch was soothing, and while not urgent, it was sexual.

They wanted each other.

They always wanted each other. That fire was always burning—even if it was banked sometimes, smoldering under the weight of busy lives.

"Thank you for the car," Jackson whispered, and when Ellery gave a choked laugh, he realized that was the coward's way out. "Thank you for the faith. Thank you for loving me and waiting for me to grow up."

"Thank you for loving me and keeping me from being old," Ellery whispered back.

Jackson pulled back and grinned at him, trying to ignore the burning in his eyes. "I thought I was making you old."

Ellery grinned back, and then, very carefully, used his thumbs to wipe away the moisture under Jackson's lashes.

"I don't care which," Ellery told him. "As long as you're at least planning on us getting older together, I'm happy."

"I *am* happy," Jackson told him. And then he heard the words in his own head, and they filled him with wonder. "I am."

Ellery gave a broken chuckle before bending over to kiss the top of Jackson's head. "You don't need to sound so surprised."

"Well," Jackson said, trying to keep his voice steady. "I... I didn't think I'd ever be that way."

Ellery was so quiet Jackson had to raise his face to see his expression. His prissy, uptight Counselor, who liked breakfast, lunch, and dinner exactly when breakfast, lunch, and dinner were supposed to be, and who knew how to dot every i and cross every t, looked as undone as a child surprised with Disneyland.

"What?" Jackson asked.

"I have no words," Ellery said. "That's the best compliment I've ever gotten. I love you."

"Those are good words. I love you back."

Jackson probably could have stared at him like that forever, but his strained stitches gave a twinge, and he must have given that away with his expression.

"You should get up," Ellery said, standing so he could help Jackson to his feet.

"Yeah." Jackson paused and saw Ellery's extended hand, remembering a time when he would have forced himself up to prove that he could. To prove that he didn't need any help, that he could take care of Jackson Rivers just fine, even though taking care of himself was probably the thing he was worst at. He reached up deliberately and took Ellery's hand, allowing the leverage to pull him up. He stood, chest to chest with the person he loved most in the world, and closed the gap between them, feeling the moment. The heat of their bodies, the heat of their tears, the heat of their emotions—all of it searing him from the inside out, making him, remaking him, strengthening him so he could be strong enough to hold all the things. What they'd said, what they'd meant. He could handle the total combined weight of the love between them.

Ellery's lips on his were salty but Jackson didn't care. So were his own. A year they'd been doing this, but they'd lost a lot of that year because Jackson hadn't known how to take care of himself, because he'd been hurt, body and soul, in so many different ways. It had taken them a year before their souls were as naked as their bodies, and a few tears were nothing, nothing at all, to kissing a person—to kissing *the* person— with his heart on his lips, his soul in his kiss, no veils of uncertainty between every touch.

They made it to the bed slowly, one item of clothing at a time. Jackson was hurt, but they'd loved each other before while dancing around wounds. This time, they brought each other off with mouths on cocks, the ultimate in reciprocation, and when Ellery cried out and thrust hard to the back of Jackson's throat, Jackson clutched him closer, swallowing everything Ellery had to give, almost surprised when his own orgasm washed over him, Ellery's eager mouth stroking him, pulling his come from his body without fear or reserve.

When they finally parted, each rolling slightly to lie faceup, their hands caressing the other's thighs, Jackson knew his own hands were decidedly shaky.

They might have lain there forever, too, but there was a clatter of silverware from the dining room table, and Billy Bob streaked by the open bedroom door.

He appeared to be holding a pork chop in his mouth.

"Oh for fuck's sake…. *Fuck!*" Jackson sat up too quickly and stretched the stitches they'd just been so careful of only moments ago.

"Is that cat eating your dinner?" Ellery asked, rolling to his side as Jackson got out of bed and limped slightly toward the kitchen.

"How do you know it's not yours?" Jackson called over his shoulder.

"I ate most of my pork chop. You didn't."

"Oh for *fuck's* sake!" Jackson repeated, and then called, "C'mere, you no-thumbs-having motherfucker. Daddy's gonna make a fur pillow out of you."

Ellery laughed softly and fell back against the pillows, obviously content to let Jackson do the cleanup and discipline for the moment.

Good, Jackson thought, limping grimly through the house naked. Ellery had taken care of Jackson plenty over the past year. It was good that sometimes he got to do the same.

Fish Bowls in the Air

ELLERY LAY on his side, watching Jackson chase his cat through the house. After a few entertaining minutes of hearing Jackson swear—and watching him run naked back and forth in front of the door—he swore to himself and gave up. Ellery could hear the muted sounds of cupboards opening and shutting and silverware on plates. When he realized Jackson was going to do dishes too, Ellery got out of bed just long enough to put underwear on and grab his phone.

There was something really sexy about a naked Jackson doing dishes in his kitchen. He had obviously set about making the night nice for Ellery—for the two of them, really—so Ellery was going to stay there and savor.

Loving Jackson Rivers had never been easy. Coming to this place, this emotionally satisfying place right here, was like waltzing with a porcupine until his quills turned to feathers. It was like skipping over rolling logs until you met a brick road and could skip down it instead. Like coating yourself with sirloin steak and walking through a panther cage—and coming out on the other side for a fresh shower and some gelato for your trouble.

A year it had taken them, to get to this place. There had been progress and there had been setbacks, and they had both kept trying and trying again, because separating after everything they'd been through together had absolutely not once been on the roster of possibilities.

And now, happily sexed but body still humming in anticipation of more, Ellery remembered a moment the year before, when Jackson had scorned the idea of a wedding because, in his words, "Who in the fuck would want to marry me?"

Ellery would.

Ellery had from the very beginning.

At first it had been a dream, a distant hope, a thing he tormented himself with before he closed his eyes on the worst nights.

The ones when Jackson had been in the hospital, for example. There'd been a lot of those.

But lately, it had become more and more an expected, hoped-for part of the horizon. Someday, Ellery was going to ask him. And when he did, he knew Jackson would say yes.

Because Jackson loved Ellery enough to give him everything. Including hope.

Ellery pulled the comforter over his bottom half and practically giggled to himself.

Especially hope.

He could have gone to sleep happy right there, but he just had to check his phone.

"Jackson!" he called, hopping out of bed. "Jackson, what did you *do* while I was gone?"

"I'm sorry?" Jackson murmured, and Ellery heard the start of the dishwasher as he rounded the curve. "I made some calls. Why?"

Ellery held out his phone. "Whatever you did, you managed to piss off the DOJ. My mother needs to talk to us!"

Jackson's eyes got amazingly big. "I... hold on. I have to go put on some pants."

Ellery rolled his eyes and turned to follow him back into the bedroom. "We're not Zooming. This isn't on Skype. How's she going to know if you've got pants on or not?"

"Oh, she'll know," Jackson muttered direly. "Lucy Satan will *know*."

"My mother's name is... you know, never mind. Call her Lucy Satan. She likes it. I think it makes her feel young."

Jackson had scooped up their clothes as he'd stalked back into the bedroom, and now he was rooting for his underwear before pulling out a pair of transparent nylon basketball shorts from the chest of drawers Ellery had bought exclusively for Jackson that summer, along with clothes to fill it.

Ellery looked at the shorts in despair. Jackson had actually volunteered to retire most of his old clothes from activewear—probably because they were rotting, thread by thread, from his body. He kept the old stuff for mooching about the house, which made complete sense until Ellery had to see him wearing shorts that were transparent and sort of slinky and threatening to reveal all of Jackson's best parts as he moved.

"Please," Ellery said through a dry throat. "If we're going to talk to my mother, could you put on some sleep pants that don't give me wood?"

Jackson paused long enough to give him a filthy, *filthy* smile of absolute ownership.

"Heh heh heh heh heh heh…."

Ellery arched one eyebrow and regarded him stonily, hoping that the knowledge of exactly how badly Ellery's mother could put a crimp in their sex life would make him see sense.

After a moment, Jackson grunted and replaced the basketball shorts with a new pair of lightly woven cotton—just as cool, just as practical, but they apparently didn't tickle Ellery's little kink.

"Thank you," Ellery said as Jackson slid them on. "Now, do I need to know what this is about before I call my—"

His phone went off in his hand just as Jackson grimaced.

"Hello, Mother," Ellery said, soothed to talk to her in spite of himself. "What can we do for you?"

His mother's voice was, as always, reasonable and measured. Ellery had very rarely seen his mother ruffled. But that didn't mean he didn't know when she was pissed.

"Ellery, is Jackson there with you?"

"We're both here, Mother," Ellery responded.

"Hi, ma'am," Jackson said, his voice taking on the reluctant-schoolboy tones he often used when addressing Taylor Cramer.

"Good. May I ask what you boys have been up to today?"

Jackson's eyes widened in apparent panic, and Ellery gave him a meaningful look. Oh, yes. There would be consequences.

"Well," Ellery drawled, "I got a seventeen-year-old boy out of prison where he should have never been, leveraged a bailiff and a prison guard into giving up the blackmailer who wanted to keep him there, and bought Jackson an economy-sized SUV."

"Really? That's good to hear." Taylor Cramer never lied, so Jackson's little smirk of triumph wasn't lost on Ellery. "That larger vehicle is quite impractical for tooling around town."

"It is," Ellery said, ignoring the urge to remind her that they usually drove his car. "Jackson came back to work yesterday, and he really does need a vehicle of his own."

"Came back to work yesterday," Taylor purred. "Hm. So, Jackson, what did you do *today*?"

"Well, I offered an assist on getting the kid out of jail," Jackson said, nodding at Ellery like he could *will* Ellery into compliance, "and then Henry and I went to the high school to do some interviews, and then I came home and rested, because I am a good boy."

"Ellery?"

"Yes, Mother?"

"Are you and Jackson sitting close together?"

They were, in fact, their naked thighs touching as Ellery held the phone.

"Yes, Mother."

"You should move, dear boy. God is going to strike your boyfriend down where he sits for telling such outrageous lies."

Ellery made a silent fist pump and mouthed "*Yes!*" in Jackson's general direction.

"I told the *truth*!" Jackson protested.

"Sure," Ellery retorted. "But you left out the part where you got shot at and cut up your leg wiggling out of the window to confront a potential assassin."

"*And*," Taylor Cramer interjected, her voice irritated in the way that only a particularly fractious child can irritate a parent, "he left out the part where he agreed to help a rogue military operative spirit a shipment of valuable property away from the officer who needs it to help with an op!"

"You did what?" Ellery asked, staring at Jackson.

"How did you know about that?" Jackson said, obviously surprised. "I didn't even have a chance to tell Ellery!"

"Why would you do that in the first place?" Taylor demanded. "I've got a brigadier general pounding down my door, telling me to get my son-in-law back in line. What product is so important that you would agree to help law enforcement steal it from a military operation?"

"*Children*!" Jackson burst out. "Children. Okay? You all remember Jason Constance?"

Ellery could hear his mother's complete stillness through 3,000 miles of fiber-optic network, and he remembered earlier that year, when Constance and his friend Burton had guarded his mother for a week because she had pissed off the wrong people in her job as a corporate attorney who often dealt with military contractors.

"I do," Taylor said softly. "Is he our 'rogue military operative'?"

"He is, ma'am," Jackson replied, his voice quiet again. "What happened, I believe, is that Ace and Jai—you remember them?"

"I remember Ace," Ellery's mother said. "I never had a chance to meet their friend."

"Well, you'd remember him if you met him," Jackson understated. The man was nearly seven feet tall and built like a refrigerator. Who wouldn't remember him? "I believe they intercepted a shipment of children being taken to Las Vegas. The young man we got out of prison had a brother and a sister who were stolen by the local mob. They wanted to silence him and basically let him get eaten by the prison system, so they threatened the kids and then shipped them off anyway."

"That's reprehensible." It sounded like her throat had turned to concrete, and Ellery didn't blame her. He and Jackson had been dealing with that feeling for the last two days.

"It is. And Ace and Jai rescued the kids and then called their friend Burton, who probably told his CO—"

"Colonel Jason Constance," she supplied.

"Yes, ma'am. And Constance is a good guy. He came to help fetch the children and was told that they were going to be used as bait to get the attention of the mob boss in Vegas who was selling kids."

"Oh no," Taylor groaned.

"Oh yes. I don't imagine he'd take to that idea too well. I...." Jackson grimaced, and Ellery gave him a look.

"What?" Ellery mouthed.

"Later," Jackson mouthed back. Then, into the phone, he said, "Well, I believe Constance found another way to address the guy in Vegas, and he decided to escort the children back to Sacramento himself."

But Ellery's mother was a long way from stupid. "Another way to address the situation in Vegas?" she asked archly.

"Yes, ma'am."

"Would you know of any of the particulars involved in that?" she asked.

Jackson grimaced. "Particulars?" He gave Ellery a helpless look. "Ma'am, would you *want* to know any of the particulars involved in that?"

There was a silence on the line that lasted at least six thousand years.

"Perhaps not," Taylor said at last. "So you are going to help your friend deliver the children?"

"That was the plan, ma'am," Jackson said, and Ellery arched an eyebrow at him. "I was going to tell you later," he murmured.

Well, fine. For once they'd put the relationship first. Sue them.

"Good, then. After he's done that, perhaps you'd offer to find him a place, an isolated sort of place, where nobody would possibly look for him. Some place out of the way. Low key. Give it a month, at least. Treat it like a vacation."

Jackson's eyebrows shot upward. "You want us to send Jason Constance to a cabin in the woods for a month?"

"That would be best, yes," Ellery's mother said. "I'm sure you can think of the particulars. By the time he comes back, I would imagine this entire situation would have blown over."

"Okay, sure," Jackson said, holding up his hands. "I, uh… well, we'll think of something."

"I'm sure you will, dear boy."

Ellery rolled his eyes. His mother really did adore Jackson. Apparently he'd almost upended the whole of the Washington, DC, military complex, and he got pat on the head.

"Ellery, you'll help him?" Taylor confirmed.

"Of course, Mother," Ellery said on a sigh.

"Good. Well, it's really very late here. I'll leave you two boys to hash things out on your end. You're doing well, I trust?"

And suddenly Ellery's earlier glow was back. He smiled at Jackson, who looked away with a crescent of color on his cheeks. "Yes. We're doing very well."

"Jackson's not overdoing it?"

"Of course he is," Ellery said, still smiling at him. "But he also really did come home to rest. I don't think he meant to cause quite so much havoc on the phone while he was here."

Jackson looked up and nodded enthusiastically, and Ellery brushed his lower lip with a careful thumb. The man just couldn't sit still—but he'd try.

"Well, good," his mother said softly. "Jackson?"

"Yes, ma'am?"

"Remember you're loved. Don't roll your eyes at me, young man. It's a true thing. We look forward to seeing you two over winter break. Jackson, you still have to bring a Hanukkah gift. You know that happens every year."

Jackson snickered into Ellery's shoulder. "I do know that."

"And don't think I've forgotten your birthday. There will be a card and a gift in the mail."

Ellery actually heard him swallow. "That's kind, uhm, Lucy."

"That's my boy." Ellery had seen the card she'd sent him last year, right when he'd gotten out of the hospital. It had been a week or two late, but then, he and Jackson had really just gotten together. She'd signed it "Lucy Satan," Jackson's personal name for her. It may not have been flattering, but she had apparently claimed it as hers.

"Bye, boys. Try not to get into too much trouble. We love you."

"Love you, Mother!"

"Bye, Lucy Satan!"

Ellery hung up and looked at him grimly. "So, what was the part you didn't want to tell her over the phone."

Jackson's face screwed up in a grimace. "It involved Burton, Ace, Jai, a few sniper rounds, and some C-4."

Ellery's eyes widened. He'd been there the last time those particular people had been involved with sniper rounds and C-4. "May God have mercy on all involved," he said, totally and completely serious. "What about Constance?"

Jackson's grimace turned deadly grim. "I think he's being chased by mobsters *and* the US military. He's planning to arrive at the courthouse tomorrow with the kids. I think you should be there to help the human trafficking division take custody of the victims, and me and Henry should maybe…." Jackson made vague motions with his hands.

"Spirit Constance away," Ellery said. "Yes, I think that's a plan. I'll reserve a cabin up near Tahoe, literally a cabin in the woods. There's a couple of small lakes up by Donner Pass. A friend of mine had a fishing cabin up there. I'm pretty sure I can find one for rent. Was there anything else you got done by phone? Because I did a bit while I was waiting for the damned auto dealership too."

Jackson laughed with only a little bitterness and sighed. "Here." He stood and offered Ellery a hand up off the bed. "Let's go sit over some ice cream and compare notes." He hid part of a yawn behind his hand. "We need to be up early tomorrow. Constance is going to be there around six in the morning, and you and I need to debrief."

Ellery took his hand and allowed Jackson to haul him up into a half-naked, chest-to-chest kiss. Jackson nuzzled his neck for a moment, bringing them both back to those few breathless moments in bed, and then gave him one last brief press of lips before pulling him to the kitchen table and back to work.

"Hey, did you ever get that pork chop back from your cat?" Ellery asked.

Jackson grunted. "I got him to eat it in the kitchen. Does that count?"

Ellery groaned. "No. No, it does not count. What are we bringing a new kitten into? Have you thought of that?"

Jackson stilled and looked at him soberly. "A better life here than in a cage," he said.

Well, couldn't argue with that. "Let's make sure it's a tough kitty," Ellery decided.

"The battles will be epic."

Of course they would be.

HALF AN hour later they'd basically killed a small container of lemon-raspberry gelato, and Ellery was still in awe.

"You got all that done on the phone?"

Jackson shrugged. "Well, yes. K-Ski has protection, we're going to meet Constance tomorrow, and we may have Tage Dobrevk's siblings recovered before this thing is done. Wasn't much. Now you tell me yours."

Ellery grinned. "Oh boy, did Jade and AJ dig up some information for you."

Mostly Ellery's discussions had consisted of downloads of files from Jade on Ziggy Ivanov and bookmaker's odds, but it was still a wealth of information.

Jackson grinned. "I knew they would. Shoot!"

"Okay, so, Ziggy Ivanov is actually nearly thirty years old."

Jackson's jaw dropped. "No, really?"

"Yessir. He spent his youth in a gymnasium"—he pronounced it the Eastern European way, in which he drew out the *A* and made it "ah"—"as a competitive gymnast and tumbler. He didn't make it to the Olympics, but that was fine. He was recruited by the Siderov family in his teens. It's estimated he was their grease man or thief from the time he was fifteen. When he washed out of the gymnasium, he went to work for them full-time. When Siderov moved his operations to California via the influx of Russian emigres here, his skill as a thief and pretty face made him a natural to infiltrate the high school. Siderov's organization has a couple of businesses—"

"Let me guess," Jackson said. "Drugs, gambling, and sex trade."

"You cheated," Ellery said, taking a modest bite of ice cream.

"Cheated?" Jackson rolled his eyes. "I got that information the hard way!"

Well, couldn't argue that.

"So," Ellery said, "about the gambling...."

Jackson banged his head gently on the kitchen table. "I was going to text Fetzer and Hardison."

"No need," Ellery said smugly. "Turns out AJ's delinquent boyfriend—"

Jackson gave him a hard look. The gentle AJ had managed—quite without guile, they were both sure of it—to snag the attention of a kid a little younger than he was who'd just finished a six-month sentence for distribution and was now doing his best to go clean. Their courtship had been a little down, a lot of up, and now AJ's roommate was happy to report there had been actual sleepovers.

Ellery took a deep breath and tried again. "AJ's reformed and much-improved boyfriend," he said virtuously, "knows some guys."

"Doesn't every ex-con 'know some guys'?" Jackson asked.

"You're the one who runs the little transition condo," Ellery told him, although in fact Ellery was very proud of the fact that Jackson used his half of his old duplex to help transition nonviolent offenders back into the real world. "You'd know."

Jackson shrugged. "Okay, okay, AJ's boyfriend knows some guys. What do these guys know?"

Ellery took the spoon and blopped a little bit of ice cream on the end of Jackson's nose. "You're so impertinent," he said grandly, while Jackson giggled like a kid and tried to wipe the ice cream off and then licked it from the back of his hand.

"Oh my God. We have to be up in, like, five hours. You know that right?"

Ellery let out a breath. Well, yes. And Jackson was looking tired, although he didn't want to point that out. He may have been champing at the bit these last weeks, but he was supposed to ease into his workload, not hit the ground at full speed.

"Okay," Ellery conceded, setting the pint down and watching as Jackson picked it up and took a bite. Oh, nice. Jackson's constant struggle against what was very probably an eating disorder was never going to go away in spite of his resolution to live healthily. It was nice to see him eat something unforced, with joy, because it was a human thing to do. "So Ty Townsend apparently had the bookies in a real spin this year. You know that I know very little about football, but he was, in AJ's words, 'the shit.'"

Jackson snickered. "Yes, the kids are calling it that these days."

"Whatever. So, Ty's 'the shit,' and he's going to a Pac-12 school, and people are really excited about him. Now, we've worked really hard to keep Ty's arrest out of the papers, and Ty is still, as far as anyone knows, scheduled to start training camp at the end of this week."

"Yes," Jackson mumbled over another mouthful of sweet.

"Anyway, *somebody* in the gambling community let something slip because betting just went up considerably against Ty's school this year. All of the longshot bettors just changed their odds, and I have no idea how that works, but AJ's roommate seemed to think it was very exciting."

"Yeah. That's what Henry suspected."

"He was very humble about that when I told him," Ellery said with a completely straight face.

"How many fist-pumps?" Jackson asked dryly.

"A complete lap around the car dealership," Ellery said, although he suspected part of that had been to let off steam. Ellery and Jackson weren't the only ones to be a little stressed over the last two days.

"What car did John and Galen get?" he asked idly, because in spite of the fact that they really did need to catch up, the fact was, they were used to exchanging parts of their day at the end of it. Small conversations about the people they cared for had become part of their routine, and Ellery's heart gave an extra special throb when he realized how important it was to both of them.

"Galen apparently let him pick," Ellery said with a snort, and then he sobered. "And Henry asked first about the amenities for the back seat. I was thinking he'd go SUV, but he made it a luxury sedan because it would be harder for Galen to get in and out of an SUV."

Jackson held a hand to his chest and blinked rapidly. "Our little redneck is all grown up and emotionally available in three short months. It happens so fast!"

"Of course, right after he told me that, I confirmed the hunch about the gambling, and he did the lap around the dealership."

Jackson pretended to wipe a tear. "But still a good ol' boy at heart. Does a body good."

"God, you're obnoxious."

Jackson grinned with all his teeth. "It's an art." Then he sobered. "Okay, so Ty was *not* a random target, and it wasn't just because he's of color. They wanted him out of commission to make money on the gambling front, but I'm still betting they were trying to get those cops somewhere else. Have we checked out those empty buildings that Fetzer said were left unpatrolled?"

Ellery rolled his eyes. "Yes, Jackson, because there's an army of us and we can all split ourselves up into clones and multitask like that."

Jackson snorted. "Okay, okay. It's on the to-do list after we get Jason to safety. Have you—"

Ellery held up his tablet, which had been open on the table as they'd debriefed. "I've got a couple of places scoped out," he said. "One local, one in Tahoe like you suggested, and one down on the coast."

"Monterey?" Jackson asked, his voice rising eagerly.

"Yes. You liked it there?" Ellery asked.

"So much." His voice dropped, and Ellery smirked as he seemed to remember that reality bites. "But maybe next summer."

"Or did you want to do San Diego again?"

Jackson blinked. "Hm, I'll have to think," he said. "Balboa Park versus the aquarium…." Then he paused. "You know, we're planning for next year."

Ellery bit his lip. "Yeah. I know. We planned for winter holidays too."

Jackson nodded. "This planning for the future thing—gotta tell you. Used to freak me out, but I'm starting to get into it."

Ellery leaned in to kiss him, and Jackson opened his mouth to let the kiss linger. The mix of cold ice cream and warm man was practically irresistible, and they necked at the table for an embarrassingly long time before Jackson pulled away and covered his mouth with his hand. "Night," he mumbled. "Getting on."

He took what was left of the ice cream, put the lid on, and threw it in the freezer, moving with just enough stiffness to let Ellery know his stitches were hurting. Ellery stood to join him in the kitchen, fetching the ibuprofen while he was there and setting the bottle down in front of Jackson at the counter.

"Fine," Jackson muttered, but he downed the painkillers with a quick swallow of water. "Okay. Have we covered everything?"

"Dima Siderov's organization," Ellery said promptly. "I was getting to that. You know Tage's address?"

Jackson screwed up his eyes. "Mob central?"

"Yes. And James Cosgrove was Dima Siderov's nephew."

Jackson gasped as the implications hit him. "Wait—no, that's not right."

"I assure you it is. That's what AJ pulled up. Why?"

Jackson flailed. "Because… because you do *not* order a hit on your eighteen-year-old nephew because he asked for mercy! I know we've all seen the John Wick movies, but usually there has to be some *action* involved before somebody takes another person out. A betrayal or something. All James Cosgrove did was ask his uncle if it was necessary to set Ty up. That's it. That's the end. I mean, worst-case scenario, Dima says, 'You are a sweet adorable little summer child. Now, don't talk to me again or I backhand you.' But he doesn't order Ziggy to make a *hit* on his *nephew*."

Jackson suddenly rocked back on his heels. "Oh my God," he said.

Ellery did the same thing. "Oh my God," he echoed.

They both looked at each other and said it almost at the same time.

"Ziggy acted alone."

"Dima really thinks Tage did it!"

Jackson scrubbed at his scalp with his fingertips. "That explains the kids. They kidnap the kids and then ship them off. Arrest Tage and then have him killed in prison. Don't give the family a chance to even so much as hint that Tage didn't do it. *Ziggy* did it—we've always assumed that. But *Dima Siderov* has not!"

"But why?" Ellery asked. "Why would Sergio Ivanov kill his boss's nephew? What practical purpose would that serve?"

Jackson started to prowl the kitchen, stiff movements and sore ass notwithstanding. "Pink pills," he muttered. "Pink pills. They've been bothering me. Pink pills with butterflies on them." He paused. "What sort of drugs does Siderov deal?"

"Kitchen meth," Ellery said promptly.

"No opioids? No shipments of anything from anywhere?"

"No. Remember the case that put you in the hospital in June?"

Jackson grunted. "Robert Sampson and Candy Cormier, yes. They held a corner on the pill and opioid trade. I'm sure that void's been filled."

"Well, yes, but according to Jade's intel, Siderov only deals kitchen meth to his own community. It's a side gig for him, not his bread and butter."

"So what in the fuck is Ziggy doing with pretty pink tablets of X with little butterflies on them?"

Ellery sucked in a breath. He remembered that detail too. "That's not Siderov's MO," he said slowly. "Ziggy is working for somebody else."

Jackson nodded. "And Ziggy killed James to keep him from going to his uncle about Ty Townsend because that would give Ziggy away. That's why the attempt at the entire family. He flat out didn't want Dima Siderov to know…." Jackson trailed off, then, "Uh-oh."

Ellery stared at him. "What?"

"When Mira called, she said Maxim and Sophie were a shipment to the big boss. Dima's superior."

Ellery nodded. "Yes, and…?"

"And, uhm, remember how I talked to Burton?"

Ellery's nod was slower this time. The last time Jackson had "called Burton," Burton had taken out a psychotic drug dealer with one impossible sniper shot. They'd had a tough time explaining how one of their main bad guys had come to be missing half his head, but Jackson's heart had been giving out at the time, so Sean Kryzynski—and through him, the department—had given them a pass. Ellery wasn't so sure how another Burton save was going to go over.

"Yes."

Jackson swallowed. "Well, like I said, there were some shots fired and a big explosion, and Burton said he'd get here tomorrow to help watch Constance's back."

"Which is good," Ellery said, because Burton did have a way of managing things.

"Well, if Burton's explosion did what I think it did—"

"Kill off the big boss Siderov reported to," Ellery said, seeing the horizon Jackson was waving from, waiting for Ellery to catch up.

"Yes. Exactly. If Burton's explosion killed off Siderov's superior, then Ziggy is running out of options. Siderov is either growing suspicious or about to start, and Ziggy just killed his nephew and used his supply train to cover it up. He's too hot on the street right now to so much as stir a whisker outside whatever rat hole he's hanging out in. If Siderov's superior was the guy he's sucking up to, Ziggy doesn't have any cover whatsoever, and if he *wasn't* the guy Ziggy was sucking up to...." Jackson frowned.

"There's a power vacuum," Ellery said, finally seeing what Jackson saw. "And if there's a power vacuum, now is the time for Ziggy and his new friend to make a move."

Jackson stood up suddenly, looking exhausted and intense. "We need to warn Tage's parents. We... I can't believe we're saying this, but we need to warn Dima Siderov."

Ellery stayed put. "Why? Dima Siderov is a bad man, Jackson. He traffics children and sells bathtub meth. He's no better or worse than the guy who's taking his place."

Jackson scowled. "No, I could give a rat's ass about Siderov, but look at Ziggy's scorched-earth progression right now. Tage's in protective custody, but his parents are relying on Siderov's protection. They're going to get hurt. Everybody in that apartment complex is going to get hurt, and some of them are just people looking for affordable housing!"

Okay. "Well, we're not SWAT!" Ellery retorted. "Look, you know people, I know people. I'm going to call Arizona Brooks and tell her to get ready to start processing people. You call Christie and Fetzer and Hardison and give them a heads-up. And while you're on the phone, get our Kevlar out of the closet. Tomorrow promises to be a *treat*."

"But shouldn't we *do* something?" Jackson protested, and Ellery *did* stand up now, because having this fight was much more impactful if they were standing three feet from each other and yelling.

"We *are*. We're telling people with guns and vests and tactical gear where to find other people with guns. *Jackson*, it's time to *think*. This isn't meeting a bad guy on accident, or rescuing someone from a situation because nobody has your back. This is having valuable information for people who are better equipped to deal with it. If we go out tonight and get shot because we're in the middle of a gunfight, who's going to have

Constance's back? Who's going to take care of Sophie and Maxim? This thing we're in the middle of? It's bigger than us. It's *huge*. And we're not out in the desert where we can just shoot a bunch of shit up and blow up a car and hope for the best. If we go cowboy here, we will get hurt, we will get others hurt, and we will not do the good things that we are capable of doing because we were someplace we had no business being. Now get on the phone and call the cavalry, young soldier, and I'll do the same thing."

"The cavalry was a bunch of racist pussies who tortured women and children, you realize that, right?"

"Well, Custer was a bad man, but not all of them were—"

"Genocide, Ellery."

"Well, sue me for a bad example. And make your goddamned phone call before I blow on you and knock you on your ass!"

Jackson's face went absolutely blank, and then Ellery heard it too. "Don't," he muttered.

"You're gonna blow me and knock my ass?" Jackson asked, his lips quirking up reluctantly.

"If that's how you want to do things," Ellery said, pinching the bridge of his nose. His voice gentled. "Make your calls, Jackson. I'll make mine. We have to be up in—" He looked at the microwave over the stove. "—less than five hours. Let's do what we can."

"Fine," Jackson muttered. "Hate this."

"Yeah, mortality's a bitch. Call."

Jackson stalked off, muttering to himself, and for a heartbeat Ellery mourned the quiet moment they'd just been sharing.

Then he remembered that he'd won. Jackson had conceded that— this once—being in the thick of the battle wasn't the best way for the two of them to win the war.

Oh God, they might survive to see forty.

Hell, they might survive to get *married*.

Ellery was going to give a *truckload* of money to his synagogue to spend on good works, because whether the rabbi thought so or not, he was *sure* somebody was looking down on them and perhaps just once had whispered in Jackson's ear.

Swimming Fury

GOD, IT sucked when Ellery was right sometimes. By the time Jackson had gotten off the phone, he'd woken people up and pissed people off, but he'd gotten Fetzer, Hardison, Andre Christie, and the entire SWAT team mobilized to the Dobrevks' apartment complex.

Christie had been particularly glad Jackson and Ellery weren't in the thick of things.

"Stay home," he'd muttered, apparently texting someone else while he got out of bed and got dressed. "You don't know these apartment complexes."

"The fuck I don't," Jackson replied shortly. Rabbit warrens, with ins and outs and often no rhyme or reason. It was easy to lose a suspect in one and easy to be ambushed while you were finding your way.

"Okay, maybe you do. But if there's a gang takeover going on, there will be a boatload of guns out there and too many civilians as it is. This is a good tip—and you could save some lives tonight—but not if we're watching your ass too."

Jackson growled, hating being sidelined, but then he remembered Kryzynski. Odds were, even if Sean and Jackson trained together every day for a year, there would have been no way to predict what had happened when Ziggy Ivanov had leaped over that railing and stabbed Sean Kryzynski.

But Jackson couldn't know that. Not for sure.

He'd spent nearly ten years expecting nobody to have his back and counting on good luck and good reflexes to save his life. Relying on those things to keep everyone else safe while he ran around and stirred shit up was a good way to get other people killed, and that was no goddamned fair.

And the fact was, the cops didn't know who he was and didn't trust him to wipe his own ass. He could be doing everything right, and he'd still get people killed because they'd be watching him instead of the bad guys.

"Fine. Whatever. But if this pans out, I want you all to remember this the next time shit goes down. I'm one of the good guys, and just like you, we want the innocent people safe and the real bad guys off the street."

Christie blew out a breath. "We're starting to get that. Let me go be a cop, and I'll let you know what goes down."

"Fine. Be safe. Don't get dead. If I have to visit you in the hospital, I might have to wipe the floor with more beat cops, and that's not what Ellery had in mind when he told me to make nice."

Christie's chuckle was bad-guy dirty. "I heard about that. You beat the crap out of some of the guys who've given Sean the worst time for being out. So, well done." He sobered. "And I'll keep you in the loop. That's not bullshit. You're doing good work here. Later."

"Later," Jackson grunted and hit End Call. Okay. Fine. He could do this. He called Fetzer next, and she was a little grouchier about being woken up.

"Seriously? You are being serious here calling at this hour? Some of us have to work, Rivers!"

"I'm one of them," Jackson retorted. "And I've got a 6:00 a.m. meeting that promises to be a bear. Did you know that Dima Siderov's boss got blown up tonight, and Ziggy Ivanov is probably working for his archrival? Because that's our theory right now, and if that's the case…."

Fetzer had stayed alive on the streets for too long to not understand the implications.

"Oh holy Jesus," she muttered, and Jackson could hear waking-up noises in the background. "This could get bloody. This could get…. I'm going to hang up now and call the dispatch sergeant, and I will call you if we all survive the night."

"Be safe out there. Keep Hardison safe. You're the only blue uniforms I can actually stand."

Fetzer's grim chuckle echoed over the phone line. "Don't gush on, my boy. I've got shit to do. Stay put, you hear?"

"That 6:00 a.m. meeting is really important," Jackson told her. "If I don't make that, this other shit might not matter."

"Well, we all got a job to do. Stay safe."

"Will do."

Jackson signed off then and swore. Oh, he hated this. Sending other people out into the thick of things while he hung back was one of the hardest things he'd ever had to do.

But Ellery had been right. They had people counting on them in the morning, and this thing was bigger than the two of them.

Irritated and unhappy, he stalked to the closet and got out their Kevlar, then unlocked the gun safe and pulled out their guns. While Ellery finished his calls, he grimly set about cleaning and loading their weapons and hoped their regular trips to the gun range since March had made Ellery a better shot.

It certainly hadn't made Jackson happier at seeing Ellery with a gun, but there was grim shit going down. They needed all the backup they could get.

Ellery came in while he was packing up the cleaning kit and putting the guns back in the safe for the next morning. By the time Jackson had washed his hands and brushed his teeth, Ellery was in bed, setting his phone to go off at unholy buttcrack a.m., and Jackson was feeling the exhaustion of the day seeping into his bones.

"God," he muttered, yawning and turning out the light. "So much for a nap."

"So much for recovery," Ellery fretted. "You were supposed to ease into things."

"I *am* easing into things," Jackson told him soberly. "If I'm not out at that apartment complex getting my ass shot off, I'd say I'm being a model citizen."

Ellery's brow furrowed, and his chin jutted. "That's not funny," he said. "Dammit, Jackson—"

Jackson put two fingers over Ellery's mouth and then removed them for a quick kiss. "Don't. We're both tired. We have to be up at fuck-all in the morning. Let's go to sleep and not argue so we can wake up and not argue and do the shit we need to do because it's important, okay?"

He saw the reluctant curve to Ellery's lips, and a little bit of triumph soothed the parts of his soul left raw by staying out of the fray.

"I would love to go to sleep and not argue," Ellery said.

"Good." Jackson smiled a little. "Now roll over so I can spoon you."

Ellery's mouth quirked. "Can I be big spoon tonight?"

Jackson searched his eyes in the dark. "Why?"

"Because I need to is all."

He sounded so much like Jackson himself that Jackson's heart gave a little throb. He hadn't been easy on Ellery Cramer in the past year. Maybe Ellery just needed to feel in control of Jackson, of the two of them.

"Sure."

Jackson rolled over and Ellery's arm wound around his middle. "Thank you," Ellery whispered. "Thank you for staying with me."

Jackson laced their fingers together and spoke the truth. "Nowhere else I'd rather be."

His phone rang less than fifteen minutes later.

"Jackson?"

Jackson recognized the voice, but barely. Tage's cousin, Sascha, fresh from prison, working hard to get his life back on the straight and narrow.

"Sascha? What's up?" God, fifteen minutes. He actually had *drool* on his chin because he'd been asleep.

"My aunt and uncle," Sascha said fretfully. "They are at their apartment building, and there are shots and shouting. Jackson, they're crouched in the bathtub, and they're freaked the fuck out, and there's cops all over the apartment complex, and if they get caught talking to the cops, they're *toast*. You know it, I know it. Tage will never be able to come out of hiding." His voice caught. "Even if Sophie and Maxim come home, they will always be in danger. Jackson, you have to get them out of there. Please. For me. They can't be seen talking to cops! That's the only way I could keep Tage safe in jail was because he didn't have any connection to the police."

God. And what Sascha wasn't saying was that his only hope of staying gang- and bullet-free while he got his life together was to avoid any notice whatsoever, and that meant his family too. Sascha, in fact, was one of the people Boris and Olga Dobrevk were trying to protect by not going into hiding with Tage.

He swung his feet over the edge of the bed. "I'll get 'em," he muttered. "Can I bring them to you?"

"Yeah." Sascha had been born in Sacramento, and he had no accent and no connection, really, to the people probably in the middle of starting a war. He just had his aunt and uncle. His parents had gone back to Russia when he'd been in middle school.

And he'd called Jackson because Jackson was his only hope.

"Be ready for me to bring them by," he said. "Tell them I'm coming."

He stood stiffly and slid on yesterday's jeans while Ellery rolled over in bed. "What in the hell...?"

"The Dobrevks need me," he said, his voice dropping, hoping Ellery understood. "It was one thing when it was just a big cop clusterfuck and nobody needed little ol' me in the middle. But this is different. If the Dobrevks are taken in by the cops and not arrested, they're fucked."

Ellery sucked in a breath, and Jackson knew he couldn't argue.

"And even if they're arrested, they're still fucked," Jackson said softly. "Just like Tage was about to be. One way or another, they're going to be material witnesses to people with a lot more money and a lot more power, and not even the world's best defense attorney will be able to save them." Jackson gave what he hoped was a conciliatory smile, and his heart hurt when Ellery looked away.

"I'll be back," he promised rashly. "I'm just going to sneak in, grab the little old people, and sneak out. I promise—"

"Stop," Ellery said, voice shaking, and Jackson felt it in the pit of his groin.

He could lose Ellery over this.

It's why he'd backed off before. Why he'd called the police and gave them the tip and told them he'd stay put. Because Ellery was scared, and goddammit, hadn't he put Ellery through enough?

But this was different. When it was going to be a police roundup of different gang factions gunning for each other, Jackson had absolutely no place in the battle. There was nothing for him to do, and he'd promised he'd think twice about putting himself in danger. But the Dobrevks were innocent, and Jackson had a tie to them, and someone had asked— begged—that he keep them safe.

This was who he was. If Ellery couldn't understand this, all of Jackson's "being good" was not going to save them.

Ellery had gotten out of bed, still in his underwear, and was looking pale and awkward and vulnerable in the faint light from the bathroom.

"Ellery—"

Ellery put a shaking finger over Jackson's mouth, and Jackson closed his eyes. Then Ellery's voice, nothing more than a trembling rasp, whispered in the darkness.

"Come home to me."

Jackson's eyes flew open, and he pressed Ellery's fingers to his lips and kissed them.

"If there's breath in my body," he said, and then took Ellery's mouth, hard and urgent, because the blood surging through his chest was hard and urgent.

He hadn't lost him. Ellery understood.

Jackson would die for this man.

He could damned sure live for him.

HE DROVE the Tank and parked it behind the line of cherry tops on the side of the block covered by the apartment complex, searching out a familiar face.

The complex itself sat under the grainy luminescence of the soda lights, looking deathly still. Nobody in the quad, nobody walking from their car to the pool in the humid light. No lights on, no windows open to catch a stray breeze.

Every now and then came the *pop-pop-pop* of gunfire, and then silence.

Jackson's gut churned. It was a meat grinder, fuck him if it wasn't.

Fetzer and Hardison were easy to spot. They were hanging behind the SWAT vehicle, exchanging dry looks as the commander barked instructions to everyone *not* SWAT. Fetzer was the one who saw Jackson first, and she nudged her partner's elbow. Together they edged their way behind the crowd completely and directed him to a dark corner in the shade of what was probably their own vehicle. Only the shop's cop would lean on it.

"What in the hell is that?" Hardison asked, nodding at Jackson's converted SUV.

Jackson squinted. "Well, it used to be something fancy, but now it's bulletproof, and I really don't think it has a name."

Fetzer's eyes went wide. "Bulletproof, you say?" she asked with interest.

Jackson nodded. "Some friends tricked it out for me after I, uh, well, it's a long story, and we've got no time."

"I thought you were going to wait this one out," Fetzer said, her mouth pursed in a look that probably terrified children and grandchildren alike.

Jackson smiled gamely. "I got called in?"

They both just looked at him, their eyes weary as only old cops' eyes could be.

"There's civilians inside," he said, looking at the sprawl of the apartment complex. He'd had Ellery text him the address—and some specs on where, exactly, the Dobrevks lived in the multiunit area—and studying it now gave him stomach cramps. More *pops*.

And hey, there was a scream. Aces.

"We know that," Fetzer snapped. "That's what we're for!"

Jackson shook his head. "No, you don't understand. These civilians have children who were trafficked because one of the players in this little shindig wants to keep the family quiet. Their son was the kid we bailed out of jail—and both sides want him dead. They refused police protection because they hoped the gang wouldn't turn on their extended family. If they're seen taken into custody, it'll be a death sentence. They need to just disa-fucking-pear and not surface until we get them into WITSEC with their son."

Fetzer's and Hardison's eyes had gone wide. "So you're going to… what? Walk in there and say, 'Come with me'?"

Jackson shrugged. "As good a plan as any?"

"It's a shitty plan!" Fetzer burst out. "It's a hellaciously shitty plan." She and Hardison met eyes. "What can we do to help?"

Jackson met both their eyes and then flickered a glance to where the young, fit SWAT commander was going over protocol and planning.

"Show me where *they're* not going to be," he said. "Get me in, get me to the Dobrevks' apartment, help me slip in and out. The rest of this—" He indicated the massive police presence, everybody focused on the SWAT commander. "—it's going to go down, and it's going to be bloody. I just need to get these guys out."

"Here," Fetzer said, pulling out her phone. "We've got a readout of where the cops are going to go. We used to patrol this place all the time. I can tell you where they're *not* gonna be!"

Jackson grinned at them. "I'm point—"

Fetzer shook her head. "*I'm* point, civilian. You're in the middle, and Jimmy's riding cleanup. Our job is to get you there and get you out, and you need to look like you're with us or one of these assholes in uniform will shoot you, and we'll have to pretend we have no idea who you are." She nodded and flicked his tactical helmet. "Give us a sec to get ours from the shop and we're going. All that gear you're wearing is the only fucking reason I'm doing this. Most sense you've shown since you wandered into the precinct yesterday afternoon."

Jackson grinned wolfishly. "Like it? It was my boyfriend's idea."

Hardison chuckled. "Yeah, well, let's hope you see him again to thank him. This is truly the dumbest thing we've done in thirty years."

"Twenty," Fetzer said. "We spent our first ten years lucky to be alive."

"Yeah." Hardison looked nostalgic. "This is like a second honeymoon for Adele and me. Let's not get dead!"

TWO MINUTES later they were following Fetzer's floorplan and ghosting through the shadows of the complex while Fetzer broadcast their location quietly over the radio at her collar.

Jackson could hear the squawk of Lieutenant Chambers as Fetzer finished. "What? Fetzer, you get your ass back to the insertion point—"

"Will do," Fetzer said, and she released the Talk button and chuckled to herself. "Me and Jimmy will get back there just as soon as we're done with this."

"Aren't you going to get in trouble?" Jackson asked.

"Sure," Hardison said behind him. "Lieutenant'll yell at us when the op is over, maybe. If she remembers. Right now they've got ten more minutes to set up, and shit's going down there. We can hear it."

Fetzer took them to the deepest shadow under a stairwell, and they all crouched for a moment, getting the lay of the land. "You got infrared goggles on that helmet?" she asked.

"Nope," Jackson said, although he knew she did.

"Too bad." With three well-placed shots, Fetzer took out the three lamps in their corner of the quad, and they all stayed still and held their breath at the flurry of shots afterward. None of the shots were aimed at their location, and they eased up after a few painful heartbeats.

"Dobrevks are upstairs," Fetzer whispered. "Up this staircase and directly overhead. Jimmy, you want to stay here and cover us while we go up there?"

"You asking or suggesting or telling?" Hardison asked, pulling deeper into the shadows and aiming his service piece through one of the gaps between concrete steps.

"Telling," Fetzer told him, and he grunted.

"Thought so. Sure, Adele. Love to stay here while you two make yourselves targets. Jesus, don't get dead."

"You neither. Got extra clips?"

"You ask that now? Do I look stupid? Now go!"

With that, Fetzer left the safety underneath the stairwell, Jackson on her heels.

God, he hated these complexes—had some shitty, terrible, frightening memories of running through them—but this moment here? Crouching behind Fetzer and running as quickly and quietly up those goddamned concrete stairs in the darkness? This was one of the worst. A shot echoed through the quad, and then another, and the staircase rang as a piece of concrete ricocheted behind them. Fetzer put on a burst of speed, and Jackson followed just as Hardison's pistol echoed beneath them: one, two, three shots, and a muffled scream that followed.

They reached the landing, and Fetzer grabbed Jackson's chest, tugging until they were in the shadows again, at a doorway. Jackson checked the apartment number and nodded.

"Your people," she muttered.

Jackson stood to one side and tapped on the door. "Mr. and Mrs. Dobrevk? Are you there? Sascha sent me." He paused for a moment and listened—heard a struggle and upended furniture and a muffled scream.

He met Fetzer's eyes, and she shook her head, reaching over to give the door a quick knock before yanking her hand back.

Just in time for the door to explode in a shotgun blast of pellets and splinters raining over them, making Jackson grateful for both the helmet and the goggles. Fetzer risked a look through the night vision and jerked back.

"He's got her to his left so he can use the gun," she said. Jackson's ears were still ringing from the blast, but he heard her.

"I'm dropping down for the shot," he said, waiting for her hard nod before crouching and peering over the bottom edge of what was left of the door.

His eyes had adjusted to the darkness, and he could make out the young man, thin at the wrists and neck, holding poor Mrs. Dobrevk across the shoulders while staring eye-level out the door.

Jackson aimed carefully and took out the gunman's kneecap.

He howled and dropped Mrs. Dobrevk, his gun drooping, and Fetzer crashed through the door in time to hold her gun to his unprotected head.

Jackson followed her, scrambling upright, getting there to relieve the young man of his weapon as he dropped to the floor and moaned.

Jackson holstered his own gun and cracked the shotgun, removing its ammo before shoving it through his belt, where it hung, heavy and useless, thank God.

Fetzer was speaking into her radio, saying, "Suspect apprehended in apartment 220A. Please advise." She nodded at Jackson and whispered, "Get them out," while she waited for a reply.

Jackson showed her the shotgun and set it on the counter that stood between the kitchen and living room in the humble apartment and then turned to Mrs. Dobrevk, who was crouched on the floor, sobbing.

"Where's your husband?" he asked.

"Tied up," she hiccupped. "Tied up in the bedroom. He used me to keep my husband silent. He said Dima's men would be after us, and that we would bait the trap."

Which was what Jackson had suspected; one way or another, the Dobrevks were going to be in the thick of it tonight. He grabbed a knife from the butcher's block and strode down the darkened hallway, thinking that he really did need to get night-vision goggles, because it was all he could do not to knock into shit as he walked.

Mr. Dobrevk was tearful and grateful to be cut from his zip ties and reunited with his wife. Jackson told them to stay down behind the door while he went to scope out the sitch with Fetzer.

The situation wasn't good.

They could both hear Hardison down below the stairs, the reports of his pistol precise and specific—and usually followed by a scream or shouted swear word from somewhere across the quad. But the fact that he was still down there firing meant that going back through the quad was not a good situation.

"I've got nothing," Fetzer said. "The captain says to stay put and protect the civilians, but—"

Bullet fire crashed through the window, and she and Jackson dropped to the floor.

"Yeah," he muttered in the silence that followed, a silence punctuated by the original gunman's moans. Fetzer had administered first aid, tying a scrap of fabric around the wound with a towel to keep pressure on it, but this kid—and he was truly only sixteen, if that—was going to bleed out before anybody got to this corner of the complex. "That doesn't work for me. I've got an idea." He looked at her, making sure she could see his eyes. "I'm going to disappear for a minute. Tell your captain not to shoot me when I come back."

"How's he even going to see you?" she demanded.

"Oh, trust me. Everyone will see me." Although Jackson rather hoped Ellery wouldn't, because he was really keen on the idea of just getting home in an hour or so and saying, "Danger? Not so's you'd notice."

"All right," she muttered. "What's your plan?"

Fish in a Bulletproof Bowl

ELLERY STARED at his television screen in absolute shock.

"Kill him," he muttered. "I'll kill him."

"You can't kill him," Jade said on the other end of the phone. "You can't kill him because this is as safe as I've ever seen him."

Ellery tried to swallow the pounding of his heart, but it wasn't going anywhere. "Sure," he said in a weak voice. "I guess."

It wasn't like he was going to get any sleep anyway. As soon as Jackson had left, the Tank making an obscene amount of noise through the modified muffler and exhaust manifold, Ellery had wandered around the house aimlessly, finally settling down on the couch with the cat next to him and the computer in his lap. He'd managed to cruise politics and humor for a good half hour before his phone vibrated against his thigh with Jade's ringtone, which Jackson had programmed with the theme from *Wonder Woman.*

"What are you doing up this late?" he asked, tired to his bones.

"Turn the TV on to the local news," she had ordered, no preamble. "Or the computer, but it's going to be on the TV—yes! There!" She named the station, and Ellery had fumbled with the remote on the end table.

And watched in horror as Jackson's modified Infiniti SUV drove over the curb and onto the lawn of what appeared to be the Dobrevks' apartment complex and then circled around to the back.

"What in the hell…?"

"Wait," Jade muttered. "We've got another angle coming."

Some enterprising soul had brought their phone camera—it had to be a phone, because the picture was grainy and shaky—and taken footage of Jackson pulling the vehicle behind the apartment complex, then scrambling to the roof to assist three people from a balcony looking over the field behind their unit.

Two of the people appeared to be civilians, and the third—the one who stayed to help the civilians down off the balcony while Jackson steadied them on the top of the Tank—was a police officer.

Jackson was, as promised, dressed in full tactical gear, with a helmet and Kevlar and armor plates inserted over his chest and back. He moved fluidly, not like he'd been injured. Or even like he'd been the man who'd needed a break and some water after getting injured in the heat that afternoon.

Ellery watched breathlessly as Jackson set the two civilians on the ground and then assisted the officer down, all of them seemingly unnoticed by the cadre of officers surrounding the apartment complex and getting ready to go in.

Once the passengers were secured, Ellery expected Jackson to simply drive off the lawn and drop everybody at the curb, but to the horrified fascination of the person taking the video, and to Jade's and Ellery's, he didn't do that immediately. Instead, he installed the officer—Ellery remembered her, Officer Adele Fetzer—in the driver's seat and had her pull the vehicle into what appeared to be a breezeway that led into the complex itself. Jackson ran even with the vehicle on the passenger side, and as soon as Fetzer stopped the SUV, he dodged into the breezeway.

"Come out, baby," Jade said over the phone, and Ellery made an incoherent noise of agreement.

"Come out," he whispered.

"C'mon, Jackson, where'd you go?"

"Oh my God!"

They both said it at the same time, as Jackson appeared with another cop, this one with an arm draped over Jackson's shoulder as he limped, obviously injured. They had just emerged from the breezeway when Jackson's body jerked, but he didn't go down.

"Fuck," he squeaked. "Was he hit?"

"He's got a vest," Jade muttered.

"But he was hit, right? That was a hit."

"He's still walking," Jade told him. "Maybe the other guy was hit."

"Augh! I don't want to hope the other guy was hit."

"Well, hush. They're getting into the car right now!"

Ellery wanted to correct her—it wasn't a car, it was an SUV—but he figured correcting her on that point, at this moment, might actually be grounds for a he-had-it-coming defense in court.

There. Jackson was assisting the second cop—probably Fetzer's partner, Hardison—into the back, and then he swung into the front passenger side himself, and Fetzer gunned the engine, taking them all out of the camera's reach and hopefully to safety.

"God," Ellery burst out.

"Right?" Jade muttered. "Motherfucking werewolf Jesus, *right*?"

"Fuck. Me."

"Not on a dare," she retorted but didn't wait for a response. "Ellery, what in the hell was he doing there?"

"Getting the Dobrevks out," Ellery told her. "Apparently our, uh, friends down south blew up Alexei Kovacs tonight, and I know you don't know who that is, but—"

"He's Dima Siderov's rival," Jade said promptly.

"Wow."

"I've been researching!" she defended. "So the gangs blew up, and the Dobrevks were vulnerable. Either side would want them dead."

"Pretty much," Ellery agreed. "So Tage's cousin called Jackson to go help and…." He made a helpless sound. "And he did."

Jade's own helpless sound gave him a little bit of heart. "And he's fine," she said softly.

"He's going to have a hell of a bruise," he muttered. "We saw it. He was hit."

"But did you see him?" she said, and then her voice pitched to beyond the phone. "Good choice in tactical gear, honey. That served him really well!"

"Ask Ellery if I can buy him some more. That shit's expensive!" Jade's boyfriend, Mike, was nothing if not pragmatic.

"Tell him sure," Ellery mumbled on the phone just as it buzzed in his hand. "Wait, that's Jackson." He switched over the calls, Jackson's rough, breathless timbre sending a wave of relief that took him out at the knees.

"Got the Dobrevks," Jackson said briskly. "On our way to Sascha's now. Didn't want you to worry."

Ellery burst into a cackle of semihysterical laughter then, and Jackson crooned softly, "It's okay, baby. I'm fine. Safe as a kitten the whole time."

And Ellery couldn't stop laughing, not even when Jackson had to end the call.

But the phone call must have done something for him, because by the time Jackson got home, he was asleep on the couch, wrapped in one of the afghans that had survived the trip from Jackson's original duplex to Ellery's house. It was a bright amalgam of colors, clashy as hell, and warmer and softer than it looked.

Billy Bob was cuddled up to his chest, purring like a champion, the subtle vibration working soporific magic.

"C'mon, Ellery, time to go to a real bed."

"Mm...." Ellery uncurled reluctantly and allowed Jackson to remove the cat and guide him to their bed for what was left of the night. "Everyone safe? Kittens out of trees? Tage's parents hidden?"

"Yeah. We're all okay."

"Sure you are. Strip."

Jackson made a hurt sound. "Uhm, didn't we already do that?"

Ellery was suddenly very, very awake. "Take off your Kevlar and your clothes and lie on your stomach. I'll be right back."

Jackson narrowed his eyes and crossed his arms defensively—and winced.

"Who told?" he asked, squaring his shoulders—and wincing again.

"You were on the news, Jackson. And while covering the plates with mud was a good idea, after tomorrow I wouldn't drive the Tank again anytime soon. Now stop arguing and go lie down. We have to be up in three hours, and it would be great if you got some sleep."

Ellery came back into the room with some aloe-and-arnica gel, a couple of ice packs, and some ibuprofen and water—and he was still not prepared for the extent of the bruising on Jackson's back, or the blood seeping through the bandages along the outside of his upper thigh.

"Irritating man," he muttered, setting his supplies aside and handing Jackson the ibuprofen.

"Sorry," Jackson mumbled, sounding half asleep already. He swallowed the pills with a gulp of water before turning back to rest his head on the pillow, hands under his cheek. "Thank you for not leaving me."

Ellery's breath caught, and he lowered his head and kissed Jackson's shoulder, which was about the only part of his back not sporting a swelling black bruise.

"Can't get rid of me that easy," he said softly, rubbing the topical gingerly on his back, trying to soothe and not irritate. "Thank you for only going when it mattered, and not out of pride."

"Mm…," Jackson murmured in response to Ellery's hands. "Is that what it was?"

"That made you want to be in the thick of it? Yes. Partly. You like to have control, Jackson. Being in the middle of the violence makes you feel like you can contain it, I think. Keep it from getting to the people you care about."

"If that's what the hurt is about, I suck at it."

Ellery chuckled softly and took the two ice packs and spread them out along Jackson's spine. Jackson hissed at first and then relaxed. The main bruise itself was just below Jackson's left shoulder blade. The bullet had missed the spine and the shoulder itself and that was a blessing, but Ellery was very aware that without the tactical gear, Jackson would have been dead.

He wasn't chuckling anymore.

"You wore the body armor for me," he said softly. "The helmet. You got help from Hardison and Fetzer because I asked you to. You… you're not careless with your life anymore, Jackson. You might not ever play it safe, but I have no doubts, none, that you want to come home to me."

"Good," Jackson mumbled. "Because seriously, if I'd known you'd take such good care of me when I got hurt, I would have hooked up with you way earlier."

"You lie," Ellery chided. "You would have taken me home for a night and then tried to let me be a pretty memory."

"You would have been a *beautiful* memory," Jackson insisted.

"Right up until I made you take me home again."

Jackson chuckled, barely awake. "I said that at the very beginning. You were a forever kind of guy."

"So were you," Ellery said, standing and giving Jackson a kiss on the forehead. "You just didn't know it yet."

Jackson's shoulders shook once, and then his eyes closed. Ellery went into the bathroom to wash his hands, and by the time he came back, Jackson was fast asleep. Ellery turned off the light and set his phone for twenty minutes to take the ice packs off before closing his eyes.

He took a moment in the darkness to listen to Jackson's even breathing before giving a prayer of thanks.

The Early Morning Coffee Swim

FIVE THIRTY in the slutty crotch of dawn found them gulping coffee from thermoses as Ellery drove to the courthouse, and Jackson fielded a call from Andre Christie.

"Adele Fetzer says hi," he said as soon as Jackson picked up. "She and Hardison are both a little bloody but still standing."

Jackson let out a breath. He'd dropped them both off where the EMTs were waiting before driving off into the night. Hardison had sustained a through-and-through in his calf, and Fetzer had some cuts along her face and arms from the exploding door.

"That's good to hear," he said carefully. "How about you?"

"Really fucking grateful for Kevlar," Christie said, sounding pained. "Doc says the ribs will heal. I'll live. How about you?"

"Spent the night in," Jackson lied cheerfully. "Nothing to report."

"*You*," Christie barked, "are a worse liar than my twelve-year-old son, who says he's passing all his classes. You are aware there's news footage of you helping two little old people out of that meat grinder and into a whatever-the-fuck model SUV that actually was."

"Which station?" Jackson asked, playing for time. His back throbbed—though much less than it would have without Ellery's ministrations—and he'd had to wash down some extra ibuprofen for the sleep headache and sore muscles that morning. To say he wasn't thinking at optimum was an understatement.

"No, seriously, what in the fuck were you driving? They got a clear shot of your face, but that vehicle, that was really something."

"An Infiniti-QX," he said, giving up because it wasn't worth the trouble. "Some friends tricked it out—bulletproof." Or, more, bullet *resistant*. There were little round dents in the side panels now, but no penetration. The glass had held too—only a couple of nicks. Jackson felt like the car should have had its own residence and naked sports cars to rub it in oil.

"Fucking nice," Christie muttered. "And since I saw the footage, I'm glad *your* Kevlar held. How's your back?"

"Hurts like a motherfucker, but functional," Jackson told him, slumping awkwardly in the passenger seat. Next to him Ellery grunted, and Jackson would have shrugged if it wouldn't have hurt.

"Functional is all we can ask," Christie conceded without judgment. "Can't say the same for the bad guys."

Oh damn. "Tell me," Jackson ordered, putting the phone on speaker so Ellery could hear.

Christie's account—terse and militarily precise—was both harrowing and grim.

"Well, to begin with, not sure if you saw this, but SWAT got to the apartment complex just as the first shots were fired," Christie said. "And believe me, that was the thing that saved everybody's life."

Based on Jackson's tip—and with Christie's lieutenant's backing—Christie had gotten a midnight search warrant for Dima Siderov's apartment. Since shots were being fired as they arrived, the SWAT team was able to enter apartments that housed the gunmen and not just Siderov's rooms.

About twenty minutes after Jackson had gotten the Dobrevks out of the complex, SWAT, with Christie riding point, had managed to round up three of Siderov's lieutenants and three guys who'd been gunning for Siderov's apartment.

Neither Siderov nor Ziggy Ivanov were in the numbers of those arrested, but there'd been zero civilian fatalities, so Christie was calling it a win.

"Both of them?" Jackson muttered. "*Both* of them got away? Were they even there in the first place?"

"From what we can gather, Siderov had an exit strategy, and his guys are loyal. The basic gist of all our questioning was 'Good luck catching him—he's got people everywhere.'"

"What about Ziggy?"

Christie's noise over the phone was unpleasant. "Well, from Siderov's people we got 'That little rat bastard better not show his face in this state again!'"

Jackson grunted. "That's promising. I'd be happy to find his body in a river somewhere, and I'm not gonna apologize. What about the guys he was running with?"

Christie made a sound like he was sucking air through his teeth. "That's a little more complicated. Like you said, their boss got blown up this afternoon. They're counting on Ziggy to lead them to the promised land. They were like, 'Ziggy who? We don't know any Ziggy, but if we did, we'd guess he was far away from here.'"

Jackson let out a low grown. "Which probably means he is still in the city, waiting to see what Dima's going to do."

"It's worse than that," Christie said grimly. "One of the guys—you might know him—was maybe sixteen and was lying in a room with a shattered door and a doctored leg wound. Ringing any bells?"

"None whatsoever," Jackson said flatly.

"Yeah. Fetzer said she and Hardison took him down. I showed that woman the fucking news footage, and she said she and Hardison took him down. Son, I am not sure what you do to inspire such loyalty, but we wrote in the report that Fetzer and Hardison took down an armed intruder in the Dobrevks' house before the SWAT team launched its assault, and that's my story and I'm sticking to it."

Jackson let out a breath. "Good. Fetzer and Hardison are good cops. The Dobrevks were primed to be either used as pawns or shot in revenge, depending on who was winning. I didn't want to get in the way, but...."

"But you wanted to get them out of there." Christie blew out a breath. "I get it. I mean, zero civilian casualties and theirs was the only apartment with innocent people in it that had been breached. I just wish you would have trusted us to—"

"I did!" Jackson protested. "I got help. I stayed out of most of it. I swear, I was being good like I promised."

Christie chuckled mirthlessly. "You sound about six. I hope you're going to bed later."

"If by later you mean tonight, yes," Jackson said on a yawn. "But tell me about the kid."

Christie grunted. "Sure. And then you need to tell me what you're doing now because you seem to have access to the best parties. Anyway, the kid. He was scared shitless, and.... God, Jackson. I don't even want to know what his life was like. He said, 'Nobody's safe from Ivanov. Not even Dima's product.'"

"Product?" Jackson sucked in a breath. "That was his exact word?"

"Yeah," Christie replied. "It was sort of weird. Do you know what that means?"

"Product is the word people have been using for trafficked children," Jackson said, his chest like ice. "We've got someone bringing in a busload of kids that Ziggy tried to ship to Dima Siderov's late boss-slash-enemy. Two of them might have incriminating evidence against Ziggy himself, and even if they don't, their deaths would be a big signal to anyone who wants to write Ziggy Ivanov off as just another flunky."

"Oh no. When's this bus getting to town?"

Jackson looked at the readout on his phone. "Anytime in the next hour, but I think he was aiming for 6:00 a.m. so he knows we're ready for him."

Christie grunted. "So, ten minutes? That's where you're going? Where's the meet?"

Jackson fell silent for a moment, sudden suspicion—and protectiveness for the children and for Burton's CO—assailing him. Christie seemed to be a completely clean and a stand-up guy, but last night he'd run a raid on the very group of people Jackson and Ellery had been poking with a stick for the last two days. How could he be sure Christie wasn't being followed?

"Hey, Rivers," Christie said brusquely into the silence, "don't chicken out on me now!"

"I'm not chickening out," Jackson snapped. "But you just came off an all-nighter. You gonna be ready for the fallout here?"

Christie grunted. "Are you fucking kidding me?"

"I got sleep," Jackson muttered defensively.

"Augh! Rivers, I swear to you, I want those kids safe—and the bad guys behind bars—as much or more than you do. Sean's a good cop and a good friend. I won't let you down, I promise."

Jackson took a deep breath. "Fine. We'll be at the courthouse in ten. But remember, the guy driving the freedom bus is military covert ops, and he's gonna have friends in the bleachers."

"Ooh." Christie's sound was a cross between seeing Superman and getting kneed in the balls. "I'm starting to see why Sean's such a fan. You and Cramer really do hang out with the most interesting people."

Jackson grunted; he couldn't argue with that. "Just remember to ducking fuck," he said, and Christie's snort on the other end told him the joke was appreciated.

"And try not to fuck the wrong duck. Got it. Courthouse. Fifteen minutes. I'll keep my eyes open for sparkly lights in the wrong windows."

"And your tactical gear on!"

"Amen."

Jackson hit End Call and leaned his head back against the seat. "This is going to be a hell of a party."

"I don't remember you telling me Burton was going to be there," Ellery said.

"I think he'll have Ace and Jai with him. They were, uh, blowing shit up when I called."

Ellery grunted. "This makes me happy. Can you see how happy I am?"

The temperature in the Tank had dropped about twenty degrees.

"That's a sweater full of happiness right there," Jackson responded. And then, "Shit!" Without even explaining to Ellery, he pulled out his phone and dialed Henry.

"This had better be important." Henry sounded mildly out of breath and not like Jackson had woken him up at all.

"Is Lance off today?"

"No, but he was going to be," Henry snarled.

Oh! "Well, apologize to him for me."

"No."

"Fine. But we've got a bus full of kids showing up at the courthouse in five minutes, and a driver who may or may not be injured and is deliberately disobeying orders to get these kids home. Think Lance can help doctor him up if I get him clearance from the DA's office?"

"I don't know," Henry mumbled. "Does it work that way?"

"I have no idea," Jackson said frankly. "But I'll ask. Anyway, this guy is going to need a place to hide where nobody would think about looking for him and some guys to watch his back. We have a cabin in Tahoe lined up for later, but I'm talking today. You, uh, got any ideas?"

The silence coming across Henry's line wasn't reassuring.

"Yes...?"

More silence.

"Just, you know, be ready for my text," Jackson said. "I'll let you know if we've got incoming."

And that silence changed to brooding anger. "Because where will *you* be?" Henry snapped.

"Uhm...."

"Goddammit, Jackson."

"Hey, I went home and rested yesterday."

There was an ominous sound on the other end of the line. "Do you think we don't watch the news here?"

"Good for you!"

"How you moving today?" Henry asked sweetly.

"Like buttah. I'll text you."

"I'll be there in twenty minutes. Then you and me are gonna talk."

"How do you even know where I'll be?" Jackson asked, gaping.

"You're going to tell me right now, or I'm going to pound your back like an asshole the next time I see you. Now pony up. Where the fuck am I going."

Jackson leaned his head back and groaned. "Courthouse. There will be snipers and military assholes there. Not including you, of course."

"I have tactical gear too," Henry snapped, rustling sounds in the background indicating he was putting some on at that very moment. "Ellery bought it for me while you were in the hospital. It was like Christmas came early."

"I'm sure it was," Jackson said sourly. "Look, we're pulling up to the courthouse now. If you could, I don't know, park around the block so maybe out of sight from us here, that would be aces. I'd love that."

"No," Henry said, and Jackson was amused to hear he wasn't the only one who'd regressed twenty years in age.

"Look, Junior, our guy is getting here soon. Whatever fireworks happen, they're going to start before you get here. That way you can scope out the situation before you get your ass shot off."

Henry grunted. "I actually did have other plans for my ass this morning, this is true."

Oh God. The mental images—they burned!

"I hate you. Fuck off. I'm not even kidding."

"Which is exactly what I was doing before you called and fucked up my morning. Blame yourself, geezer. I'll be there in ten if you shut up and let me kiss my boyfriend goodbye."

"Stay home."

"See you there. Stay alive."

Fuck. "Fine. You too."

And then Jackson hung up because everything hurt and shit was about to go down, and he wanted two quiet minutes with Ellery before the shitshow began.

Ellery pulled up to a loading-zone-only space in front of the courthouse and turned off the ignition. The street was deserted, and the early-morning shadows stretched long over them. It was late enough in August that the mornings had a little chill, but the day was still probably going to be a scorcher. For a moment, though, they sat in the silence and breathed.

Jackson was unsurprised by Ellery reaching for his hand, or the twining of their fingers.

"You okay?" Ellery asked.

"I could sleep for a week," he confessed.

Ellery let out a weak chuckle. "How's your back?"

A year ago, Jackson would have shined him on. He'd done it with Christie and had just tried to do it to Henry.

But he wasn't doing it with Ellery, not after the night before. He could remember Ellery's hands on his skin, so tender, and the way he'd simply... accepted. He'd accepted who Jackson was. Yes, he wanted Jackson to be more careful of himself, but the part that he couldn't change, he accepted.

Such a powerful thing, that acceptance.

It had taken them a year to get here: to the place where Jackson learned to take care of himself for Ellery's sake and Ellery learned that there were some parts of Jackson he didn't want to change.

So for once he didn't play the "I'm fine," game. He wasn't fine. They were going out into a potentially dangerous situation, and he was not moving as fast as he usually did, and Ellery needed to know that.

And Ellery wouldn't judge him for being hurt.

"Ow-ooh-ch." He punctuated the extended syllables with a grimace. "I could have used a Jacuzzi and some ice and another backrub."

"Poor baby," Ellery said, and he was only partially teasing. "Maybe the weekend."

Jackson gave him his best smile, the one that came up from his toes. "Count on it."

"Still want to pick out a kitten?"

Jackson nodded. "Yeah. Maybe we'll have some cakewalk cases so I can spend a little more time at home with it. I'd hate to bring it home and just *leave* it with Billy Bob. That's no fair."

"To anybody," Ellery said sourly. "We may want to consider separate rooms, separate cat boxes, and separate food."

Jackson grunted. "Definitely separate food. Billy Bob's fierce. Too much time on his own. He never got enough when he was younger. Doesn't share. Has trouble playing well with others."

Ellery's smile was gentle and luminous. "Bad habits, true," he conceded. "But I think he can learn."

Oof. Well, yeah. "If I can, anybody can?" Jackson interpreted.

Ellery tilted his head from side to side, playing coy with the fact that Jackson had voiced his exact intention. "Well, you've both learned fixed animals don't wander," Ellery said gently.

"No, we do not. Just, you know, takes a lot of work to fix us," Jackson apologized.

"Not so much."

And for a moment the pain fell away, and the world was the two of them, and the gentleness they brought to their bed, to their lives, and the way sometimes, when it was only the two of them, the world could be perfect.

"Worth it?" Jackson asked, his heart suddenly pounding for the answer.

"Absolutely."

And a breath, falling into Ellery's eyes, and a heartbeat of knowing their love was strong.

And his phone, buzzing on his lap. They broke away reluctantly, and he picked it up.

"Rivers."

"Burton. He just got off the freeway at J Street, and it's not looking good. Bus is belching smoke and wobbling on a tire, and he's driving like he's about fucking done. Get your shit down there. Ace has a van but we need someone to drive the transpo, if we can find a safe place for him to stop, 'k?"

"'Kk," Jackson repeated. "How will I know you?"

"When bad guys start dropping dead," Burton replied and hung up as Ellery started the engine.

And Jackson picked up the phone and started making calls.

By the time he and Ellery hit J Street and hung a right, he had Mira, as well as Sodhi and Pasternak from the DA's office, hauling ass for Mira's minivan, as well as Christie in his unmarked, and Henry in Lance's crapmobile, all headed down J Street, looking for a stuttering group transport.

Burton called him just as he saw a shambling converted school bus, painted badly in rainbow colors that were never meant for the side of an automobile. As Ellery roared past it in the Tank and then spun around in a bit of driving worthy of the most hardened stunt man, Jackson read the words Johnson's Independent Church of the Christian Republic on the side.

"Oh dear God," he muttered over the phone. "You would not believe what we're following down the road."

"Ace and Jai stole one of those shuttles from an eldercare home to take its place," Burton replied flatly. "They should be about a block behind you."

"Wow," Jackson muttered just as Ellery said, "Seriously?"

"Oh God, he's not going to make it much further." Jackson could see the wobble Burton had been talking about, and it looked like the tire was off center because the axle was cracked. And from the amount of smoke and the smell, the engine was about to catch fire.

"All right," Jackson said. "I've got an idea. Have him hang a right at Ninth and then left directly onto Capitol Mall. Have him follow the roundabout and then turn left on Ninth again. There's a park about a block down. We will be right on his tail. You got that?"

"Got it. I can spot all the things from here. Traffic is just waking up, but it's not dire yet. I think he can make it."

"Tell him," Jackson ordered. "I've got—"

Something bounced off their passenger window, and Jackson looked up in surprise in time to see the bank of windows at the top of the school bus explode into pulverized glass.

"Oh fuck. We're passing Seventh and someone was here to meet us," Jackson told Burton. "There's three SUVs full of Ziggy's guys or Kovacs's guys or who-the-fuck's guys and they're... oh."

The SUV that had passed Jackson, and then the bus full of children on the wrong side of the road suddenly went screaming onto the sidewalk, hitting a light pole before rolling down the road and stopping upside down half on the walkway and half on the sidewalk.

"Dead," Ellery said, voice blank. "Those guys are dead."

"Guess it doesn't matter who they're working for," Jackson muttered, wondering where the fuck Burton was. "Oh shit. Here comes another one for another pass." They were coming up behind Ellery, heading for the inside lane next to the bus.

"I don't have a clean shot!" Burton muttered. "If they keep firing into that bus, they're going to hit someone. I don't care if the kids *are* flat on the ground!"

"Ellery!" Jackson cried out, panicked. "We've got to—"

"Yeah, I know," Ellery muttered. "Fuck. Fuck, fuck, fuck. I will never give you shit about wrecking another car again."

And with that, Ellery gunned the motor of the Tank and made an abrupt right, standing on the brakes so the black SUV with the gunmen popping out of the driver's side, getting ready to spray the school bus, would T-bone them right in the center.

Jackson got a good look at the whites of the driver's shocked eyes right before they hit.

It Takes a Fish Bowl to
Save a School of Fish

THE TANK came specially modified, including protective webbing and a triple-lock suicide seat belt. When Ellery and Jackson braced for impact, they were flipping the last two closures of the webbing before the SUV hit them broadside, sending him and Jackson rebounding sideways and back and exploding all the airbags.

All of the modified airbags that took most of the impact and made it bearable, that cushioned their fragile bodies just enough that Ellery's head didn't smash through the window and Jackson wasn't thrown across the center console.

Turns out, there was a bag there too.

They sat for a moment, stunned, and then Jackson started issuing orders.

"Out of the car," he muttered. "They've got airbags too, and—"

There was a series of short explosive sounds coming from Jackson's side of the car, and the glass—bulletproof, yes, but not completely disaster proof—began to show fractures radiating out from the shots aimed at them by whoever was conscious in the SUV.

"Forget getting out," Jackson barked. "Does this thing still run?"

"Hasn't stopped yet," Ellery mumbled, still dazed. "Isn't the engine supposed to kill in a crash?"

"Thank Ace later," Jackson cried. "Get out of this place *now*!"

"Fuck!" Ellery's left wrist and forearm ached ferociously, enough to disable movement completely. He shifted the Tank to Reverse and lifted his right hand to the giant knob on the steering wheel that was probably illegal and spun it, giving the modified SUV enough gas to rip it off the grill of their attacker's car.

"You steer, I'll shift," Jackson commanded, and Ellery stomped on the brakes, letting Jackson shift into Drive. "Go!"

And he shot forward, squinting through the cracks in the front windshield that blocked their vision.

"See the bus?" Jackson asked tersely, making muffled grunting sounds as he unhooked his seat belt and webbing so he could rummage on the floorboard at his feet. "Fuck!"

"I'm going right," Ellery told him, spinning the wheel hard and pumping the brakes. The brakes barely responded, and the Tank screamed in pain—much like Ellery's entire body, head, spine, arm, wrist, leg…. What in the fuck had he done to his left leg?

It was not his imagination. Jackson was whimpering, bracing against the dashboard with one hand while clutching at his phone.

"Are you okay?" Ellery asked, keeping the bus in sight. "Oh fuck! Did you see that?"

He couldn't see where the car came from, but the third SUV full of Ziggy Ivanov's men turned right from the outside lane, cutting off two lanes of traffic and diving after the bus. Ellery groaned and dove right, following the bus and the bad guys.

"Are *you* okay?" Jackson asked irritably. "We're not okay. Catch them!" His phone started buzzing, and he looked at the face of the thing. "Well, shit."

Ellery spared a glance at it and saw that it was cracked beyond all use, except for answering a call.

"How you guys doing after that?" Burton demanded over speaker.

"Peachy! Going skydiving next," Jackson lied, his voice cracking a little.

"Fabulous. Okay, the cops caught up with the car that hit you. They're taking down idiots with guns and attitudes as we speak."

"The third SUV is right on Jason's tail," Jackson told him. "We're doing our best, but this thing's wobbling like a motherfucker, and something keeps screaming—"

"Brakes," Ellery said shortly. "Feels like the axle's bent."

"Yeah. Big car no-go pretty soon. Where are you?"

"Passing on your left," Burton said, and to Ellery's surprise he heard a motorcycle buzzing past. Burton didn't slow down or even wave, but the bike was scary impressive—streamlined, shiny, and the helmet obviously had some sort of state-of-the-art com link in it. No wonder they hadn't been able to spot him. He could have been anywhere.

"Nice ride," Jackson said sourly. "Do we have a plan?"

"I'm going to try to take out the driver," Burton told him. "If you two can pull alongside him when I do?"

"He's going to be shooting through a moving vehicle in our direction," Ellery said, feeling the blood throb in his forehead. "How can this possibly go wrong?"

"School bus full of children," Jackson reminded him tersely. "Besides, your windows are pretty intact."

Ellery made a sound in the back of his throat like Snoopy getting a titty-twister. "Great. We're solid. We can do this."

"Was that a go from Ellery?" Burton asked over the phone. "Because they're turning left onto the Mall. Can you see them?"

"We can see them," Jackson ordered. "Stand on it, Counselor."

It was like Ellery's gas-pedal foot was a completely different creature than the rest of him, because it obeyed without question.

To say the Tank shot forward was an overstatement, but the engine made growling, screeching noises, and they lurched ahead, taking the turn onto the Mall about two car lengths behind the SUV as Burton pulled up next to it.

They were in a perfect position to watch as he pulled out a gun with a silencer on the end and shot. And shot. And shot again.

Ellery practically stood on the accelerator, and they were just starting to draw even with the SUV as it leaned to the side, slowing as it did. Ellery drew up so he could look into the passenger window, and he and Jackson made the same noise.

The car had carried four men. The driver, the passenger, and the guy behind the passenger were all dead, neat holes in their foreheads, their brains splattering the armrests and windows around them.

The guy behind the driver was screaming, terrified, no gun in his hand at all, fumbling with the door lock with fingers clumsy from panic.

"Shit," Jackson muttered. "Ellery can you roll down your window?"

Ellery made a sound like a hurt kitten, and Jackson shifted in his seat and gasped.

"Oh, baby—baby, don't worry about it. Here."

Oh God, Ellery couldn't even look at his left arm. It hurt, it hurt it *fucking hurt*, but Jackson was bleeding from a cut on his head and cradling his own shoulder like it had taken a beating.

But that didn't stop Jackson from scrambling between the two front seats to the back. He grunted a couple of times, probably from pain, and Ellery got a glimpse of blood running down from his backside, probably from ripped stitches.

But he made it, twisting with a yelp of pain and landing heavily on his bottom so he could roll down his window and stick his head out.

"Hey," he hollered. "*Hey*!"

The guy in the back seat of the SUV turned to him with saucer-wide eyes. "Oh my God!"

"Dude, reach over the front seat and steer!"

The guy gaped. "What—"

"Steer, goddammit! Right now we're the only thing keeping you from veering into oncoming traffic. Now steer. You're slowing down. Steer until someone can get in and stop you!"

"But… but… the cops!"

The guy was weeping, and Ellery could almost hear Jackson rolling his eyes, even with the blast of wind coming in through the window.

"But… but… but… *you should be dead*!" Jackson mimicked. "Now steer this piece of shit to the side of the road and get out and deal with the cops."

And to Ellery's relief, he did, the buffeting against their own vehicle stopping as the back-seat passenger began to steer to the curb that guarded the grass inset of the Mall itself.

"Slow down and let him pull over," Jackson told him. "Then go around the circle and catch up with Burton's friend."

Ellery's vision was coming in firework sparklers, but he couldn't imagine Jackson's was any better. For a few blissful moments, he just drove, the car screaming in their ears because they wouldn't scream themselves.

By the time they got around the Mall and pulled off alongside Stanford Park, their engine was starting to smell suspiciously like burning oil, and the steering wheel threatened to break his other wrist. He parked practically perpendicular to the giant school bus that was up against the curb and killed the engine before the car exploded.

"Fuck," he said weakly, and he felt Jackson's hand over the headrest, stroking his hair.

"It's okay, baby," Jackson murmured. "You did great. You stay here where it's safe. I'm going to go check on our status and get you an ambulance."

"You'll ride with me?" Ellery begged, feeling stupid.

"Couldn't stop me." Jackson rubbed Ellery's cheek. "You were a fucking hero. Man, that was some driving. Now stay put. I'll be right back."

"You're hurt—"

"Yeah, but I was premedicated," Jackson said, and Ellery could hear his smirk. "I was practically swimming in ibuprofen. When I come down from this high, they'll see my footprints on the moon!"

Ellery laughed again, and Jackson reached into the center console, digging under the airbag and swearing for a moment. He came back with a water bottle and the ibuprofen, right where Ellery kept it, and Ellery heard him chuckle.

"You're right, Ellery. It always pays to be prepared. Now, I'll be right back."

As Jackson shoved, swearing, against the warped door and then slammed it shut, Ellery could only be amused that he'd thought they'd need his legal expertise, not his driving prowess, when he left the house that morning.

One Last Dirty Stinking Crappie

JACKSON TALKED a good game to Ellery, but he could barely walk. His knee felt dislocated from the pressure on the door, and he knew he was bleeding from his stitches again. His head, neck, and back were on fire, he had blood dripping in his eyes, and he was pretty sure his wrist was sprained.

Ellery's arm was definitely broken, though, and he'd managed to drive their bustedass vehicle through a high-speed chase. The least Jackson could do was make sure everybody was okay. That didn't stop him from checking on his gun in his holster, almost groaning when he realized he'd have to reach for it with his bad wrist.

God, let there be people here in better shape than Jackson and Ellery.

Jackson limped around the front of the Infiniti, grimacing at the smell of cooking engine and burned rubber, and stepped up on the curb of the small park. There he found a stunningly handsome African American covert ops officer in bicycle leathers talking to a tallish, pale, dark-haired country boy and an almost seven-foot, bald Russian bear, who all looked like they'd spent the night rolling around in gunpowder.

"You wrecked that nice SUV Sonny made you," Ace Atchison—the country boy—said as Jackson rounded the corner in front of the school bus.

"Sorry," Jackson muttered. "Couldn't be helped. There was this SUV full of bad guys…." He frowned and looked into the school bus. "Have you checked on the kids?"

"Constance is waiting for your friends from the DA's office," Burton said, his leathers so stiff and shiny they creaked as he shifted his feet. "He doesn't want to get the kids out until it's safe."

Jackson grimaced at the bullet-riddled side of the bus. "Anybody hit?"

Burton sucked air through his teeth. "Jason," he said softly. "I stuck my head in, and he's lost a lot of blood. He's not looking great. The chatter at the moment is that if he comes in right now, he'll be court-martialed for disobeying orders. Did you mean it when you said you had a safe place for him?"

Jackson nodded. "If we can promise that the guy won't lose his residency for not reporting a gunshot wound, I might even get him his own personal-care physician. But you're right. First the DA needs to get here, and we need to make a record that the kids got here safely."

"Good," Jai—the giant Russian bear—said. "These children were abducted. They belong with their families."

Jackson nodded, watching the route from which they'd come. He saw a minivan, an unmarked SUV, and three cop SUVs all headed in their direction, as well as the flash of ambulance lights about two blocks behind the other vehicles.

Good. Ellery needed medical attention, and Jackson's entire body hurt. Of course the children and Jason Constance would have priority, but just the knowledge that there was help coming reassured him.

"I think we're in luck, then, because—*fuck*!"

If he'd been standing still, the bullet would have hit him center mass and possibly stopped his heart because after last night's blow to the back he'd been lucky not to feel any signs of arrhythmia. But he'd been in midturn, and it caught him in the shoulder, a graze, enough to send him off balance, and he fell to his knees while the next bullet hit Burton square in the chest—and the substantial body armor he was wearing under his leathers.

"*Fuck*!" Burton snarled, pulling out his gun. "Ace, Jai, get *down*!"

But Ace and Jai were never great with orders, and before Jackson could even register what he was seeing, Ace had cleared a bigassed knife from a sheathe at his belt and hurled it with force and deftness that bespoke long practice. Jackson followed the trajectory to where Ziggy Ivanov stood, just in front of the small shuttle that Ace had co-opted, gun in hand.

He looked like hell—battered, his clothes torn and bloodied— and Jackson had time to wonder which of the two wrecked SUVs he'd been in. Probably the second one, the SUV that had rammed Ellery and Jackson. They'd been close enough for Ziggy to see the trajectory of the giant school bus and to make it there on foot.

Ace's knife embedded itself deeply in Ziggy's shoulder, near his chest center mass, but not quite. Ziggy's arm fell, the gun still clutched in his hand but his arm useless to aim. He turned abruptly, the haft of the knife still sticking out of his body as he swerved into the street and started to run toward the school bus on the outside of the parked cars. Jackson and Burton were the first on their feet to give chase, Jackson dodging between the school bus and the Tank to intercept whatever he had in mind for the driver of the school bus, while Burton circled around the front of Ace's stolen shuttle to keep him pinned.

Jackson had the shortest route, so he saw what happened next, and because he'd seen Ellery's probably broken arm, his swollen wrist, he knew what true heroism was.

Ziggy came hauling ass alongside the parked line of cars, limping, yes, his arm dangling almost uselessly, the gun practically falling from his fingertips. As Jackson came out from between the vehicles, his own gun drawn, he watched as Ziggy transferred the gun from his right hand to his left, raising his left hand to aim at the driver of the school bus even as he ran.

He got off one shot, so intent on using his last strength in his pain to get revenge on whomever had stolen the children from their intended destination in the first place that he wasn't paying attention when Ellery shoved open the driver's side door of the Tank. Ziggy charged into the open door full bore, driving the knife farther into his shoulder and flailing backward onto the pavement.

Jackson's stomach rolled when Ziggy's head gave a hard bounce with the sound of a dropped watermelon. Right as he and Burton got to Ziggy's prone form, Ellery stuck his head out the door and got quietly sick, the shock and pain of doing what he'd just done with his injuries obviously hitting his nausea centers hard.

"Got him?" Jackson asked Burton, who nodded once. Jackson watched as he ripped Ace's knife out of Ziggy's shoulder and handed it to Ace, who had arrived in time to see Ziggy go down. They were rolling him over, binding his wrists and ankles with zip ties, as Jackson stepped gingerly around the mess on the ground to help Ellery back into the SUV.

"Sorry," Ellery said weakly, tears of pain rolling down his cheeks.

"There's no sorry for that," Jackson told him, voice all gentleness, as he reached over Ellery for the water. "Here. Rinse and spit, and I'll dump the rest."

They'd had nothing more than coffee in their stomachs that morning, so there wasn't much to clean up, but Jackson knew the misery of being that kind of hurt.

Ellery nodded, meek as a child, and did what Jackson said. Jackson dumped some water on his T-shirt and went to wipe Ellery's face with the hem when the pain in his shoulder stopped him.

Like wildfire and lighter fluid, the graze on his bicep roared through his adrenaline and across his nervous system, hitting him hard enough to make him weak with it.

"Oh my God," he muttered, leaning against the door frame of the battered Tank. He used the other hand to wipe Ellery's mouth and took a couple of deep breaths to clear the spots in front of his eyes.

"What's wrong?" Ellery asked. He was leaning back against the headrest, eyes closed, face pale, working hard on breathing.

"You took out the bad guy with a car door, Ellery. It was fucking epic. Once we get some breakfast and some doctoring into you, I'm going to make you call your mother and tell her that story. She's going to be so proud."

Ellery's shoulders started to shake, and his rusty chuckle told Jackson that he was going to be all right.

In spite of the *many* places on Jackson's body that felt like shit, Jackson was pretty sure they both were.

JACKSON MADE sure Ellery stayed put until the ambulance got there, but as soon as Ziggy was bound up and rolled to the sidewalk, where he lay limply and bled without pity, Jackson, Ace, and Jai went to check on the kids. And on their driver, who had been frighteningly quiet.

The children were all seated, two by two, in the first four rows of the bus, and they greeted Jai with tentative smiles and waves. He crouched near the front of the aisle and began to speak to them, low and in what was probably Russian. Jackson heard his own name mentioned, and he turned and waved over his head, relieved beyond words.

Sophie and Maxim were sitting together, wearing travel-stained clothes and clutching each other's hands. They looked tired, but Jackson could see a trash bag full of fast-food wrappers and empty water bottles in the back of the bus, so he was pretty sure everyone there had been fed and watered and might even have gotten some sleep.

They weren't battered or bruised—scared, possibly for a long time to come—but not hurt physically, and that was a win.

For a moment, Jackson let his heart slow, let some joy seep into his chest. Tage, who'd gone through hell in the hopes that he could save them, would have at least part of his family back again.

But the joy was short-lived. Their safety had come at a price, and while they were going to walk away from this school bus unaided, the same couldn't be said for their driver.

Jackson could barely remember seeing Jason Constance before, when he and Ellery had gone into the desert and almost not come back.

The man had looked tired then, but fit, in command, militarily crisp and ready to go face the bad guys.

This was not the same man. This man had his shoulder and arm wrapped in a dirty bandage that might have once been a cheap T-shirt. His face was bruised, and he was as worn as a discarded shoe.

One with no sole—or soul—left to speak of.

Ace got there first, wrapping his arm around Constance's waist and helping him out of the bus. He stumbled when he got to the stairs, and Jackson reached around him, he and Ace forming a sling between them and walking sideways to get Constance to the sidewalk and help him sit on the grass.

"What in the actual fuck?" Ace said, his twang more apparent than ever. "You were in one piece when we left you on the road."

Constance glared at Ace sourly. "And you still had eyebrows," he muttered.

"Well, I lost my eyebrows blowing up a dirty, no-good, child-trafficking, drug-selling mob boss," Ace said defensively, handing Constance a water. "What's your excuse?"

"The US military wanted the children to get to the dirty, no-good mob boss," Jason said, weariness etching lines in the corners of his eyes. "So they could say how they knew he was dirty and no good. I guess they'd been trying to pin down his operation for a long time, and part of it involved stealing guns from the military itself. The kids were their way in."

"Fuck that!" Jackson couldn't help it—he flailed when his shoulder and his back and his neck all hurt and then everything hurt more. "They actually—they shot you so they could do that?"

Constance grunted. "The mobsters shot me. Someone in the military who was making money from the guns told the mobsters where I'd be."

"Well, that sucks," Burton said, giving Ziggy a fuck-you kick in the ribs before moving over to crouch at Jason's side. "Are those people dead?"

Jason shook his head. "Not all of them. And the guy in the military is still there. We haven't figured out who it is yet."

"Goddammit, Jason," Burton muttered. "There is now a price on your head. That's just swell."

"I got nothing," Constance said, stifling a yawn. "I... God, I need my wound irrigated and some antibiotics and some sleep and a computer and...." His voice trailed off, and whether he was about to pass out from exhaustion, blood loss, or illness, Jackson couldn't be sure, but he knew the man was done.

He looked down the block to where everybody—*everybody*: EMTs, rescue vehicles, DAs, detectives, and police officers—had begun to park, and singled out Henry's brand-new luxury sedan almost immediately.

"Ace," he said urgently, "can you help me get him?"

"I'll do it," Burton muttered. "You go talk to your buddy, and we'll follow you."

Jackson shot him a look, and Burton rolled his eyes.

"You are bleeding, asshole. Now move it so you and Cramer can get some first aid. You both have head wounds, are you aware?"

Ugh! No, he hadn't been. "Bleeding before breakfast," Jackson muttered. "*Not* a good idea." With that, he headed toward Henry, who was looking pissed off.

"Twenty minutes. It took me *twenty minutes* from a cold start to get dressed and get my ass down here, and you still managed to wreak havoc across three city blocks."

Jackson couldn't help it. "Heh heh heh heh heh."

Henry shook his head, his blond hair looking seriously sex-tousled, and Jackson didn't feel bad at all. "Lance says he's down to help. What do we have?"

Jackson nodded to Ace and Burton, who were on either side of Jason Constance, helping him walk toward the brand-new town car that Henry had driven up in. As far as Jackson knew, Henry didn't own his own vehicle; he just drove Galen's car, because most of the time, it had Galen in it.

"We have one battered military guy whose whereabouts need to be unknown," Jackson told him.

Henry nodded. "Yeah. I explained to Lance how the guy is pretty much a hero. He said he could deal."

"Well, there's the ADAs in charge of human trafficking cases getting out of their vehicles now. Let me go talk to them for a minute, make sure everybody's on board with 'No, sir, that bus drove itself.' I would really like Lance's name to not even get mentioned, but there are still bad guys out there who might be very interested in where Jason is, and someone on the inside in the military who might be giving them tips."

Henry sucked air in through his teeth. "Now that just hurts. Goddammit. Drove a school bus full of children through a meat grinder to get them to safety. Guy should get a parade."

"I think he'd settle for some painkillers and a good night's sleep," Jackson told him. "But if you've got a parade in mind, go for it."

Henry snorted and called to Burton and Ace. "Here, let me put a towel down first." He grimaced to Jackson. "All-new leather upholstery. Feels disrespectful to let someone bleed on it the day after we bought it."

Jackson felt an absurd chuckle coming on and went to where Burton and Ace stood, most of Constance's weight supported between them. "Guys, Henry's going to take him to safety. I, uh, know where he's going to be, I think, but if we could, I don't know, keep watch over the place? There are some really innocent dumbass kids in that building, and I'd love for them not to get hurt."

Burton let out a sigh. "Me and Jai can do it," he muttered, and Ace made a hurt sound. Burton shot him a glare. "Ace, I love you, and I love Sonny, but if you don't drive something back to Victoriana in the next ten minutes, Sonny is going to lose his shit. How many times has he texted you in the last three days?"

Ace's high cheekbones went dull red. "Not so many as you'd notice."

Burton blew him a raspberry, which was so far out of character that Jackson stared. "Bullshit," he said, to follow up the rude sound. "You probably used up your entire data plan telling him to hold tight. Jai can follow what's going down on the street, so we know who to worry about. You need to go back to Sonny."

Jackson watched as a part of Ace seemed to shore itself up to accept his fate and another part lit the man up from the inside. Obviously he was missing Sonny as much as Sonny missed him.

"Well, fine. If either of you two get your asses shot off without me, just remember, I know where your boyfriends live, and I can sic them on you with one goddamned phone call."

Burton looked like he'd swallowed a bug. "You would not—"

"Hell I wouldn't. I would drive Ernie and George up here and kick them out of the SHO, aiming them at you two like a tank gun." Ace scowled. "No fun without me, hear?"

"Zero fun, sir," Burton intoned levelly, and only Ace's cocky grin showed that he recognized the movie reference.

"That's a good friend right there," Ace said, and they both moved forward as Henry finished his business with the towel and the back of the car. "Here you go, Colonel. We'll keep you safe, right?"

Jason gave Ace a weak smile. "Thanks, soldier."

Ace and Burton helped him into the car, and Burton squatted down by the curb to speak earnestly to his boss for a moment. Jackson took that as his cue to go talk to Mira and her bosses.

Eleanor Sodhi wore another black suit, this one accented with a gloriously threaded gold-and-scarlet scarf. Her hair and outfit were impeccable, but her expression was haunted.

"Fourteen children?" she asked, voice rough. "You've done an amazing thing, Mr. Rivers."

Jackson scowled, gesturing with his chin. "Those folks over there did this," he said, meaning Jason Constance, Ace, Burton, and Jai—who was still in the school bus, getting names from the children. "I just poked a hornets' nest and tried not to get stung."

"You failed," Mira said dryly.

"You *are* seeking medical aid, aren't you?" Ethan Pasternak asked. He did *not* look like he'd just stepped off a magazine cover. His thinning hair was sticking out in all directions, and his shirt was haphazardly shoved into his slacks. No jacket or tie either. Jackson realized he sort of liked his lawyers rumpled, and he gave Pasternak a sober nod.

"I need to get Ellery to the ambulance first," he said, nodding to the three busses that had parked up the street as he'd been talking. "One more minute. I need to make sure you can process all the children," Jackson told them. "Get the kids to their homes?"

"We need an interpreter," Eleanor began, but Jackson shook his head.

"You have one, and here he is now."

Jai emerged from the bus, his face set into its usual implacable lines, and Eleanor Sodhi and Ethan Pasternak both took a terrified step back.

"Guys, you do not need to know this man's name, but he's got—"

Jai held up his phone and nodded briefly to Jackson. "Forwarded," he said.

Jackson grimaced. "Jai, my phone is toast. I can't forward it to them."

Jai huffed. "Cramer?"

"Yeah. Do that."

"Done." And then he turned away to stride toward where Burton and Ace stood after Henry had pulled away from the curb.

"Give me a moment," Jackson told them. "You can go talk to the kids. I need to get Ellery's phone."

"Jackson," Mira whispered, eyes on Jai's enormous retreating back. "What *was* that guy's name?"

Jackson gave her a half smile. "I told you, honey, you don't need to know."

And then he absolutely had to go see Ellery.

JACKSON MANAGED to retrieve Ellery's phone and forward the information to Mira and her bosses before the same EMTs who treated Ellery's arm with a pressure bandage and helped him into the stretcher for the ride to the ambulance focused their attention on Jackson.

"All right, all right," he muttered. "I'm riding with Ellery. Let me get in, and you can do whatever."

Whatever proved to be a lot, and Jackson was in a foul mood when they arrived at the hospital and the two EMTs—strangers this time, which was unusual—insisted on admitting both of them for treatment.

"I don't do hospitals," he muttered.

"Yes, Jackson, but you weren't going to leave me in there alone anyway," Ellery told him, looking less woozy but still in some pain. "You might as well come in, get it over with, and deal."

"I'm so pissed," Jackson said, his voice sounding peevish to his own ears. "I was so going to stay out of them this go-round. That was, like, my driving goal! I was going to visit *other* people in the hospital if I had to, but I wasn't going to need to go myself." Some of his peevishness bled away under the roar of the ambulance, and some of his exhaustion seeped in.

"And by 'other people,' I didn't mean you," he added miserably.

Ellery's chuckle had an edge of hysteria in it.

R.O.R.

X-RAYS AND CT scans and painkillers, oh my! Jackson kicked up a fuss about not leaving Ellery's side, so he sat, shirtless, in the hallway while a pretty physician assistant, with tawny skin and wild curls pulled back in a ponytail, irrigated and stitched his arm and his head wound and then had him shuck his pants so she could apply more glue to the stitches in his backside.

Ellery remained in the stretcher, blissed out on painkillers, with temporary splints on his forearm, wrist, and knee, listening to Jackson shamelessly flirt with the PA in order to hide the shaking in his voice and the frantic fear of the hospital that had not stopped dogging him just because he hadn't been incarcerated in one for the last two months.

"You've had a busy couple of days," the PA muttered, prepping more gauze and another needle. "Were you trying collect as many small injuries as possible so you could win a free week in ICU?"

Next to him on the stretcher, Ellery snorted. "I'll remind him you said that the next time he gets stitches in his ass."

She glanced up at Ellery, taking in *his* recent stitches and the temporary splints on his arm and leg. "You appear to have no room to nag," she said bluntly. "Is this *your* first trip to the ER?"

Ellery paused to think about that, because the painkillers were *good*, but Jackson answered for him. "No. Would you like to hear how he kicked bad-guy ass with a broken wrist and a dislocated knee?"

Ellery regarded him with true horror. "No. No. That is not how we're telling that story. I refuse!"

The PA gave Jackson a wicked smile. "Is that really how it happened?"

"Oh yeah." Jackson nodded. "Totally badass. I left him in the car because... well, look at him. Sad, right?"

Ellery glared at them both, wishing he could just pass out and wake up at home, while the PA gave him another once-over.

"Like a sad little kitten in the rain," she confirmed.

"See? And I'm talking to some total badasses—like blowing shit up and motorcycle assassin badasses—and suddenly, a bad guy shows up!"

Ellery heard the thread of hysteria in Jackson's voice and let him go. If he could flirt a little, tell a good story, pretend to be someone else who was some*where* else, he might get out of the hospital without having another heart attack.

"How do you know he was a bad guy?" she asked. "And speaking of badasses, I need to see more of yours so I can get these stitches under the thigh."

Jackson obliged her, turning a little more, while Ellery answered.

"He was the bad guy because he shot Jackson in the arm. You just stitched that."

She snorted. "You guys are a laugh riot. It's like Abbott and Costello in here. Okay, so, bad guy shoots and…."

"And one of the badasses throws a *knife.* Into his *chest*—well, a little north and west, so his shoulder, but I swear, it was a thirty-yard throw and he missed the heart by that much. And bad guy can't aim the gun anymore, so he turns to run away, and one badass chases him one way and I chase him another. And Ellery here, whose only job was to stay put, waits until the bad guy is too close to stop and throws open his door—"

"With a broken arm from a car crash that just occurred?" the PA double-checked, sounding like she didn't believe a word of it.

"Sweartagod," Jackson confirmed. "And the bad guy goes over backwards, and his head bounces off the pavement like a watermelon—"

"And I keel over and vomit," Ellery inserted dryly.

"True story," Jackson averred. "And that, yer honor, is how we ended up here."

There was a round of applause from the edge of the corridor, and Ellery looked over—slowly, because his back and neck were also pretty stiff—and saw Dave, Alex, Jade, and Mike standing there taking in the show.

"That was an amazing story," Jade said, moving gracefully to look over the PA's shoulder as she worked on Jackson's backside. "Thank God I got that version because I'm sure what really happened would give me a stroke."

"You mean the part where Ellery swerved the Tank in front of an SUV full of bad guys?" Jackson asked, some more of his veneer cracking. "Because that was true-blue hero stuff right there."

"Witness his bleeding head wound and wrist splint," Ellery told them all.

"And that beauty of a bruise on his back," Mike said, coming to sit on Jackson's other side.

Jackson grunted. "That was entirely different," he said with dignity.

Mike nodded. "So says the news footage." He didn't wait for a reply but looked at Ellery. "How long you got here?"

Ellery closed his eyes and shook his head. "No idea. What's it been, Jackson? An eternity and two millennia?"

"Two eternities, one millennium," Jackson corrected. "Ouch!"

The PA hissed. "That was *not* my fault. You ripped your stitches so badly you need another line of stitches. Good God. I'm not sure how much of that story was true—"

"All of it," Jade and Mike said in tandem.

"Or how much of it is bullshit," the PA continued, rolling her eyes. "But you two definitely need some downtime before you do whatever it is you do some more."

Jackson grunted. "He's a lawyer," he said.

"So boring." Ellery didn't need to feign his yawn. He was exhausted.

"And what are you?" the PA asked.

"Nothing," Jackson told her. "I'm on medical leave."

And that was the last intelligible thing she got out of any of them until they carted Ellery away for X-rays.

AN HOUR later Ellery had a temporary cast on his arm and wrist—because the whole thing sported a total of three hairline fractures—and a splint on his leg to immobilize his knee. Mike was pushing his wheelchair while Alex and Dave led the way for them to visit Sean Kryzynski.

"There are some benefits to being a frequent flyer," Alex burbled. "You guys get a personal escort service and a group discount at the viewing."

Jackson grunted. "Expedited visiting hours?"

"You got about five minutes," Dave said dryly. "And by that I mean I give you five minutes before you have to get the fuck out of this place or go hurl in a trash can, so we won't keep you long. He just got an update from his detective pal and wanted to make sure you two weren't dead."

"Well, it'll be good to see him too," Ellery said with dignity. Hell, *he* didn't have a hospital phobia, and hey! Someone else was pushing him around.

Alex slid open the door to Kryzynski's room, and Sean and Andre Christie started clapping as Ellery was pushed in.

"Hear you're looking to change professions," Christie told him. "NASCAR, I understand?"

"Monster truck," Ellery told him, feeling mellow. "That way I can just *vroom* right over the bad guys!"

"That's fantastic," Sean wheezed. "Jackson, how stoned is he?"

"Three sheets to the wind and tallyho," Jackson replied. "How stoned are you?"

Sean grunted. "Not so stoned I can't see how much you need to leave," he said gently. "Christie here has been waiting for you guys to show so we can get the wrap-up. Andre, go fast."

Christie nodded. "Okay, so by the time I got there, this was the sitch." He took a breath and gave Jackson and Ellery a sideways look. "There were three wrecked SUVs, two with drivers who had taken bullets to a noggin by, witnesses report, 'a badass guy in black motorcycle leathers with a black motorcycle that was so shiny it looked like it was from outer space.'"

"Which witnesses were those?" Ellery asked, exchanging an alarmed look with Jackson.

"ADA Sodhi and ADA Pasternak," Christie told them grimly. "They claim to have no idea what the 'badass motorcycle guy' looks like without his helmet. So there's that."

"What a shame," Jackson said, obviously trying not to bounce on his toes. "Isn't that a shame, Ellery?"

"I'm wrecked," Ellery said and then let a giggle escape. "Get it? Wrecked?"

Christie aimed a level look at both of them. "Hang tight, guys. Four more minutes to go."

"Continue," Jackson said. He attempted a bow and then pulled up with a grimace and made an elaborate hand gesture instead.

"So, no leather-clad badass, and no knife, which apparently made a rather large divot in would-be social climber one Ziggy Ivanov, who is currently in surgery but who may not survive."

"I'm all broken up about that," Sean Kryzynski breathed.

"Devastated, destroyed," Jackson seconded.

"Wrecked!" Ellery giggled some more.

"No more oxy for you," Jade said sourly, and Ellery beamed at her until she booped him on the nose.

"You're so pretty," he said. "Why aren't you a lawyer?"

Her eyes widened in horror. "Dear God, no. Not in a million. I'd kill someone. Christie, he's flying. You need to hurry."

"Who *was* left?" Jackson asked.

"A nearly seven-foot bystander with no eyebrows and first-degree burns on his face and hands who happened to speak Russian and who helped the ADA contact the children's parents and then disappeared," Christie said sourly.

"That was nice of him," Jackson said. "Don't you think that was nice of him, Ellery?"

"Jai's a peach," Ellery said. "I mean he. *He's* a peach."

"Yes, he's a peach," Jackson echoed. "Go on."

"There is no sign of the driver," Christie continued, "although there was a considerable amount of blood in the driver's seat, so I hope he's gone somewhere to get medical attention."

"God, so do I," Jackson muttered. "Anything else? Any word on the street about Dima Siderov? The swiss cheese apartments? The state of the gangs in the area?"

"Dima Siderov remains at large," Christie told him soberly, "although his gang is much diminished. Besides the split due to Ziggy trying to get his lieutenants to join Alexei Kovacs's gang, there were the arrests made last night and"—Christie's face went very grim—"the number of deaths this morning. Apparently Siderov is terrified of whoever killed all of Ziggy's men, and Siderov's men are too. I think if… people wanted to, say, move out of state with a little bit of government assistance, then Siderov would be fine with that. He's got other cats to skin and fish to fry."

"Erk!"

They all looked at Jackson in alarm as his face washed almost green.

"Detective, you need to up your metaphor game," Dave said crossly. "Now, is that everything we need to know? Can Jackson and Ellery go home now?"

"One more thing," Christie said, standing up and extending his hand. "Thank you."

Jackson took his hand and shook it, and then Christie moved to Ellery, who said, "You really want to thank us?"

Christie nodded. "I do."

"There's a kid named Ty Townsend who got busted because Ziggy set up a scam and who would really love to have all his charges dropped."

Christie frowned. "Wait. What scam?"

Jackson wobbled on his feet. "We could never figure it out. Fetzer and Hardison thought there were a couple of abandoned big-box stores on Lindstrom and Craft's beat that were supposed to be patrolled. Ziggy gave them Ty as an easy bust to keep them away from the big-box stores, but we still don't know why."

"They also picked Ty because Ziggy was running odds on the team he's supposed to play for—*if* he doesn't get his scholarship revoked because of bullshit charges," Ellery added. "He's supposed to leave for school *tomorrow*, Detective."

Christie nodded. "Understood. You guys go home. I'll call you in a couple of hours. I have the feeling there are a few more loose ends here."

There were, but Christie was right. They were done.

Jackson leaned over Kryzynski's bed and locked hands with him, gently bumping foreheads. "Get better. Call us when you can give us a ration of shit again."

"I saw the video. Count on it," Sean breathed, sounding stronger than he had the day before but by no means full strength.

Jackson gave him a weak smile, and then Dave and Alex literally turned him around and escorted them all out. Mike had pulled Ellery's Lexus to the front and pumped up the air-conditioning, and the trip home was made in blissful silence.

Tails, Scales, and Epic Fails

THEY GOT home and went to bed.

For nine hours.

Jackson rolled over at around eight o'clock at night keenly aware that Billy Bob was licking at the salt from his hairline. He groaned, because everything hurt, and checked on Ellery.

Ellery was lying on his side, his wrist on one pillow, his knee on another. His eyes were closed, but he was muttering in his sleep, squirming.

"Ellery," Jackson mumbled. "El. Wake up!"

Ellery glared at him through slitted eyes. "My hair hurts," he said succinctly.

"Mine too. What's wrong?"

Ellery whimpered. "I have to pee."

Jackson let out a weak laugh. "Okay, then. Me too. I'll go first and come back and get you, how's that?"

"Deal."

They finished their tasks with a lot of hopping and swearing and a little bit of laughing, and Jackson got him back into bed with pillows propped up behind his back and the remote control for the TV mounted on the wall.

Jackson limped to the shower and took a quick one, dressing in basketball shorts and one of his favorite disintegrating T-shirts. He looked up from pulling it over his head when he heard his phone vibrating on the chest of drawers.

"Rivers," he said shortly, looking at Ellery.

"So, did you enjoy that nap?" Christie asked. "Because I could use a good nap. Was it a good one? Tell me, so I remember what sleep feels like."

Jackson looked at the maze of cracks on his ruined phone. "I see no messages from you. For all I know, you spent the last ten hours facedown on your mattress."

Christie let out a broken laugh. "I wish. I can't even believe you two. 'Yeah, hey, we got a tip about something going down at these two vacant stores. You may want to check that out.'"

"Uhm, for the record, our tip was from your people. I mean, Fetzer and Hardison told us that might be a place to check out, but, you know, shit went down."

"Yeah, well, Fetzer and Hardison can get commendations. I don't know what to give you two besides pain-in-the-ass awards."

"Commendations? What did you find?"

"An auction house," Christie said. "With locked rooms in the back for girls, many of them underaged. It's taken hours. We're still processing them. Chambers finally sent me home because—" He cleared his throat. "—I had a few choice words for her and how her beat cops apparently hadn't checked this part of their beat for almost a week."

Jackson blinked. "Ty Townsend was arrested five days ago—that's a very coincidental time frame."

"Yeah, you were right about that. Ziggy Ivanov had the usual beat cops who scoped this place out arrest Townsend to keep them away from an auction night. Apparently Lindstrom and Craft had gotten calls or tips from their CI a couple of times since—"

"To keep them away from that area," Jackson said.

"Yeah. And we had cops canvass the neighborhood, and boy did the neighborhood have some shit to say. Apparently there were a couple of ginormous fucking parties here that they used to cover the sale of the girls. So you and your boy busted up a human trafficking ring."

"Did we find the CI?" Jackson asked shortly.

There was a hesitation on the other end of the line. "No," Christie admitted, reluctance tinging his voice.

"Do we know where Dima Siderov is?"

"Also no."

"Do we know how Ziggy or the mysterious informant got their intel on which two cops to bait?"

"And no," Christie snapped. "Goddammit. Like, god*dammit*! We saved lives today, Rivers! There were fourteen kids on that bus and over thirty girls in that godforsaken vacant store. You can't save the world in two days. You have to be glad you survived a day like this one and go on to work some more."

Jackson grunted. "I've heard that before," he said, hating to admit that.

"Yeah, from whom?"

"My boyfriend."

Christie gave a weak chuckle. "Well, he is the brains of your operation. Take care of him."

Jackson looked over to Ellery, who was flipping through channels dispiritedly.

They'd survived another one, and Christie was right. The best they could do was live to fight another day.

"That's my best job," Jackson said fondly. Ellery looked up from his channel flipping and gave a warm smile. He looked peaked, Jackson decided. He needed food. "Thanks for the update," he said into the phone. "Now seriously, you really should get some sleep."

Christie yawned into the phone. "So sayeth my wife," he said happily. "I'll catch you later."

"You too."

Jackson rang off and threw himself across the bed, catching Ellery by surprise with a kiss on the cheek.

"How you doing?" he asked, resting his chin on Ellery's shoulder. "Ready for another pain pill?"

"Yes," Ellery said, because macho posturing was not part of his makeup. "But I need something to eat first."

Jackson smiled. "I smell Chinese takeout. I wonder if Jade and Mike brought some over while we were sleeping."

"The takeout fairies?" Ellery asked. "I could deal with that. How come we never bring takeout to their place?"

"Because they remain disgustingly healthy and unhurt," Jackson told him. "Also, we bring Jade coffee and a pastry four mornings out of five and take Mike to basketball games. I think we're doing okay as far as not mooching off our family." He kissed Ellery's cheek again, wanting to rub his face all over Ellery's body and just revel in the fact that they were alive and the world was quiet—for the moment. Instead he pushed himself off the bed with a sigh and went to check on dinner.

Chinese takeout it was!

Jackson came back into the bedroom with two laden plates, setting one on each end table. He left again and returned with two glasses of milk and some pain meds for each of them, set those up, and hopped into bed, sitting cross-legged and facing Ellery, who was using a throw pillow for a table.

"What did Christie say?" Ellery asked, and Jackson briefed him, the two of them chewing over the case's dangly bits as they ate.

When they were finished, Jackson took the plates away and rinsed them off, then returned to find Ellery swallowing his pain medication and looking thoughtful.

"What's wrong?" he asked.

Ellery shook his head. "It's just… you know. The last time we had a case with so many far-reaching implications, it almost killed us both. You more times than me."

Jackson gave him a hopeful smile. "But look at us now! A little battered, but we didn't even do any hospital time. It's like an entire learning curve."

Ellery answered with a look that was almost shy. "Look who's suddenly optimistic. It's practically glowy in here."

"Well, anytime we get a meal together, Counselor, it does tend to leave me all aglow."

Ellery rolled his eyes. "Come here," he said nakedly. "Lay on me. Watch some television. Let's pretend there's no criminals of Damocles dangling over our heads. Just for tonight."

"Sure. What time is it in Massachusetts, though?"

Ellery groaned. "Do we really have to?"

"Bet you she's seen my video too. And I really *do* need to tell her the your-son-is-a-badass story.'"

"God," Ellery said. "You really *have* matured if you're looking forward to talking to my mother."

Jackson reached over his body carefully for the phone.

"It's always important to give Lucy Satan her due," he said earnestly. "I mean, if we don't call her, she could, you know, show up unannounced." It had happened before.

"Fine," Ellery grunted. His eyes on Jackson weren't unhappy, though. "Here," he said, nodding to his shoulder. "Lay there, though. I'm going to take a picture."

"Matching head wounds?" Jackson asked as they looked at the selfie screen and saw the identical patches of white gauze.

"No. I just want her to see we're okay."

He sent the picture right as the phone rang. It was Ellery's mother, and telling the story of how Ellery Cramer, mild-mannered attorney and badass stunt driver, had saved the day was the last thing Jackson absolutely had to do that night.

Besides lie next to the man he loved and be grateful, oh so grateful, that they had this moment, had survived this day, and would live to fight again.

They had so much work to do.

Belly Up or Still Swimming

AFTER A week, Ellery could limp along with a cane, and the bruising on Jackson's back had almost faded.

Ellery was so grateful to be mobile again. He'd been forced to sit, knee elevated, for five days, until the swelling went down. His wrist cast was one of the new 3D printed varieties—breathable and waterproof—and he was grateful. The hated plaster cast was a thing of the past. Not that he'd broken a bone in childhood but he'd seen a few.

Jackson had been back to the office two days after their adventure with the not-so-magic school bus, and he'd kept Ellery up-to-date with new clients, interviewing a couple with Jade and providing background so Ellery could do his job. Jackson had been the one to bring a small bouquet of flowers and a box of chocolates from Ty Townsend, his mother, and—sweetly enough—Nate Klein, all of whom were so very grateful that Ty had the chance to go south to school and live his dream.

Nate had even left an envelope full of coupons for sandwiches, 20 percent off.

And Ellery, forced into immobility so soon after Jackson returned to work, was given a whole new perspective on how hard Jackson must have worked to stay home for seven weeks.

God, he thought fondly, that man really *did* love him.

Loved him enough to get him crutches so they could help Andre Christie escort Sean Kryzynski home.

Jackson had—without any prompting from Ellery—made a bunch of small microwavable meals and packed them in plasticware so they could stock Kryzynski's refrigerator. The two of them arrived at the hospital in time for checkout, and followed Christie to Kryzynski's apartment, blissfully downstairs, so they could make sure he was settled in.

The place looked like it had been hit by a tornado.

"Uhm," Jackson said, looking at the piles of DVDs on the floor and the clothes all over the bedroom. "Is… I mean you *look* like a fully functioning adult."

"Goddammit, Jesse," Kryzynski muttered. "Jesus. He broke up with *me*. In the *hospital*."

"I thought firemen were the good guys," Christie said, upending the DVD shelf and starting to put them back.

"Well, he was, mostly," Sean grumbled, allowing Jackson to settle him on the couch and prop up his arms with pillows to make breathing easier. "All except that 'I'm not out of the closet, and I'm not prepared to deal with heavy emotional shit when I can't tell anybody all my feels' part."

"Asshole," Jackson said succinctly. "Are you sure it's him?"

"Andre, is my *Baby Driver* DVD in there?"

Andre grunted. "Nope. Neither is *Inception* or *Fight Club*."

"Fuck," Sean muttered. "Fuck, fuck, fuck."

Ellery was the one to say it. "Sean, do you have anybody to stay with you this week? You're going to need some help, you know."

Sean looked away. "I... I called my sister in Turlock, but her boss wouldn't let her go."

"Fuck," Ellery muttered just as Christie said, "I can stay a couple nights until you're back on your feet."

"I'm on it," Jackson said. He grabbed his new cell phone and ducked out of the room, coming back in about ten minutes with a really pleased expression on his face.

"What?" Sean asked, eyes closing as Jackson got busy helping Christie clean up. "What is that look?"

"It's no worries," Jackson told him. "I got you sort of a live-in helper. You have a guest room, right?"

"Yeah."

"Got a bed?"

Sean grunted. "It has a bed, yes."

"Good. Because we, uh, made this kid's living situation a little crowded with an unexpected roommate earlier this week, and this way he can have his own bed."

Sean narrowed his eyes like he was trying to put two and two together. "Wait a minute...."

"Henry will be driving him over in the next two hours. As soon as he gets here, we can leave you to get some rest, and Ellery and I are going to go see another patient."

"What other patient?" Christie asked with interest.

"Avi Kovacs just woke up in intensive care at Mercy San Juan," Jackson said smugly.

"Who in the fuck is Avi Kovacs?" Sean asked, confused.

"Well," Christie began, "remember how, right before you got skewered like a piece of meat, some asshole tried to steal a file from the goddamned public defender's office?"

Sean gave a long blink. "Oh my God. He's been in a coma for a *week*?"

Jackson nodded. "Yup. And I'm betting he'll be so surprised at how much the world has changed."

"Gonna tell him about Ziggy?" Christie asked. "And Baldwin Schroeder?"

Ziggy had died in surgery. Ace's knife had been pretty close to his heart, and his collision with Ellery's door had driven it home. By the time the surgeon realized he'd been bleeding into his chest cavity, his heart had stopped, and the world was short one more bad guy and up a couple of questions about the whereabouts of Dima Siderov and what remained of his organization. The apartment complex had been eerily vacant over the past week. Only the innocent and bewildered were left to call the place home. Some of the vacated rooms had been full of drugs and guns, but no cash, leaving the police to speculate that Dima might have gone somewhere else to start over.

Ellery and Jackson weren't so sure.

Baldwin Schroeder and his little brother—a member of the Capitol Valley High swim team, which had been practicing the day Jackson and Henry had been shot at—had both been in the SUV Ziggy had been riding in, the one that Burton had taken out with his first shot.

Baldwin had been the driver shot, but his brother, Klaus, had been left alive. There was nothing to charge him with besides suspicion of gang activity, but once his hospital stay was over, he would be spending a good year at the California Youth Authority Boys Ranch. Out in the boondocks, it was like juvenile hall except with a focus on rehabilitation. Police were still looking for the gun he'd used to shoot at the school with, but Ellery and Jackson suspected it was long gone.

But Ellery had put in a request to Boys Ranch to let them know if Klaus was released early—or escaped—so he and Jackson would know to watch their backs.

Baldwin's cousin Kurt, the SRO at Capitol Valley, had simply failed to come in to work the first day of school and disappeared. At first they'd thought maybe he'd gone into hiding with Dima, but the more they thought things through, the less sure they were of that. It was possible that the Schroeder family had a different set of loyalties.

"What about Alexei Kovacs?" Jackson added. "Because Ziggy and Baldwin are actually small potatoes if he's wearing the family name. But yeah, we would really love it if some of this rampant speculation was confirmed."

Although some of it had been. Some of the surviving gang members in the SUVs had told them that Ziggy had aligned with Kovacs, and that some of them were Kovacs's men that Ziggy had co-opted, and some were Siderov's men who had been either lured or coerced to turn on their boss.

But one last interview, to tie up loose ends, to get a feel, maybe, for where Dima Siderov would go, where he could come from next. And who the mysterious confidential informant had been, the one who had called Lindstrom and Craft to tell them where their small busts would be but kept them away from the real action.

Christie had told Ellery and Jackson privately that the two policemen'd had their financials thoroughly investigated. They were too poor to be dirty, just not smart enough to get promoted. It wasn't going to make them any friendlier, but knowing they weren't on the take had made Jackson, at least, feel a little better about the last ten years since he'd been on the force.

"I hear you," Christie said now about the interview with Kovacs. "I'd love to be in on that, but me and Sean have some shit to do here."

Jackson nodded, and Ellery felt better for poor Kryzynski. No, Andre Christie wasn't a lover, but he was a brother, and sometimes that was what a person needed.

Jackson and Christie cleaned up the rest of Sean's breakup mess, and Jackson ordered pizza for lunch. The moment the delivery person left, Henry knocked on the door.

Standing behind him was one of the most beautiful—and haunted-looking—young men Ellery had ever seen.

"Heya!" Henry barged his way in, the young man coming in on his heels with a backpack over his shoulder. "I understand you've got a job for Billy?"

"Billy?" Kryzynski said, brows furrowing. "Why do I know that na—"

And then he saw the young man—dark haired, sloe-eyed, with a blocky build and muscles that could have been chiseled from marble. Billy had a lean mouth and thick, dark lashes that most women would kill for.

He also had a square jaw and a chiseled chin, and altogether, as a package, he looked like a model for one of those military magazines that seemed to fetishize guns as much as they fetishized muscles.

Ellery's eyes grew wide, and he glared at Jackson over the couch while Jackson looked blandly back.

"Hi, Billy," Jackson said, reaching out to shake the kid's hand. "Pleased to meet you. Did Henry tell you what you'd signed on for?"

"A little bit of nursing, some light housecleaning, and basically making sure Detective Kryzynski here is okay before we leave him to his own devices." Billy gave a brief smile then, the kind that indicated he was as competent as he was good-looking and valued the competence more. "I'm getting my degree in engineering, but I've been in sports all my life so I've got some basic first aid knowledge, and I'll be good at giving baths and helping with physical stuff." His smile changed, became kind and professional. "And not much shocks me, so you don't have to worry. Your secrets are safe with me."

Sean gazed at the young man with a slightly opened mouth and blue eyes that had gone as round as a cartoon character's.

"Uhm...."

Jackson grinned, so full of himself that Ellery wanted to smack him. "Well, our job here is done. Ellery and I need to go question a scumbag, but you all feel free to stay here and have pizza and welcome K-Ski home."

"Hold up," Henry said. "I'll follow you out. Let me make sure Billy here is settled."

They waited, Jackson making small talk to fill in the rather awkward silence as Christie tried to draw Billy into conversation and Sean just stared at him like a man slaking his thirst after a long dry spell. By the time they'd left, Sean was managing entire words but no complete sentences, and as soon as the door closed behind them, Ellery smacked him in the arm.

"Ouch!" Jackson complained. "What was that for?"

"*That*," Ellery growled, "was for hiring a porn model as your friend's live-in nurse and not warning him!"

"Heh heh heh heh…." Jackson was practically dancing on his toes he was so proud of himself.

"That was pretty sweet," Henry added. "Oh my God, I thought he was going to swallow his tongue!"

"And *you*!" Ellery continued, leaning heavily on his crutches. "You just sort of threw that poor kid in like a lamb to the slaughter. You know Sean's going to find out what he does for a living and—"

"Oh no," Jackson said, shaking his head. "I've seen that look. Sean knows. Believe me, Sean knows."

Henry started to laugh too. "Heh heh heh heh…."

If Ellery could have managed it without falling over, he would have whapped them both with a crutch. "You two are supposed to be Sean's *friends*!"

Jackson took a deep breath and rolled his eyes. "Look, Ellery, Sean has had a positively miserable week in the hospital and getting dumped by a boyfriend he thought was one of the good guys. I knew some of Henry's boys are mostly trying to get through school, so I thought, you know. A pretty nurse. And I've met the guys. They're all sweet as hell. A pretty nurse who's not an asshole and who knows how to be kind to someone having a shitty month. What's so bad about that?"

"And Billy is so ready to get out of the flophouse," Henry added. "Jason was touch and go for a little while. One of the other guys has sort of taken on his care and feeding full-time, but it's crowded in there. Billy's one of the guys who's been there the longest, and he's so ready to get his degree and an apartment of his own. And probably to get out of the business too. But first—"

"Graduation and a job," Jackson said, and Henry nodded.

"Yeah. So this is sort of like a rent-free vacation for Billy: one fairly reasonable guy to take care of and his own room with his own bed. It's win-win."

Henry's boyfriend, Lance, had worked as a porn model for a couple of years during his residency. He'd roomed with a revolving roster of other models, and the place had been—according to Henry—every bit as sexually charged as one might imagine. Lance had pretty much left that life behind when Henry had been forced to room in the flophouse for financial reasons and they'd fallen in love, but Henry had gotten to know the guys pretty well and had sort of taken on the role of big brother, along with Lance. The two of them had since moved out of the flophouse, but only to the downstairs apartment. Jackson had sent Jason Constance to the flophouse to heal because, in his words, the last place anybody would expect to see a special ops officer was in a two-room apartment that was balls-to-the-walls sex workers and starving students.

Also, he'd added, all the guys were incredibly muscular. They wouldn't be easy targets.

Ellery let out a sigh. "Fine. Whatever. If this ends badly, I'm blaming you two. Both of you. Because apparently you've corrupted Henry beyond all redemption."

This time they both laughed. "Heh heh heh heh heh…."

"Where you guys off to?" Henry asked when they caught their breath.

Jackson narrowed his eyes. "You know where we're off to. We're going to the hospital to interview coma boy." They'd called into the office that morning; Henry would have been briefed.

"Well, yes," Henry admitted. They were drawing near the parking lot, and Ellery saw the town car parked next to his Lexus. "I was sort of angling for an invite. I, you know, want to see how this ends."

"Yeah, sure," Jackson said with a shrug. "Climb in. We'll drop you off back here."

Henry grinned. "No worries. I left the keys with Billy. Drop me off at the office and play musical cars later."

Ellery regarded him through narrowed eyes. "Awfully damned sure of yourself, weren't you?"

Henry's grin didn't dim one iota. "Yup. Face it, you guys cut me out of the fun last time. Maybe *I* wanted to get into a car wreck and shot. Did you ever think of that?"

Ellery's knee was down to a low-level throb, and his back and shoulders were flexible enough to not hinder movement, but his wrist was going to be in that cast for another seven weeks.

"Frankly, no," he said shortly as Jackson opened the car door for him. He slid inside and waited for Henry to hop in the back. "I think you and Jackson are insane, and if you didn't have keepers, you'd pretty much be self-extinct by now."

"Word," Henry said, holding his fist up over the front seat for Jackson to bump.

Jackson didn't leave him hanging.

HENRY AND Jackson kept up the shits and giggles on the trip to the hospital. Ellery let them because Jackson's fear of hospitals would have been hanging over their heads otherwise, and they managed to contain themselves as they gained entry to Avi Kovacs's room.

Kovacs was probably a good-looking man when he was well. He had high cheekbones and a full mouth. Today, pale and grief ridden, he looked like a wraith, a tragic ghost, and Ellery had a moment to pity him. Not the best of men, no, but his entire world had been turned upside down in the space of a week, and he'd been asleep for the whole thing.

"Mr. Kovacs?" Ellery asked while Jackson brought him a chair. Ellery sat, conscious that Jackson and Henry were both standing behind him like twin blond bodyguards.

"Da," Kovacs said, but he had no accent. Maybe he used the word as habit—or irony.

"How are you doing today?"

It was a courtesy, really, but Kovacs jiggled his wrist against the handcuffs that held him to his hospital bed and looked dourly at the two armed officers who stood guard at the room's entrance.

"I'm champagne and fucking roses," he said sullenly, closing his eyes. He opened them, though, and sighed. "And that was rude. I'm not normally such an asshole."

"You threatened to shoot up the public defender's office," Ellery pointed out.

Avi groaned. "God, yeah. Not my finest hour."

Ellery and Jackson exchanged glances. A self-aware bad guy— apparently they existed.

"Then why'd you do it?" Jackson asked.

Avi looked at him, frowning. "Do I know you guys?"

"We're the guys who stopped you," Henry told him. "Last time you and me saw each other, I was barring a door against you with a fireman's axe."

Avi groaned again. "Bathtub meth is bad," he said seriously. "So bad. Stay away from drugs, kids. They will make you stupid."

"You don't look like a habitual user," Jackson observed. "The doctors didn't say anything about withdrawal symptoms. What happened?"

"My fuckin' cousin," Avi muttered. "Ziggy Ivanov. Sacramento happened, because God, Vegas was such a clusterfuck."

"So…?" Ellery led, because apparently the jig was up for Avi. He didn't see any reason to be discreet. Well, that worked for them.

"So," Avi said with a sigh. "About Vegas being a clusterfuck. So a year ago strange shit started to happen."

Ellery and Jackson met eyes. "Strange shit?" Jackson asked cagily.

"Yeah. Like small cells just taking each other out. Cars getting busted for no apparent reason. Guys dying in what looks like accidents but we know are actually hits. Anyway, weird shit. Vegas and the surrounding areas are toxic as hell. So Alexei starts looking for ways to get the fuck out of Vegas. We've got rumors of Batman in a yellow car with an eight-foot-tall Robin and assassins who can literally predict where we're going to be when we don't know ourselves. Life ain't fun in Vegas. Alexei starts fishing around for somewhere else. LA's too big, and their mob life is covered. So he looks up in Sacramento. Now, Dima's got a decent operation, really. Smooth, doesn't draw attention to itself, lots of respectable Russian community going on to cover our bullshit. But he hasn't done anything to us, and we got no reason to move in on him."

"You guys don't just take each other out for kicks?" Henry asked, and Ellery winced.

Avi, however, didn't take offense. "Not if we can help it. Man, every man in your organization is a fucking investment. They're either raised in the life or trained in the military. Russian, American, it doesn't matter. You think we've got a Bad Guys 'R' Us outlet where you can lay down cash and get some brothers to have your back? We wish!"

Jackson and Henry chuckled, and Ellery rolled his eyes.

"So you weren't going to move into Sacramento. What happened?"

"Ziggy Ivanov and Karina Schroeder." Alex shuddered. "And her husband, Dietrich. God, especially Dietrich, the sick fuck. Anyway, Dietrich and Ziggy were Dima's guys, fresh off the fuckin' boat. They were in dance school together, and they'd done their time in the brothels, you know? So they know sex trade inside and out. But Dietrich, he's got a head for numbers, and he's thinking they can up their gambling operation, and Ziggy wants to start kidnapping little kids and shit, because, hello, they're both sick fucks, and they were used like meat and they want to share the pain."

Schroeder—the name was definitely familiar. "Any relationship to Baldwin and Klaus?" Jackson asked, getting right on that.

"Uncle—why?"

"'Cause we took Baldwin out a couple days after you went to sleep, and we were wondering how they got sucked into this mess."

Avi groaned. "Sick fucking family—Schroeder can't even speak decent fucking English, man, has an accent you can cut with a knife. Anyway, Dietrich and Ziggy want to expand the operation to more trafficking 'cause that's their fucking kink."

"I take it Dima wasn't on board for this?" Ellery asked.

"No," Avi said shortly. "Alexei wasn't either, frankly, but then Ziggy and Dietrich started showing up with shipments of girls. Alexei did girls—can't lie. And then they showed up with shipments of kids, and buyers lined up, and Alexei, well, there was money to be made, and all Ziggy and Dietrich needed was muscle."

"And then all they needed was to take over Dima's operation," Ellery supplied coldly.

Avi sighed sadly. "It was more complicated than that. Ziggy and Dietrich supplied us with traffic, and Alexei, he gave them drugs to sell, and at first, it didn't seem like we were so much as taking over Dima's shit as we were just doing the jobs he didn't want."

"Human. Trafficking," Jackson said, his voice also cold, and Avi shrugged.

"We are not good people," he said candidly. "You think saints take a snort full of bathtub meth and haul ass into a PD office with a semiauto?"

"No," Jackson replied, voice still arctic. "But I didn't think reasonable guys with a modicum of self-awareness did either."

Avi's gray eyes met Jackson's without flinching. "When your brother puts a gun in your hand when you're twelve years old and tells you to kill the guy who tried to knife him in a drug deal, you lose your high-fucking-morality really quick. Doesn't mean I like it. That's just how the world works."

But it wasn't. Not for Jackson.

"My mother sold me to her boyfriend for a hit of crank when I was eleven," Jackson said. "I became a cop so it didn't happen to someone else. You only lose it when you want to lose it."

Avi's face went blank. "Yeah, well, I did want to lose it. Life's easier when that part of your soul is empty."

Jackson hadn't wanted to lose his humanity, though, Ellery thought. He remembered that moment when they were bracing for impact and he realized Jackson would be the one to suffer the worst if the Tank didn't hold up. There hadn't been a moment's hesitation in his eyes, and not a moment's regret.

There'd been children in that school bus, and if they had to throw themselves in front of the SUV to save them, that's what Jackson would do.

He would have done it without the Tank. He would have stood in the road and laid down his life if he hadn't been able to think of a better way.

Any pity Ellery might have felt for Avi abruptly vanished.

"Easier," he said softly, thinking of his colleagues who would have defended Avi without question or qualm. "But not good. So, why *did* you end up hauling into the PD's office with a semiautomatic weapon?"

Avi crossed his eyes. "Because Ziggy screwed up. He assumed that Tage Dobrevk would be just another kid lost to the system. Same thing for Ty Townsend, actually, but it didn't matter so much if Townsend got off. Townsend didn't know anything. Ziggy's sources in the courthouse told us Dobrevk's case was going to someone good, Ziggy told Alexei someone needed to make sure that didn't happen, and that—*that*—was his plan."

Avi swallowed, his face carefully blank. "I know what you think of me, and it's all true. I'm a murderer. I'm a trafficker and a drug dealer. But I've never—and you probably don't care about this, but it meant something to me—I've never killed someone not in the life. Alexei never killed the girls who slept with the wrong mobster. He relocated them to a different state, but he didn't kill them for that. I've never killed a witness 'cause they saw too much. Ziggy's plan was to go in like a random shooter, and Alexei, God, he was so tired of all Ziggy's shit. The heart went out of him when he realized Ziggy had killed James Cosgrove. It was like he knew he'd gotten in bed with the devil, and he was just waiting for the devil to fuck him to death and get it over with. He gave that order and I... I had to do something or I wouldn't have been able to go through with it, and the next person on Ziggy's list to kill would be me."

There was silence in the room then, and Ellery tried a little harder to hate Avi Kovacs and failed. He wasn't a good man—would never *be* a good man—but he hadn't been pure unadulterated evil either.

"Why'd Ziggy kill James Cosgrove?" Ellery asked. "Was it because he was asking Dima to back off?"

Avi's expression grew haunted. "Yes. The kid was going to his uncle to help get Townsend out of jail. Ziggy was begging for Jimmy to wait because he wasn't ready for the takeover yet. He had a few guys on his side and a couple of Alexei's guys ready to come up. He'd had a football coach working for him for the last two years to help him get contacts at the school for girls and drugs, but things weren't quite in place. So he… he killed Dima's nephew, which was too fucking bad because he wasn't a bad kid. Dima had tried to keep him out of the business. That's why he changed the last name. So Dima was all fucking ripped up about it, and Ziggy pinned it on the Dobrevk kid, thinking it would be easy to take him out. Who was going to care about an immigrant kid, right?"

"We did," Jackson said. "We cared for the immigrant kid, and the Black kid, and the dead guy named No Neck who bled out on the laundry room floor."

Avi nodded again. "Yeah. I figured as much when you guys asked if you could come talk to me."

"So why did you agree?" Ellery asked, but he figured he knew what was coming.

Avi looked at him and shrugged. "My brother's dead. Most of his contacts are in the wind. I got no reason to go home and nothing to stay here for, but I don't want to be a snitch. Ziggy's dead. Dietrich and Karina are fuck knows where, and I just told you everything I know about them for free. I got my own money in an account that's got nothing to do with the mob. All I want is for you to plead me out and let me do my twenty-five years someplace nowhere near Sacramento or Vegas. Let me serve my time in fuckin' Washington or Colorado or something. Let me close my eyes and pretend I was born someplace else."

Ellery's eyebrows went up, and for a moment, he thought of saying no. But he had a better idea.

"San Quentin?" he asked. "It's on an island near the ocean, if that helps."

"You can get me something near the ocean?" Avi said, with a sort of wistfulness that actually hurt.

"Can you pay Tage Dobrevk's and Ty Townsend's legal fees?" Ellery asked, ignoring the suck of breath through Jackson's teeth and Henry's hum of surprise.

"You get me near the ocean and I'd pay Ziggy's," Avi said starkly. Then his face relaxed into a sort of smile. "Lucky me, I don't have to, so I'm glad the fucker's dead."

Ellery agreed, and they shook hands on it. Then he told the guards to make the necessary arrangements to allow him to represent Avi Kovacs, and they took their leave.

As they neared the car, the weighty heat of August tapering off a little in the late afternoon, Henry said, "But I thought you were going to do Townsend and Dobrevk for free."

"I was," Ellery said. "But don't tell him that. This way I can keep you and Jackson in vehicles and health insurance for all of the other 'free' cases I do."

Henry smirked, but after they'd gotten into the car, he still had one more question.

"Rivers?"

"Yeah?"

"Did your mother really sell you for a hit of crank?"

Jackson grunted. "She made me a perk. I elbowed the guy in the windpipe and became a liability."

"And did a week in juvenile hall for attempted manslaughter," Ellery added darkly, because stories like this from Jackson's past were one of the reasons he defended kids like Ty Townsend and Tage Dobrevk for free.

"Who got you out?" Henry asked, his voice neutral.

"Jade and Kaden's mom," Jackson said softly. "She was a paralegal in a public defender's office. Didn't make much, but boy, she put the fear of the law into us."

She'd also given him the love and stability his life had been missing until Kaden had brought Jackson home. The debt Jackson felt toward Toni Cameron was not something he could ever repay or work off. It had taken Ellery a while to understand that Jackson's entire life had become dedicated to making the sacrifices she'd made for all three of them absolutely worth it.

"Good," Henry said softly. "I'll light a candle for her if I ever go to mass again."

Jackson gave a sweet smile. "I think she'd like that." The smile faded. "Why do you ask?"

Henry shrugged. "Just… just an odd thing to tell a guy like Avi Kovacs."

Jackson was silent for a moment. Then he said, "Don't you think the bad guys need confession?"

Henry grunted, and Jackson tried again.

"Didn't *you*?"

"I was nowhere near—"

Jackson's turn to grunt. "No, no, you weren't anywhere near an Avi Kovacs. I'm just saying that when people are being human to you, you try to be human back. Even the bad guys. Every now and then someone pays it forward, but even if they don't, it's like Avi said. He gave away that thing that tried to be moral when he was twelve years old. You need to decide right now what the price is inside *you*." He shrugged, but Ellery knew it wasn't that easy. "Being human to a guy who's about to go away for twenty-five years and who just made our job a little easier is not anywhere near that price, you know?"

Henry made a thoughtful sound. "You never think about it in the military. You assume the people telling you where to go and who to shoot have done the math. But here...."

Jackson's eyes slid to Ellery's before they refocused on the road. "Second thoughts, Junior?"

"God no," Henry answered smartly. "But I do have a small request."

"What do you need?" Ellery asked, knowing what it would be.

"Absolutely not," Jackson told him, because Jackson wasn't stupid either.

"Next time there's going to be high-speed chases and daring rescues out apartment windows, you have *got* to let me in."

"That doesn't happen every day," Jackson said with such a straight face that Ellery had to look at him twice.

"That ends with a *y*," Ellery finished dryly. "Henry, I'll tell you what. *I* will have you on speed dial so I can tell you what we're doing next. How's that."

"That's a deal," Henry said smugly. "Jackson? Piss up a rope. I'm your backup, dammit. Treat me like it."

"His boyfriend's gonna kill us," Jackson muttered to Ellery, and Ellery just laughed.

LATER—AFTER HENRY was dropped off at the office and Billy came by with the car, Jackson and Ellery took an early day home.

"Is everybody getting nice and rehabilitated?" Galen asked, his voice arid.

"No," Ellery told him, and then heat crept up his cheeks. "I mean, yes, we are both healing nicely, thank you, but that's not why we're going home early on a Friday."

Galen's eyes lit up. "Could we... could it possibly be... are you two having a *date night*?"

"It's an anniversary of sorts," Ellery responded with dignity, and Galen smiled back.

"You know what happened in mid-July?" he asked.

"The heat spiked to 110?"

Galen made a face. "Yes, but it was a *dry* heat," he returned. "Besides that."

"Not a clue," Ellery said. "Besides perhaps that may have been about the time Jackson got so bored he took an online criminal-justice class specializing in children's crimes, because why be a lawyer when you can take all the classes, right?"

Galen snorted. "Of course. But no, this was for me. See, two years ago in April, John and I met in Florida. I was in a really bad place, and John was coming out of a worse one. And we did all the things we weren't supposed to do if you're recovering addicts, and we fell in love. But John had to run his company, so he came back here, and I still had rehab, so I stayed out there. I could barely walk back then, even with the cane, and I was about thirty pounds underweight, and I was a *mess*. But John still loved me. Can you imagine that? Surrounded by some of the prettiest men in the world, and he still loved *me*."

"He's got good taste," Ellery said, feeling his eyes sting for some reason.

Galen inclined his head modestly. "You are too kind. Anyway, I was working, not just on rehab, but also on physical therapy. So I could walk around the house without the cane. So I could drive in an emergency. So I could be the best man I could be for a guy who professed to be a porn mogul with no conscience. Do you know why?"

Ellery had met Galen's boyfriend, and he was goofy and awkward and sweet, and he put 60 percent of his profits into things like health insurance and college funds and financial counseling and job placement so the kids who were young and sexy and excited to be naked and free with their sexuality when they started the business weren't old and used up and cynical when they left it, usually a year or two later.

"To make him proud?" Ellery hazarded.

Galen shook his head. "To be good enough for him," he said. "So mid-July, he and all those beautiful men are having a picnic by the zoo, and here he comes with his niece, wearing zinc oxide and a hat and carrying a giant gorilla, and I was there waiting for him, and it was the best moment of my life."

Ellery swallowed hard. "A year ago," he said gruffly, "sometime this week—neither of us remember the day—after Jackson and I had danced around each other for nearly seven years, pretending to hate each other, sneering when we passed each other in the hallways, making snarky comments when we knew the other one could hear...." He smiled slightly. "We finally gave in."

"Ah," Galen said, nodding. "That's a good day to remember."

"So much has happened since then," he said, feeling this in his chest. "So much. You've seen part of it."

"And researched a lot more," Galen said with a half laugh.

"Yeah. And it all comes down to that moment, I guess. When we gave in. And I knew I wouldn't ever go back. There was nothing I wouldn't do to keep him. He was mine in all the ways that counted, whether he knew it or not."

Galen gave him a luminous smile. "So this is a *very* good day," he said. "Happy anniversary, Counselor Cramer. May your celebration be lusty and good."

The heat that had threatened Ellery's cheeks washed over him completely. "Thank you, Counselor Henderson," he said, suddenly very grateful for this man who had pretty much declared himself Ellery's business partner and then made it so. "Our lives are very much richer because you're in them."

Galen's cheeks washed pink as well, and he grimaced. "You are a gentleman, sir. Now kindly get the fuck out of the office. I do believe I need to see my boyfriend."

Ellery laughed and limped away.

Fishy-versary

JACKSON HAD been prepared to try to cook, but Ellery had insisted on takeout. Fancy, fancy takeout that they actually put on plates and ate with silverware the moment they got home.

Neither one of them had been in a restaurant mood, although Jackson had offered.

"No," Ellery replied, shaking his head. "Sometimes all I want is you and me."

Jackson made sure Ellery had some of his favorite wine, and he drank pinot grigio to keep Ellery company. He cracked wise about getting the sweetest wine he could find for his unsophisticated palate, but the truth was, he was starting to appreciate other tastes too.

It was like cooking or classes in law or getting used to letting Ellery have enough control to let him feel comfortable about the times he *wasn't* in control and Jackson had to be Jackson; it took practice, it took getting used to, and it took effort.

They'd put in both over the last year.

Their dinner conversation wasn't profound. They chewed over the case, making all the pieces fit. At the end of dinner, as they shared a piece of divine cheesecake—a thing Jackson had never ordered before Ellery—he could sense Ellery's exasperation.

"We're not going to get Dima, Jackson. We're not going to get Dietrich and Karina. I mean, we *might*. They're out there. Dima can rebuild. Dietrich and Karina know how to make money gambling. They're going to be a problem." He shrugged. "But it's nothing we haven't faced before."

Jackson had felt it then, the profound shift inside him that told him Ellery was right in this moment. Just like the night he'd had to rescue the Dobrevks. Things might change tomorrow—hell, they might change in an *hour*, or fifteen minutes from now.

But right now—*right* now—Ellery was dressed nicely for Jackson Rivers, of all people. He'd shaved twice, put on aftershave, and worn slacks and a button-down just to eat in their dining room.

Jackson had done the same.

Ellery's hair wasn't gelled. Because he wasn't at the office, yes, but also because Jackson liked it without the gel, liked the way it fell softly forward, liked the way Ellery looked at him shyly sometimes, when Ellery was one of the sharpest people Jackson had ever met.

Jackson was looking shyly back.

"What?" Ellery asked, biting his lip.

"I am feeling lucky, tonight," Jackson said softly.

"Well, we did just escape death," Ellery said, rolling his eyes, and Jackson had to laugh.

"Not that way." He raised his hand to cup Ellery's cheek. "*This* way. I'm feeling lucky *this* way. That a year ago, we… well, we had some serious sex in the span of about two days. I mean, like record-setting pace."

"We gave in," Ellery agreed.

Jackson nodded. "We gave in. And you know what?"

Ellery shook his head. "No. What?"

"It saved my life. This last year has been a roller coaster ride, that's for damned sure. But as rough as you and me are on each other sometimes, I don't think I could have made it through if we hadn't started with all that arguing and a fuckton of sex."

Ellery laughed. "I guess we are lucky." He sobered and covered Jackson's hand with his own. "Watching you just… be *you*, I guess, isn't easy. It's never been easy. It's why we did the dance for so long, I think. But getting to be with you? Best thing I've ever done."

Jackson gave a shaky grin. "Think we'll make it another year?"

Ellery returned it. "You mean, you and me or, you know, make it out alive?"

"I mean you and me," Jackson said. "Because if I've got a you and me to live for, you can bet your ass I'll make it out alive."

"My ass?" Ellery said, arching a playful eyebrow. "Really?"

"Go get undressed, Counselor, and I'll show you how it's done."

When Jackson had finished putting everything away, he ventured into the bedroom, not surprised to see Ellery naked but under the covers.

He started to unbutton his own shirt, shaking his head in mock annoyance. "No," he said. "This isn't naked."

"I can assure you—"

"Pull back the covers, prop your bum knee up with a pillow, and spread your legs for me with your ass on the edge of the bed, Ellery. We may both be the walking wounded here, but I really think we should mark our anniversary with some serious sex."

Ellery glared at him in challenge.

"Well, that's romantic."

Jackson cocked his head. "Do you really want me to get in there and go to work on you?" he asked sweetly. "Because I'll do it!"

Ellery threw back the covers and splayed himself out for Jackson's eyes, and Jackson smiled in satisfaction as he stripped off his own slacks and laid them on the dresser.

"You're insufferable," Ellery muttered, naked and vulnerable and so, so hot. His long-fingered hand was unconsciously stroking his own cock, and Jackson shuddered seeing it.

"I want you," Jackson said evenly. "I want all of you. I want your ass, I want your come…." He grabbed the lube from the end table, where Ellery had set it up to be prepared. He leaned over the bed, bracing his weight on his elbows, and kissed the side of Ellery's neck. "I want your body," he murmured and nipped his ear. "Your sex, your soul."

Ellery smiled just a little as Jackson kissed his way down Ellery's chest.

"Oh," he said simply. "Okay, then. Carry on."

And Jackson did. He knew Ellery's body now—nipples, cock, sweetly giving asshole. But he loved it more now too, wanted to take his time on every part. He kissed and he teased as Ellery thrashed beneath him, begging, pleading, *needing*.

When they'd first started, he'd done this out of pride. He only got to have someone in his bed if he was a good enough lover to give them the full e-ticket ride. Ellery had figured out what he was doing and put a stop to it, and now, when Jackson did the full-court arousal press, he was doing it because he enjoyed playing with Ellery's body, enjoyed his noises, enjoyed knowing he and he alone could make Ellery Cramer happy.

He had Ellery's cock down his throat, his fingers spreading Ellery's ass, making him ready, when Ellery cried out, "Please, baby. I need you inside me. Please!"

And Jackson couldn't tease him anymore.

Ellery Cramer was the kindest, smartest, *hottest* man Jackson had ever known, and if he needed Jackson in any capacity, that was Jackson's right, it was his privilege, it was his *pleasure* to give it to him.

He stood at the edge of the bed and lifted Ellery's good knee, careful of the one propped on the pillows, and entered him slowly, enjoying the way Ellery's exposed throat patterned red with his sex flush and the way his body gripped Jackson's cock like a slick fist. He slid all the way to the hilt, both of them letting out little groans of completion, and Ellery forced his hooded eyes to meet Jackson's.

"Jackson?"

"Yeah?"

"Hard and fast."

"*Yes!*"

Jackson was careful, even in the throes of the monster orgasm that was roaring in his blood, not to hurt Ellery's healing body.

And it was so easy to let that monster roar through him as it was, spurred on by Ellery's cries of pleasure, turned on by the sight of his hand stroking his own cock, his body stroked by Ellery's asshole as he clenched so, so tight.

"Now!" he begged, and a year ago he would have been too proud to beg. And a year ago, Ellery would have forced him to take what he needed anyway.

But now, he could ask, and Ellery tilted his head back and cried out, his come jetting across his abdomen and chest.

The sight pushed Jackson over, and he closed his eyes and thrust one more time, spilling all that he was with his spend.

He stayed still for a moment, rutting, because his body was so locked in the action of fucking that it didn't want to stop. Finally he opened his eyes and slid out, collapsing to Ellery's side so he didn't force Ellery to move the knee wrong.

Their heavy breathing filled the room, and he watched Ellery's face avidly for a clue, any clue, to what he was feeling.

The slow smile curving his lips was a good sign.

"How was that?" he asked, feeling hopeful and a little wicked.

"I'm not sure," Ellery said, the smile deepening. He opened his eyes and turned his head, capturing Jackson's mouth in a hard kiss. Jackson returned it and then frowned.

"Wait a minute. You're not sure?"

Ellery's warm chuckle rippled up from his stomach. "We may have to do it again," he teased breathlessly. "So, you know, I can see."

Jackson laughed and kissed him some more before pulling back. "Okay, we can do it again. And maybe two or three more times after that. But then we have to stop and get some sleep."

"On our anniversary weekend?" Ellery asked, eyes widening in mock outrage. "Why would we have to stop and get some sleep?"

Jackson propped his head up on his hands and began to run his fingertips desultorily over Ellery's chest. "Because we," he said, "have to get a kitten. Remember?"

Ellery's surprise showed Jackson that he'd forgotten. Then he captured Jackson's fingertips and kissed them. "I do now. I'd love to. Happy anniversary, Detective."

Jackson laced their fingers together. "Happy anniversary, Counselor. I love you."

"Love you too."

They would make love again soon, he knew, and maybe even a third time, because he always wanted Ellery.

And then they would sleep and have a normal, everyday weekend filled with small things like visiting friends and playing with kittens.

They would rest, fill up with the good things in their lives, make sure their hearts were good to go again.

It was a rough world out there, and even the best of men were asked to make hard decisions sometimes.

They had so much work to do.

And as always, I've included the shorts written between Fish Out of Water novels. The last short is—by request—about Dave and Alex, the two adorable, competent, compassionate nurses who take such good care of our guys.

Thanks to all my health-care people out there—you are remembered and treasured. And even before the 2020 pandemic, you've always been heroes.

Cold Water

A Jackson and Ellery Story

Necessary Journey

"I DON'T want to leave Billy Bob," Jackson said mulishly.

"Cat's fine." Ellery labored to throw both their carry-ons into the trunk. He'd packed Jackson's with cargo shorts, tees, hooded sweatshirts, and tennis shoes because that was pretty much all he wore anyway.

"Aren't I supposed to go back to work in six…?"

Ellery got into the driver's seat of the Lexus and sent Jackson a deeply tired look. "Finish that sentence," he said, exhaustion hurting his bones. "I dare you."

Jackson took a deep breath—a gratifyingly clear deep breath—and nodded.

"I'm sorry, Ellery," he said dutifully.

Ellery let out a cracked laugh. "You got out of surgery a week ago. You're doing fine. You just need to relax, and you're not doing it at home. Can we…?" He looked at Jackson in honest supplication. "We're the bosses, and I say we take a vacation."

Jackson nodded. "You're planning to work during my mandatory nap time, aren't you?"

"Yes," Ellery said without repentance. "But we have a hotel room overlooking the ocean, so it will feel like a vacation."

Jackson smiled faintly and yawned. "You need to not worry about me for a week," he said, and that new understanding he'd shown when his heart murmur had really started getting bad hadn't gone away yet.

Ellery was grateful.

"Yes," he said gently.

Jackson regarded him with narrow eyes. "Am I going to get sex? Finally? Because the doctor said I could go as soon as I felt up to it."

"And when do you feel up to it?" Ellery closed the door and started the Lexus, drowning out Jackson's automatic "Always!"

"I'm sorry," Ellery said, holding his hand to his ear. "I didn't hear that."

"You did too, you big baby. How do you know it's not true?"

Ellery took one more look at him before backing the car out. He'd gained a little weight back, and since the surgery clearing out the scar tissue from his aorta, his cheeks were a normal color again. But Ellery had almost lost him so many times, the idea that he could lose Jackson *now*, to Jackson's stubbornness, still filled him with fear.

"It's true when you're not trying to prove something to me," Ellery said, his face relaxing a little. The garage door was open; they were going to see free air. "I don't just want you for the sex—and yes, it's a perk. I really, really need to know you're okay."

Jackson closed his eyes, the shadows under them indicating he'd about used up his awake time for the moment. The doctor said he'd sleep a lot in the first couple of weeks, but as long as he kept up a regimen of *moderate* exercise and ate well instead of like a fifth grader running away from his parents, he would be back to five miles a day and a hundred miles an hour in no time at all.

Ellery needed him to sleep.

"You have said that before," Jackson said softly.

"Which part?" Ellery backed out and hit the button for the garage door. Jade and her boyfriend, Mike, would be by to water Ellery's plants that evening, and Henry would be by to take care of Billy Bob in the mornings. Between the three of them using the pool and taking advantage of the air-conditioning and the privacy, the house should look well lived in for the next week. Ellery wasn't worried about it.

Jackson on the other hand…. Ellery would never not worry in that direction.

Never.

"That you don't need sex from me."

"I don't! I—"

"No, no." Jackson held up a languid hand. "I believe you, Counselor. I just need to remember I have to work at being better company."

"You do not! That's the point. You don't have to work at being anything but yourself."

Jackson let out what might be a laugh when he woke up. "I'll parse that in a few hours. Are you sure you're up for driving?"

"Monterey here we come." Ellery had literally pulled it out of a hat. Jackson had loved the beach in San Diego, but they needed someplace cooler. Some place Jackson wouldn't be tempted to surf, swim, or otherwise dive into the water.

Some place they could walk easily, not sweat too much, and eat clam chowder, and Ellery could remind him that his entire existence was more than his ability to solve mysteries or sex Ellery up.

Not, of course, that the sex would be unwelcome. It was just that Jackson needed to remember that he was loved.

He'd come through the surgery with flying colors—and too many people worried about him. Once everybody had gone away, he'd been alone with the voices in his own head and a body that wouldn't let him outrun them. Ellery had learned all sorts of things about being in a relationship with this man over the past year, but as he drove out of Sacramento and down toward the Monterey Peninsula, he thought that maybe the biggest thing was that Jackson didn't have a roadmap for how a normal life looked.

Ellery needed to give him some pointers, and he couldn't do that in a place where every breath was measured against how he'd felt healthy and how he'd felt dying.

A week in Monterey sounded like the perfect getaway. And every time they'd gone out of town before now, they'd had a case. Ellery was really curious to see what they could manage without one.

Getting a room at the hotel in the center of downtown Monterey, overlooking the bay, was expensive and ostentatious, and Ellery didn't give a shit. He had princess diamond tiara status or whatever in the hotel chain, and he wanted Jackson to wake up every morning and look out at the crystal waters of the bay.

Ellery had never really wanted to abuse his wealth until he'd loved someone who had grown up not having enough to eat.

Jackson had looked around with shy appreciation as they took the elevator to the top floor. "There's a skyway across the street," he said.

"Yeah, that's sort of Monterey's main street," Ellery told him. "There's shops, tourist kitsch, antiques, fudge."

Jackson laughed softly. "We can walk to the aquarium," he said. "It's the one they had in *Star Trek IV*, but they called it something else."

"You want to go?"

"Go see about the smart fish? Yeah, why not. I hear they have a mantis shrimp there. Do you know those little bastards have a dozen or more color cones in their eyes? They can practically see sound. They can power punch through six inches of fiberglass. It's like a little karate death underwater butterfly. I want to see that."

Ellery looked at him, appalled. "You want to go see a karate death underwater butterfly?"

"I hear they have otters too." Jackson smiled sleepily, the combination of little-kid wonder and snarky asshole almost irresistible.

"Tomorrow," Ellery told him. "We can go tomorrow. And maybe drive down the coast some the day after. The shopping in Carmel is really wonderful."

Jackson grunted. "Shopping?"

"We can get my mother's Hanukkah gift early."

"Sure." Jackson wrinkled his nose. "And yours, I guess. And your birthday gift while we're at it. I sucked at your birthday gift."

"You got me a very nice tie." It had Siamese cats on it, like Billy Bob except with four legs. Ellery sort of treasured it, as tacky as it was, because Jackson had tried—hard—to reconcile their two different worlds.

Jackson's laugh cracked. "I got a pass because last year was fucked way up. No more passes. I have to give better gifts."

No. No, you don't.

"Then we have to go shopping together," Ellery said, voice thick. "It's a skill."

Like resting.

"WHAT ARE we going to do this evening?" Jackson said it with bright interest, but his steps dragged. People don't like to admit that traveling is exhausting, particularly people like Jackson who felt like they were cheating at life when sitting still.

"You're going to go sleep some more, and then we can go walk around and find a restaurant." And Ellery could research the three cases they'd gotten in the past week. He'd be super excited about how he and Jackson kept attracting media attention with their high-profile cases if it didn't mean Jackson ended up in the hospital all the fucking time.

"Aw, come on, Counselor. At least let me use my Google Fu and help you brain words."

That was actually not a bad idea. Jackson's instincts—whether he was up and around or not—were usually spot-on.

"Fine. Nap first."

"Lay down with me?" And Ellery might have said no if Jackson had done that suggestively. But he didn't. Instead, it was couched as a simple request, bare and particularly vulnerable.

Ellery couldn't ignore those. Jackson so rarely made them.

"Sure."

Jackson lay down dutifully as Ellery set up their luggage— Jackson's battered duffel, Ellery's Samsonite Rollaboard. Ellery put both their shaving kits in the bathroom and came back to the bed, where he kicked off his loafers and arranged himself neatly next to Jackson. Jackson had brought a blanket from home, something he'd owned before they'd gotten together that he'd picked up at a craft fair, and he was curled up underneath it, watching Ellery with hooded eyes. His hand on Ellery's middle was warm and welcome, and Ellery closed his eyes, relaxing into the comfort he'd insisted upon.

"Going to nap with me?" Jackson asked. "The traffic was pretty awful on the way down."

Yes, it had been. And, well, Jackson needed a roadmap. It was up to Ellery to provide. He slid lower on the bed so their heads were even on the pillows.

"You're good at that," he murmured.

"What?"

"Taking care of me when I'm trying to take care of you."

Jackson smiled faintly, allowing his eyes to close all the way. "I do my best," he said. "You're just difficult."

Ellery chuckled, and as he drifted into a truly necessary nap, he realized that it had been a while since he'd laughed.

Appreciating the Scenery

JACKSON REGARDED the giant cephalopod with wonder. "Look," he whispered, not wanting to disturb the guy—he was, after all, just sort of chilling. "The sign says he's super smart. He changes colors when his favorite people are nearby." He could swear the thing was regarding him with a friendly eye.

"Is that favorite as in friends or favorite as in foods?" Ellery asked, and while he tried to sound persnickety, Jackson had the feeling he was charmed too.

"As in friends." Jackson scowled at him, but mischief was in his eyes. "They're really gentle creatures, you know. A little shy, and they don't like light or loud noise. Hey!"

That last part was aimed at a kid—maybe eleven—who had elbowed his way in between Jackson and Ellery to take a picture with his phone. Without compunction, Jackson stuck his hand over the flash.

"Hey!" the kid yelled, and Jackson shushed him.

"Buddy, as I was saying, this thing is *sensitive*. When you flash him like that, it hurts his eyes. And yelling is just as bad. It's like throwing a rock concert with a baby in the house. It's *rude*."

The kid sneered, a blond, blue-eyed master of the universe in the making. "*You're* rude!" and he set up to take another picture.

Jackson reached over his shoulder and took the phone from him.

"Hey!"

"You want it back?" Jackson asked, eyes flat.

"Yeah, man, gimme my fuckin' phone!"

"Go get your parents and bring them to this spot, but do it quietly or I might lose the phone before you get here."

"My dad's a cop. He'll kick your ass if you don't give me my damned phone."

Jackson's turn to sneer. "And I look forward to that," he said with sincerity. "Now scoot. We'll be here when you get back."

The kid took off through the aquarium, screaming "Dad!" at the top of his lungs, and one of the docents, a young man with ebony skin and gentle eyes, stepped forward in relief.

"Thank you," he said softly. "I hate it when kids do that. The giant octopus is really shy. If someone flashes him, he disappears for days. And he *cries*."

Jackson raised an eyebrow. "No, seriously?"

"Okay, we can't tell if he's shedding tears from his two big eyes, but he turns… just gray. And sad. And it's so nice to see someone speaking up for him." The young man turned toward a group of seven- or eight-year-olds getting ready to tap on the glass. "Please don't do that," he said. "It really hurts their ears."

The kids backed up and nodded, eyes big. "Sorry," one of them whispered.

"I know you want to get its attention," the docent told them. "And it's great that you want to know more, but these creatures are out of their element here. We try to make them comfortable, but when they have to people too much, it stresses them out."

"My little brother is like that," a little girl said. "We'll be nice. We promise."

They gathered closer, talking in low voices, and Jackson grinned at the docent, who smiled back. It was good they got a reminder that not all kids were little assholes, because as soon as they had that moment, that kid came back with his father in tow.

Dad was ginormous—six-five, three hundred pounds of ball-playing muscle with bristly black hair from pale skin, and he did not look happy.

"Did you take my kid's phone?"

Jackson gave his best party smile and hoped he didn't look like he wanted this guy to eat a sea urchin in the shell. "Did you ask your son what he was doing with it before I did?"

Dad's eyebrows went up, and he turned toward his son, who suddenly looked sullen. "I was just taking a picture."

Jackson pointed at the sign in the cephalopod area that read No Flash Photography.

The docent took a deep breath and addressed the situation. "We are actually authorized to ask anybody hurting our animals to leave," he said with a swallow. "Please, the flash hurts them, and that's no fun for anybody."

"Trevor, we paid a fortune for these goddamned tickets. If you get us kicked out because you can't keep your phone in your pocket, I'm making you pay that back with your allowance!"

"But Dad—"

"I'll take the phone, sir," his father said, extending his hand.

Jackson met his eyes solidly, and Dad looked at his kid again.

"Don't worry. He won't get it back."

"But you said it was so I didn't get lost."

"Well, you're not leaving my side now, are you? Mom's got the little kids, and you and me, buddy, we're like glue. It looks like you need to learn how to read again, doesn't it?"

The kid's eyes got huge, and his face got red, and Jackson turned the phone over, feeling reassured.

"Thanks," he said soberly. "I don't like it when people hurt the defenseless."

The guy nodded. "I'm a cop. It's my job to protect, so I get what you mean."

Jackson stared at him as he retreated, his kid complaining bitterly with every step. It looked like Dad was holding firm, though, and Jackson let out a deep breath.

"A cop," Ellery said, his first words in some time.

"Yeah, I know. Surprised me too."

Ellery was looking at him like he did sometimes, his eyes wide and a little glossy, his face open and full of wonder. Jackson didn't understand that expression; he didn't know what he'd done to warrant it.

"Surprised the hell out of me," the docent muttered, and Jackson grinned at him.

"Well, may we all meet more cops like that," he said, thinking that his own attitude may be a teeny bit biased against law enforcement.

"May there *be* more cops like that," the docent said. "I've got to go, but thanks so much for the assist." He smiled fondly at his friend the giant octopus. "Buddy here is grateful too. He just doesn't talk that much."

Jackson chuckled and was surprised by Ellery's grip on his hand.

"What?" he asked, turning to him again.

"Nothing," Ellery said, eyes bright. "You… you do things like that. It will never cease to amaze me."

Jackson was about to shrug him off, make light of the way he was looking, pretend he hadn't done anything.

But the thing he'd just done—trying to fix something small, teaching someone something valuable about the world—it was apparently one of the reasons Ellery stuck with him through fifty-dozen trips to the hospital and the unpacking of copious stacks of emotional baggage.

He swallowed, and disregarding any curious onlookers, he linked his fingers with Ellery's as the two of them wandered through the darkened environs of the rest of the cephalopods.

"What?" Ellery said softly, and Jackson squeezed his hand. Maybe a younger, friskier, Jackson would have pulled him into a corner and kissed him, and maybe an older, healthier Jackson would do that too. But this Jackson, in this moment, was just so happy to know he'd done something real, something that made Ellery look at him like that.

"Thank you," he said softly. "That's kind."

Ellery paused in a dark corner and tugged on his hand before kissing Jackson softly. Jackson regarded him in the black light of the aquarium and smiled slightly.

"What was that for?"

"I am so in love with you."

And Jackson didn't flinch or shrug or get embarrassed. "I love you back, Counselor. I'm so glad I'm good enough for you to love."

Another kiss, and then they separated, mindful of the bustling families and excitable children around them. They kept their hands linked, though, as they wandered the aquarium, open to the experience of wonder.

That night they ate practically downstairs from the hotel, consuming big bread bowls of the best clam chowder in the world. They took their bowls to a concrete wall that overlooked the beach below, watching children as they ran in and out of the waves. The ocean was too cold to go swimming. Even Jackson knew that now. He'd been hurt too badly plunging his feverish body into brutally cold water to ever take his heart for granted again.

For the moment, he would welcome the man beside him, the light sparkling off the sea, and this moment in the sun.

THAT NIGHT as they walked into the hotel room, he tugged on Ellery's hand and took him to the window.

"What?" Ellery asked, his voice as wondering as a child.

"The view's nice. I... you know. Wanted to share it with you."

"Jackson?"

"Yeah?"

"Can we make love tonight?"

Jackson kissed him gently, like it was their first time. As Ellery opened his mouth and gave underneath his hands, Jackson's heart beat loudly in his ears, and he was grateful for how strong it sounded. How alive.

Their clothes disappeared, and they lay on the bed, skin to skin. Their hands were reverent, and every touch sang. Ellery thick and hard in his hand was as important to the moment as Ellery's touch on his own cock. Jackson's stroke grew harder, faster, and Ellery sighed. Jackson kept it up, bending to catch Ellery's spend in his mouth.

Ellery arched and came, and the joy of it was enough to send Jackson over into Ellery's fist.

Jackson rested, his head on Ellery's stomach, and Ellery stroked his hair.

"Jackson?"

"You love me," Jackson said, confident of it as he never had been.

"For quite some time," Ellery said, his voice thin. "And you love me."

"But I think I finally believe it. Believe there's a reason you'd love me."

Ellery let out a strained and broken laugh. "There's several. God, you're dumb."

"Yeah. I am. I'll try not to be so dumb in the future. I don't want to miss any moments like this."

Ellery's breath quickened, and Jackson looked up in time to see him wipe under his eyes.

"What?"

"You could have. You could have. So many times." His voice shattered, and Jackson moved to pull Ellery's face against his neck.

"I can't do that anymore," he said. *Oh, Ellery. You deserve so much better.* The least Jackson could do was give this man the healthiest, most real person he could be.

"No," Ellery whispered. "Please, baby. We have so many more moments like this. Don't end them before you have to, okay?"

"Not if I can help it." Jackson kissed his temple, and the darkness protected them like it had protected the giant octopus. Sometimes the dark was needed, because the light hurt too much, and sometimes it was needed to see the light in a lover's heart.

And sometimes it was both.

That One Shirt

A Jackson and Ellery Story

THE IRONY of being on medical leave forced vacation was that the bedroom was set up so that Jackson's side of the bed was right next to the phone chargers.

Ellery's phone went off, and Jackson woke up and handed it to him; he wasn't allowed to get up.

He'd tried a couple of times. Couldn't they at least go running together? And when the weather was milder, it worked. But not in mid-August, after their trip to Monterey. Yeah, sure, Jackson was doing better. He had everything, including his meeting with the rabbi, down on the planner.

But Ellery wasn't about playing fast and loose with the rules, and the rules seemed unhealthily obsessed with the temperature on the steamy Sacramento streets.

Like this morning, about two weeks before Jackson was due to go back, when Ellery's phone went off to—oh dear God—the Shins playing "New Slang."

Jackson rolled out of bed hopefully, reaching into one of the two drawers he had in Ellery's dresser for running clothes.

"No. It's already ninety outside. You can go to the cooled gym and use the treadmill or wait until I get home and swim."

"My dick's getting pruny. It might never inflate again."

Even with his hair rumpled and pillow creases in his face, Ellery could still manage a deadpan look that would freeze solid rock.

"You. Would find. A way."

And with that, he got out of bed and quite literally glared Jackson back in.

"I have to get back in bed?" Jackson threw the covers back and slid his hand down his boxers. "If I have to get back in bed, I might as well do something useful." He'd been soft when he'd rolled out of bed—morning wood had come and gone—but his own hand, squeezing, defining, sorting things that had been all crumpled, into a place where they could air out... well, it did make a helmeted warrior stand to attention, as it were.

Ellery's eyes widened in surprise, and he stood, wearing his tank and boxers, scratching his head like he'd never seen Jackson stroke himself before.

"That's... that's your alternative? I tell you to go back to bed and you're going to masturbate?"

The fact that it made Ellery uncomfortable was an even bigger turn-on. "Sure," Jackson said happily, spreading his knees and arching his hips, getting *really* comfortable. "Just me, here on the bed, my good right hand."

Oh wow. He was getting hard. He closed his eyes and enjoyed knowing Ellery was watching with his mouth open. With his other hand he reached up to pinch a nipple, enjoying that too.

"I'm... uh...."

Jackson slitted his eyes to see that Ellery's boxers had tented, and his eyes had gone from wide to half-lidded and heavy. Jackson allowed his to close again, pretty sure he could get what he wanted without needing to see.

Jackson shoved his boxers down his hips and stroked hard enough to bring a pearl of precome to the tip. He let out a breath and smoothed it around his cockhead and then sucked it off his thumb.

He registered Ellery's mouth on his cock before he even heard the two footsteps to his side of the bed.

"Oh. Oh wow. Counselor, you're going to be... oh... late...."

Ellery didn't even bother to reply, just pulled him in deeper, kneeling by the side of the bed where, dammit, Jackson couldn't stroke him off in return. Jackson settled for massaging Ellery's scalp through his hair while Ellery sucked him hard and slow and then wrapped a fist around his cock and plied the end with this tongue while looking Jackson dead in the eyes.

"Hello." Jackson breathed. "You were doing something?"

"I would like nothing more than to finish this," Ellery said, his eyes lighting up in that particularly wicked way he had when he was about to do something Jackson might not like but would do only for Ellery.

"Feel free," Jackson told him, not wanting to beg. "If it's not you, it'll be me."

Ellery gave him a half smile. "But I won't have time to get off myself," he said. "You'll just have to deal with that. I—" He deep-throated Jackson's cock, hard and fast, and came up with his mouth swollen and glazed with spit. "—won't 'get mine,' Jackson. You'll have to trust that I'll come home anyway. Can you live with that?"

Jackson tried to pull his feet underneath him to sit up, because no, that was not something he did. Instead, he drove his cock all the way into Ellery's throat, and Ellery took advantage, tapping on his entrance just enough that Jackson quivered, shaking, needing to come.

Ellery kept his grip on Jackson's cock and pulled back, eyes watering, looking as debauched as Jackson had ever seen him. "Do you trust me?" he taunted.

"You think I'm letting you out of this house without coming, you're sadly mista—*augh*! *God! Ellery! Dammit!*" He was too far gone. Between his own self-pleasure and Ellery's masterful power play, Jackson was done for. He arched his back and came, loudly, without inhibition or shame.

When he fell back onto the bed, Ellery was standing by the bedside, stroking his face with a messy hand. "Now go back to sleep," he ordered gently.

Jackson lay there, panting, eyes half-closed, and nodded.

He waited until Ellery was in the shower before he stood up, dropped his boxers where they fell, and stalked into the bathroom with lube in hand. He was already mostly hard again when he stepped into the shower and started to kiss Ellery's neck.

"Jackson," Ellery breathed, "this wasn't in the agree—oh my!"

Jackson thrust two fingers into him. Not roughly, but firmly, because he knew Ellery would still be slack from the night before. Ellery cried out and bent, hands against the wall, as Jackson parted his cheeks and pushed inside.

"Jackson—"

"Don't start what you can't finish," Jackson growled, hips rocking as the water pounded on them both.

"Oh God," Ellery moaned. "Okay, fine. Fine. Uncle. Oh God. Jackson—faster. Faster, please. Oh my.... *Yes!*"

He was primed—he must have been—from blowing Jackson, from taunting him, from the power reversal, all of it, because in a few strokes he was quivering, hand working his own cock, which made Jackson even hotter. Jackson rocked harder, faster, even as the water ran cold. Biting Ellery's neck when he gave a choked groan of climax and shuddered against the tile wall weakly before Jackson rutted once, twice, and a slow aftershock rolled through him, half residual from the first climax, and half inspired by Ellery's tight body, his responsiveness, and his surrender.

Jackson caught him around the waist when it looked like he was going to slide down the wall. "Nah-nah," he rasped. "You have work today, remember? I have to stay home 'cause I'm fragile, and you have to go to—"

Ellery straightened with alacrity. "Shit!" he swore. "Shit! I *do* have work. I've got two cases, and I have to meet Henry at the office." He turned in the spray, using the washcloth to get his private places before stepping out. Jackson grunted and grabbed the washcloth from him, resigning himself to tepid water for the rest of the shower.

"I don't even get a kiss?" he complained.

Ellery turned irritated eyes toward him. "Isn't that my line? Get out and dry off, and I'll give you a kiss goodbye. But hurry. You don't want to get caught naked either!"

Jackson squirted some soap into his hair and tried not to hiss at the cold water.

"Caught naked by who?" he asked as he soaped his hair and private places.

"You have delivery men at nine. They'll be bringing a dresser to put in the far corner against the wall. There's plenty of room there, but you need to supervise and make sure the cat doesn't get out."

"I know not to let the cat out," Jackson muttered. "But why are we getting a new dresser? What's wrong with the old one?"

"The old one is mine. The new one is yours. You need more clothes."

"How can I need more clothes? You keep buying them for me. I've got my own section of the closet!"

"Well, I've bought you some more. Casual clothes. Jeans, T-shirts, those weird shorts that make me think of you naked."

"Basketball shorts?" Jackson chuckled and turned off the water in a hurry because he was freezing. "You ordered me new basketball shorts? I have three pairs already!"

Ellery waited until he stepped out of the bathtub to greet him, towel around his waist, with a chaste kiss on the cheek. "This way you can throw those out," he said calmly. "And some of those T-shirts that are hanging on by threads. And some of the underwear you got in high school. And some of the socks that peel off your feet."

Jackson gaped at him. Ellery had been on a not-so-subtle campaign to change up Jackson's wardrobe over the past year, and granted, a lot of their adventures had taken out parts of the wardrobe in general attrition. But this wasn't a skirmish or even a battle. This was D-Day on Jackson's remaining clothes, and he was unprepared.

"But... but...." Ellery smiled, cat-like, and Jackson was suddenly indignant. "*You*," he said in irritation, "do *not* get your way all the time!"

"Of course not. If I got my way, we would not have just had sex in the shower, and boy, you showed me. I learned my lesson about daring you, didn't I?"

Jackson glared at him. "Shut up."

Ellery kissed him on the lips. "Shutting up now, Detective. Wouldn't do to make you mad. You might blow me next, and then I'd be in real trouble."

"I know where you keep your sex toys, Counselor. Don't make this a contest."

To his everlasting joy, red crescents appeared high on Ellery's cheek, and his bluster drained out of him, replaced by the color. "I... those were from when I was single and, uh, you know."

Jackson's turn to capitalize on his discomfort. "Sure," he placated. "I'll never mention them again. They'll just, you know, sneak up on you. By surprise."

Ellery's eyes narrowed. "But not this morning, unless you want to *really* surprise the guys delivering the dresser." And with that, Ellery turned on his heel and went to get dressed.

Jackson dried off and brushed his teeth, then did the same, picking nylon basketball shorts that, he had to admit, were almost transparent, and a T-shirt with a collar barely hanging on by the threads, that read "Duct Tape: It Can't Fix Stupid But It Can Muffle the Sound" with a little silver line of duct tape weaving through the words.

Or it *had* a silver line of duct tape weaving through the words, but that was the first thing to go before the lettering started to flake off. The shirt was dark blue—or had *been* dark blue—but it was getting sort of greenish with overwashing, and there were holes in the armpits.

Jackson looked at it mournfully as he tugged on the hem and realized that even though he'd put on some much-needed weight that summer, it still flapped around his hips because it had been stretched out beyond all repair.

"Are you touching it like that because you're trying to say goodbye?" Ellery assessed as he walked past Jackson and into the hall. "And I'll make you some oatmeal for breakfast. Don't worry, I won't forget the margarine and teaspoon of sugar."

"Why would I say goodbye?" Jackson retorted to his retreating back. "It's got a few good years left!"

He tugged at the hem again and sighed when another portion of the neck gave way.

Goddammit. Did Ellery always have to be right?

Jackson was still feeling sulky when the furniture guy arrived. Just the fact that the dresser had to be *moved* instead of *assembled* meant that it was not only pricey, but also that it wouldn't interfere with Ellery's tastefully heavy furnishings.

In fact, it looked like a twin to Ellery's dresser, and Jackson sighed. It was official. After a year of sharing the same house, he was living with a guy who didn't seem to want him just for sex and was prepared to deal with all of his baggage.

Weird, but the thought was getting less weird as time progressed, so that was something.

The clothes, on the other hand....

"Did you at least put them away?" Ellery asked during his afternoon phone call.

"I didn't have a choice," Jackson told him. "I don't have anything else to do!" He had to admit, Ellery had taken his taste into account. The T-shirts had snarky sayings on them, and in addition to the slacks and button-downs, there was a share of stone-washed 501's and basketball shorts.

And the underwear didn't have a single hole in it—and neither did the brand-new, squishy-soft comfy socks.

Gah!

"You could try assembling those files I sent you and making that to-do list for Henry…. Oh, yes. I see. Wow, that was quick."

"I'm bored," Jackson said flatly. "Are you sure I have another two weeks?"

"Doctor's orders," Ellery said, that edge of irritation in his voice that said his last nerve and Jackson were getting to be friends again. He let it out in a sigh. "Do you want to walk to frozen yogurt when I get home? It'll be nearing evening. The heat won't be so bad."

"Really?" And oh! He sounded pathetic. But the promise of getting out of the house and doing something physical—with Ellery's approval—was probably his best thing right now.

"Promise." Ellery's gentleness told Jackson he understood.

Ellery changed into tasteful Bermuda shorts and a casual T-shirt, gray with a matching madras shirt to go over the ensemble. Jackson stayed in his basketball shorts and shredding T-shirt out of sheer perversity.

As they were walking into the yogurt place, Jackson was surprised to find that they were the object of a quiet conversation between a mother in her late forties and her daughter, probably in her late teens.

"Oooh," Mom said, sending Ellery a surreptitious look. "Hotties incoming."

"Mom!" daughter wailed, looking them over. Her eyes lingered on Jackson. "Okay. Fine. They have come in, and they're hot. Green eyes. Mm."

Jackson turned his attention to the line of different yogurts. It was one of those places that weighed your choices at the end and then charged you. He decided on pistachio with lots of chocolate and cookies while he listened to the rest of the convo.

"Oh, honey, not that one. The other guy."

"The other guy looks boring. *That* guy looks hot!"

"The other guy looks like he could pay the rent," Mom said. "And believe me, when you get to be a grown-up, that's *sizzle*. I mean, oh, baby, pay that bill for me one more time!"

Her daughter cracked up. "I'll crush on the guy who looks like he could dance on motorcycles while juggling chainsaws. I mean, I'm not gonna marry him, right? Just ogle him at fro-yo!"

Her mother laughed, and Jackson and Ellery went to get their frozen yogurt, and Ellery finished talking about the caseload Jackson would be walking into when he got back to their firm.

But he did notice Jackson was thinking about something. "What's up?" he asked as they were walking slowly home, savoring their treat.

Jackson looked at his T-shirt, which was actually letting in gusts of the river breeze as they walked. "I was just thinking how sexy you are," he said, and he smiled a little, but he was really thinking, *When you get to be a grown-up, that's* sizzle.

Ellery snorted, and Jackson shook his head.

"No," he said, taking another thoughtful bite. "I mean it. You have this grown-up thing mastered, you know? But… you still know how to have fun. I may need to take Ellery lessons."

Ellery grunted over his own bite of ice cream. When he'd swallowed, he said, "You're worth more than an 'ogle at fro-yo,'" with complete understanding.

"You heard that, did you?" Jackson asked, smiling.

"Mm." Ellery nodded and scraped at the bottom of the little plastic container. "The girl thought you were pretty special."

"She thought I was dangerous," Jackson said with a half laugh.

"You are," Ellery told him seriously. "Just…." He trailed off, and things were suddenly very serious.

"I've already promised to not be so much a danger to myself," Jackson said, just as serious. "I remember."

Ellery relaxed a little.

Jackson paused his stride long enough to bump Ellery's shoulder. "Look, I can't promise to be a new man—"

"I like the old one, mostly," Ellery said mildly.

"Yeah. But this isn't about me. It's about you. And how being a grown-up is hot too."

Ellery's smile went slow and then wicked. "Does that mean we can have sex in the bed tonight instead of the bathroom?"

Jackson laughed. "That means that I'll maybe save the geriatric T-shirts for hanging out at the house," he said. He stroked the front of the shirt he was wearing and more of the lettering flaked off. "I mean, you're already hot, Counselor, but let's see what I can do to make *you* look good."

"Don't bleed," Ellery said, completely sober.

Jackson just laughed.

That night they made completely serious, totally sober, very adult love. They smiled and laughed a lot, but they both knew the other would be there when it was over.

In fact, as they gave that final kiss good-night before melting into the mattress, they counted on it.

When Dave Met Alex—

A Fish Out of Water Story (with a few cameos by the String Boys)

Dave Meets Jackson

DAVE SAW the young police officer coming out of the boy's room looking tired and sad. He'd been in the hospital on occasion with his Daddy Cop, a man Dave disliked on principle because he was an asshole, called Dave "sweet cheeks," and was a rude fucker to the people he was talking to.

Baby Cop was different. Young, blond, green-eyed, he still had a toughness to him, a hardness to his jaw that said he'd seen too much too young. But he'd been kind—if distracted—to Dave when Dave had needed to interrupt police business to tend to patients in the ER.

"How is he?" Dave asked as the cop emerged, but what he was really asking was "How are *you*?"

"His ass hurts," the cop said bitterly. "Because some dirtbag tried to rip it open with a four-by-four."

Dave let out a breath. The kid had been beaten and sexually assaulted. The damage was done, and the kid was a wreck. But he was also funny, and his family—parents, sisters, a punk-ass brother, and a bestie who looked like he'd die for the kid—gathered around him like they'd give him strength through a tube if they could.

"I know that," Dave said dryly. "But how's he doing?"

The cop gave Dave a sideways look and a reluctant smile. "He's a tough kid. Man, I'd be losing my shit, but he's... he's holding steady." The cop closed his eyes and shuddered. "But he's also lying his ass off, which is unfortunate."

"Lying?" Dave was surprised. All that genuine family warmth.... Lying didn't seem in their wheelhouse. "About what?"

"Someone got into a fight with the guy who assaulted him last night."

"Good!" Dave blurted, relieved when the cop laughed a little.

"I would agree with you, but whoever it was practically cut the guy's head off. So that's one dead scumbag in the morgue and one freaked-out kid wandering the streets." Cop boy rubbed his eyes. "After what happened to Kelly, I don't think whoever did it as revenge would end up doing too much time, but...." He looked at Dave, taking in his magnificent Blackness (as Dave liked to call his pale brown skin) and quirked an eyebrow.

"Your people aren't good to the brown, are you?" Dave asked, disgust lacing his voice.

"I wish I could say that wasn't true." The cop sighed. "I just... there's got to be a halfway point between 'Hey, he was protecting his family, give him a break,' and 'People who cut people's heads off should not just get to walk away.'"

Dave grunted. True words, right there. "Do you know who it was?" he asked.

"I've got a couple of ideas," the cop said. "Unfortunately, not enough from anybody talking to even ask the right kid the right questions."

"Mm." Dave let out a sigh, and the new blond nurse who'd been recently hired sashayed down the adjoining corridor. "Mm, mm."

The cop turned and grinned. "Do you have plans I should know about?" he asked.

Dave shook his head. He and Malibu Ken had never even crossed paths, but boy howdy, did that kid's ass fill out a set of scrubs. "I only wish," he murmured. "Cute as hell, isn't he?"

"Not my type," the cop said dryly, and he yawned again.

"Well, whoever your type is, I hope they're waiting for you when you get home. You look...." Dave narrowed his eyes on Baby Cop. "You look like you haven't eaten or slept in months." Scrawny, bags under his eyes, shaking hands. This cop wasn't doing well. "The job getting to you?"

Baby Cop gave a tired shrug. "Shouldn't it?" he evaded. They came to the corridor that led to the entrance of Davis Med Center, and he started to veer. "Nice talking to you, Nurse Dave," he said, indicating Dave's nametag. Sure, he could have had his last name on it, but Nurse Dave put people at ease.

"Stay safe, Baby Cop," Dave murmured. Dammit! He'd already lost track of Malibu Ken. God, he should at least learn that guy's name if he wanted to nail him to the wall, right?

The day went on, and he stayed busy. Med Center was a bustling metropolitan hospital, so there was a lot to do. The kid eventually healed enough to be released from care, and Dave hoped for the best for him.

The next time he saw Baby Cop, he was being brought in on a stretcher, a big fucking hole in his chest, sucking up pints of blood through his arm like a sponge while his heart stuttered like a skipping record.

Alex Meets Dave

"Fuuuuuck…," Alex muttered, exhaling smoke with the word. He was leaning against the wall near the back entrance of the hospital, the sort of no-man's land where everybody took their smoke breaks in shame because health-care professionals weren't supposed to have vices, and fuck that all anyway.

"God, that was rough."

Alex turned his head to check out the nurse next to him. Tall, built, with dramatic, sweeping gestures and honey-brown skin with sloe-brown eyes. Alex had caught "Nurse Dave" checking out his ass more than once.

He liked it.

But right now, he liked the companionship more.

"That… I can't believe that guy is still alive," Alex said. "Whatever he was shot with, it practically pulverized his chest."

"The day's young," Dave said, his voice shaking. "Fuck. He was a sweet kid too."

Alex felt a little pang of jealousy. "You hit that?"

Dave shook his head, his lips quirking up in a bitter smile. "Nice that you think I'm in his league, but no. He was just a good cop. Liked to talk to people. Liked to do the right thing. His training officer—"

"DOA," Alex said, because he'd been there when that bus had opened its doors, and it had looked like a slaughterhouse inside. Not that the live cop's bus had looked much better.

"Yeah, well, he was a bastard. Not sure he deserved to go out like that, but our live guy—"

"Rivers," Alex told him. "Jackson Rivers."

Dave grunted. "You got his name?"

"I charted him," Alex said. He swallowed. "Twenty-one." His own age.

"He really is a baby," Dave said, and for a moment their eyes met.

Alex saw the wistfulness in Dave's eyes, and thought he was, what? Maybe five years older than Alex? Not too old. Definitely not too old.

"Hey," Alex said gently, taking another drag of his cigarette and watching as Dave mirrored his actions. "Us babies can still get around."

Dave's laugh was still a little broken. "Be careful, Baby Nurse. I'll take that as an invitation."

Alex's entire body shook with the adrenaline of the job, with worry, and with the need to let some of it out. "I invite you to try me," he said, meeting Dave's eyes, and he felt it. The moment the same wildfire swept them both. They hadn't even touched.

"I've got twenty minutes left on my break," Dave said, brown eyes daring him.

"I can blow you in ten," Alex told him, suddenly needing it that bad.

"My car. Seats fold down. Come on."

Dave grabbed his hand and hauled him to the parking garage, which was just across the thruway. Alex jogged to keep up, surprised when the used SUV came into sight. It was a little battered, but well cared for, and Dave opened it and shoved the seats down in the back in less than a minute. Alex climbed in and shut the hatch, glad, suddenly, for the early-spring day, because otherwise it could be damned uncomfortable in there. For a moment, they simply looked at each other in the breathless dark, and then Alex practically jumped forward, taking his mouth that quickly.

Hard, quick kisses—this wasn't tender, and it wasn't sweet. Everything was hard and quick. Alex took his mouth, took his throat, nipped his way down that long body, and then shucked his scrubs halfway down his hips, along with his underwear.

Ah! God yes. He couldn't think about the awfulness he'd just lived through with his mouth full of cock. Couldn't think about how his hands were shaking, or how the young, hot guy his age might be dying even now when cock was shoving down his throat, leaking precome. Couldn't be afraid, or horrified, or sad when his body was shaking with the need to taste come, with the need to release too.

Alex had been a total slut in college, and he used every trick now. Cheeks, tongue, throat, fist—and Dave wove his fingers through Alex's hair and held on until his body arched and he shot down Alex's throat.

His orgasm triggered Alex's own, in his shorts, and he came as he swallowed, the shakiness not getting any better.

He became aware of Dave's hands in his hair, soft, tender, and of the fact that he couldn't get his breathing under control.

"Come here, Baby Nurse," Dave said gently.

Alex nodded and squeezed his eyes shut, pushing back up in the confines of the SUV and letting Dave pull him close, wrap long arms around his shoulders, and nuzzle his temple.

"You okay?" Dave asked, and the tears Alex had been fighting since he'd opened the first bus and seen all that blood took him over.

"Sure," he said, but his voice broke, and then he broke, sobbing in this stranger's arms while his spunk cooled in his shorts.

He tried to hide his face against Dave's chest, but then he realized that Dave's chest was shaking as much as Alex was.

And Dave was sobbing too.

They held each other until Dave's watch went off, and he swore softly. "We are a fucking mess," he said, his throat tight.

"I've got jizz in my shorts," Alex mumbled, because it had been sitting, cold and yucky, against his skin as their crying jag eased.

"Do you have extra scrubs and shorts?" Dave asked. "Like, in your car?"

"In my locker," Alex said. And they both paused. "How am I going to get through with… oh my God."

"Here, baby. I've got clean scrubs and shorts with me. You can wear them and return them tomorrow."

Dave twisted and pulled extra clothes from a bag down by the front, and the next two minutes were filled with awkward fumbling as the two of them got undressed and redressed in the damned SUV.

"Return them tomorrow?" Alex said as he pulled up the briefs, which fit just fine—Dave was taller than Alex, but Alex apparently had the fuller ass.

"You off tomorrow?" Dave asked, wriggling into his own scrubs.

"No, but I thought we could, uh, maybe come in together tomorrow." He paused and looked Dave in the eyes.

There were still tears in his lashes, and Alex reached out and wiped his cheek with his thumb.

"After," he rasped, "you know, we spend some more time together."

Dave smiled slowly. "Not just one and done?" he said lightly.

Alex shook his head. "I… hell, I'd like dinner at the very least."

And that smile just got wider. "Dinner I can do," he said softly. He reached out and rubbed his own thumb under Alex's wet cheek. "You seem like a pretty sweet guy. I bet we can find something to talk about."

"I bet we can."

Jackson's First Stay

PAIN AND drugs and pain and fear and pain and… wait. Jade and Kaden and Rhonda. Good. He liked those people.

And pain and drugs and pain and fear and pain and… "No!"

He thought he was screaming, but what came out of his throat was more like a kitten's whisper.

"Shh, Baby Cop" came an almost familiar voice. "You are not sleeping, are you?"

"Can't sleep," Jackson whispered. "What if they know?"

"Mm." There was a soft touch on his brow. "What if your cop friends know you were wearing a wire?" the voice asked. "Given that only your family seems to be happy you're alive, I'd say they know."

Jackson groaned. "Where are they?" He knew they'd been there. J and K had his back. Always had.

"Well, you've been here for about two weeks, son. They probably went home to worry some more. You've been giving the whole world fits, do you know that?"

"Jade and Kaden and Rhonda," he muttered. "All I got."

"Well, you got me. Nurse Dave, remember?"

Jackson remembered now. The young nurse who'd been kind to him when he'd come to check on Kelly Cruz.

"You're my nurse? Thank God. Probably the only reason I'm alive," he said, meaning it. The guy had a sharpness about him; Jackson had trusted him to do his job right.

"Well, there's a few decent health-care professionals here," Dave said, that ever-present snark in his voice. Jackson liked him. "Just—" He lowered his head. "—watch out for Dr. Scheideman. He tried to give you a colostomy bag when your lower intestine is probably the most intact part of your body. He's dumb, and he's in charge. So you ask for me, or ask for Alex—you know, little blond nurse?—and we'll make sure you don't end up shitting in a grocery sack. Deal?"

Jackson closed his eyes, trying to picture Alex. Allies. He needed allies.

"Deal," he murmured under his breath.

The next time he woke up, there was a perky blond twinky checking his vitals.

"Hello, Baby Cop," Twinky purred, and Jackson squinted at him. "Alex?"

"Ah, Dave's been by. Yes. You can trust me. I'll treat you right."

Jackson smiled a little. "Good," he said. "Good to have people have your back."

About two weeks later—still in the fuzzy time when days bled into surgeries, bled into weeks, and then just bled—he saw Dave walk by, giving a little wave into his ICU unit.

"No flirting," Alex said, putting his vitals on the tablet by his feet. "You're slated for surgery in the next few days. Flirting puts strain on your organs."

Jackson chuckled weakly. "I don't even know if that organ works anymore," he said. Sex? Sure. He'd probably have it. But not in this fucking ICU unit, that was for sure.

"Mine does," Alex said with a saucy wink. He looked up at the clock. "And it's time for my break. See you in two hours, Baby Cop."

It took another month for Jackson to realize they both called him the same nickname.

But that day he realized they were banging each other silly, practically every break.

It gave him something to look forward to, really. Those two kind men, working hard, doing something good with their lives—and falling desperately in love.

Award winning author AMY LANE lives in a crumbling crapmansion with a couple of teenagers, a passel of furbabies, and a bemused spouse. She has too damned much yarn, a penchant for action-adventure movies, and a need to know that somewhere in all the pain is a story of Wuv, Twu Wuv, which she continues to believe in to this day! She writes contemporary romance, paranormal romance, urban fantasy, and romantic suspense, teaches the occasional writing class, and likes to pretend her very simple life is as exciting as the lives of the people who live in her head. She'll also tell you that sacrifices, large and small, are worth the urge to write.

Website: www.greenshill.com
Blog: www.writerslane.blogspot.com
Email: amylane@greenshill.com
Facebook: www.facebook.com/amy.lane.167
Twitter: @amymaclane

Choose your Lane to love!

Orange

Amy Lane's Dark Contemporary Romance

Guess who's swimming in the same pond...

FISH
OUT OF
WATER

Amy Lane

Fish Out of Water: Book One

PI Jackson Rivers grew up on the mean streets of Del Paso Heights—and he doesn't trust cops, even though he was one. When the man he thinks of as his brother is accused of killing a police officer in an obviously doctored crime, Jackson will move heaven and earth to keep Kaden and his family safe.

Defense attorney Ellery Cramer grew up with the proverbial silver spoon in his mouth, but that hasn't stopped him from crushing on street-smart, swaggering Jackson Rivers for the past six years. But when Jackson asks for his help defending Kaden Cameron, Ellery is out of his depth—and not just with guarded, prickly Jackson. Kaden wasn't just framed, he was framed by crooked cops, and the conspiracy goes higher than Ellery dares reach—and deep into Jackson's troubled past.

Both men are soon enmeshed in the mystery of who killed the cop in the minimart, and engaged in a race against time to clear Kaden's name. But when the mystery is solved and the bullets stop flying, they'll have to deal with their personal complications… and an attraction that's spiraled out of control.

www.dreamspinnerpress.com

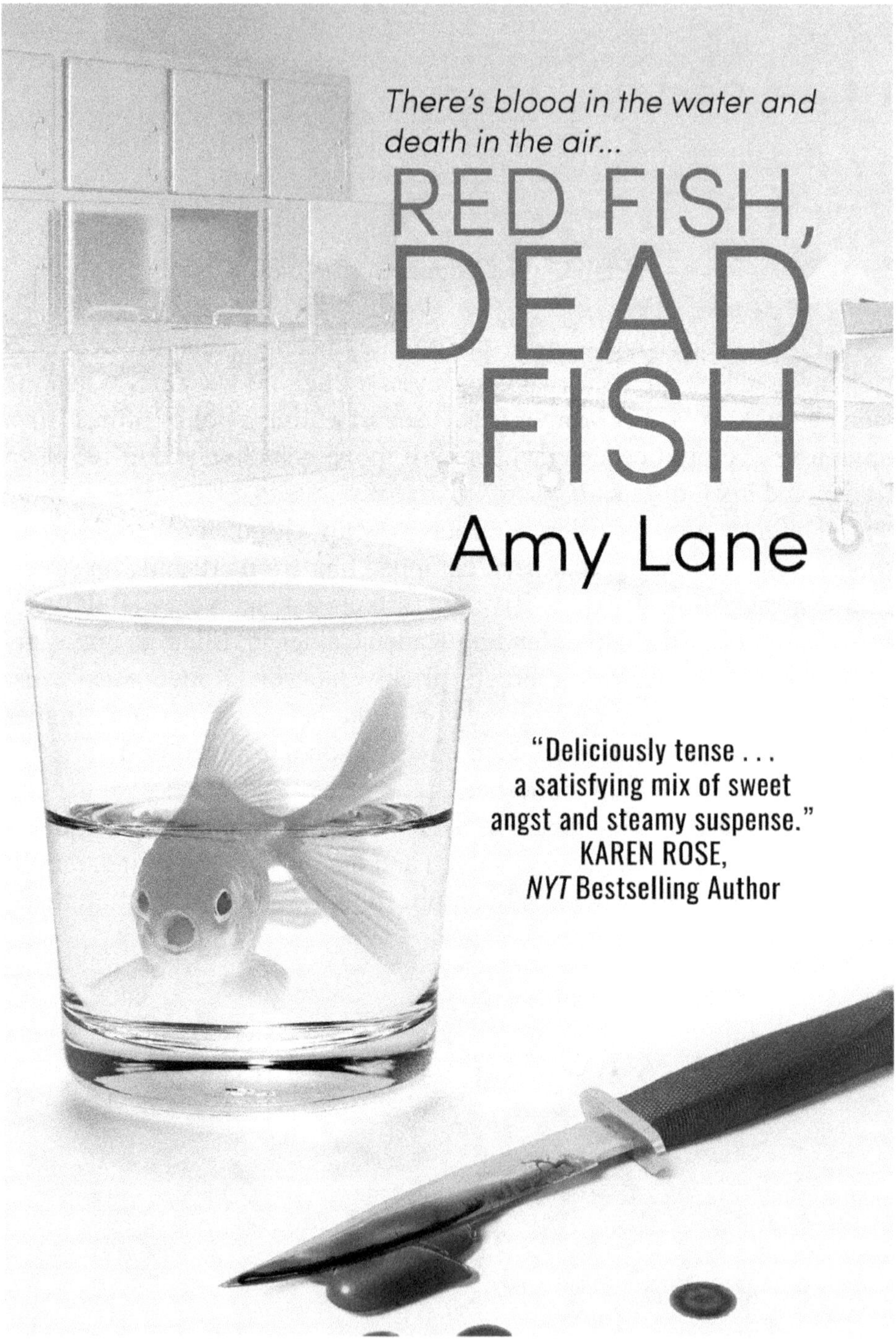

*There's blood in the water and
death in the air...*

RED FISH,
DEAD
FISH

Amy Lane

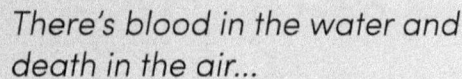

"Deliciously tense . . .
a satisfying mix of sweet
angst and steamy suspense."
KAREN ROSE,
NYT Bestselling Author

Fish Out of Water: Book Two

They must work together to stop a psychopath—and save each other.

Two months ago Jackson Rivers got shot while trying to save Ellery Cramer's life. Not only is Jackson still suffering from his wounds, the triggerman remains at large—and the body count is mounting.

Jackson and Ellery have been trying to track down Tim Owens since Jackson got out of the hospital, but Owens's time as a member of the department makes the DA reluctant to turn over any stones. When Owens starts going after people Jackson knows, Ellery's instincts hit red alert. Hurt in a scuffle with drug-dealing squatters and trying damned hard not to grieve for a childhood spent in hell, Jackson is weak and vulnerable when Owens strikes.

Jackson gets away, but the fallout from the encounter might kill him. It's not doing Ellery any favors either. When a police detective is abducted—and Jackson and Ellery hold the key to finding her—Ellery finds out exactly what he's made of. He's not the corporate shark who believes in winning at all costs; he's the frightened lover trying to keep the man he cares for from self-destructing in his own valor.

www.dreamspinnerpress.com

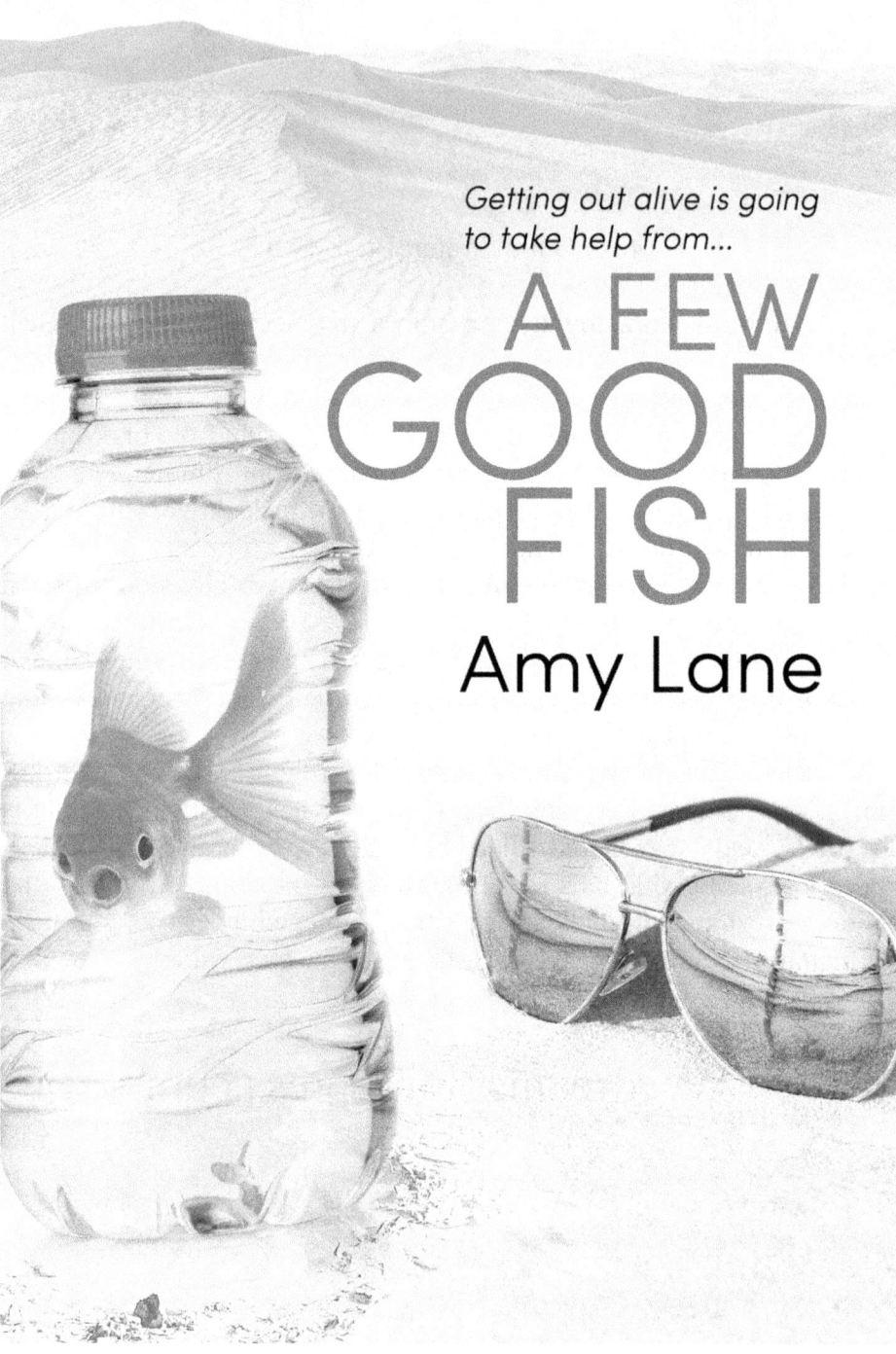

Getting out alive is going
to take help from...

A FEW
GOOD
FISH

Amy Lane

Fish Out of Water: Book Three

A tomcat, a psychopath, and a psychic walk into the desert to rescue the men they love…. Can everybody make it out with their skin intact?

PI Jackson Rivers and Defense Attorney Ellery Cramer have barely recovered from last November, when stopping a serial killer nearly destroyed Jackson in both body and spirit.

But their previous investigation poked a new danger with a stick, forcing Jackson and Ellery to leave town so they can meet the snake in its den.

Jackson Rivers grew up with the mean streets as a classroom and he learned a long time ago not to give a damn about his own life. But he gets a whole new education when the enemy takes Ellery. The man who pulled his shattered pieces from darkness and stitched them back together again is in trouble, and Jackson's only chance to save him rests in the hands of fragile allies he barely knows.

It's going to take a little bit of luck to get these Few Good Fish out alive!

www.dreamspinnerpress.com

Hiding the Moon

AMY LANE

Fish Out of Water: Book Four
A Fish Out of Water/Racing for the Sun Crossover

Can a hitman and a psychic negotiate a relationship while all hell breaks loose?

The world might not know who Lee Burton is, but it needs his black ops division and the work they do to keep it safe. Lee's spent his life following orders—until he sees a kill jacket on Ernie Caulfield. Ernie isn't a typical target, and something is very wrong with Burton's chain of command.

Ernie's life may seem adrift, but his every action helps to shelter his mind from the psychic storm raging within. When Lee Burton shows up to save him from assassins and club bunnies, Ernie seizes his hand and doesn't look back. Burton is Ernie's best bet in a tumultuous world, and after one day together, he's pretty sure Lee knows Ernie is his destiny as well.

But when Burton refused Ernie's contract, he kicked an entire piranha tank of bad guys, and Burton can't rest until he takes down the rogue military unit that would try to kill a spacey psychic. Ernie's in love with Burton and Burton's confused as hell by Ernie—but Ernie's not changing his mind and Burton can't stay away. Psychics, assassins, and bad guys—throw them into the desert with a forbidden love affair and what could possibly go wrong?

www.dreamspinnerpress.com

FISH
ON A
BICYCLE

Amy Lane

If you give a
fish a bicycle,
how's he going
to swim?

Fish Out of Water: Book Five

Jackson Rivers has always bucked the rules—and bucking the rules of recovery is no exception. Now that he and Ellery are starting their own law firm, there's no reason he can't rush into trouble and take the same risks as always, right?

Maybe not. Their first case is a doozy, involving porn stars, drug empires, and daddy issues, and their client, Henry Worrall, wants to be an active participant in his own defense. As Henry and Jackson fight the bad guys and each other to find out who dumped the porn star in the trash can, Jackson must reexamine his assumptions that four months of rest and a few good conversations have made him all better inside.

Jackson keeps crashing his bicycle of self-care and a successful relationship, and Ellery wonders what's going to give out first—Jackson's health or Ellery's patience. Jackson's body hasn't forgiven him for past crimes. Can Ellery forgive him for his current sins? And can they keep Henry from going to jail for sleeping with the wrong guy at the wrong time?

Being a fish out of water is tough—but if you give a fish a bicycle, how's he going to swim?

www.dreamspinnerpress.com